MELEE MAGE

MELEE MAGE
Fledgling God

Book 2

Michael Taggart

Copyright © 2020 by Michael Taggart

All rights reserved. This book or any portion thereof may not be reproduced or used in any manner whatsoever without the express written permission of the publisher except for the use of brief quotations in a book review.

This is a work of fiction. Names, characters, places, and incidents are the products of the author's imagination or are used fictitiously. Any resemblance to actual persons, living or dead, businesses, companies, events, or locales is entirely coincidental.

Cover by Michael Taggart
Collector Edition print of the cover available on Etsy.

www.etsy/shop/MichaelTaggartPhoto

Editing by Judi Davidson

Print Copy, Book Spine and Back Cover by Cynthia D. Griffin
www.CynthiaDGriffin.com

Editing by Harold Phipps

Beta Readers and Editors:
Thomas Costa
Blaine Gray
Steve DeHart

ISBN Number:
9798667315070

Printed in the United States
First Edition

This book exists because of the encouragement and support of one person—Judi. She listens like a wise monk on a mountaintop and encourages like a mother duck. If everyone had a friend like her, then they would feel loved, safe, and emboldened to be all they can be.

Judi, thank you for laughing at all my jokes and pretending all the book ideas I had were good ones. In short, You Rock!

To my nephew Shane, thank you for listening to all the mechanics of magic in this world. It's a much better place with your input and support! It's also been a lot more fun.

To my editor Dawn, you tackled this book like it was your own. You made the pages run red! And the book is so much better for it. Thank you for your notes of encouragement at the end of each chapter. They helped beat back the doubt demons!

To Bermuda Moses, you are my furry muse! All the loving looks, purrs, standing on the keyboard, sleeping on the keyboard, and bird watching has somehow gained a life in these pages. Love you, little fella.

To my Beta Readers, Steve, Thomas, Blaine—You guys gave me a whole new insight on how the book could be read and received. Your time and attention has created a much better flow. Thank you for your feedback!

To my husband Harold, you are the soundtrack to my world! You give me the life that lets me follow my dreams. Thank you for getting down in the mud and sweating Caps and Commas. Here's to many more happy years together!

Table of Contents

Recap of Misfit Mage...1
1 Three on Two.. 7
2 Fixing Sandy... 24
3 To Nest An Egg... 52
4 Colonel Mustard in the Park................................ 80
5 All by Myself... 100
6 Surprise... 116
7 A New Journey.. 135
8 Hit Like Moose.. 149
9 Physician, Heal Thyself...................................... 167
10 Making Tea.. 188
11 Gem Cells.. 203
12 Anna Lykit... 220
13 Watering the Flowers....................................... 232
14 My First Star.. 255
15 Her Darkness... 279
16 There Can Be Only One................................... 299
17 Asylum.. 320
18 The Secret to Power... 341
19 Terraforming Penny... 365
20 Second 10k.. 376
21 Pigeon Steps.. 387
22 What About John... 397

23 Oath and Vow 415

24 Twin Sinks 448

25 Arena 462

26 Behold... 477

27 Going Mousing 490

28 Big Ugly 517

29 Epilogue.. 537

Thank You!.. 548

Recap of Misfit Mage

Our story begins with Jason being pursued naked through a hotel by a squad of hitmen. Cornered and caught, his Death Experience is both brutal and ugly. Just when the hitman, "Thing One", is about to administer the killing blow, Jason taps into the Source of Creation and transforms into a supernatural being. In the process, Jason absorbs all the energy in the hotel room, including that of the four hitmen.

Jason's power cocoons him with vines and healing moss before he is rescued by two unlikely individuals: his landlady, Sandy, and the maintenance man, John. With the help of his fellow tenant, Annabeth, Jason is nursed back to health and welcomed into a new world of magic and danger. He also discovers that Sandy is a battlemage, John is part Mountain Troll, and Annabeth is a mage who can hear and influence magic with sound. Even the House, an old mansion converted into apartments, is magical, and part of a network of magical Houses all over the world.

At Jason's first House orientation, he reveals that he has been able to do magic since he was a little kid and can already do things with his power. His demonstration, showing how he can levitate a penny, goes very wrong. But in the end, his "Penny" has turned into a fully awake and self-aware charm.

When Jason wakes up from the botched demonstration, he discovers he is in bed with Tyler, a good incubus, who is trying to save him from his Remnants. Apparently, parts of the four hitmen now live inside Jason and are trying to get their revenge. Tyler tries to remove them, but they fight back, knocking him through a wall. With no other option, Tyler decides to stick around and gently remove the Remnants at a slower pace.

After recovering from the Remnant attack, Jason and Annabeth go for a walk in the nearby park where they are attacked by a rock golem. Annabeth tries to stop it, but the golem is too strong for her. To save Annabeth, Jason angers the golem into pursuing him as he runs away. While running for his life, Jason makes some little magical creations that take the golem apart and drain it of magic.

As Jason makes his way back to the House, he is again attacked by another one of his Remnants. This time he's rescued by a little black-and-white kitten that seems to have the power to tear the smoky Remnant apart. The kitten is called Bermuda Moses, and he adopts Jason and quickly starts training him to be a good human and provide treats and love upon demand.

A few days later, the members of the House are in the process of charging up their depleted charms when they are ambushed by Isobel and the Louisville Mages. In true villain fashion, Isobel reveals she was the one who killed one of their former Housemates by sucking out all her magic, and that she now plans on stealing their charms and doing that to the rest of them.

While Sandy and John take on the Louisville Mages, Isobel confronts Jason. She is furious at the loss of her golem and wants to know where it is. When she discovers Jason destroyed it, she attacks him. Bermuda tries to defend Jason, but Isobel kicks him through the air. She then delivers a brutal beat-down on Jason. John intervenes in the nick of time and fights Isobel, running her off.

Even with John's help, Jason is left in a bad way with his face smashed in, ribs broken, and arms fractured. Tyler reveals that having a high concentration of magic in the body can repair all damage, although he isn't sure how Jason can do that. Highly motivated to figure it out, Jason eventually discovers he can see down to the cellular level, and how to take his magic and infuse it into his cells. Once he awakens enough cells in an area, the process takes on a life of its own.

Helping in her own way, Annabeth talks to him about acceptance—how it can take any situation, no matter how bad, and allow him to process it and start to figure out how to handle it. Jason takes this to heart, and in the process of accepting his situation, finds the Center of his Magic. Visualized as a Throne Room, it is in bad shape but is a safe place for him to finally rest and regroup.

As Jason continues awakening his cells, he discovers he can group the small capsules of magic in spheres, which he then uses to make a Magic Matrix. This allows him to have vastly more magic in his body and significantly speeds up his recovery.

While Jason heals himself, the Louisville Mages attempt a full-scale assault on the House. They cause a lot of damage to the House shields but are eventually defeated by John and Tyler.

Jason and Bermuda finally make a full recovery, except that Jason can't see. He still has his Magic Sight, but his natural sight is gone. Regardless, Jason is ready to start learning how to be a Mage, and he and Sandy get together for his magic assessment. Jason discovers he has a very powerful soul, an affinity for air magic, and a huge magic capacity. However, he has a big disadvantage with distance. His magic is most powerful when he is touching something, and the maximum size he can work magic on is about three inches. Sandy then gives him his first charm, and he discovers the biggest disadvantage of all—he can't use regular charms.

Mundane chores continue, so Jason and Sandy head out to get groceries at the nearby Kroger. In the process, Sandy is kidnapped. John runs home, gets Jason and Annabeth, and they run back to the grocery store. Jason is able to use his magic sight to track the kidnappers back to a local warehouse where they find Isobel and several enemy mages. An epic battle ensues, but they are able to find Sandy and free her from a magical circle that was siphoning her power and feeding it to Isobel.

The House sends out an alarm, causing Annabeth to rush back to the House to handle the shields. Jason uses a little stone rocket armed with a light rune to blind and disorient Isobel, who finally falls to John's assault. A sphere of magic forms around her broken body, lifts her out the roof, and whisks her away. John goes to Sandy as Jason runs home to help Annabeth protect the House.

Jason arrives to discover the House is being attacked by what looks to be ghosts and a Necro Golem riding a saber-toothed tiger. Bermuda shows up, and with the help of all the Granny Godmothers, takes on the saber-toothed tiger. That leaves Jason on his own to handle the Necro Golem.

The golem is powerful and tireless, and eventually knocks Jason to the ground and runs him through with a magic sword. The golem can't get the sword back out of the ground, though, so he leaves and attacks the House shields without it.

The last of the Remnants, Thing One, decides this is the perfect time to appear and take over Jason's body. Jason fights him in his Throne Room, and Thing One reveals this was his plan all along. All seems lost, until Jason realizes Thing One is using Jason's own power and has no power of his own. Jason takes back his magic and grinds Thing One into dust.

Jason then communicates with the magic sword and discovers it is almost out of magic. With its Source gone, it is lonely and just wants to die. With Penny's help, Jason convinces the sword that he could be its new Source. The sword agrees to help him with his battle against the Necro Golem.

The sword transforms into liquid metal armor with powerful claws, and together they hack the Necro Golem apart. With everyone finally safe, Jason collapses on the front lawn. He later wakes up with Tyler and discovers that John and Sandy are home, but they are not doing well. The sword is now an egg-shaped piece of steel. With most of its magic gone, it is now sleeping. Penny absorbed all of Jason's creations he used to fight, and because of all the diluted magic, she is sleeping too. Jason still has a sword-shaped hole in his chest, so he needs to take it easy and recover. Just when all seems calm, Tyler vanishes.

Our tale continues right after the events of the first book, so it seems wise to name the characters and their current condition.

Jason: recovering from getting run through with a sword. Other than that, he is glad to be alive and safe.

John: currently a nine-foot-tall stone Mountain Troll, sitting on Sandy's bedroom floor and keeping an eye on her.

Sandy: in her bedroom and drained of almost all magic.

Annabeth: healthy and cheerful as always.

Bermuda: safe and happy.

Penny: currently sleeping after absorbing a huge amount of magic from all the Granny Godmothers.

Sword: currently sleeping and almost out of magic.

1

Three on Two

It was three on two, and not in our favor. I haven't been in many battles, but somehow it seemed like it was never in our favor. Just once, I would like to have a nice one-on-one, or even a two-on-one with us having the "two"! I could actually relax and enjoy the fight then.

We've had worse odds before, but that wasn't what gave me pause. What made me nervous were their auras. They were rotten.

The mage on the left had the best aura, but not by much. I could see his natural aura of yellow peeking through in spots, a bright lemon color. Overlaid on it, though, was a hodgepodge of other colors, mostly brown and green. And it wasn't a nice brown like dirt. It was the type of brown you find in the toilet bowl after a night of Mexican food, beers, and too much hot sauce. It was the type of brown that smelled bad and looked like it burned coming out. The green wasn't much better. It was pond scum green mixed with radioactive waste. Even mosquitoes would think twice before diving into that green mess.

I'd seen this type of rot before. Isobel, the former master of their school, had everything this guy had and so much more. She had leached magic from others for decades. But without a living person to refresh it, the aura rotted over time. I'd never experienced it myself, but I could only imagine that having an aura like this would eat away at the core of a person.

Taking others' magic by force was one way to get stronger, but it wasn't anything I wanted to try. The evidence in front of me was a cautionary tale. As bad as Lemon guy on the left was, the other two mages were worse. They had the same rotten colors, and even a few more. The guy in the middle had the most power with a base of purple. I guess he was a purple people eater. I thought that was funny, but we were trying to look tough, so laughing out loud was probably not the thing to do right now.

The last guy had a yellow base as well, but it was more like a darker mustard color. The three of them were staring us down, putting on their best tough guy sneers. I looked over at Annabeth to see how she was taking all this.

"I think they've watched too much Netflix," she murmured, before putting on her own tough face. She was only five foot two inches. Normally she smiled a lot, so hanging tough was not her strong suit. I don't think she could intimidate a pizza guy, much less the three rotten mages. Still, she tried, and that's what counts.

I settled for a neutral poker face. Being a backroom poker player, I was good at that. Despite the amateur posturing, the stakes were real. Three Realm Gate groundhogs were lying in the grass, encased in some sort of spell, and struggling to get out. They looked pissed off and very scared. They should be. These three wackos were planning on eating their magic and tossing their corpses.

Because the groundhogs were from another realm, they were high in mana. To me, that didn't seem like a good enough reason to eat them. I can handle seeing people getting injured a lot easier than seeing helpless animals getting hurt. Being cruel to innocent creatures is one of the highest evils in my book.

The House had alerted us to the impending magic heist, so Annabeth and I were here to stop it. Although it was late in the evening, our standoff was illuminated by the lights along the walking path in the park. I'm sure it looked dark and sinister, but I had only my Magic Sight, and it showed me everything regardless of the actual illumination.

We didn't look that imposing, I'm sure, but we were ready to rumble. Annabeth had her charm bracelet on. Although she had only been a supernatural for around six months, she was a charm prodigy. I'd seen her hold off three mages on her own. I was not a charm prodigy. Actually, I couldn't use charms at all. I was still hopeful that I'd figure it out soon, but right now my main offensive weapon was a shillelagh that John had given me. It is a strange Irish club made out of blackthorn wood and capped with silver.

The only reason we hadn't started rumbling yet was because I was hoping for some information. That last time I'd seen Isobel, her shattered body had been airlifted out in a magic bubble. Had she recovered somehow? Was she back? If not, what was happening in their school? Who was in charge now? I decided to get this party started.

"Does Isobel know you are here?" I asked. I made it sound like they were naughty school boys and I was going to call their mother. Nobody likes that tone of voice, so I was hoping to get a rise out of them.

"Isobel is gone," Purple sneered. "We have our own crew now. We are the Magic Ninjas."

He and Mustard struck kung fu poses. Lemon just looked confused. I'm guessing he wasn't the brightest crayon in the box. I looked at Annabeth. She still had her tough look on, but I could tell she wanted to burst out laughing. This was like a bad after school special.

"So what's up with the Louisville school? They let you go? Just like that?" I asked. I added some disbelief in my voice. They seemed anxious to let me know just how tough and independent they were. I could work with that.

"It's chaos over there, man," Mustard spoke up. "Nobody is in charge anymore, and everyone is sucking magic from someone else. I doubt anyone knows we've left, and we like it that way."

I was surprised. I thought maybe there would be some turmoil with Isobel gone, but nothing like this. It sounded like a free-for-all. If so, there shouldn't be any more major assaults on the House for a while. Yay for us!

"What do you mean, sucking magic? You guys can pull magic directly from something else? I thought only

Isobel could do that, and she passed it on to you guys inside a circle."

"We thought that too." Mustard seemed very willing to talk. Maybe he wasn't looking forward to the fight either. "It turns out that the tattoo we got for her inner circle had the Sucker Rune in it. Apparently, she was pulling some magic for herself, but kept it quiet. Now she's gone, we've discovered that the rune is completely open. As long as you have the rune, you can pull from anyone else that has the mark. No circle or ritual needed."

Purple gave Mustard the stink eye. I'm sure he wasn't supposed to be that free with information, but I wasn't arguing. It was some interesting info to have. I gave Mustard a smile of appreciation.

So Isobel had not only been draining any sups she found, she'd also been pulling from her own students! That was just diabolical. It certainly explained the major chaos her inner circle was in now. Now that they could pull magic from each other, it meant every one of her former students was a meal ticket. No wonder these three decided to split off and do their own thing. Purple seemed anxious to cut Mustard off (cut the Mustard?), and get back to business.

"Anyway, we need more power. That's why we're harvesting these mana bags." He got a sly look on his face. "Maybe we can work something out where you harvest these for us in the future. In exchange, we will leave you and your precious House alone."

"These aren't mana bags." Annabeth looked furious. "They are living, breathing creatures that have done you no harm. You should respect the world around you, not exploit it. This isn't the nineteenth century, you know."

"Looks like we got a tree-hugger," Purple sneered. "These mana bags aren't even from our world. They are probably messing up the environment, or something. We're probably doing this park a favor by taking them out."

Things were starting to heat up. Time to get my Flashers ready.

"Besides, have you seen the teeth on them? They are mean little buggers. When they bite, it hurts!"

"Of course they bit you," Annabeth said. "You're trying to eat them! If you were going to eat me, I'd bite you too. And for the record, I'd much rather hug a tree than hug you any day!"

Okay, that wasn't the snappiest comeback in the book. Annabeth was too nice to have any real zingers. I was concentrating too much on making my Flasher to care. I had the lightning bug body and the trench coat set up. Now I was working on adding the light runes. That's where the real boost happened.

I'd had a lot of luck with my Flasher creations before. If the enemy can't see someone, then it's awful hard to aim their spells. They might have magic sight also, but so far I hadn't run across anyone else that could see like I could.

"You're gonna bite me, huh?" Purple said. He walked closer, looming over her. "Maybe I'll eat you too. Maybe I'll go all wolf and eat you up like a little piggy." He flexed at her.

That was the wrong thing to do. Annabeth doesn't like bullies at all. I poured magic into my mostly finished Flasher as she hit him with a spell, blasting him backwards through the air.

His shield saved him from most of the damage, but still, that had to hurt. I sent the Flasher to Lemon. Hopefully, we could take him out quickly, which would even the odds.

Mustard advanced on me as Lemon started firing on Annabeth. It was show time! I realized I'd forgotten one critical component: I hadn't put a duplicator on my Flasher. Crap. In a perfect world, I'd have six Flashers, one for each of their eyes, and they would be blinded and out of commission quickly. I'd waited too long to start my creation, and I'd screwed up.

Mustard wasn't going to give me any time to make another one either. He started slinging spells at me, and unlike Annabeth, I didn't have a shield. Actually, I didn't have any useful charms at all. Sandy had given me a light charm, but I couldn't get it to work. It was just a useless piece of metal on my wrist.

What I could do was make my little creations. They were like little cartoon characters that I filled with magic. They could do all sorts of small things, but it took time to make them, and Mustard wasn't going to give me that chance.

He was flinging spells, moving quickly towards me. I'd faced a couple mages before, and they liked to hang back and throw magic. That made it much easier to dodge. By walking towards me, his spells came faster, and more accurately. I was able to dodge three of them, but the fourth one scored a partial hit. I stumbled, and that's when he really tagged me.

His spell hit low, knocking my feet out from under me. I hit the ground hard. Fortunately, we were in the grass in the park, so it wasn't that bad, but it still shook me up pretty good.

My Flasher made it to Lemon, flared his coat, pointed his tail, and let him have it. Right in the eyeball. I'd lost my natural sight when I got punched in the face by a stone golem, and my magic sight doesn't do it justice, but I hear that the light created by the Flasher is insanely bright. Being that it was dark out, I'm sure Lemon's pupils were wide open and vulnerable too.

He screamed bloody murder and staggered back. Even though my Flasher had directed his light, the indirect light must have been brilliant since Annabeth, Purple, and Mustard all started blinking and rubbing their eyes. I hadn't planned on affecting Annabeth, but I was happy that it had stopped Mustard for a moment. Hopefully, Annabeth would recover quickly and finish off Lemon, so I decided to direct the Flasher to hit Purple next.

I still had my shillelagh. It had a thong in the handle that was looped around my wrist. Trying to be stealthy, and yet quick, I grabbed it and rushed Mustard. I swung it hard and fast, but it just bounced off his shield. Damn it! Was I the only mage in this world without a shield? That didn't seem fair.

I saw Annabeth shoot a slow heat spell at Lemon. These shields typically worked on speed. They blocked anything incoming that was fast. If something was slow enough, it would get through.

I decided to follow her example. But going slowly in the middle of battle was not an easy thing to do. I put the head of the shillelagh up against Mustard's shield and waited for it to fall. If I could just get part of the club inside his shield, I could batter him with short punches. It wasn't the best, but it could work.

Unfortunately, Mustard's eyes cleared up just as his shield fell, and he grabbed the shillelagh before I could use it. That sucked. I was too close to effectively dodge his spells, and yet I didn't want to release my only weapon. If I did that, he would have a club *and* his spells to hit me with.

He cast a spell with his free hand, but I grabbed his wrist, jerking it away from me. The spell shot off into the park. We grappled for a moment: me trying to get my shillelagh free, and him trying to get his spell hand free. Mustard was bigger than me, and he was using his weight to his advantage. It didn't help that I'd been stabbed through the chest with a sword only a week ago. I'd worked a lot on healing myself, but I was nowhere near at full strength yet. Suddenly, the night lit up with a second light blast and a scream. My Flasher had made it to Purple.

Annabeth's heat spell made it to Lemon at almost the same time. It slowly ghosted through his defenses, setting his clothes on fire. He started screaming as he flailed around. He needed to stop, drop, and roll—not fan the flames. I'm sure it was much easier to think about this when flames aren't tickling your keister.

I was still wrestling with Mustard when I heard a second whoosh, and Purple's clothes caught on fire too. Annabeth was taking the groundhog murderers out! She might be short and sweet, but she was a badass in a fight. Being hit by a heat spell was no joke, but I wasn't that worried about the mages. They would end up with some burns, but we are supernaturals and can recover from just about anything if we have time. They were planning on doing much worse to the poor groundhogs, so a little pain and distraction was worth it for saving lives.

Two down, one to go. Annabeth was headed my way. Mustard was going to be a toasted marshmallow soon.

Unfortunately, he knew that too. We were still grappling together, and I was just trying to keep him occupied, when he pulled me in close and kicked me—right in the nuts. Normally, guys don't kick other guys in the baby makers. It's just not done. I could see, however, that the possibility of being flambéed would make him break the rules.

He didn't just score a glancing blow either. He hit me solid. I had a brief moment of reflex where I was up on my toes trying to alleviate any testicular compression, and then I was on the ground, in a ball, whimpering.

Getting kicked in the nuts is intense. It is one of the few pains in life that is both sharp and deep at the same time. It's sharp and immediate, like getting your finger shut in a door jamb. It's also deep, like breaking a bone, and it takes your breath away.

The pain doesn't stop either. It flows through you in waves. I was crying, trying to catch my breath, and wanting to throw up. All at the same time.

Needless to say, I was out of the fight for now. Mustard whirled around, reached towards his two crew mates, and pulled magically. For a moment, I thought he was trying to help them. Then I saw a thick ribbon of power flow out of them and into Mustard. He was draining his friends!

The ribbon was a tight band of energy. It left one specific part of their body and was absorbed by Mustard into his forearms. I'm guessing that was where their tattoos from

Isobel were etched. The ribbon flashed with different colors. It wasn't just their magic that was being transferred. It was all the additional stolen magic as well. Lemon and Purple were already rotten, and now all of it was going to Mustard.

His aura doubled, and then tripled in size. It was so thick I could barely see him. He screamed as the new magic rolled and churned through him. It was a primal, guttural sound. It was fear and anger and agony all rolled into one.

Annabeth couldn't see auras, so she was still charging at him. From her perspective it probably just looked like he reached for something and then started screaming. She had already fired off a slow heat spell, but it hit his new aura and died. It was going to take a carefully crafted spell to get through that mess now.

Mustard didn't use any finesse, he just used raw magic. You can do that if you have lots and lots of magic to spare. He swiped up at her, and his magic reached out and flipped her into the air. Then he smacked at her with his power, sending her flying. It looked like she was a baseball, and he was hitting it out of the park. She even went over a couple trees. I'm sure the flying part was fun, but the landing was going to be a bitch.

I got to find that out for myself when he turned to me and did the same thing. A powerful force smacked my huddled body into the air, and then flung me through the park. I tried to uncurl a bit and catch some of the air to slow me down, but the pain from my private parts was too much.

I went through the branches of one tree, which slowed me down, but set me to spinning, before I crashed into a second tree. My magic sight is a full sphere of vision. I can see up to about twenty feet around me. Normally, that is a good thing, but when I'm spinning, it amps up the vertigo exponentially. I couldn't keep track of what happened at that point. I crashed into things and broke branches, and finally landed on the ground, where I threw up. Again.

I threw up a lot. I threw up supper, then lunch, then breakfast. I'm pretty sure I reached way down into my lower intestines and threw up supper and lunch from the day before too.

For what seemed like a long time, I just lay there. I'm so glad nobody came after me. I couldn't have defended myself from a hostile fly.

I was covered in blood, leaves, and bark, and I was scratched and bruised all over. It didn't feel like I'd broken anything, but I was afraid to find out. I'd gotten punched in the face by a rock golem before, and shortly after, the crap kicked out of me by a powerful mage. I was very familiar with broken bones and how awful they can be.

My performance in this battle had been pitiful. I'd been feeling useful, and even a little badass, after helping take out Isobel and four mages. This time, though, I hadn't even been able to take care of one guy. I desperately needed a better offense. If I could have taken out Mustard quickly, I wouldn't be in this mess.

I heard the pitter-patter of little feet, and Bermuda Moses popped into view in my magic sight. He was a little black and white tuxedo kitten, and he had saved my keister on more than one occasion. I've learned that all cats are magical, but he seemed to have extra abilities.

He must have been napping, because he stopped to do a big front stretch—butt in the air, head down, front paws way out, like he was reaching for treats. Then head up, butt down, and back legs stretched out like he was a rocket and his hind legs were thrusters. It was the perfect yoga for cats, a full body wake up in two moves.

Bermuda had more courage than sense, so I was glad he hadn't arrived earlier. He probably would have tried to take Mustard out all on his own. He's still only a kitten, so that wouldn't have ended well.

Bermuda took one look at the puke puddles in front of me and decided he would go around behind me. He was purring to beat the band, and soon I felt his raspy tongue on my neck. Surprisingly, that felt good, and the world stopped spinning a bit. Then he hopped up on my head, deciding to clean my ear.

There is nothing like a kitten rooting around in your ear to get you moving. I was still afraid of broken bones, so I started out cautiously. I flexed my hands, then my arms. So far so good. I pushed Bermuda off my head. His tongue was rough! Feet and legs seemed to be okay, so I took a chance and rolled over.

Everything hurt. I felt like I'd been the favorite whipping boy at an S&M convention. I was covered in cuts and bruises, and my clothes were shredded, but I was alive. Thank goodness for that.

Bermuda started cleaning my face. He didn't seem to mind how scratched and dirty I was. He was just purring and making sure I was okay. That's love of the kitty kind. I didn't know where Annabeth was, or how she was doing. For all I knew, Mustard had gone after her. I still had work to do.

I slowly pushed myself to my feet. I ached all over. Considering what had just happened, I wasn't doing too badly. I got my bearings and slowly headed back to the area of the fight with Bermuda scampering along beside me. I wasn't sure how much use I would be, but if Annabeth was still fighting, I needed to find a way to help.

The park was quiet. I came up on the park bench and all the wild magic in the air. Mustard was gone. So were the three groundhogs. Two piles of burnt clothes and dust were all that was left of Yellow and Purple. They weren't dust from the fire. They were that way because Mustard had sucked all the life and magic out of them. I'd seen something like that before in my Waker Moment. I'd pulled the life out of four guys who were trying to kill me. Actually, I'd pulled every bit of life from everything in the room and had left only ash behind.

I shuddered at the memories. The whole event still felt raw. I shook myself and pushed the thoughts away. What was done was done. If I had to go back, I'd choose life all over again. Sure, this magical existence was very different than my life before, and it involved a lot more fighting, but it had its perks too. I just needed to get better at the fighting part.

Annabeth wasn't here, and with all the raw magic in the air, I wasn't sure if she had even come back. Hopefully, she wasn't chasing Mustard on her own. My magic sight was limited, so I walked around a bit to see if I noticed anything else. I did a small circle around the area, and then a larger one. That's when I saw my shillelagh. I guess Mustard had tossed it away. It wasn't magical, so he probably didn't value it. He was also toting around three captive groundhogs, so he certainly had his hands full. I picked it up and continued walking the loop.

I had just finished, when Annabeth showed up. She was bruised and dirty too, although her shield had protected her from most of it. We both agreed that Mustard was long gone at this point, and neither of us were in any sort of shape to chase after him. Annabeth checked out the two piles of dust, and then we limped home.

Annabeth was quiet. The loss of the groundhogs was eating at her. We were okay, but they weren't. We'd failed, and they would pay the price. The next time we ran into Mustard, he'd be sporting some extra rodent magic. I can understand wanting to be stronger. Stronger equaled being safer in this mystical world, but to get stronger by ripping the mana out of something else was just wrong. Very wrong.

I didn't say much either. I wasn't sure what to say. I felt like this was my fault. Annabeth had taken on more than her share of the mana raiders. I'd been the one to drop the ball.

When we got back to the House, we agreed to meet up later with Sandy and John, and I headed to my apartment. I was covered in dirt, tree debris, and puke and I desperately needed a shower.

Bermuda hopped up on the back of the toilet like always. That was his throne from which he surveyed all cleaning activity. My clothes were shredded from the fall through the trees, so I took them off and threw them away.

I took a moment to examine myself with my magic sight. I was one giant bruise. Mustard had really done a number on me. Actually, given how bad I looked, I was surprised that I wasn't in worse shape. No broken bones, I had all my teeth, and nothing appeared to be torn or dislocated. This wasn't my new normal at all.

I'd been working on waking new cells every night before I went to sleep and every morning when I got up. During my recovery from one of the many fights where I had gotten beaten to a pulp, I discovered I could take my Sight all the way down to the cellular level and awaken my individual cells by infusing them with my magic. Once I did that for a large enough area, the awakening continued on its own. I'd healed several of my ribs, my arm, my teeth, and my face using this technique. My new magic cells were much more resistant to damage, and I felt like that was what saved me today. The only things that hadn't healed right away were my eyes. They appeared to be all healed up, and I should have been able to see. I had no idea why I was still blind.

I got into the shower, letting the water wash all the grime and blood away. The scratches stung like crazy, but at least they were clean now. I lathered, rinsed off, and then decided to do that one more time. I needed to clean off more than just the dirt. I needed to clean off the sting of my failure. Today had really sucked.

My testicles were a constant reminder of that fact. They were swollen and sore, and I made sure to clean them very gently. It would be a while before I was walking normally again.

I toweled off and climbed into bed naked. The sheets felt nice, and it was so wonderful to lie down in my own bed. Bermuda hopped up on my pillow. He started purring and butting me with his head. For a good while, I just loved on him and basked in his warmth and companionship.

That was the wonderful thing about my kitten. He didn't judge me or tell me how sucky I was. Certainly not like I was judging myself. Instead, he just loved me and showed me that he wanted to be with me. I didn't deserve to, but I felt better.

Finally, Bermuda curled up to nap, and I started working on my healing. I zoomed into my chest where the sword had gone through me. It had missed my lungs and heart, but it had done damage to my muscles. I'd already awakened many cells in the area, and the whole region glowed with power. It wasn't enough, though. I still had a lot of work to do. I picked a new area and started infusing cells with power. Waking cells is simple, repetitive work, and I lost myself in the process. It felt good to accomplish something, and after a few hours I finally fell asleep.

2

Fixing Sandy

The next morning I couldn't move. Literally, I could not move. I tried, and nothing happened. It only made me feel even more sore for trying. It felt like a construction crew had taken turns whacking me with sledgehammers. I groaned and resigned myself to lying there for a while, gradually waking up. I played over the events of yesterday in my mind, and despite the all-over body ache, took a moment to be grateful. I'd been chucked into a tree. It was a small tree, sure, but still, nobody likes to be thrown that hard! I was sore, but things could have been so much worse.

Bermuda was on my pillow, belly to the sky, all four paws stretched out. I started rubbing his soft tummy, and we had a nice snuggle moment. He's so cozy and warm when he first wakes up. Unfortunately, that didn't last for long.

Kittens have a huge amount of energy, and soon he started tearing around my bedroom chasing something only he could see. He raced over the top of me a few times. It was just too much motion for my morning.

I hurriedly summoned Dot, my little red laser light in a sports car, filled him full of energy, and sent him off. Bermuda was after him in a flash, and they tore off into the living room in a fun game of chase.

I used my moment of peace to slowly stretch out. I started with my hands, then arms, and gradually got everything movable again. The frantic chase was still going on as I slowly rolled out of bed and stumbled to the bathroom. I took a moment to see how I was doing. It seemed like even my bruises had bruises. I was bruises squared.

Ha! I made a math joke. Not bad for first thing in the morning. Not really funny either, but at least it was something. A long hot shower kept the wake up process going. I was feeling halfway human by the time I finished. When I exited the bathroom, the final game of chase was winding down. I pulled Dot back into Penny, my awakened charm, and got some cereal.

Bermuda hopped up on my lap, and we played a fun game of "Paw the spoon and see if we can get Daddy to spill his cereal." I won. I didn't feel like wearing my cereal, and he wasn't trying that hard. He just liked to make sure he had my attention.

I really wished I could watch Netflix. That was my usual routine. My magic sight let me see shapes very well, but I couldn't see regular colors. I could see magic colors just fine, but the TV was not magic. Without colors, a TV was just a flat, boring panel of nothing.

At some point, my regular sight was going to come back, but until then, I didn't have anything to do other than work on my magic. That was probably a good thing as I still had so much to do. I needed to awaken even more cells and speed up my healing process. I also needed to exchange magic with Penny and wake her up too.

She had absorbed all the magic from hundreds of thousands of flying Granny Godmothers and, in the process, had gone back to sleep again. Penny needed a certain level of my personal magic to remain awake and present. Too much neutral magic diluted her essence, and she had to shut down. The only way to get her back was to restore the balance between neutral magic and my personal magic. This had happened once before, early on, when she had taken in all the mana from a golem. It had taken a lot of time and effort to get her back to normal. This last round she had taken in all the magic from a Necro Golem, a saber-toothed tiger made of this necro dust, and the dust controlling thousands of House-shield-bashing spirits. That was a lot of magic.

I put the cereal away and spent a few moments exchanging power with Penny. I pulled in magic from her until I was buzzing with energy. It was kind of like taking in a really deep breath and holding it. The magic I pulled in from her was almost a neutral white. I mixed it with the rich emerald green and sapphire blue of my magic, and then I'd push as much of this saturated magic back into her as I could. I kept that up until I noticed my normal color level dropping a bit. It didn't drop much. It was still my magic in my body of course, but the saturation level wasn't quite as rich. I discovered that if I gave it a few minutes, it would refresh itself.

I also needed to push magic into my sword. Its capacity was way beyond my level, but I needed to keep giving it my magic and growing the bond we had. Penny was all mine. She was my first awakened charm. The magic sword had saved my life, though, and Penny had agreed to share me as a source and gradually make it fully aware and awake again.

Since we were bonded, I really needed a good name for my new awakened charm. I'd started calling him Swordy, but he wasn't really a sword anymore. Now he looked like a shiny egg, although what he really wanted to be was a vase. A very fancy, fifteenth century looking vase, but still a vase. Plus, he didn't want to be a sword anymore, and I didn't want to call him something that reminded him of what he used to be.

Vasey? Cherub? (The perfect vase in its mind had lots of scroll work on it and little, naked flying babies. Don't judge.)

Baby Face? Bob?

After a few minutes, I gave up and decided to check on Sandy and wait for Annabeth. Bermuda was tired now, but he didn't want to leave me. He wanted me to pick him up and carry him with me like a baby. I told him "No." He yawned, giving me his sleepy cute look.

So I picked him up and carried him like a baby. He purred all the way down to Sandy's place. What can I say? My kitten is spoiled rotten.

I was glad he was with me, though. Sitting with Sandy was depressing. When I got to her place, I let myself in. Sandy was still unconscious and John wasn't moving, so nobody was going to get the door if I knocked. I went to the bedroom; nothing had changed. Sandy was in her bed, looking like a sleeping fairytale princess. John was still sitting beside her, all rocky nine feet of him. He had eaten some sort of rocks during the battle and transformed himself into a nine-foot-tall stone monster. It had worked, and in the end he had smashed Isobel into a bloody paste. I knew Isobel was strong, but I had underestimated just how strong she was. We all had.

After I'd defeated the Necro Golem, Tyler and Annabeth had returned to the warehouse. John was still sitting there like a pile of rocks, but they'd managed to get him moving, and he'd brought Sandy back to the House. Once Sandy was in bed, John had settled down beside her and hadn't moved other than to help take care of her. That had been a week ago, when Sandy had been captured and had lost almost all of her magic in a draining circle. Thankfully, I'd managed to break that circle while she still had enough magic left to live. Without magic she would turn into a pile of dust just like Lemon and Purple People Eater.

I was worried about her. As the week passed, there was still little sign of recovery. She just lay there, like she was paralyzed or something. Even sleeping, she should have shifted around a bit and rolled over. But she didn't even seem to breathe. She was alive. My magical sight confirmed it, but there was little on the outside that showed Sandy still lived.

I checked her out again. My magic sight could easily read her and see how she was doing. Her aura was present, but felt hollow. It also didn't block my sight like it had before. I could see a faint orange mist inside her. It seemed just a tiny bit more substantial than yesterday, but only a tiny bit. Normally she was thick with magic, with viscous, rich swirls in her power centers.

I'd have thought she could come back fairly quickly. She was a magical prodigy after all. But this wasn't looking good. I was also worried about John. He seemed distant, like he was listening to something else and only partially paying attention to us. He was a far cry from the fun-loving, beer-drinking man I knew him to be. This John was more like a stone golem, silent and unmoving.

I went over to Sandy and began moving her around a bit. Annabeth had done some Googling, and apparently it was bad for a person to stay in the same position for an extended period of time. She needed to move and get some blood flowing. Since she couldn't move herself, we were doing it for her.

John opened his eyes and checked me out. "You seem a bit banged up this morning."

That was a good sign. At least he had noticed and said something. I told him about our adventures yesterday and how badly it had gone. He grunted in a few spots, but didn't say much else.

I finished up with Sandy and went over to sit on John's lap. It was like curling up on a giant statue. I wasn't sure if he could feel me, or what was going on with him, but he needed human contact too. I finished my story. John didn't say anything else. He just closed his eyes and continued to sit on the floor.

I checked him out with my sight. His magic was gray with small touches of black and white, and it sparkled. He was thick with magic. It flowed over and around him like molasses. If I had to guess, he had the opposite problem to

Sandy. He had too much magic. He'd pulled so deeply on his connection with the earth that he couldn't get rid of it now. I guessed it was going to take a long time for him to recover too.

Sandy's bedroom was quiet as a cave, so I settled in to do some magic work. Bermuda crawled up on my lap to do some napping. We were like a set of Russian dolls; nine-foot golem man, regular-sized human, and cat. Biscuit and Snowy, Sandy's two cats, joined us, and for a while all was quiet. I exchanged magic with Penny, pulling and pushing the magic in a steady rhythm, like it was the tides flowing in and out of the shore. When I got tired of that, I pulled in more and more magic, until I was buzzing with power, and started working on my cells. This time I stayed near the surface and worked on creating lots of awakened clusters in my skin.

It was weird being this quiet. Normally, Sandy was cooking supper or talking shop, and John was hanging around cracking jokes or telling stories. Sandy's apartment was the hub of activity for our crew, and it always felt like it was full of life and happiness. Now it felt as silent as a tomb.

I lost track of time, but it was at least a few hours later when Annabeth showed up. She had bruises on her bruises too, and she was moving around like an old lady. I told her she looked old, at least seventy-two, and she stuck her tongue out at me. She was really mature like that. Seventy-two was her actual age, but due to her magical awakening, she was growing younger. Now she looked like she was in her early fifties, although sticking out her tongue made her seem like she was five years old. I stuck out my tongue back at her, because I'm mature too, and we laughed. It felt good to laugh.

I caught her up on what I was seeing with Sandy and John. She didn't have the sight like I did. Instead, she could hear magic. What she could hear was matching what I was seeing. Sandy barely had any sound at all, and John sounded like a landslide.

"So the question is, what are we going to do?" I asked. "We have to do something. Sandy isn't recovering her magic, and John can't let go of his power."

"Agreed," Annabeth said. "It is going to take Sandy years to recover, and we've been attacked twice in the last few weeks. We can't keep the House protected without our two heavy hitters."

"Let's start with Sandy," I said. "The question is, how does a supernatural recharge their magic? If we can figure that out, we can help Sandy, and if we can reverse the process, we can help John."

Annabeth laughed. "Recharging your magic is the big million-dollar question. If mages knew how to do that reliably, then they would throw around a lot more spells. It's easy to run out of your personal magic, and it takes time to recharge again."

"This is all new to me," I said. "I'm coming from the other side. I have too much magic. Penny can absorb the extra magic, but then she goes to sleep. My problem is taking all that extra neutral magic and converting it to be all mine. What has Sandy told you about the charging process?"

"She said that if someone were to figure out how to recharge quickly, they would keep it a secret." Annabeth paused a moment, thinking. "She said that life creates magic, so everyone generates a bit of magic on their own. Give it enough time, and a person will recharge their magic pool with their own energy. That doesn't really help us in this case. If Sandy could recharge quickly, then it would have happened already.

"She also said that some people have an affinity for getting their magic back. They can cast spells all the time because they are always refilling quickly. Again, that doesn't help us, as I don't know how to boost an affinity or know of any sort of rune that does."

"Since we are covering everything we know, let's talk about Isobel," I said. "She would recharge by pulling magic from someone else. I know that isn't anything we want to do here, or even that we know how to do it, but I'm just listing it as a way to get magic."

Annabeth nodded. "Isobel sucked, like literally, but she did know a shortcut to getting power." She paused in thought. "Sandy also said something about the environment. She believed that it wasn't just personal power. She felt that magic-rich areas produced more powerful mages and naturals. She told me a story about a mage that left his House to live by a volcano. It stuck in her mind because that seemed like an exotic place to live. She asked around, and some people said that volcanoes and caves have more natural magic than regular places. It was more of a rumor than anything, though. She couldn't find anyone who knew for certain."

"If I'm ever near a cave, I'll have to check it out," I said. "There are some caves near here, but I'm not sure about transporting Sandy there and having her stay long term. She is much safer here, behind the House shields. Even with all the crazy battles we've been in recently, they still have held up. A lot of the mages got hurt in the last House battle, and

Isobel is gone now, so hopefully we won't get attacked again soon. Maybe she'll have enough time to heal before something else comes for us."

I fell silent, lost in thought. A theory was percolating in my brain, trying to come together. I had a talent for seeing underlying patterns. That's what made me a good poker player. I could feel the flow of the cards and the way the players were using them.

Annabeth left me to work on the problem while she started moving Sandy. She started humming as she moved around, and soon her cheerful pink magic filled the room.

"What if we are sort of like charms?" I said. "I noticed when we were charging charms that magic calls to magic. What if we are denser vessels of magic, moving through space? As we do, we call to the neutral magic in the air and attract it to us. As the neutral magic is absorbed, we convert it to our own personal color of magic.

"That would kind of fit the story you told. Sandy said that no mage she has ever known has the sight like I do, so they wouldn't be able to see neutral magic in the air and if it was being absorbed or not. There isn't that much neutral magic floating around, so absorption would be too slow to notice. If volcanoes and caves do have more ambient magic, then supernaturals would absorb it faster, and therefore, become more powerful."

"It sounds possible," Annabeth said. "It's the best theory we have at the moment. So you are thinking we need to boost the neutral magic in this room? How do we do that?"

"I'm thinking that first we need to experiment and see if we are on the right track," I said. "Let's head down to the Circle Room and see if we can figure this out."

I've always loved the Circle Room. It was the first place I'd contributed an idea that worked. Using Penny to gather the energy and get it into the charms had been a real breakthrough. I'd felt like I was finally becoming a productive member of the team.

Plus, the door was just cool. It was blue with sparkles that swirled a bit. It really did look like a magical door.

Once we were inside, I could see all the motes of neutral magic in the air. There are always a few sparkles of magic floating around, but they were really dense in the Circle Room. I guess that is why this was such a great place for recharging charms.

The room had a few benches and a gold ring in the center of the room. The ring wasn't magical that I could see. It was just a placeholder for where the mages should stand. In this case, I didn't want to make an actual circle. I just wanted to gather some neutral magic and experiment with it.

"So, what do we do now?" Annabeth asked.

"I thought we would gather some magic together, and then see if you could absorb it." I tried to sound like I knew what I was doing. I was really just winging it, though. "Now we are actually here, I'm not really sure how to gather it together. I can see it in the air. There is a lot of it just floating along, but I'm not sure how to influence it."

"Can we do what we did last time?" Annabeth asked. "I know we don't have all four people here, but even two of us should be able to do something."

I shook my head. "Penny is sleeping. Last time she was at least partially awake—enough to transform herself and make a thin band. She absorbed all that power from the Necro Golem, and I haven't been able to talk to her since."

"Can you do your energy exchange thing again and wake her up?" Annabeth was going through all the logical steps, like I had. Maybe she would think of something I'd missed.

"I've been working on that for days now," I said. "It will work eventually, but I don't know how long that will take. Until then, Penny is just a ring on my finger."

"How about using one of your creations?" Annabeth suggested. "We know a circle works. Your creations are made of your power, so maybe we can spin the neutral magic around one of them and condense it."

"It is certainly worth a shot," I replied. "If it does work, it would be pretty awesome. That means I could make lots of circles and condense magic wherever we are."

I held out my hand and made a magic circle. It was a band, about two inches across. That wasn't a big area, but hopefully it would work as a test. I could make creations up to three inches wide, but it takes a lot more power.

I put a twisty texture on it. It wasn't fancy or anything, but it was a little something to give it some uniqueness and life. I spotted a fairly large wisp of floating magic and held my ring right up to it. Then I concentrated, attempting to spin the magic around it.

Nothing happened.

When we had done this before, Penny had been the base of the circle. It had felt easy and natural to wrap my magic around her. Then John, Sandy, and Annabeth had layered on top, and we were able to spin our power in a perfect circle. The neutral magic was attracted, and that had been the base of our charging circle.

This time, my magic just wouldn't wrap about my creation. It was responding to me, but it seemed confused. I guess that made sense as my creations were basically my magic, and I was asking my magic to wrap around itself.

I tried imagining my magic flowing around it like water. The circle was on my palm, so my magic flowed up and over the circle, but it didn't spin. I tried separating my colors. Trying first the emerald green, and then sapphire blue. That didn't work either.

I did notice one thing. When I held the ring right next to the wisp, the neutral magic drifted closer to the circle and stuck to it. I tested if this was some sort of coincidence by moving my hand around. The wisp stayed stuck to the ring.

So my creations could attract magic, but I couldn't seem to spin it, or compress it. I took a moment to tell Annabeth what was happening. She couldn't see magic, so from her perspective I was just waving my arms around and looking intently at nothing.

"Have you tried spinning the circle itself?" She suggested.

That was a good idea. Two brains are better than one.

Spinning the circle was easy, but it didn't really do anything. The wisp stayed stuck to the ring until it started spinning too fast, then it was just flung away. It didn't go far, though. The wisp was acting a bit like a soap bubble. It just drifted along and sometimes stuck to something. It seemed to have almost no mass, so it wasn't like it could be thrown far.

"Good idea, but it didn't work," I said. "I do have another idea, though. We've been thinking of making a circle because that is what worked before. How about instead of spinning, we try gathering and compressing?"

Annabeth just looked confused, so I kept going. "When I was building my matrix, my magic felt like a dust bunny. It was just a bunch of strings of magic loosely meshed together. This neutral magic kind of reminds me of that. I can't control it directly because it's not my magic, but what if I make something that goes around it and then compresses it. Think of it like stuffing feathers in a pillowcase. On their own, a pile of feathers is very light and spread out, but if you stuff them in a pillowcase, then they become much denser."

"That makes sense," Annabeth said. "We are just experimenting at this point, so it's worth trying anything."

I felt hopeful. I'd learned to trust my instincts, and this just felt right.

I dismissed the ring, and this time made a box with an open lid. I moved the box until the wisp of magic was inside. That was a bit harder than I thought it would be as the wisp kept sticking to the outside. Finally, I got it stuck to the lid, and it was just a matter of closing the box. Then I put the box between my two hands and smashed it flat. I opened the lid. The magic inside looked flat and much denser. My idea had worked!

I quickly ran into a problem, though. The magic didn't want to come back out of the box. Denser magic meant that it was even more attracted to my creation, so it really didn't want to come out.

I was on the right track, but I couldn't spend all my time running around the room trying to catch wisps. What I needed was something that was bag shaped and would run around the room for me. What I needed was a magic-eating octopus!

I dismissed the box. It was boring anyway. An octopus was much more exciting. I gave it a big head, because it needed to carry a lot of magic, and made it purple. For some reason, that just seemed to be the right color. Then I added on some tentacles for swimming and gathering magic. It needed to see where it was going, so I added two eyes and gave it some nice, long eyelashes.

My new creation gave a twirl, batting her lashes at me. The little Octopus looked so pretty, I decided it had to be a girl. Since she was going out for a magical dinner on the town, I decided to give her some diamond earrings and an emerald necklace. She didn't have any ears, so I just put the diamonds on the side of her head. I put some diamonds around the emerald in the necklace to tie everything together. Her eyes were still her best feature, so I decided to add a row of tiny diamonds along the edge of her eyes. Perfect! Now she looked flashy and classy!

She could swim through the air, so there was no need for jet packs or anything like that. After some debate, I added a duplicator ring. I felt like this was going to work, even if she might need a few more modifications. I was done making changes for now, so she left my hand and went for a test swim through the air.

"Hello, Octa!" I waved at her. She was so cute. She waved back. "This is Annabeth. She can't see you, but if she could, she would think you are adorable."

I caught Annabeth up on what I'd done, and she gave a happy wave in Octa's direction. That's the nice thing about Annabeth. She was always willing to play along and enjoy the moment. A magic swimming Octopus didn't faze her at all.

"Okay, Octa, let's gather your first piece of magic." There was magic everywhere, so Octa swam a few inches to the nearest mote. It was on the small side, but it had a nice twinkle. It only took a couple tentacles to catch it and pull it toward her mouth. With a sip, it was gone.

So far, so good. "Did you like that?" Octa batted her eyelashes at me, so I took that as a yes.

"Try gathering some more magic. Stop when you feel full and come back here again," I instructed.

Octa didn't really seem to hurry, but she sure ate a lot of motes quickly. As she stored more magic, her head started glowing with all the power inside. She began to look like a cute, purple light bulb with tentacles. In a few moments she was done, so she swam over and settled back on my hand again.

I did a scan. Everything seemed fine. Octa still appeared healthy and happy. There weren't any ill effects from holding neutral magic. The magic itself was compressed into a ball. It wasn't compressed to a liquid state like when we had been filling charms in the park, but it was much better than the motes floating through the air.

"Octa did a great job gathering the magic," I said to Annabeth. "Now it's time to see if you can feel it and absorb it. Hold out your arm and let Octa land on it."

Annabeth held out her right forearm, and I moved my hand right beside her. Octa left my hand to gently settle on Annabeth's forearm. Her tentacles weren't long enough to wrap around Annabeth and keep her steady, so I had her come back and made a few modifications. I added some suckers to her tentacles so she could stick to Annabeth better. I modified her beak a little so it could open wider and let the magic rest right against Annabeth's skin.

Modifications completed, Octa swam over to Annabeth's forearm and tried again. This time she stuck to Annabeth just fine.

"So far, so good?" I asked.

"I don't feel anything yet," Annabeth said. "I'm hearing some interesting sounds, though. I'm hearing a simple flute melody, which I think must be Octa, and behind that is some white noise, which I'm guessing is the neutral magic. It's like a radio playing flute music, but it isn't quite tuned in all the way."

Well, that was certainly interesting. It didn't help me right now, so I kept going. I directed Octa to open her beak and let the magic sit directly against Annabeth's skin. I could tell as soon as it touched her because Annabeth jumped.

"Are you okay?" I asked.

"I'm good. I'm good." Annabeth waved my concern away with her other hand. "It just surprised me. The good news is I can certainly feel it."

"What does it feel like?" I asked. I had a lot of experience with neutral magic, but it was always Penny that pulled it in. I hadn't ever touched it myself.

"It's got a little tingle to it. And maybe a bit of heat," Annabeth said. "It doesn't feel bad or anything, and it's not even that intense. It just feels different." She seemed to search for more words. "I guess that's it. It just feels different."

"Okay. If you are good with it, then I'll take a closer look," I said.

"Oh, yes. It's fine. Look all you want. Now I'm getting used to it, I think I kind of like it."

Using my magic sight, I zoomed in to get a closer look. The first thing I noticed was that Annabeth's natural aura was resisting Octa. That made sense as Octa was my magic and looked like an invader from Annabeth's perspective. Her aura was there to protect her, and that is what it was doing. It wasn't fighting Octa hard, though. More like a passive resistance.

There wasn't anything I could do about that, other than keep an eye on Octa and refresh her structure when she needed it. The other thing I noticed was that the neutral magic right next to Annabeth was gradually turning pink, which was Annabeth's magic color. I watched it for a while. Was it just turning pink but staying separate, or was it actually merging with her magic? It took several minutes, but I could see the level of neutral magic in Octa go down. Since it wasn't going into Octa and it wasn't going back into the air, it had to be going into Annabeth.

We had found a solution!

I told all this to Annabeth, and we did a happy dance. I was a little surprised, but Annabeth could shake some booty!

It still wasn't perfect, though. Octa didn't have any problems gathering the magic, but I needed a better delivery system. The whole point was to get magic in Sandy as quickly as possible, so I needed to get more of the magic in contact with her skin.

I told Annabeth to keep in mind how this felt, and then sent Octa back out to refill her neutral stores. It took less than a minute, and most of that time was spent swimming. I estimated that Octa had only been able to deliver about 25 percent of her payload to Annabeth. She filled up so fast it might even have been less than that.

After refilling, Octa settled back onto my hand. Distance mattered a lot with my magic. I used to make changes to my little creations as they hovered in the air in front of me. After my magic assessment, I learned that I could make changes a lot faster and easier if I was actually touching them.

She fluttered her beautiful eyes at me and her diamonds sparkled. I smiled back. She didn't really need it, but I added some bright red lipstick. Her beak was on the bottom of her head in the middle of her tentacles so no one would see it, but I'd know it was there, and so would she. A girl should always feel pretty.

I also added some swirls to her purple skin. It gave it a bit of texture and would help her resist Annabeth's aura a bit better. I've discovered that the more detail I gave my creations, the stronger and more durable they were.

The last thing I added was a better delivery system. I made a tube in each of her tentacles for the neutral magic to flow through. Then I added tiny output holes right beside her suckers. The magic should now come out like lotion and coat her skin in a much wider area.

I decided to try it on myself first. Annabeth was a much better neutral party to test on as she couldn't see what I was doing and didn't have any expectation of what was going to happen. She had certainly felt something, though, and I wanted to experience it too.

Octa shifted down to my wrist, spread out her tentacles, and suckered in. It tickled just a little. Then Octa activated her new delivery system, and I felt the tickle replaced by a pleasant glow. This was going to be perfect.

"Annabeth, let's try this again," I said. "I've made some changes, but I'm not going to tell you what they are. You just tell me if you notice a difference."

This wasn't exactly a double-blind scientific study, but it would have to do. I knew where Octa was and what she was doing, so my mind could anticipate where and what I should be feeling. Annabeth couldn't see my creations, so I was going to mix things up and see if she noticed.

Octa left my wrist and swam over to Annabeth, topping up her neutral magic on the way. When she left my arm, I could see the neutral magic shining there, like a neon tattoo. It quickly faded away.

This time she went to Annabeth's other arm. Annabeth was still holding out her right arm, waiting for Octa to land. When she landed on her left, Annabeth knew it right away.

"Ahhh, trying to surprise me," Annabeth said. "She's right here." She pointed to where Octa had landed. Clearly my creations could be felt, even if they couldn't be seen. Octa activated her delivery system, and the neutral magic started flowing.

"Oh. Wow," Annabeth said. "I can feel the magic again, but it is stronger this time. Like much stronger."

"Last time it felt like a poke. Not in a bad way. Maybe like someone was pressing the tip of a pen against my skin. This time it feels more like a warm band aid." She waved her other hand in the air. "I'm sure that doesn't sound clear at all, but I'm not sure how else to describe it."

"Oh no, that's perfect," I said. "That fits exactly with what I did."

I told Annabeth all about it. We bounced ideas back and forth a bit, looking for an even better solution. We were limited by how big I could make Octa. She was about two inches long, half of which was her head. Her tentacles were about an inch long, and when they spread out in a circle, they made for about a two-inch round coverage.

In the end, we decided this was good enough. We might come up with another idea later, but right now this was the best solution. It was worth taking the time, because once I started duplicating Octa, it would be a lot harder to make future changes.

I did have one final idea. It would be nice to see at a glance how much neutral magic Octa had remaining. I could always scan her, but once I had lots of these creations, that wouldn't be very efficient. She also glowed when she was full of neutral magic, but that faded out completely when she was half full. I called Octa back and made a slight change to her color. Now, when she was full of magic, her skin would be a bright purple. As she delivered her magic to Sandy, she would gradually change to a darker tone. Based on the color change, she had delivered about a third of her magic to Annabeth in a much shorter period of time.

That was the final change, so I added more of my personal magic and triggered the duplicator. Now there were two magic gathering Octopuses. More magic and some duplications later we had four, then eight, then sixteen beautiful ladies.

I decided to stop there. This was enough for a good first run. I turned them loose in the room, and they went to work. I was surprised at how fast they worked and how much they could hold.

I caught Annabeth up on how things were developing. She said she could hear a whole bunch of flute melodies now. It sounded like a very strange orchestra as they swam around the room.

Once the ladies had eaten their fill, we headed back to Sandy's place. We made quite the parade. They couldn't swim that fast, so Annabeth and I were walking slowly in front while all the Octopuses were swimming through the air behind us.

"I kinda feel like a mama duck," I told Annabeth. "I wish you could see them. The Octopuses are as cute as can be, and the way they are all floating through the air makes me feel like I'm underwater.

"This is kind of like Mary Poppins. She goes on these magical adventures and pops into paintings. It's like we are in an animated adventure." I thought about my bruises. "Although this animated adventure can smash your face in and suck out all your magic—or knock you into a tree."

Annabeth laughed wryly. "There is that. This new supernatural world is certainly dangerous sometimes. At least it is beautiful too.

"And I think the word you are looking for is octopi," she said.

"Huh?" That took me by surprise. I thought we were still on the beauty and danger discussion. Not a grammar discussion.

"I think the plural of octopus is octopi. The correct way to say it is we have several Octopi swimming through the air behind us." Annabeth was using her lecture voice. I was used to that from Sandy, but this was the first time Annabeth had slipped into teacher mode.

"So what would octopuses be?" I asked playfully.

"I guess, if you had an eight-legged cat, it would be an octo-puss. Then, if you had several of them, they would be octo-pusses."

"Hmmm. Now I want to make an eight-legged cat," I said. "So what do you call a bunch of octopi? A herd? A flock?"

"Maybe a school? Like a school of fish?" Annabeth played along. "Or a colony?"

"That's boring," I replied. "If you can have a murder of crows, then there should be a cool name for a group of octopi. How about a sucker of octopi?"

Annabeth gave me the look. "That sounds like they are a bunch of card sharks looking for a sucker to take his money."

"True," I said. "And bonus points for sticking with a nautical reply. How about a tangle? A tangle of octopi?"

"A tangle of octopi," Annabeth said, trying it on for size. "It does have a nice ring to it. You know, I'm going to have to Google this later and see what the term is really supposed to be. For now, though, I think a tangle will work."

And, with that, we and our Tangle of Octopi made it to Sandy's apartment and into her bedroom. Annabeth held the door open so all the little Octopi could swim inside. As they started settling on Sandy, I realized we had a problem. A problem of the cat kind.

Bermuda was stretched out napping on John's lap. Since John didn't move much, Annabeth had covered his lap in pillows. It was the perfect place to work on magic or have a think. When we came in, Bermuda gave me a sleepy, 'Oh, you're here. Hi, Daddy.' kind of look. That all changed when sixteen purple, tentacled creations swam inside. Then his eyes got big. Like 'Oh, Daddy! What did you bring me to play with?!' kind of big.

He hopped off of John and stalked over.

"Bermuda! No!" I yelled at him.

Snowy and Biscuit just looked at us like we were crazy. They couldn't see my creations, so it didn't bother them at all. Bermuda, however, shared the same magic as me, so he was able to see all my works. I think it was the waving tentacles that fascinated him the most.

Bermuda's other ability was that he could shred spells. I first saw it when he protected me from a remnant, and I saw it again when he helped me win my necro battle. He can't destroy magic. I don't think anyone can do that. Somehow, though, he ruins the form the magic takes. It then becomes harmless magic that just dissipates in the air. That's great if someone is throwing a fireball at me. It's not so great if it's something I've made and I really need it to work.

His tail started swishing, and I quickly picked him up before he could pounce. I tried to distract him with some love and kisses, but he was having none of it. He had a one track mind: check out those strange purple things!

I had to take him out into the hallway and summoned Dot to keep him entertained. Even that didn't work. He wanted back inside.

Dot was clearly old news, so it was time for an upgrade.

I'd made Dot like a sports car, with a shiny red spotlight in the back. He had special tires so he could run up walls, but otherwise he didn't have any special powers. That was going to change.

I added a propeller on the front of the car and changed the doors so they would transform into wings. Now it could fly! I modified the light in the back so it was blinking, instead of always on. That would make it feel more dynamic.

I gave Dot 2.0 some power and sent him out for a spin. Bermuda was certainly interested, but it didn't take his mind off the Octopi like I wanted.

I didn't want to put tentacles on the car. That would just give Bermuda the idea that tentacles were something you played with. I needed something else.

Feathers. Cats liked feathers.

What if the feathers weren't attached to the car? What if they trailed behind and could be caught? That certainly sounded exciting to me.

I made a bunch of feathers, and then made a string. I attached the string to Dot, then attached the feathers to the string. Dot 2.0 kicked into action, and this time the feathers shimmied in the air behind him.

This was too much for Bermuda. When Feather Dot raced down the hallway, he was not far behind. I made two more Feather Dots, and they joined the fun. Now my kitten was in sensory overload. He was trying to catch all three of them and going into frantic overdrive. Hopefully, they would last long enough to wear him out.

I left them there and went back to the bedroom. This was supposed to be all about Sandy after all.

All the Octopi were docked onto Sandy, and the transfer had started. The neutral magic glowed. It looked like

Sandy had a bunch of light bulbs attached to her. It was kind of pretty. Now it just needed to work.

We waited for several minutes, chatting to pass the time. Then Annabeth had another idea.

"Sandy is a fire mage with orange magic," Annabeth said. "Right now we are pumping her full of neutral white magic. Maybe providing a fire near her would help her convert what Octa is providing."

"It's possible," I said. "I don't want to burn the House down, though, so we would need to be careful. Maybe John could make a fire pit, and we could break up the furniture for wood. Sandy won't be happy about that, though, when she wakes up."

Annabeth just looked at me like I had a hole in the head. "What?" I said. I thought I was being pretty responsible about all this.

"Candles, Jason. Candles."

Ohhhh. Yes. That would clearly be a better solution.

It turned out Annabeth was a candle hoarder. She had all sorts of candles: smaller candles in jars, large fat three-wick candles, candles with wooden wicks, and even a giant candle that was three feet tall.

It took a lot of trips to bring them all down from Annabeth's apartment. It felt good to be moving around, even with all the bruises. I was initially afraid to leave Octa in case Bermuda started stalking her and the Tangle again. The new Feather Dots had worn him out, though, and when we let him back into Sandy's bedroom, he went back to sleep on John's lap. There would still be trouble in the future, but for now he was okay.

We got about half the candles set out, and once they were lit, Sandy's bedroom became a beautiful sanctuary. It felt like something out of a movie. Now all it needed was rose petals strewn about and two star crossed lovers to complete the look.

Actually, we already had the two tragic lovers. I felt a chill at the thought. I didn't want to lose John or Sandy.

The Tangle was about half finished delivering their magic, so I zoomed in for a closer look. I could see a slightly denser cloud of magic inside of Sandy where each of the Octopi were. The absorption seemed to be much slower with her than with Annabeth.

I guess that made sense if magic attracted magic. Sandy was very low on power, so she wasn't attracting much. Even being spoon fed magic like this was slow. I guess the good news was that the process would eventually speed up. For now, though, it took four hours for her to take in all the magic.

I took all the Octopi back to the Circle Room to get a refill. Since the first round was a success, I doubled the number of purple magic eaters. The Circle Room only had a limited amount of neutral magic in it, and the Octopi gathered up everything it had. Hopefully, four hours would be enough time for the Circle Room to refill. If not, I'd have to go back to using less of them again.

Once we were back and the Tangle was infusing Sandy again, I checked out her overall status. It did seem like the candles were working. I thought the little bit of magic she had was a touch more saturated than before. She also definitely had a bit more magic inside her.

We had a long way to go, though. I felt like we had dumped a few gallons of water into a nearly empty swimming pool. Sure, there was more water than before, but it was going to be a long time before we went swimming.

3

To Nest An Egg

The next three days passed in a blur. Every four hours I needed to take Octa and her Tangle on a refill trip. The Circle Room couldn't regenerate magic sparkles fast enough, so I ended up having to supplement it with trips to the park.

The place by the picnic table, where Annabeth and I were attacked by a golem and where I first met Isobel and her goons, still had the densest source of neutral magic. There were other spots as well with a few sparkles, but it took longer to reach them, and the fill up was a lot less. Still, I'd take whatever I could get.

I felt the candles around Sandy were helping, and Annabeth said she could hear a slight difference, so she kept them burning. Despite the fact that she was a candle hoarder, Annabeth still didn't have enough to keep the room lit twenty-four hours a day for who knew how many days. Annabeth decided that she would ask the House for help, and

I got to see the famous House request in action for the first time.

Annabeth simply walked around the room, pointing out where she would like candles and what type they should be. Annabeth and I then left to refill Octa, and when we got back, all of the requested candles were there. Annabeth's pink magic, however, was missing from the room.

Annabeth was always humming, which expelled her happy, pink magic into the world. It was like cheerful fairy dust and that ended up sticking to everything. I was so used to seeing it all the time that it felt strange when the walls and floor didn't have a slight touch of rose. When the candles showed up, the rose color disappeared. I figured the House absorbed her magic and somehow turned it into the candles.

I decided to try it for myself. My sword, now an egg shape, was still sitting in my dresser drawer in my bedroom. This was not what we had agreed to. It liked sunlight and a window from which to watch the world go by. It wasn't like I just let it sit there all the time. I pulled it out at least once a day and gave it some magic. I told it how pretty it looked now and thanked it for all its help in the necro battle. Annabeth said I was like a mother hen, brooding over her egg.

Spending time with the egg was fun. Taking care of Sandy was rough. I felt like a new mother, having to make sure her baby was fed every four hours, which came around really quickly. Bermuda had a new thing where he liked to be carried everywhere, so I often found myself walking to the Circle Room with a kitten in one arm, steel egg in the other, and a Tangle of Octopi swimming along behind. I was discovering that taking care of an injured housemate was almost as hard as being injured myself. Anyway, I couldn't carry the egg with me everywhere, and it needed a much better resting spot than a dark sock drawer, so I took the time to have a talk with the House.

I stood in front of my bedroom window, considering what I needed. The former sword was an egg right now, but it wanted to be a very ornate vase. Like, very ornate. Like scroll work, angels, cherubs, all that. It was a "more is more" kind of egg. Because it was now one of my awakened charms, it could be whatever it wanted. It didn't feel right to just throw a cat bed on the windowsill, plop the egg in it, and be done with it. The charm needed more pizzazz than that.

"Okay, House," I said tentatively. I felt strange talking to the air. "I need something to put my egg charm on so it can look out the window and enjoy the sunlight. It likes fancy, older stuff, so I was thinking maybe an elaborate column and a nice, luxurious cushion to rest on. I'm not the greatest decorator, so use your best judgment."

I'm not sure what type of judgment the House had, but it had gone to work on Annabeth's apartment, and it was simply stunning. Hopefully it would do something nice here too.

"House, I'm also not sure how to pay for all this," I said. "I think I just give you some of my magic, and you do the rest. If I'm wrong, then please find a way to let me know." I waited, but everything looked the same. The House didn't give me any sort of sign it had heard me.

"While I'm here talking to you and feeling a bit strange, I wanted to say thank you for letting me stay here. Thank you for the housemates. They are truly unique and wonderful. And thank you for keeping me safe. I sleep better at night knowing I'm behind your shields." That seemed a bit formal to me, but this was my first time talking to a wall. Hopefully, it got the right idea.

I wasn't sure exactly how to do this, so I just put my hand on the wall and pushed out my magic. I'd gotten very used to doing that now. It seemed to go somewhere, but nothing changed in the moment. I wasn't sure how much to give, so I just kept pushing until I had given it almost everything I had. I wasn't low on magic for long, though, as I easily pulled in more from Penny. Hopefully, what I'd sent into the House would be enough.

I'd been using my magic a lot recently. I was constantly having to repair an Octopus or make a new one. Sandy's aura was very weak, but it was still breaking down the Octopi when they rested on her. Despite my best efforts, Bermuda was still fascinated by them, and sometimes he'd catch one and it would vanish with a pop. I was also pushing magic into my steel egg all the time. The egg formerly known as a sword was still very low on magic and was asleep at the moment. It was going to take time to fill it back up again. Especially since it needed someone with a lot more magic capacity than I had.

In addition to all that, I continued spending time awakening my cells. Every chance I got, I was awakening a new cluster of cells and helping my physical magic grow. It seemed like I was getting injured all the time, so I needed as much power in my body as possible. Awakened cells didn't just heal over time, they transformed right away into healthy tissue.

That was why three days later I was feeling fully recovered from my trip through the trees. The bruises were mostly gone, and I felt good. In addition, my sword wound was pretty much healed. I still felt a little twinge from it now and then, but even that was fading away. I wasn't up to Tyler's amazing transformation abilities, but I was certainly doing a lot better than I had before.

Speaking of Tyler, I missed him. I missed him a lot. I really enjoyed waking up with him and having our morning time. He'd just started to open up to me right before the House took him away. He looked perfect to me, and he had been a supernatural much longer than I had, so it was easy to think his life was impeccable—that his life was exactly the way he wanted. It wasn't, though. Tyler was still finding his way in life. He didn't have it all together yet, and it was nice seeing the vulnerable side of him.

I admit I was crushing on him. I liked him. I wanted to see him. I wanted to spend time with him. But that wasn't happening. I'm sure the House was keeping him busy, and he was fixing a problem for another new supernatural. Maybe many new supernaturals.

I had gone up and checked his door. It was still there. That meant the House was planning on him coming back. I held onto that hope. It was much better than the thought that he had moved on. I was fixed now, my Remnants were gone, so I didn't need his incubus powers anymore. We had talked about physical training, though, and Tyler had thought the House wanted him to teach me how to defend myself. He would be my Jedi Master, and I would be his padawan.

That would certainly work for me! I'd seen Tyler in action. He was deadly. We'd already had one sort-of training session and dodging had been a lot harder than it looked. He had said that once a mage comes into his or her magic powers, then every problem starts to look like it should be solved with magic. Mages rely heavily on magic shields, but there are other ways to defend yourself. That was what he was offering me.

He also inspired me to awaken my cells. By doing this, I was getting a bit stronger and faster. I was healing better. I had advantages other mages didn't, and I needed that edge. I didn't have big, powerful magic like Sandy, and I couldn't use charms like Annabeth. My magic was small. It took time to work. Fights demanded power and speed, and I wasn't suited for that. Developing myself as a Natural in addition to a Mage was my way around those limitations.

I have my own insecurities, though, and they're usually headed up by my Analytical Side. That side of me keeps me from doing really stupid things—especially in poker. He's got an English accent and a cutting sense of humor, and usually I enjoy hearing a fresh perspective—but recently he'd been talking to me a lot about Tyler.

Jason, old chap, you do realize that Tyler is very hot.

'Yes, I do realize that.'

He's not just hot, he's like an amazing, supernova hot.

'Yes, I realize that too.'

So, on a scale of one to ten, he's a fifty.

'Fifty? Really? That seems a bit high.'

On top of all that, he eats bad emotions. People feel better just being around him. When they have sex, it's a religious experience. They feel out-of-this-world amazing. Like a dog-with-two-tails amazing. Like tingles-from-head-to-toe amazing.

'Yes. Yes. I get the idea. I had Remnants, so I couldn't tell you myself.'

What I'm trying to say is, he is out of your league. Like way, way out of your league.

'Really? That much?'

You're a solid seven. Eight on a good day. You have a nice smile, and you have some muscles. You're only mildly jaded by the world, and you have a quick mind with a fun sense of humor. You're not bad, and to the right person, you could be a ten.

'Thank you. I think.'

What I'm saying is don't get hurt. You can crush on this guy all you want. He is very crushworthy, but don't think he's going to return the same level of feelings. He can literally have anyone he wants. He's interested in you right now. A unique set of circumstances helped you catch his attention. Just don't expect to have it forever.

'I... That does make sense. Damn it.'

Enjoy your moments. Love every minute together. But it can't last.

I felt sad. Like Tyler and I had already been together, and now we were breaking up.

Ahhhh—who am I kidding? You're going to dive in and get hurt anyway. That's just who you are. Life is a journey and all that jazz. Just remember to smell his roses along the way.

'Hopefully, I'll do more than that!'

I'm sure you'll try.

I mentally stuck my tongue out at him. 'Buttface.'

It's your own face you're insulting. So sad.

'Buuuuuuttttttt face! Buttface! Buttface! Buttface!'

I'm rubber, you're glue; whatever you say bounces off me and sticks to you.

I mentally chewed some gum, took it out, and stuck it in his hair. I'm creative like that.

You are just horrid!

My Analytical Side disappeared in a huff. It's a crazy three-ring circus in my head sometimes. Do other people have these types of thoughts too?

He wasn't wrong. Tyler was a one-of-a-kind supernatural, and I'm sure lots and lots of people have become infatuated with him. Still, a guy can't help but hope for the best, while being afraid of the worst. That's life. If you don't have hope, if you don't try, then what's the use of living?

I gave myself a mental shake. Enough wool gathering, it's time to give the Octopi a refill, and then see if the House made something for Eggy.

That was the former sword's name at the moment, Eggy. I'd have to change it again when it became a real vase.

I sent out the call, and my Tangle of purple creations followed me out the front door of the House, across the street, and into the park. I'd already cleared out the Circle Room on the last trip. It needed time to refill. I didn't take them all the way to the picnic table. There was plenty of ambient magic in the air. It was surprising how dense the sparkles were in the park. Maybe it was because people came here all the time? I knew there was a Realm Gate around here somewhere. Maybe it was because of that? Regardless, I was happy I had it. Sandy needed all the help she could get.

When they were refilled, I dropped them back off with Sandy, played with Bermuda for a few minutes to keep him away from Octa and her Tangle, and then picked up Eggy and headed up to my room. I'd been checking every recharge cycle to see if the House had done its thing yet.

My apartment was beginning to feel a bit strange. I was spending so much time in Sandy's bedroom and catnapping on John's lap, that I was losing touch with my own space. It would be nice when all this was over to sleep in my own bed and have a relaxing morning.

I opened the door and went through the living room, mentally saying hello to my tattered old couch and TV. 'Hang in there guys. I'll be back again someday. I promise.' When I entered the bedroom, I stopped in shock. The House had provided a stand for Eggy! And it wasn't just any old stand.

It was like a spray of water coming out of the ocean. The base was wide and frothy with sea-foam. The column itself was a thick pillar of water, ending in a wide splash about waist high. The whole thing looked like it was made out of blown glass. It was thick, shiny, and organic looking in the way that only blown glass can look. It had all the shades of blue in it, almost white-blue for the bubbles, light blue to show the rush of the water, deep blue for the core. Right at the top there was an indent, a perfect dip, just right for the bottom of an egg.

I took a moment to just take it all in. It was beautiful. It looked like it should be the centerpiece of an art exhibit by Chihuly. It occurred to me it must have magic in the design for me to see the color with my magical sight. I put Eggy in the indent and stepped back to admire it.

It was perfect. All the white and blue reflected off of Eggy's polished steel, making it the crown jewel of the entire stand. It was just the right height too. Eggy would get the morning sun, and it could look out the window. The House had done a truly spectacular job.

Eggy was still sleeping, but when it woke up, I'm sure it would be very happy. I sat on the bed for a moment just enjoying the sight. It was so perfect, it made the rest of my bedroom look very bland and boring. Annabeth's place was spectacular, but she said she had changed only one thing at a time. Maybe I could do the same?

What goes with a column of water? I wasn't sure, but I wanted to find out. I put my hand on the wall to give it magic.

"House, thank you for the stand! It looks better than I could ever have imagined. I'm not sure what would go with it, but let's work on the window next. Let's give Eggy something fun and beautiful to look through."

I pushed magic into the wall for several minutes until I was almost empty, then refilled from Penny. This was exciting! My apartment wasn't going to be a bland living space anymore. I wondered what the House was going to do next.

I spent a few more moments appreciating the glass sculpture, when I noticed a slight change in Eggy's reflection. There was a prominent streak of blue on the lower right side from where I was sitting. It had shifted. I sat and looked at it some more. The whole thing was moving!

I watched a tiny bubble in the foam at the bottom gradually shift and flow up the column before it popped and vanished. It was super slow, but the glass was somehow in motion. I had a moving, magical piece of art in my bedroom. How cool was that?

The motion was snail-like for me, but Eggy was used to sitting in one spot for long periods of time when it was a sword. Maybe the changes to the glass fountain would be fascinating to it? If not, I could always request something else later. For now, it was everything I wanted, and so much more.

My bed felt so comfortable, I decided to stretch out for a bit and just enjoy being in my own space. The slow change to the fountain was hypnotic and peaceful. I started nodding off to sleep, and I didn't try to fight it. I had time for a catnap, and this was a nice place for it. Bermuda wandered in and jumped up on the bed to snuggle with me. He curled up in my arms, licked me a few times on the cheek, and then gave a long sigh as he snuggled in. The bedroom was calm, tranquil, and together we drifted off to sleep.

I woke up gradually. I felt for Tyler, but he wasn't there. Damn. Bermuda was, though, curled up on my pillow. He gave a big yawn and rolled over so he could touch my face with his paw. He gave me this look that said 'Come on, Daddy. Love me already!' So I did.

I loved, he purred, and we were happy together. He was so damn cute I had to kiss him. He decided it was play time, so I switched to making fart noises on his belly. He started growling, and it was on like Donkey Kong! Growling seemed to be his new thing. He growled when we played, and he growled when I called for him. He even got mixed up at times and purred and growled at the same time. My kitten was talented like that.

I had to stop soon, though. He was getting too excited, and those little claws were sharp. He was wide awake now and wound up, so I made a couple Feather Dots and turned them loose to play. They tore off into the living room where the fun continued. I lay in bed for a few minutes more. It was just so nice to be here in my own space. I checked out the glass column again. It looked even more beautiful than last night with the sunlight shining on it now. It really brought out the depth of the colors inside the thick glass.

Wait a minute. Sunlight? I could see sunlight?!

Omg! I could see! I had my sight back!

I sat bolt upright in bed, my heart pounding. I checked the clock. I could see the time! The digital numbers showed 5:39. I grabbed my phone and turned it on. I could see the screen! Omg! I could play Sudoku. I could actually text people, make phone calls, and do all my normal stuff again.

I loved my magic sight. I really did. It had kept me going, and I hadn't gone crazy when I'd lost my normal vision, but it wasn't a substitute for the real thing. I hadn't been able to watch Netflix, play Sudoku, see the sky, tell time, or any of the other normal things I'd taken for granted.

I wanted to run and tell Annabeth right away. She had been so helpful and encouraging. When I'd started to doubt that I would ever get back to normal, she'd told me over and over again that I would be alright. She'd said that someday I would see again. I couldn't wait to tell her that that day was today.

I also couldn't wait to play a game of Sudoku. Playing a few games was usually how I started my morning. I had really missed my normal routine. Watching all the numbers line up just felt right.

I could also smell something in the air. It smelled a little ripe. Oh, wait, that was me. Without a clock or knowing when the sun was out, I'd lost track of time. Apparently, the time to take a shower was now.

Well, it was just me here, so it would be fine if I was ripe for a few more moments. I fired up my phone and played a few rounds. I was rusty, so I left it on the easy setting. I had the gift of seeing patterns and being able to figure out how things worked. The numbers just flowed out, and I felt more rested and relaxed than I had in a long time.

I could have played all day, but I'm sure Octa and her Tangle needed a refill. There was time for a shower, though. When I got out, Bermuda was lounging on the back of the toilet, and the roll of toilet paper was on the floor. In other words, everything was normal.

Feeling much cleaner and smelling a lot better, I headed up to see Annabeth.

"I can see!" I said to Annabeth as soon as she opened the door.

"Oh? What are you seeing?" Annabeth clearly had her mind on something else.

"No, I can see," I said. "Like really see. Like see-with-my-eyes see."

" Oh? Ohhhhhh. You can see! That is wonderful." She gave me a big hug, and we did a happy dance together.

"How did it happen?" She wanted to hear all about it. I told her about waking up and seeing the sunlight.

"Oh, that reminds me, you have got to see the new stand for Eggy." I told her all about my first decorating project.

"It's nothing like this place." I gestured at her beautiful Tuscan villa apartment. "But it's a start."

"I'm sure it's beautiful," Annabeth said. "I can't wait to see it later. At least your former sword will have something nice to sit on now." She didn't like to call it Eggy, saying it sounded too much like something you'd have for breakfast.

"Have you eaten?" She switched topics on me. I realized I was famished. She pulled out all the fixings for a killer sandwich, and we went to town. I had a turkey sandwich with lettuce, tomato, relish, mustard, mayo, and some crushed up potato chips for a bit of crunch.

I'm a "more is more" kinda guy.

Annabeth had a sensible ham sandwich with lettuce, tomato, mayo, and pickle. We munched and chatted, and had a nice few moments together. Life was strange with Sandy down and John not communicating. Having a few normal moments was a welcome respite.

After lunch, we went down to check on Sandy.

"How is she looking?" Annabeth asked.

"Her magic is filling in," I replied. "There used to be no orange at all. Then there were little wisps of orange magic floating around. Now there is a definite fog of orange. It also seems like she is starting to absorb the magic a bit faster."

"That's what I'm hearing," Annabeth said. "She is starting to sound like Sandy used to. It's still really faint, though. Any idea how much magic she needs before Sleeping Beauty wakes up?"

"I have no idea." I shook my head. This was familiar ground for us. We'd asked each other that question before, hoping one of us had gotten some new insight. We could agree that she was doing better, but we didn't have any idea of how far we had left to go.

"I'm assuming our purple people need a refill?" she asked.

"Oh, yes," I replied. "They are already up in the air ready to go."

"Let's refill them in the park," Annabeth suggested. "Now you have your sight back, you need something bigger than this House to look at."

That sounded great to me. I checked out each of the Octopi and repaired and refilled them with my magic as needed. Sandy's aura was only doing minimal damage, and Bermuda had stopped chasing them as often, so the Tangle was looking pretty good overall. I gallantly offered Annabeth my arm, and the both of us and the purple parade slowly made our way outside.

The park was beautiful. Like it was the most beautiful thing I'd ever seen. I was blown away. I even teared up a bit. The colors were so rich and vibrant. I felt like I had never seen green before. The leaves on the trees and all the shades of grass, wow. Just wow.

And the sky, wow again. There were lots of fluffy clouds with so much texture that towered up and up and up. I have always enjoyed nature, but this touched me on a whole new level.

I stood for a while, just taking it all in. Annabeth didn't talk or ask any questions. She just let me have my moment. She's good like that. Finally, I started telling her what I was seeing, and she gave me another big hug.

"I just didn't think it would be this good, you know?" I gestured to all the beautiful nature in front of me.

"Whenever I thought about getting my sight back, I always thought about my phone, or being able to watch my shows again. I didn't realize how much I missed all this."

Annabeth just nodded and took my hand. The purple parade was doing its thing collecting neutral magic. They'd already gathered all the easy sparkles, so they had to go out much farther to get refilled. They weren't fast swimmers, so we had some time before we had to head back.

"How about we have a nice walk and just enjoy the day?" Annabeth asked. "You've been working so much recently. Taking a few minutes won't kill you."

That sounded nice, so we set out at a leisurely pace. A cool breeze tickled the trees and provided the background music of nature. The sun felt pleasant, not too hot, and it felt good to just stretch my legs a bit. I like the House, but sometimes it's nice to have lots and lots of space.

"You know, I think something is different," I said. "I know seeing again is obviously a big deal, but this feels like it is more than that."

"How so?" Annabeth asked.

"Everything seems so much more vivid than I remember," I replied. "I'm trying to think about what the park looked like before, and it wasn't like this. It's like the colors were muted and they weren't as sharp. Like they were muddled together. Now everything is super sharp and crisp. It's like the whole world has gone high definition on me."

"Is this as big a change as when you first used your magic sight after your Waker Moment?" Annabeth asked. "You were shocked at how much you could see and how easy it was when you were looking around the kitchen."

"I'd forgotten about that," I said. "This is a lot like that. It's maybe not as big of a change, but it is pretty significant."

"Well, you did have to regrow your eyeballs," Annabeth said. "Maybe your new eyes are better. Have you ever had glasses?"

"Are you saying my old balls were fuzzy?" I cocked an eyebrow at her. "And my new balls are smoother and more colorful?"

"I think you are taking what I said out of context," Annabeth said primly.

"Or maybe my new balls are bigger." I gave her a wide-eyed look. "Do my balls look bigger to you?"

She playfully smacked me on my arm. "You think you are so funny." Annabeth was fun to play around with. She acted all miffed, but her eyes were sparkling.

"To answer your question, I've never had glasses. I had a test in school, and they said I was okay. That was a long time ago, though, and I don't know how good my eyesight was. It just seemed normal to me." I looked around at the details I'd missed before. "Maybe I needed glasses more than I thought.

"So how good is your eyesight?" I asked her.

"I used to wear glasses," Annabeth replied. "After my Waker Moment, my sight just kept getting better and better, and I finally threw them away. I think my eyesight is better now than it has ever been, even with glasses."

"How about we play a little game and see how we compare?" I suggested.

"Sure," Annabeth replied. "I'll go first. Let me see..." She looked around for something to test me with. "Way over there are the doors to the restroom. Just to the side of them is a trash can. Can you see it?"

"Got it," I said.

"Right in front of the can is a piece of trash. Someone probably went to throw it away, missed, and didn't go back to pick it up. Can you tell what it is?"

She had picked out a hard one. The way my eyesight was before, there was no way I could've picked out what it was.

"It's a Cool Ranch Doritos bag," I said. "The opening is pointing to the right, and a few inches in front of that is a silver gum wrapper."

"That's really good," Annabeth said. "I can't see the gum wrapper at all." We walked a bit closer. "Okay, now I see it."

"My turn," I said, looking around for something good for a test. "Do you see that house with the columns and all the flowers out front?" I pointed to a house that was quite a distance away at the edge of the park. Annabeth nodded. "There is a bit of yellow in the upper left window. Can you see what it is?"

"It looks like flowers in a vase," she said. "Although it's fuzzy and I'm not sure."

"How many flowers are there? And for extra credit, what color is the vase?"

She peered at it for a while. "I think there are five flowers, and I have no idea on the color of the vase."

"I think there are six flowers, and the vase is dark green," I said. This was fun! I couldn't believe how well I could see now. It's like I had super vision. We started walking towards the house to see how accurate we were.

Annabeth tripped over a tree root. She didn't fall down, but she didn't recover gracefully either.

I grabbed her arm to steady her. "Are you okay?"

"I'm fine," she said. She took a deep breath, steadying herself. "I'm still sore from our mage fight the other day." We started walking again. "How are you feeling?"

"I was feeling really rough the next morning," I said. "I thought I wasn't going to be able to move for a while there. I feel fine now though." I took a mental inventory. Was I really completely over it? I stretched my arms and rotated my torso. "Yep. All good now."

Annabeth gave me a funny look and kept walking. Something was up.

"Are you sure you're okay?" I asked.

"Can I ask you for a favor?" she said.

"Sure," I replied. "Whatever you need. Just ask."

Annabeth stopped and looked at me. She had her serious face on.

"I want a matrix."

"What?" That totally caught me by surprise.

"I want a magic matrix like you have, Jason," she repeated. "I want to be able to heal like you do. This new world is tough. I've been kicked by a golem, knocked through a tree, and been in some tough battles." All of this was coming out in a rush. "I haven't been injured as badly as you have, and I'm scared. One day my shield will come down at the wrong moment, or I'll be in the wrong place at the wrong time, and I'll get really hurt. Like punched in the face by a golem hurt."

She started to tear up a bit. "We keep getting attacked, so it's just a matter of time until it happens. When

I do get into trouble, I want to be as ready as possible. I want to have done everything I could to prepare. This is my second life, and I'm not going down without a fight." Despite the misty eyes, she looked fierce, determined.

What she was saying made total sense. If I had known a golem punch was coming, I would most certainly have done everything I could to be ready. Broken bones were no fun.

I was going to work on the same thing when Tyler got back. I still couldn't use charms, so learning how to fight was my best option. Annabeth was right. More battles were headed our way. It was smart to be prepared.

"Annabeth, you're my best friend in the House. Of course, I will do everything I can for you." I pulled her in, giving her a big hug. I felt her relax a bit as she hugged me back. Was she afraid I'd say no? She was used to being the mom and the grandmother. She needed to learn that it was okay to ask for help.

"I'm excited about a matrix, and I'm nervous too," she said. "I mean, look at you, you feel no pain from getting knocked into a tree, and it's only a few days later. I had a shield and I'm using a healing charm, and I'm still feeling it."

"Going through the experience to get the matrix was no fun, but it is great now that I have it," I said. "I can see these little flashes inside me. I call it twinkle lightning, and I know that every day I'm getting better at healing myself. So what are you nervous about?"

"I'm nervous that since I only hear magic that there won't be any way for me to create a matrix," she said. "I have been giving this a lot of thought, and I do have some ideas about how to proceed."

"Hold that thought," I said. We had arrived at the house, and I pointed at the upper left window. There were six yellow flowers in a dark green vase, just like I had said.

"I think you win the vision test," Annabeth said. "I was just guessing when I said it was five flowers. It looked like a bunch of fuzzy, yellow clumps to me."

"It's my new balls," I said with mock seriousness pointing at my eyes. "I got the long-range model." I was trying to lighten the mood a bit.

She poked me in the arm and laughed. "Seriously, though, being able to see that clearly is going to be an advantage. I'm not exactly sure how, yet, but I'm sure it will come in handy." She gave me her serious look again. "Maybe as handy as having a matrix."

I got the hint. Annabeth was resolved about this, and she wanted to talk about it now. We started walking again.

"I'm sure you have tried this on your own already. How did it go?"

"It was frustrating," she said. "I felt a lot like you did when you first tried. I could feel my own magic, but I couldn't figure out how to compress it. I tried squishing it, kneading it, talking to it, singing to it, and even slapping it around a bit when I got irritated. I tried zooming in like you did and dealing with just a tiny part of it, but I don't have your ability to see that small. Basically, I've tried everything I can think to do on my own, and nothing has worked."

Wow. She had really worked at this. The key for me was the ability to zoom in to a microscopic level and work with my magic from there. That was the only time it hadn't been a mist. It had finally been real magic components that I could manipulate. If she had spent this much time and thought on her attempts so far, she probably had a plan already.

"So what do you need me to do?" I asked.

"I need you to do your zoom thing on my magic and start compressing it. You said that once you got a big enough matrix, the magic had started compressing on its own."

"That sounds like a plan," I said. "Except for one very big problem. I can't work with your magic."

Annabeth nodded. "I've thought of that. Remember when we had our celebration after you recovered from getting golem punched, and Sandy asked you to look at her magic?" I nodded. That event was how I knew how much magic Sandy could hold and how far she still had left to go. "She swore on her magic to let you in so you could see her spinning cores. What if you could do more than that? What if you could actually manipulate someone else's magic?"

I thought about it. Would that be possible?

"That sounds like a solid maybe. We would need to get the wording right on what you were swearing, but it would be worth a shot. There is one other possible problem. It's not just magic; it's your aura. Your aura is your natural defender, and it will keep me from zooming in too far. Bermuda and I share the same magic, but his aura makes it hard for me to see what is happening. I'm sure we will run into the same thing with you."

"Then why don't we include my magic and my aura in one swear?" she replied. "I think auras are just an extension of magic, so they might follow the same rules."

"It's worth a shot," I said. "If it doesn't work, then nothing bad will happen. You'll have the magic level you have now, and we'll just have to figure out something else. When do you want to try this?"

"How about now?" she said.

This was coming together quickly. Almost too quickly. Was I ready to do this?

"We probably want to write down what you are going to swear to. You don't want to swear something that is going to backfire."

"I'm way ahead of you." Annabeth pulled out a small notepad from a pocket of her pants, flipped to a page, and then handed it over. Her handwriting was very neat and legible, unlike mine. My handwriting was awful. It looked like a pen threw up on the page. Her letters had little flourishes, and it made the writing flow like a script. It was artistic in a way.

What she had written was a great start, and we talked about a few additions for her aura, as well as how long we should go for. Sandy had said that you should always put a time limit on a swear since we are immortals and situations can change quickly. I was thinking a few days, but Annabeth was thinking a few months.

When I'd made my matrix, it had taken days, and it was the only thing I'd worked on. Now I was busy with refilling Sandy, waking up Penny and Eggy, and hopefully training whenever Tyler came back. I had a full life, so I wasn't going to be able to take a lot of time and work on Annabeth's matrix. After thinking it through, I agreed to three months. If it wasn't finished by then, we could always swear again. I thought we should be sitting down for this, so we made our way to the famous park bench where our first battle had started.

Once we sat down, I sent out a call to all the Octopi to meet me here. This was a good spot to regroup and head back when we were finished. I was on one side of the bench, and she was on the other. She held the paper notebook with the finished swear in one hand, so I took the other one. I squeezed her hand, and she smiled and squeezed back. This seemed like a big deal, and it was nice to have the support. The wind died down, and the park seemed to pause, waiting for her to begin.

"I, Annabeth Matz, swear on my magic to grant full access to Jason Cole for the purpose of creating a magic matrix. He can see and use my magic like his magic, my body like his body, my aura like his aura. My power and my aura will assist him in every way possible to compress my magic and awaken my cells. So long as he does no harm to me, he will have this ability for three months, starting now."

She stopped, and the breeze started blowing again. The sun was still shining. I heard a bird singing. Annabeth seemed okay. I breathed a sigh of relief.

"Are you feeling okay?" I asked.

"Yes," she said. "So far, so good. I wasn't sure what to expect. We are swearing a magic oath, so I kinda feel like the sky should go dark and lightning should start flashing."

"I feel the same way," I laughed. "And now for the first test." I closed my eyes and looked at her with my magic sight.

I could see everything. I could see her pink magic like a thick fog floating inside her. I could also see all her physical parts—her heart beating, her blood flowing, all her muscles and bones. So far, this was a success.

"So far, so good!" I said without opening my eyes. "I can see your magic and your body. Your aura isn't blocking me at all. Now for the next test. Can I zoom in to the same degree and actually manipulate your magic? I don't think I can both talk and zoom in at the same time, so I'll give you an update in a minute. Stay tuned."

Sandy squeezed my hand in acknowledgment. I didn't waste any time. I zoomed into her hand and picked a spot right in the middle. Before she knew about making a matrix, Annabeth had been working on making her own swirling core in her hand. She wasn't working on it anymore, but it had left a higher concentration of magic. That would be useful.

I kept zooming in. Past the level of muscle and bone, past the level of muscle fibers, and down to the cellular level. This used to seem strange and unworldly, but I had been down to this level so often, awakening my cells, that it now seemed familiar. Test number two was successful. I could zoom in close enough. Time for test three, controlling her magic.

I called her magic to me, and a few moments later a pink dust bunny cloud showed up. It was smaller than my magic clouds had been. They had been as big as a house. Hers was as big as a truck. I called an individual strand of power down to me. It reformed from a long, hair-like strand into a fat, oblong capsule of power. It looked like one of those big fish oil capsules you get as a supplement from the drug store. So far, so good. I could call and manipulate her power. Now to make the first magic ball. I called down more magic and started stacking the capsules together. My green magic took about 60 capsules before it condensed into a much denser sphere. Her pink magic only took around 15. Her finished sphere was much smaller than mine, but then her clouds were smaller too. I guess that made sense.

I called in more clouds, pulled down 15 more capsules, and made my second sphere. I held it close to the first sphere. They repelled each other, just like I expected. They were quite a bit closer together than my spheres, though. That meant I was going to have to make a lot more of them for her matrix.

Since I was here and already zoomed in to this level, it seemed a shame to leave now without at least putting together a small matrix. I split clouds, made spheres, and it wasn't long before I had a 20 by 20 by 20 matrix. This was going so much faster than when I'd been injured. It had all been so new and experimental to me then. It was old-hat now.

I noticed that there was a delay between the time of my command and her magic responding. It was kind of like those delays when the news anchors go to a correspondent in the field. The news anchor in the studio says something like, "Let's go to Connie, who's currently in the eye of a hurricane. Connie, how is the wind?" Connie stares at the viewer with a blank smile on her face during the delay. Then the feed hits, and she starts talking about how she almost got blown off her feet. The delay of working with Annabeth's magic was like that. I'd command a cloud to split, it would pause, and then I'd get a shower of magic capsules. It wasn't bad, just annoying. I could work with it though.

The matrix still seemed fragile as there weren't a lot of spheres holding it together. Before I zoomed out, I thought I'd grow it just a bit more. The work went quickly. It was all repetitive effort, but I enjoyed it. There was something satisfying about seeing the cube grow. I hit roughly a hundred spheres on each side when I quit. I wasn't sure how much time it took, but it didn't seem like much. I let the matrix go and zoomed back out to the real world.

To my complete surprise, the sun was starting to set. I looked around a bit befuddled.

"How long have I been working?" I asked.

"More than three hours." Annabeth sounded a bit exasperated.

"No way."

"Oh, yes way." Annabeth took her hand back and started kneading her arm. Three hours was a long time to have someone holding your hand in the same position. "I would have thought that you would have stopped and given me an update a lot sooner." She glared at me. Grandma was not happy. Actually, I wasn't happy either. I'd been sitting in the same spot for three hours, and my butt was asleep. I groaned and stretched, and tried to get my blood moving again.

"The good news is..." I paused for dramatic effect. Annabeth was peeved, but she couldn't help herself—she leaned in and held her breath. "It worked."

"Really?" she asked. Irritation was giving way to excitement.

"Yep," I said firmly. "You are now the proud owner of a pink matrix. It's really small right now, like really small, but it's a solid foundation to build on."

"Yay!" She threw her hands in the air and did half a happy dance. I guess her butt was asleep too, or she would have probably run around the park trailing pink puffs of happiness. "So where is it?"

"It's right there." I touched the center of her palm. She stared at her hand for a long moment, then her face lit up.

"I can hear it!" She bounced up and down in excitement. "It sounds so different. It has a harmony to it, like a whole choir made up of the same person." Her eyes were shining. "I had no idea my magic could sound like this. So pure. So powerful."

She closed her eyes and hummed a note. "There is so much random noise in the rest of my magic. Now I know what it sounds like, I just need to tweak it." She hummed again.

Suddenly there was a flash. All of her magic condensed and shot to her hand. She stared at it for a moment as it glowed with beautiful matrix magic.

Then she fell backwards off the bench and started convulsing.

4

Colonel Mustard in the Park

"Oh, crap!" I jumped up as best as I could and limped to the other side of the picnic table. Annabeth's lower half was still on the bench with her upper body bent backward at a weird angle, flailing about on the ground. I grabbed under her arms, pulling her all the way off the bench. She was still shaking, but at least she was flat now.

What the heck happened? One moment she was fine, and now this. I gave her a quick scan with my Sight. Two things jumped out at me right away. The first was that her matrix had grown. It had grown a lot. It wasn't a tiny cube in her hand anymore. It was now a fully formed and dense matrix going all the way up to her elbow.

The second thing I saw was that the rest of her didn't have any magic at all. Somehow she had aligned all her magic in one spot, leaving no magic for the rest of her body. Matrix configurations are much denser than a fog of magic. That's why they are so useful. You can hold a lot more magic, but it has to come from somewhere. In this case, the magic had come from the rest of her.

A feeling of dread came over me as I realized my mistake. When I'd been building my matrix, I could pull from Penny. She had too much magic from the first golem I destroyed, and pulling it from Penny had woke her up and fueled my growth. Annabeth didn't have a Penny. She had nowhere else to pull from.

Her hand was doing great, but the rest of Annabeth was devoid of magic. That included her brain, heart, lungs, liver, kidneys, etc. As creatures of magic now, we depended on magic to keep us alive.

'Octa!' I hollered magically, and she was there. Her beautiful eyes batted at me in concern as she made a distressed whistling sound. I looked up. All of her Tangle was there, filled up, and ready to go. Thank goodness I'd asked them to meet me here!

'Help her!' I said, and they all swooped down over Annabeth and began spreading neutral magic on her. As the magic started being absorbed, her shaking stopped.

I saw I had another problem, though. Whatever Annabeth had done to start growing the matrix was still in effect. As she absorbed the neutral magic, it was converted to pink energy that zipped across her body and down her arm to join the matrix. She was going to need a lot of neutral magic. A whole heaping lot of it.

This sucked. This sucked big, huge donkey dicks. I now had two unconscious friends that desperately needed neutral magic. Sandy's problem wasn't life threatening, unlike Annabeth's. I had to get her as much magic as possible, as soon as possible. I started feeding my magic into Octa for duplication. I had about fifty Octopi. I needed loads more. I kept duplicating until I had amassed a Tangle of around two hundred. I felt light headed and a little sick from pushing so much magic, but it was worth it. The neutral magic around the picnic table was denser than anywhere else in the park, and the new purple creations sucked it up like beans at a church picnic.

With two hundred Octopi on Annabeth, she looked like she had caught a case of purple measles. They were all layering on life-saving neutral magic, so I didn't mind.

I had no idea how long this was going to take. How was I going to deal with this long term? I could keep her out here close to the magic for now, but having an unconscious woman on the ground in the park wasn't going to go unnoticed. People would think I was some sort of psycho and call the police. I was going to have to take her back to the House at some point soon.

The bigger question was, where was I going to find enough neutral magic for both Sandy and Annabeth? I was already using all the available magic in the Circle Room and most of the park for Sandy. There wasn't anywhere near enough neutral magic for two, and both of them seriously needed it.

Annabeth was stable at the moment, so I stood up and stretched, hoping an idea would come to me. Instead, I saw something that made my blood run cold.

Mustard was back.

He was back in a big way.

The last time I'd seen him he had just absorbed his two friends and made off with the magic groundhogs. His aura had been huge and nasty then. It was humongous now. It looked like he had drained the groundhogs and a couple more mages at least. He wasn't at Isobel's level, but then she had spent years slowly leeching off of others for her power.

Mustard looked powerful, but he looked rough too. His eyes were so bloodshot he looked like a demon, and they kind of bulged a bit, like there was too much pressure inside his skull. His body was thin and wasted, as if he hadn't eaten for a long time. His skin looked wrong too, almost like he was covered in old bruises. Mustard was powerful, but he was paying a steep price for stealing that much magic.

He spotted us and came charging. Despite how awful he looked, his movements were fast. When he stepped inside the range of my magic sight, I gagged. The stench of his power was that bad.

I thought about grabbing Annabeth and running, but there was no safe place that I could reach in time. The House was on the other side of the park. I would be too slow carrying Annabeth, and he would simply blast me in the back. Then we would both be out of it and end up in a draining circle. Goodbye magic, and goodbye second life.

No. Instead of running, I needed to take this guy out. I didn't have my shillelagh or any other weapons. I still couldn't use charms. But I'd thought about what to do after our last battle, and I had an idea for a new creation that might help.

I stepped in front of Annabeth, putting up a brave front. Hopefully, I looked a lot braver than I felt. He stopped a few feet away. He looked even worse up close. When he opened his mouth to speak, his teeth were stained yellow, and I could smell his stinking breath.

"I thought you'd be back," he said.

His rotten magic penetrated my senses, as a flashback to my fight with Isobel came over me. I felt sick. I didn't want to get hurt like that again. Recovering from that had been hell. Actual roasting in fire, getting stabbed with pitchforks, hell.

Chin up! You can do this! my British Analytical Side stepped in for a quick pep talk. *You have your sight now, and you're feeling fit as a fiddle. Just because he has overwhelming magical power and looks like he fights crazy doesn't mean you can't take him.*

'Gee, thanks,' I thought sarcastically. Now back to Mr. Smelly.

"I thought it would be a beautiful day for a walk," I said cheerfully. I gestured at the sunset. "Well, it was a beautiful day. Now it's going to be a beautiful night."

He grunted and pointed at Annabeth on the ground.

"What's wrong with her?" He kept shifting and twitching, like he had too much energy to stand still. He looked like a meth head or a twitching zombie.

"She's taking a nap," I replied lightly. "You know women and their naps. They can't say no when it's time for some shut eye." God, my banter was just awful. Good thing Annabeth couldn't hear me. I think I'd just insulted her.

I used this time to move a bit closer to Mustard. He had a huge advantage in power, so I didn't want to stay too far away. He could utterly blast me apart at will. If I got in close, I might be able to take him out. Last time we had physically tangled, it had been a draw, but I'd still been recovering from being impaled with a sword. This time I felt good. I felt ready. I'd better be. Annabeth was counting on me. I was counting on me.

I'd also been using this time to conjure a new creation of mine, Bob the Basher. He kind of looked like Wreck-it Ralph, but that was trademarked so I needed to call him something else. Bob the Basher had huge arms and huge hands with the ability to bash things very quickly. That was key. He sported a jetpack with wings for extra speedy maneuvering and heavy work boots with suckers on the bottom. I'd added baggy overalls and shaggy hair to complete the look.

"I was waiting for you to come back," Mustard said. "I got to thinking, why settle for the groundhogs when I can have you two?"

I moved a bit closer. "I'm sure we won't taste as good," I said. "She's old and tough, and I'm..."

I lunged at him.

And slammed into a shield.

Damn. I was hoping his shield amulet would have run out by now. Surely, with the mages turning on each other, there wasn't a way for him to recharge it. Plan A, get in close and hope to overpower him, was out. Time for plan B.

An evil, maniacal smile spread over Mustard's face. It stretched his features out way too far, making him look insane. Like Joker-crazy insane. He started to launch a spell, and I launched Bob.

Bob was fast. Space Ranger fast. He jetted over to Mustard, and his speed triggered Mustard's shield, exactly like it was supposed to. He landed feet first, suction boots locked down tight, and he went to work bashing the shield. The timing was perfect. Bob triggered Mustard's shield just as Mustard threw his spell. With nowhere to go, the spell bounced off and came back at him. It must have been some sort of force spell, because it hit him hard, and he slammed against the back of his own shield.

'Drop it,' I commanded Bob, and he disengaged. Without something speedy to defend against, Mustard's shield dropped, and he flopped back on the ground, stunned. Speed-based shields are great for defense against mindless ranged spells, but Bob was anything but mindless, and he was going to use Mustard's own shield against him.

Since I had a moment, I fired up a couple Flashers. They looked like lightning bugs, but with trench coats. They were Flashers, after all. I'd been practicing on summoning them, and I was much quicker now.

Mustard sat up and glared at me, and that's when the Flashers attacked. They couldn't get too close to him since his rotten aura was corrosive to my creations, but they didn't need to. They had a secret element, a light rune, and they let him have it.

It was as if the sun suddenly exploded between us. I knew what was coming, so I closed my eyes and threw up my arm to block the light. The flash was so bright I could see through my eyelids and through the flesh part of my arm. It only lasted for a moment, but I swear I could see the bones in my forearm. Freaky.

Mustard screamed and clawed at his eyes. Then he screamed again, going ape shit crazy. Power exploded out of him in all directions, and I was hit with a wall of force. I sailed through the air and then slammed into the ground hard. At least it didn't spin me like last time. The force rattled the trees, sending the picnic table tumbling away. Annabeth was on the ground, so most of the force just rolled over the top of her.

The real danger to her was the type of magic Mustard used. It was stolen power, and it had turned rancid. Although she wasn't physically hurt, the air around her was now filled with toxic power, and she was on full inhale mode. She was bound to absorb some of it into her system, and that was not going to be good. Not good at all. I needed to get her out of there now.

'Lock him up, Bob. I'm going after Annabeth.'

Bob the Basher darted in again and locked Mustard up behind his own shield. I sprinted to Annabeth, grabbed under her arms, and dragged her out of the blast radius as fast as I could. There was a group of three trees several yards away. I pulled her behind them. It wasn't anywhere near as much protection for her as I wanted, but it was better than nothing. The trees should shield her from any direct damage. Now I just needed someone to take care of the contamination.

It was Granny Fairy Godmother time!

These little ladies are some of my favorite creations. They had helped me out a lot before, and it was easy to create them again.

I began imagining a plump, female figure with gray hair worn in a bun in the back. I changed the color of her dress to pink, in honor of Annabeth. Then I gave her fairy wings and a cute little apron covered with images of cherry pies. She needed all the wholesome goodness she could get to cut this Mustard.

She was going to be cleaning, so she needed some rubber gloves and goggles (safety first). For her weapon, I gave her a dustbuster. And what's better than one dustbuster? Two dustbusters! I even threw in two holsters, western style, for that extra badass look.

The dustbusters didn't have any storage capacity, so I added two hip canisters with a vortex cleaning system and a chrome plated exhaust. She could now suck up the magic, spin it like a Dyson vacuum cleaner, and expel the bad stuff out the back. This had worked with the Necro Golem. Hopefully, it would work here as well. Finally, I added her duplicator belt and took a brief moment to add in as much detail as I could. I'd found out that the more detailed I made my creations, the more powerful they were and the longer they lasted. This contamination was no joke. She was going to need all the help she could get.

Finally, she was ready. It wasn't a perfect job, but it was pretty close. With her holsters and her fairy wings, she looked like a cross between Annie Oakley and Tinkerbell's grandmother. She rocked! I poured my magic into her and gave her some quick directions.

'Your main job is to keep Annabeth, Octa, and her Tangle as safe as possible from this nasty magic. Duplicate as much as you need to, but don't overdo it. The clean magic can go to the Tangle for Annabeth to absorb. I'm off to the fight. I'll try and keep it away from you as much as possible. Good luck!'

I held up my hand as she gave me a tiny high five. Then she fired up both dustbusters and went to town. I wanted to make sure this would work, so I waited for a moment. In no time at all, she had cleaned up enough magic to duplicate. Now there were two of them, then four. I didn't wait around any longer and sprinted back to the fight.

I'd been keeping an eye on Mustard, and Bob the Basher had been giving him fits. Every time he went to throw a spell, Bob activated the shield, and Mustard got hit with his own magic. It was driving him insane. Well, more insane than what he already was. Nobody can see my little creations except for me, so he probably had no idea why this was happening to him. He finally gave up on magic and just started running toward me. Bob waited until he was in midstep, then he activated the shield. Mustard slammed into it. Bob dropped the shield, and Mustard landed on his face. Bob was a genius!

It was too good to last, though. I had almost reached them, when Mustard threw another spell. Bob went in to shut it down, and this time the shield didn't trigger. His shield amulet must finally be out of juice. Fortunately for me, Mustard was probably still trying to recover from the Flashers, because his spell was way off. I closed the distance between us, hitting him with everything I had.

This time there wasn't a shield to stop me. Plan A, beat the crap out of him, was back on. I hit him four times, as fast as I could, and it knocked him back. Unfortunately, I hit his face wrong, and my right wrist popped. My hand went numb. I couldn't form a fist anymore. That sucked.

I compensated by stepping in and kicking him in the balls.

He'd done it to me, so turnabout's fair play. He screamed, grabbing his nuts. I expected him to drop to the ground and cry for his mommy. Instead, he went ape shit crazy again.

He hit me with another one of his walls of force. I was thrown back. This time I was able to twist in the air and hit the ground running. It was a good thing I did, because he was still screaming and shuffling towards me. He was throwing a crazy amount of magic in my direction, trying to hit me. It was happening too fast for me to react, so he hit me again.

Once again, I was airborne, but I just rode it out. I was going to be really sore tomorrow, but for now I was too amped up to even feel it. I hit the ground, but couldn't keep my feet. This time I slid along the ground face first. I got up, spitting out dirt and leaves. At least I hadn't spun around. Vertigo is no joke. I felt blood start to run down my face. Fortunately, this was a fight, not a beauty contest, so I was still in it.

Getting thrown even farther away was a blessing in disguise. He still couldn't see well, so he was just shooting wild. The farther away from him I was, the less likely I was to get hit. That gave me a quick moment to evaluate the situation to see if I could find a way to turn this around.

My right hand was out of commission, so getting in close wasn't a good idea anymore. His shield was out of juice, so Bob the Basher wasn't useful anymore either. I didn't have any powerful distance magic to hit him with, and his toxic aura would dissolve any of my little creations. Basically, I didn't have any good ways to attack him. Without any way to deal damage, how was I going to take him out?

Mustard had stopped screaming. Now he was laughing. Joker-esque, maniacal laughing. He was doing a shuffle walk and gradually getting closer to me. Spit rolled down his chin, and his eyes were completely red. He really looked like a rabid zombie. And that gave me an idea. Maybe I could win with defense.

I called in my Flashers, and they lit him up again. This time he didn't even notice. His eyes were so red and bugging out so badly, I'm not sure he was capable of seeing anymore. But he must have had some way to find me, because he kept almost facing my direction. I needed him to keep using his magic, so I started yelling.

"Over here, Mustard! Over here!"

He threw three fireballs at me. Or at least where he thought I was. One was actually pretty close, so I got the hell out of the way.

"Liar, liar, pants on fire." I really need to work on my taunting skills. They suck. I'm usually the person who's being bullied, not the one doing all the name-calling. I had no idea it was a skill.

Although my taunt had nothing to do with our current situation, it still worked. He reoriented and kept firing. This time he was using force, and I paid special attention as it whizzed by my head. That's when I noticed it. Buried in the big mass of rotten magic was a mustard core.

I was right. He was augmenting his spells with all the stolen magic he'd sucked up, but he still needed his own magic to be the base. His spells were big and powerful, but they were still his spells. This could work.

For the next few minutes, we kept up the dance. I would circle around him and call him stupid, childish names. He'd focus on me and hurl spells in my general direction. The air grew thick with contamination. It hurt to breathe. I felt like I was locked in a room filled with the stench of diarrhea and paint thinner.

He couldn't throw that much magic without some of it landing. Fortunately, they were glancing blows rather than solid hits. One time, I even pushed a spell out of the way slightly. I wasn't sure how I did it. I was off balance, the spell was going to hit, and I threw up my hands. I could feel it, somehow, and I pushed. The spell changed course slightly, only grazing me.

I'd have never gotten away with this with the old Mustard. He seemed smart, able to read the situation, and react. Zombie Mustard, though, was as stupid as they come. Much more powerful, but stupid.

I kept an eye on his spells as best as I could. The kernel of mustard magic was getting smaller and smaller. I think I could have finished wasting his magic on my own, but I didn't need to. The cavalry showed up. And by the cavalry, I mean a bounding streak of black and white fur. It was Bermuda Moses coming to my rescue.

He growled as he ran, and it wasn't the playful growling like when I was trying to kiss him. This was a fierce howl of dark alleys and moonlit nights. This was the cry of bitter fights where only the winner limped away. This was the battle cry of his people.

I thought he would stop and hiss, do his fuzz and posture thing. He was way beyond that. He'd faced this type of magic before, and this was his retribution. There would be no warning this time, no chance for retreat. It was time for blood.

He flew across the ground and leapt onto Zombie Mustard. Bermuda landed on his thigh, climbing his back like a squirrel up a tree. When he reached Mustard's skinny neck, Bermuda sank in his front claws, bit like a tiger, and started kicking with his back feet.

Bermuda tore him up. Mustard shrieked and flailed, but Bermuda would not let go and his back feet didn't stop. I'm sure it must have hurt like crazy on a physical level, but the major damage happened in the magical realm. Bermuda's claws tore up his aura, and Mustard's personal magic poured out.

Then it happened.

Mustard just stopped.

No screams. No laughing. No spells. Just stopped and stood there.

Bermuda let go and raced over to me. I picked him up and ran for cover.

Mustard was still, but his stolen magic was churning. It seemed to fold in on itself, getting smaller and thicker. I'd never seen anything like this. What was it doing?

It disappeared inside him, and for a moment he looked normal, like he didn't have any magic at all. The moment stretched on, and then there was a sound. It was the thump of a resonating bass. The pulse so low I felt it more than heard it.

It felt like an approaching storm. Or an earthquake.

Then his eyes started shining. His whole body shook.

And then, he exploded.

A wall of force and filth shot out from him like the blast from a bomb.

Trees shook and branches fell. One tree split down the middle and fell over. Fortunately, it wasn't the tree we were hiding behind. Following the force was a thick fog of contamination. It must have been corrosive because I heard a faint hiss as it started eating into the trees, leaves, and grass. It got on me, and my skin turned red and irritated like a twelve-hour sunburn. I pulled my shirt up over my nose and mouth and closed my eyes. I didn't want anything to happen to my eyes. They were brand new!

In the middle of all this, Bermuda snuggled into my arms and started purring. He liked being held, and I guess he felt happy now that he'd taken care of the bad guy. I rubbed his head, but I felt like this was the wrong time for a love moment. Then I noticed the strangest thing. The fog was being pushed back. It wasn't gone completely, but there was now an area around me that was clearer than all the rest. I always knew Bermuda was extraordinary, but now it looked like even his purrs were magic.

Annabeth. I needed to get to Annabeth. All this contamination was going to be terrible for her. Hopefully the Granny Godmothers were keeping her safe.

I could feel my little creations. Thankfully, they were a good distance away. I guess in the heat of battle we had moved farther away than I'd thought. That was a good thing. The more distant she was from the blast site, the less dense the fog would be.

I started moving towards her as quickly as possible. I couldn't move too fast as Bermuda needed to clear a path for us. He purred, I walked. We finally made it.

The Granny Godmothers were holding their own, although barely. The fog tore them up, eating through their pink dresses and cherry pie aprons. The worst was when it ate through their wings. When they took enough damage, they puffed out, unable to hold together anymore. They were still cleaning the air, though, and they used the pure magic they collected to duplicate and make more valiant Granny warriors.

I could feel all this happening, and I picked up the pace even more. Finally, I arrived and poured my magic into them. The boost of energy was what they needed, and the dome of clear air over Annabeth gradually expanded.

Could I make it to the House with Annabeth? Maybe. My right hand wasn't working well, and my wrist was throbbing. I couldn't hold Annabeth in my arms and walk with her, but maybe I could do a fireman's carry. If Bermuda stayed close to help clear the way and the Grannies provided additional protection, then we might be able to make it. The House was farther away from the blast, so hopefully the air would get clearer as we went. It was worth a try.

I went to pick up Annabeth and discovered that picking up an unconscious person is really hard. They aren't holding a shape, so they have a tendency to flop around and spill out of your arms. I couldn't grip well with one hand, which was causing this to be a lot more difficult. Eventually, I was able to get her up in the air and over my shoulder. Now it was time to march.

With Bermuda leading the way and a host of Guardian Godmothers around us, we set out. Progress was slow, but we were making it. My main goal was to keep Annabeth safe, and we were making that happen. We were an oasis of clean air in a desert of hot waste.

We were approaching the House side of the park, when we heard the sirens and saw our first flashing lights. The police had arrived in force. Through a screen of trees it looked like there was at least one fire truck and a couple ambulances too. There were probably more of them on all sides of the park. In the middle of all the magical mayhem, it hadn't occurred to me that the mundane world would be involved in this too. They couldn't see the magic, of course, but the blast had been physical. That had surely gotten people's attention. Actually, it had probably started before that, during the fight. Mustard had been throwing fireballs and force bolts all over the place. I'm sure I wasn't the only one in the park. We must have made a real ruckus.

The police got out and started cordoning off the area. This wasn't good. I needed to get to the House. If they saw me like this, bloody and carrying an unconscious woman, I'd probably end up in jail, and she'd end up in the hospital. Annabeth needed more magic, and that wasn't something a doctor could give her.

I couldn't turn invisible, and I didn't see any way to slip unnoticed between them. I hated to do this to Louisville's finest, but the only way I could think to make it home was to cause another disruption.

I cut off my power to the Grannies, and started making Flashers. When I had about twenty of them, I sent them off, and they flew up and down the street. I sent most of the Grannies on ahead to clean up a corridor for us. We were going to make a run for it.

It was the best we could do, and in a moment I sent a thought to the Flashers.

'Go time!'

They lit up the sky.

I heard cries and cursing. I started running. It wasn't easy, but I gave it all I had. The tape almost tripped me up. I thought that caution tape would be flimsy. It wasn't.

It wouldn't break, so I lost my momentum and backed up. I'd stretched it out, so now it was hanging low enough I was able to just step over it. One police officer headed my way. I don't know if that was by accident or if he heard something, but I picked up speed. I was on the sidewalk and then through the House shield before anyone's vision cleared enough for them to see me. At least, I hoped that was the case. I didn't hear anyone yelling at me specifically, so I counted that as a win.

I burst through the door, leaving the confusion behind. We had made it!

With the energy I had left, I struggled to Sandy's bedroom. My grip slipped when I tried to take Annabeth off my shoulder and gently put her down. She hit the floor and bounced a bit. Oops. That was going to leave a mark. She was unconscious, so hopefully she wouldn't feel a thing.

Since there wasn't a second bed to put her in, I made a pallet on the floor out of pillows and rolled her onto them. It wasn't the best, but it would work for now. I thought about taking her up to her own bed, but then I'd have two patients in different places that desperately needed magic. Everyone that needed help was currently in one room. I decided to keep it that way.

I grabbed a couple of the leftover pillows and curled up on John's stony lap. Bermuda hopped up, curled up next to me, and started purring. I gave my fierce warrior the loving he so richly deserved.

As I tickled his ears and gave him some full body stroking, it occurred to me that he wasn't a kitten anymore. He was now in those awkward growth months, almost like a teenager. His legs were too long, and his ears were too big. He wasn't a kitten, but he wasn't an adult cat either.

My baby was growing up.

I felt sad for a moment, but I felt fiercely proud too. He had really put a hurting on Mustard. Isobel was gone, but if she ever came back, she was going to find a very different warrior waiting for her.

I took a moment to check myself out. I was covered in bruises, and my face looked horrible. Swipe left on me right now. I'd fractured a bone in my hand. Guess that was why it wasn't working so well at the moment. My right shoulder also hurt a lot. I'm not sure when that was injured. Maybe one of the times I'd been tossed around by a spell.

Bermuda finished purring and started napping. I didn't want to disturb him, so I juiced up all the Grannies and Octopi in the room and told them to keep cleaning and gathering magic. I left Octa and the first Granny in charge, then zoomed in to work on my hand and shoulder. Pulling down magic and awakening cells was simple repetitive work, and it felt nice to do something easy and safe after all that excitement. I lost track of time as I awakened several spots and got the twinkle lightning going.

I finally finished, zoomed out, and checked on everyone. Sandy and Annabeth were covered in a Tangle of Octopi, absorbing neutral magic. A steady stream of Granny Godmothers were flying in and out, bringing fresh neutral magic and heading out for more. There were several Octopi and Godmothers hanging around in the air that needed my attention. I repaired them, filled them with fresh energy, and sent them on their way.

The adrenaline that had kept me going was long gone. Now I just felt sore and tired. I was safe and comfortable, and Bermuda was cozy. I closed my eyes, relaxed, and drifted off to sleep.

5

All by Myself

The next several days were incredibly lonely. I was quite literally the last person standing.

I missed Sandy. Not only was she an amazing cook, she also made her space feel like home.

I missed John and his big laugh. He always teased me or the girls, but in a good way. Somehow, his humor made me feel included, a part of the team.

I missed Annabeth and her happy sunshine. She was a great listener and always made me believe anything was possible.

I missed Tyler and how he made me feel. Somehow, his presence helped me relax so I could just be me. And waking up next to him was a real treat too. Plus, he was great at teasing John back. I liked having a pint of John's special brew and watching the two of them go at it. Good times.

I suppose that's what I was missing the most right now. The good times.

Instead, I was being Mr. Responsible. I spent most of my time making sure the network of Octopi and Godmothers was up and running. Being the responsible one was a new role for me. I was used to being responsible only for myself, but now the lives of my friends depended on me. That felt very heavy.

I knew how to fix Sandy and Annabeth, but I wasn't sure how to cure John. He just sat there, a big statue of rock and stone, and didn't move. He did wake up briefly, though, on the first day after I'd brought Annabeth back.

"Jason." His deep voice rumbled right behind my head, scaring the crap out of me. I'd been chilling on his lap again while healing some of the Godmothers. The contamination took a real toll on them.

"OMG! You're back!" I jumped up, giving him a hug. He was too big to get my arms all the way around his torso, but it was the thought that counted. "How are you? How do you feel?"

"I feel... " he trailed off.

Okay. Bad question. Whatever was going on with him, the last thing he needed now was to focus on it even more. I might have lost him again with one dumb question. He needed to focus on something else.

"Never mind," I said quickly. "Can you still hear me?"

He nodded. I filled him in on everything that had happened. I took my time to paint a complete picture. Maybe this would help get him out of whatever magical funk he was in. As I talked, he seemed to focus more. Maybe I was reaching him. I hoped so. I could use the company, and the help with Sandy and Annabeth.

"Annabeth is out too?" he asked. I nodded, pointing to where she was laid out on the pillows. Then I had an idea. He had too much magic. I needed changes to the House, which required magic. Maybe I could kill two birds with one stone?

"I could really use your help," I said. "Dealing with the contamination and making sure Sandy and Annabeth have magic to absorb is taking all the power I have. I need a bed for Annabeth. I also need the House to keep taking care of the candles. Can you do something?"

John seemed lost in thought. Had he gone back to la-la land again?

"You are the maintenance man, after all." I forced a laugh.

Suddenly, John leaned forward, putting both stony hands against the floor. He took a deep breath and began sending his magic into the House. I could see his gray, sparkly magic shooting off of him in waves. It went on and on and on. I don't have any way to measure magic, but it was clearly a lot more capacity than I had in my entire body. It was so much energy I could feel the room starting to hum. And still, he kept going.

Finally, he stopped and leaned back. "That should do it."

"What the heck did you do?" I was in awe. Clearly, I still had a long way to go in the power department.

"Give it time," John said cryptically as he closed his eyes. Panic coursed through me. I was going to lose him again.

"John! What's happening?!" I jumped on his lap and yelled in his face. I needed answers.

"The earth is calling," he said simply. "It is strong. So strong."

"Stay with me!" I yelled at him.

He opened his eyes briefly. "I can't." His words sounded heavy, like he was trying to lift boulders.

"Next cycle." He struggled to say something else. I think it was something about Sandy.

Then he relaxed and was gone. I yelled at him some more, but he remained still and silent. Statue John was back.

Frustrated with John and more than a little worried about him, I decided to take a break and get out of the House for a while.

I stepped onto the front porch and let out an exasperated sigh. Being outside brought up a whole other set of issues that needed fixing. The neighborhood was coated in a layer of contaminated magic. It wasn't in the air anymore. Instead, it had settled on every available surface. Everything had a dirty taint. It was like the outside world had been neglected by God, with layers of black muck coating the trees, grass, and cars. I ran a hand across the porch railing, feeling the magical grime on my skin. I felt a little ill at the contact. Who knew that one mage could create such a big mess?

The mundanes knew that something was up too, even if they couldn't see the magic. The sun was shining and it wasn't too hot, although you'd never know that by the way the people on the sidewalk acted. Today there were no strolling couples with happy smiles. Instead, they hurried along with anxious looks—fearful of something, although they weren't sure what that something was.

The bright yellow caution tape didn't help things either. It was strung along the entire perimeter of the park, a clear warning for people to stay away. There were also a couple of flyers noting that Shakespeare in the Park was no longer "in the park". It had been moved to the local high school until further notice.

The neighborhood was in a sad state of disrepair, and I felt responsible. It wasn't my fault, I knew that, but I still felt responsible. That's why I had thousands of my little cleaners working on clearing it all up. They were everywhere, like little bees, sucking up the bad stuff and taking the nuggets of pure energy back home again. It was going to take weeks to clean it all up, but I was committed to making it happen. This was my neighborhood, my little slice of the world, and a scummy mage wasn't going to take that away.

Besides, all the extra magic was going to help Sandy and Annabeth. That was a pretty big silver lining in this otherwise dark cloud.

I walked around the perimeter until I reached the far side of the park. Nobody was around, so I ducked under the caution tape and headed to the blast site. It was easy to find the spot. There was a ten-foot circle where the grass was gone. Nearby trees had their leaves stripped from them, while broken branches littered the surrounding area. There was a metal lump that used to be a lamp post right by the blast. It looked like it had been knocked over and partially melted.

I stood there for a while, taking it all in. Magic was no joke. It could be a beautiful and wonderful thing, but it could also be destructive as hell too. Seeing all this, I felt lucky to be alive.

I turned and walked away. It wouldn't be this summer, but the park would grow back again. I'd clean it up, and hopefully nature would take over and regrow everything next year. I felt sad. This new supernatural world was just as destructive to nature as the mundane one. With all this new ability, why couldn't we be better to the world we lived in?

I finished the loop around the park and went into the House. Outside had been just as depressing as inside. When I got back to the infirmary, aka Sandy's bedroom, I stopped in shock. The room had been completely rearranged. There were now two beds, one for Sandy and one for Annabeth. Well, two and a half. There was a cot for me to sleep on too. The room itself had been enlarged, and the floor was now covered in thick rugs with pillows scattered everywhere. There were even three shaggy-looking round beds for the cats to sleep in. They were ignoring them, of course. Bermuda was somehow taking up three pillows on John's lap, and Snowy and Biscuit were curled up with their mama, Sandy.

The room wasn't only bigger floorwise, it was much taller too. John had almost touched the ceiling before, even sitting down. Now the ceiling went way up, twelve feet at least, and had massive wooden beams and two chandeliers. It made the whole room look much more like a space for John to hang out in. The most amazing part, though, was all the neutral magic in the air. It was just sparkling and floating along, looking like little candles in the sky. I'm guessing that John had somehow turned this into a magic generator just like the Circle Room. That was brilliant! Now the Octopuses could refill from three sources: this room, the Circle Room, and from all the Grannies flying in. Surely that should be enough for my two power starved patients.

Speaking of Octopuses, I'd finally had a chance to ask Google what the plural of octopus was. Turns out, it isn't octopi. It's octopuses. (It was so nice being able to see with my real eyes again!)

It also said there wasn't a formal name for a group of octopuses, so I was going to stick with "tangle". That just seemed like a fun name for them.

Using my friend Google, I also looked up how many cells there were in the human body. I'd already awakened thousands of cells in more than a hundred different spots. They were now slowly converting even more cells and gradually changing me into an awakened being. The goal was to be able to transform like Tyler. So when I became injured, I'd just concentrate, and bye-bye cuts and bruises! I was feeling really good about what I'd done so far, until Google told me there are 37.2 trillion cells in the average human body. Suddenly, my thousands of cells didn't seem like that much anymore.

I tried not to let that discourage me, though. I still spent part of every morning and evening healing my bruises and fixing my hand. It wasn't transformative healing or anything, but it was nice to start feeling better so quickly.

I'd had a tiny bit of success with John. After he gave lots of magic to the House, I noticed his aura wasn't sparkling with his natural magic anymore. Now his stony exterior just looked like stone. Maybe I could finally chip away at that and get him just a little bit back to normal? It was worth a shot. Time for the League of Flying Miners!

Well, a League was a bit much for a test. Starting with one Miner would do for now. I held out my hand and made a little guy about a quarter inch high. I gave him blue overalls, a miner's helmet with a light, and work boots. Since he would be working with stone, I gave him goggles to protect his eyes (safety first!), a pickaxe, and a mustache because he was going to be doing some manly work. Next came a jetpack—because you can't have a flying miner without the flying part! I added a green duplicator ring so he could replicate if this worked.

I took a moment to fill in all the details, making him as solid as possible. Something still seemed missing, though. I wasn't trying to pick apart a golem this time. I was trying to dig John out of his rocky shell. I needed something extra, something just for John on this mission. I had the perfect thing! I started grinning as I modified the miner's helmet. Now it had two giant beer cans on either side with a straw connecting everything. The straw ran down to a sipper attached to his shoulder for easy access. Now he was John's type of miner!

I filled him full of magic and turned him loose. He wiggled his mustache at me, hitched his overalls up, and blasted off. With a 'Weeee' he did a few loops in the air and headed for John's head, trailing little puffs of white smoke. When he arrived, he took a generous pull on his beer. He seemed to like it as he smacked his lips a few times, giving me a thumbs up. Then he hoisted his pickaxe and got to work.

The tiny sounds of pickaxe on stone filled the air as I anxiously waited to see if anything would happen. For a long minute, it looked like it wasn't going to work, and then I saw the first crack. It was a tiny crack, and it took the Miner even longer to turn the crevice into an actual chip of stone. I looked at the tiny chip, maybe a quarter the size of a grain of rice. Despair filled me as I took in John's over-sized body. This was going to take a while.

I called the Miner back and upgraded his pickaxe. I'm not sure what stone John was made of, but it was going to require a better weapon. I changed his pickaxe from regular steel to adamantium and gave it a +10 bonus when powered by beer. That seemed to work a lot better. I duplicated the Miner and watched them work. They did great, until the beer ran out. I'd already duplicated him over twenty times. I didn't want to start over, so I ended up making another creation, "The Endless Kegger" and putting it on John's shoulder for easy refills. That worked very well until I had over a hundred Miners, and then there started to be a line for the beer. I needed them chipping away at John, not standing in line chatting, so I made several more Endless Keggers, lining them all up on John's shoulder.

Watching them drink and work was kind of fun. John was going to get a kick out of this story later. Some of them were having a bit too much fun and ended up flying around the room trailing puffs of white smoke. Somehow it fit right in with the Purple Octopuses and the Flying Godmothers. There was also a lot of belching going on. Maybe the beer wasn't such a good idea after all. Mostly, though, they stuck to working on John, and little bits of stone were gradually flaking off. I could see that John was going to be covered in a haze of rock dust and small chips soon. I liked napping on John's lap, so it was time to bring back the companion to the League of Flying Miners— the Ass Blaster 2000s. After all, what goes better with a belch than a good fart?

I started with a worm body, then gave it a big mouth and long tongue to suck up the dust and rock chips. The middle of the body would crush the rock down, making rock pellets. On the back side, I gave him powerful legs. They would be used to scoot the worm around, but mostly to point its butt into the sky. The back end of the little guy I made a bit like a shotgun. It would cock itself, then pew—shoot the rock pellet at high velocity into the air. I added a duplicator ring, walkie talkie, goggles (safety first!), and GPS. As a final touch, I added a mustache as well, because this little fella was also going to be doing manly work, even for a worm.

My Ass Blaster 2000 was now complete! I pumped him full of magic and sent him off. He didn't go 'Wheee', but his mustache wiggled, and his little legs pumped the air. I think he was happy. He landed next to the Miners and started munching on freshly chipped rock. At first, nothing happened. He just munched, chewed, and sucked up rock dust. Finally, he got full enough, planted his little feet firmly on John's head, cocked his ass, and "Pew" shot a rock pellet into the air. It actually went pretty far, considering how tiny it was.

Everything seemed to be working well, so I duplicated him several more times. Bermuda came up for a snuggle, so I gave him some love and ended up dozing on John's lap for a while.

I woke up to utter chaos.

Apparently, while I was sleeping, the Miners had started sharing their beer with the Ass Blasters. The extra gas started giving their rock pellets some real range and force. I guess they had decided it would be fun to shoot at the purple Octopuses. Octa and her Tangle had decided they were not amused and started fighting back. The Octopuses were picking up the rock pellets in their tentacles, spinning like a top, and firing them back. They were getting a slingshot effect, and it was pretty effective.

So, basically, I woke up to an all-out war. Bermuda had woken up, and he was in the middle of it too. He was all wide-eyed and hyped up, trying to catch the pellets as they flew through the air. He seemed to be having a blast, so I put a stop to the fighting between my creations and let them shoot at Bermuda instead. He went wild. He was jumping around like a ninja, although he wasn't catching hardly anything. Still, a good time was had by all.

When Bermuda finally got tired, I had them shoot the pellets at the wall. That wasn't as exciting, but it kept the peace. The Miners had been able to make a dent into the stone covering John. His aura was starting to peek through. That meant there was sort of a cure for John. He just needed to keep spending magic, and maybe he would finally shrink back down to his normal human self. I was worried about all this inactivity, though. John's father had listened to the call of the earth, and one day he had just walked into the mountain and was never heard from again. I didn't want that happening to John. We needed him here. We were his friends and family now.

The Flying Tipsy Miners and the Ass Blasters were the most exciting part of the week. Other than that, it just dragged on. There was plenty to do, but none of it was that fun. I fixed up any of my injured creations and made new ones as needed. I kept magic going into Sandy and Annabeth, and more rock slowly came off of John. I made a crap-ton more Granny Godmothers and continued to clean up the park outside. I kept exchanging magic with Penny to try to get her to wake up, and I continued to give magic to Eggy to keep his progress on track. This was all good stuff, but I still felt lonely. I missed my friends. They were with me, but I still missed them.

The only thing that made it all bearable was spending time with my furry baby, Bermuda Moses. He was my little buddy. I got into a rhythm of cat naps, and that suited him just fine. We played together and snuggled together. Sometimes we even purred together. He would stand on my chest and make biscuits. He'd get that half-closed, happy look in his eyes and just purr away, and I'd purr right back. He didn't have to worry about magic or saving my friends' lives, so everything was just fine in his world. Life was naps, loving his daddy, and play time. This was his version of heaven.

The days passed.

I made progress on all the things I was working on. The park gradually was cleaned of some dirty magic. Annabeth gradually filled up with magic. I thought she would wake up when the matrix filled in enough to reach her heart and brain, but she didn't. Sandy gradually filled up with magic too, but she wasn't waking up either. I got an entire layer of stone about two inches thick off of John. He was still lost in the call of the earth. Penny wasn't back yet, but I could finally feel her starting to get restless. The little bit of magic I had to spare I gave to Eggy. He was sleeping too. So it was just me, Bermuda, Biscuit, and Snowy. I prowled the House, gave out snacks and love, kept my army of creations going, and watched Netflix.

I had become used to being on my own. So it was a complete shock when I left the bedroom and ran into Tyler. I just stopped and stared. There he was. In the flesh. He looked so solid, and yummy.

I'd thought about this moment. What I'd say. What I'd do. I thought I'd say something cute. Something funny. Or maybe I'd be all cool. Like I didn't miss him at all. I never once thought I'd tear up.

I couldn't say a thing. My eyes welled up, and suddenly it all came crashing down. I didn't feel strong or responsible anymore. I just felt lonely and small. I wanted someone to hold me, and that was what he did.

He wrapped his arms around me, kissed me on the neck, and just held me. Finally, I took a deep, quivery breath and held him back. He felt so solid. So warm.

He didn't say anything. He just lifted me off the floor. I wrapped my legs around him as he turned, carrying me back to my apartment. He opened the door and swept me right into the bathroom.

"We'll talk and catch up with what's going on later," he said. His voice was gentle, playful. "But first, I think a shower is in order."

"Oh?" I said as he put me down.

"Someone looks and smells a little ripe," he said. He smiled his perfect smile, taking any sting out of the words. I realized I wasn't sure how long it had been since I'd taken a shower. Or even changed clothes. The days had all run together. I probably looked like crap.

I suddenly felt shy and embarrassed. I wanted to run away. I never thought we'd meet again and I'd look like ten miles of bad road. He just laughed and started undressing me. Somehow it was all okay in his world.

In no time at all, we were both naked with hot water cascading over us. It felt like heaven. He took the soap and wouldn't let me wash myself. Instead, he lathered up his hands and took his time cleaning every part of me. His touch was the ultimate luxury. I'd been on my own for so long, and now the one person in the world that I really wanted to spend time with was here. And he was giving me his complete, personal attention. My loneliness washed down the drain with the soap, and I started to feel human again.

Then I felt *very* human.

I felt hot. I wanted him. I wanted him on a primal level. I wanted to do bad things to him, and I wanted him to do really bad things to me.

He slowed me down enough to wash my hair, but we didn't even dry off before he picked me up and carried me into the bedroom. I had a stray thought that I could get into being carried around as I kissed him hungrily. I couldn't get enough. I felt real. I felt human. I felt desirable, wanted.

I wanted more, and I wanted it now.

His incubus magic wrapped around me, and this time there weren't any pesky Remnants to stop us. My magic was still too dense, though. His power could touch me, but it couldn't get inside.

I growled in frustration.

"That's okay," he said. "It's more fun to do it the old-fashioned way." And that was what we did, but we didn't stop there. I thought I knew what love making was all about. Compared to Tyler, I didn't know nothin'.

I was in the hands of a master. He was Leonardo da Vinci, and I was his Mona Lisa. He certainly made me Mona alright.

Instead of giving into my urgency, he slowed down and made me appreciate in detail everything he was doing to me. It was only after I started begging him and smacking his back in frustration that he gave in and gave me what I wanted. The first high was intense. Like mind-blowing, see stars, goosebumps, shudder in ecstasy intense.

He didn't stop there either. Somehow the first time was over, and we were on to the next course. It was like I was having a five-star dinner, and Tyler was my personal Iron Chef. The first course was just a teaser, a taste of all the good things to come. It was there to take the edge off my hunger and give me space to truly appreciate what was to come. The second course was deep, meaty, satisfying. I lay breathless and quaking with pleasure, but he wasn't done with me yet. The third course was the true entree. It was the one that truly wore me out, and his magic finally started doing its stuff. He pulled the worry, the uncertainty, the tension right out of me. I began to feel lighter, freer than I'd felt in a long time. Fear and hurt I didn't even know I had were just whisked away.

I thought that would be all. I was spent, relaxed, happy. But then the dessert course arrived. Just like a real meal, when you think you can't eat another bite, the chef sends out chocolate creme brulee with a thick sugar crust, deep custard filling, and topped by chocolate pieces and fresh berries. Somehow, you find room, and before you know it, you've eaten everything on your plate.

I finished our dessert course, fully and deeply satisfied. My body was loved. My mind was blown. My spirit was light and free. My soul was still.

I felt connected to Tyler in a way I never had with anyone else. I felt connected to myself, like I was awakened on a whole new level.

I felt at peace with the world.

Tyler curled around me, and we spooned. I'd woken up like this before and I loved it, but this was the first time I'd just rested with him like this. I loved his warm body pressed up against me. I loved his strong arm around me. Our breathing meshed.

The extra icing on the cake was when Bermuda hopped up and took his spot on the pillow. He closed his eyes, purring as I reached up and stroked his belly. He looked as happy and blissful as I felt. My eyes were heavy, and I closed them. I just existed in the moment, feeling love and contentment. I wanted to talk it out at some point, but I didn't want to break the mood. So, instead, I fell into a peaceful sleep.

6

Surprise

I was in a shopping mall, and I was naked. But I didn't care. I felt happy, joyful, and I was dancing around, singing. The mall had a big fountain in the center. I twirled around it like I was in a romantic movie. People were smiling and nodding at me. More than a few were taking pictures, but for some reason, I didn't mind.

Eventually, the crowd parted to reveal a stern-looking security woman in a blue uniform. She had a face like a bulldog and a voice to match. She waved her baton at me, demanding I stop. I sang to her, and she grumbled back at me. So I took her in my arms, whirling her around on my dance floor.

I could tell she was making an effort to stay mad. But I gave her my most charming smile, and she couldn't help but give in and smile back. The girl was strong, though. She spun me around, catching me from behind. Her big arms wrapped around me, holding me close. I couldn't deny how nice it felt.

The mall started blinking its lights, and a loud voice came over the PA saying it was time to get out. We didn't have to go home, but we couldn't stay here. I didn't want to go. I refused to go. I gripped her manly arms tight and held on. She kissed me on the back of the neck.

"Good morning," Tyler said.

Tyler?

I woke up. We were spooning, and I was the little spoon. Just the way I liked it. His strong arm cuddled around me with his warm, naked body nestled against my back. I cracked an eye open. Bermuda was stretched out on his favorite spot on my pillow, fast asleep.

This was it. The perfect morning I'd longed for since Tyler went away. I closed my eyes, not ready to get up yet, and floated along in my sleepy bubble.

Gradually, it occurred to me that it was more peaceful than normal. Like amazingly peaceful. I was relaxed on a level I hadn't experienced in a long time. I felt whole. I felt smooth, like all my jagged bits had been sanded away. I breathed, allowing energy to flow into me and through me with no limitation. It was like I was breathing in time with the universe.

I stayed in this perfect space for a long time, then reached up and pulled Bermuda even closer. It seemed like the right time for a cat hug. I ran my fingers up and down his belly. He started purring. It was loud too, and he started doing paw scrunches in the air.

My kitten was happy. His mood was an echo of my own. But I guess I wasn't quite clean enough as he rolled over and started licking my face. First the nose, which wasn't too bad, but I started squirming when he started on my eyelids.

That got Tyler started. He decided a little tickling was in order. Soon I was really squirming, and it started a full-on tickle battle. This was too much for Bermuda, so he hopped down to go chill somewhere else. Pillows and sheets started flying, and it would have escalated even more, except I caught a glimpse of the window Eggy was perched in front of.

It had been transformed.

Originally, it had been a single rectangular window with a basic, white window shade. Now, two floor-to-ceiling windows were elegantly framed by white linen curtains tied back with white braided cords. The rest of the wall had changed too. Now it looked like it was made out of some sort of light-colored weathered wood. The wall and window looked like they had been lifted right out of a home in Key West. I could just imagine the windows open, a soft breeze blowing, and the curtains gently fluttering.

I loved it. It looked effortless, breezy, and tropical all at the same time. It also went very well with the magical column of water that Eggy was sitting on.

Tyler rolled over to check it out. "That looks really nice. Is it your doing?"

"It's my first renovation," I said happily. "I wasn't sure what to ask for, so I let the House do its thing. I really had no idea what to expect, but I think I'm really happy with how it's turning out."

"It looks like the House is going for a tropical theme for you," Tyler said. "That could turn out really nice." He looked around the rest of the bedroom. "It's certainly much better than what you have going on now. This is more like Goodwill-chic, or maybe First Apartment Blues."

"Hey!" I punched him lightly. "It isn't as bad as that." I looked around the rest of my bedroom and had to admit he was probably right. My bed was just a comfortable mattress on the floor. My only piece of furniture was a beat-up looking dresser. I'm more a function-over-form type of guy. It was big enough to contain most of my clothes, and the drawers did slide smoothly. I guess it did look like a refugee had set up shop. Oh, well. It was my place, and that was what mattered.

"I am excited about what the House is going to do," I said. "Annabeth's apartment is freaking awesome. It looks like someone spent thousands and thousands of dollars on her place. The big courtyard in the middle with sunlight shouldn't even be physically possible. It does make for a beautiful place to work with magic. I want my apartment to be like that too. My place doesn't have to be at that level, but having a theme would be nice."

"It will be neat to see how it all turns out," Tyler said. "The good thing is that if you don't like it, you can always change it.

"And speaking of changes," he gave me a sly look, "I've been working on a surprise for you."

"Oh? Really? What is it?" I loved surprises. Well, the good kind of surprises. Not the gang-of-hit-men-chasing-you-through-a hotel-trying-to-kill-you kind of surprises. I could do without any more adventures like that.

"If I told you, it wouldn't be a surprise, now would it?" Tyler teased me. "I can tell you it has been something I've been working on since I left, and I plan on revealing it all tonight."

Now that sounded intriguing! What could he have been working on all this time? Did he make something for me? Was it magical? I had a happy moment just imagining all the possibilities. I also had a happy moment realizing that he had been thinking about me too.

My face must have shown how I was feeling because Tyler laughed and gave me a kiss. Then he settled onto his back, and I snuggled up to him. I put my head on his chest, throwing my leg over his legs. My left hand was free to roam up and down his body, appreciating all the manly splendor at my fingertips. We had things to talk about, so I might as well be comfortable and get in some primo snuggle time.

I was still feeling sated from all the love making last night. Now I wanted to spend time nestling with my man and catching up on his adventures. He seemed to feel the same as he propped his head up on an arm and got in the first question.

"So, what's been going on since I got called away?"

I didn't really want to go first. I wanted to know where he had been, and why he was just now coming back. Still, this was a good way to get the conversation started.

I told him all about the battle with Purple, Mustard, and Lemon, and what we had found out about the mages and their sucker rune. He seemed really shocked to hear about that. He said there were lots of ways to get magic from someone else, but he hadn't heard about using a rune before.

We talked about Sandy and the ongoing attempt to fill her back up with magic. He thought that all sounded good, and he didn't know of any way to recharge an unconscious mage either. Of course, he's a natural, not a spell slinger, so this was outside of his area of expertise.

I then filled him in on Annabeth and the result of her attempt at creating a matrix. Finally, I covered the second battle with Mustard and the wrecked park as a result.

"Wow! You have really had an adventure," he said.

"I'm not sure I would call it an adventure," I replied. "It feels more like one disaster after another. I'm now the last one still awake and keeping all the magic charging." I paused for a moment. "These last several days have felt very lonely. I wish you could have been here."

"I wish I could have been here as well," he said. "I just thought you'd be recovering from your big fight and getting all fat and sassy on Sandy's cooking. I thought you would be okay. That's why I've been letting the House run me ragged.

"I had an idea for something I wanted to make for you, but it was going to take a lot of magic to make it happen. Like a LOT of magic. The House has needed much more assistance over the last year or so. I decided to put in some extra time, get some extra magic, and hopefully clear up some of the problems so I could spend more time here with you."

"That's very nice to hear," I said. "I wasn't sure what had happened. I'm glad you are alright. One moment you were here, and the next you were gone."

"Yeah, that was a real emergency. Sort of like when you called me and I woke up in Sandy's living room fighting

Remnants. I really thought I'd be back sooner than this. If nothing else, just for a brief visit. There is so much going on right now, though, that I just ended up jumping from problem to problem."

"What kind of things did you run into?" I asked. I knew I probably wouldn't get details. Tyler was pretty secretive about what he did, but just having a general idea of what was happening would help fill in missing gaps in my imagination next time he was gone.

"Some of it was defending different Houses. We didn't get into a massive battle like we had here, but there were some powerful groups making a determined effort to take out House mages. It seemed like we had to deal with everything from humans to supernaturals to weird natural events. One House was in a jungle realm, and for some reason, all the insects suddenly decided to swarm the shield. Having thousands of ants, spiders, and mosquitoes gang up on your shield is not a fun thing to watch. The thought of all of them crawling on me was just nasty."

He shuddered, which made his perfect abs flex. I loved me some well-defined abs. I could watch them all day. In this case, I had a front row seat, and they were just yummy. I reluctantly pulled my mind out of the gutter and made sympathetic noises.

"The House also pulled me to new houseguests that were having problems with their Waker Moments. It seems like the number of new recruits has really jumped. There are always a few of them that need help with the transition to their supernatural life, and that number has gone up a lot. I used to help someone once a year. Now it seems like I help someone at least once a week.

"The new recruits are causing a strain on some of the Houses, so sometimes it's not a single person I need to help, it's a whole House. Tempers get short, fights break out, and new sups aren't getting the help they need. When that happens, I line them up and everyone gets a cleanse."

"So you're saying you bang the bad right out of them?" I asked. Tyler started laughing.

"That's pretty good! I'm going to have to remember that. I've always thought of it as bringing love, or something like that. Or maybe shagging off the shitty attitudes."

"You're humping them till they're happy." I was on a roll!

"Jumping them till they're joyful." We were both laughing now. It was a nice moment.

"You seem like you are really okay with what I do," he said. I could hear a question in his voice.

"Yeah, I'm good with it all," I replied. "It helps that I've had time to think about this and process it. Being a good incubus is who you are. Having sex and eating negative emotions is your talent. Expecting you to be different would just be wrong."

I gestured at the House. "It's not just your talent; it's your job too. The House uses you to make this world a better place. If you hadn't shown up, I probably would have lost the battle to my Remnants. I'd either be dead, or Thing One would be running the show." I shuddered at that unhappy thought. Thing One had been the man who had tortured me and nearly killed me, and he'd almost taken over my mind and body as well. Tyler had given me the power to heal and take back my soul. How could I not let him do the same for others?

"It's like you're an X-rated superhero, saving the world one shag at a time."

Tyler just chuckled. "I'm not a superhero. I don't want to be one either. They get into all sorts of troubles, and they usually end up old and lonely. Or young and dead. I like helping people, and I have to use my talent, or I'll fade away. That's it for me."

"Are you sure?" I said playfully. "We could call you Captain Ab-tastic. You've got great abs, and time with you makes people feel fantastic!"

"I'm sure," he said. "I like my time alone. I don't want to be a celebrity or superhero or anything like that. I think that is why I like my time with Mr. Tubbles so much. He loves me for me, not how I look, or what I can do for him."

He ruffled my hair. "That's why discovering that I liked spending time with you was such a surprise. I've helped a lot of people while I've been with the House, but somehow time with you just feels natural and easy. I like that."

I gave him a squeeze, and we just snuggled together for a while, not saying anything. Tyler saw me as a friend, and in this case, that was a good thing. I could see where Tyler could make a lot of easy friends and lovers wherever he went. With me, he was looking for something deeper, and that suited me just fine. I'd had lots of easy relationships too, bouncing from home to home. I liked the idea of developing a deeper friendship with Tyler. It sounded very satisfying.

This whole friendship-slash-relationship was going to be interesting to navigate as Tyler would consider being a friend more intimate than having sex. He probably didn't snuggle much when he was taking care of people. It was probably wham-bam-thank-you-ma'am with little quality time. That was going to be different with me. I liked my quality time. Snuggling was great!

"I guess my Remnants were useful for something, right?" I said. "They made you stick around and appreciate me for more than just my pretty face." I was being a bit sarcastic. Tyler was the handsome one, not me.

"That is true," he said. "Spending time with you has been a surprise bonus. My powers usually get the job done in one go. You made me do it the hard way."

"I thought your usual way was the 'hard' way," I joked. I poked him. He laughed and poked me back. We almost got into another tickle war, but we settled back down again.

"Seriously, though, now your Remnants are gone, why is it so difficult for me to pull the negative out of you? I got the job done, and it was totally enjoyable watching you squirm, but I haven't had to work that hard in a very long time."

"I think it has to do with my soul density," I said. "When I had my assessment with Sandy, I tested as having very rich and saturated colors. She said that makes me highly resistant to other people's magic. They can still affect things around me, but it's going to be difficult for them to affect me directly."

"So that's generally a good thing, then?" Tyler asked.

"Most of the time, yes. I'll take any defense I can get. Having a lot of soul also gives me fine control over my magic, which is what I used to heal myself. It's got a bad side too. I think it makes me resistant to healing charms.

Annabeth seems to get a lot more use out of them than I do. It also makes me resistant to you, and I'd much rather experience everything you have to offer."

"Oh, I don't know," he said. "Doing it the old-fashioned way has its perks too." He kissed me.

It was nice, so we didn't stop, and that led us to making love again. Unlike last night, it was gentle and easy. It was like a nice "good morning", but with a lot of touching and a marvelous happy ending. Afterwards, we snuggled together again.

I could get used to this.

"So when are Sandy and Annabeth going to recover?" Tyler asked.

"Annabeth should recover very soon," I said. "Her matrix is almost done. I don't know about Sandy. I really thought she would have woken up already. She's gotten a lot of her orange magic back. It's still nowhere near what she had before, of course, but she's got almost as much as Annabeth had before she started her matrix. Annabeth was doing just fine with that level of power, so I don't know why Sandy hasn't regained consciousness yet."

"She should be back in two months, right?" Tyler asked.

I just shrugged. "I don't know for sure. I wish I did. Why? What's happening in two months?"

"That's when the Gathering happens," Tyler said. "It's all I've been hearing about recently. Since Sandy is a new Head of Household, she really needs to be there. It won't look good if she doesn't make it. Especially since she was chosen."

This was all news to me. "What is the Gathering?" I asked.

"It's when all the Heads of Household get together and catch up on what the other Houses are doing," Tyler said. "It's held every four years, so it doesn't come around that often. I've never been myself, but everyone talks about it like it's a big deal."

"So they just get together and gossip among themselves?" I asked. That didn't sound very exciting. Or very important.

"It's much more than that," Tyler replied. "There is a big tournament with some killer charms as prizes. There is also a big fair with lots of stuff for sale. I think the Houses get something out of it as well, but I have no idea how that works. The main thing is it turns into a giant party."

"So there are witches dancing naked in the moonlight?" I said mischievously.

"Something like that," Tyler smiled. "I don't know myself, but I hear it's pretty intense. One guy told me it was like part concert, part rave, and part spirit quest. He said the magic was so thick it owned him, and he felt things he hadn't felt before or since. He also said he fell in love twice and had more nookie than he could handle. So there's that too."

That did sound intense. It also sounded like the guy was pretty impressionable.

"How come you've never gone?" I asked. "It sounds like you would have a great time."

Tyler made a face. "That's not really my scene. I don't like organizing things, so I'd just get bored listening to all the Heads talking. Plus, I'm not a big party guy. I'd much rather just spend some quiet time with a good book. Give me a cool morning, a hot cup of coffee, a good book, and Mr. Tubbles on my lap. That's heaven to me."

He gave me a half hug. "I don't get that often enough as it is. I'm not going to give that up for a week-long party."

I hugged him back, and the conversation drifted into what types of books we liked and our favorite authors. He liked a broad range: mystery, spy novels, and fantasy. He even liked some of the old westerns like Louis L'Amour and the Sackett novels. I talked about Harry Dresden, which mixed the noir mystery novels with a wizard in Chicago. We also covered the Iron Druid stories by Kevin Hearne and "The Blacksmith's Son" by Michael Manning. It occurred to me I was living the real life version of these stories. Life was a lot scarier and hurt a lot more than fiction.

Of course, here I was curled up next to a warm, sexy man who was quite capable of doing some magic all on his own. Real life was a lot nicer that way too.

Finally, it was time to get up and start the day. We made plans to get together that evening, as Tyler needed to go home and spend some time with his kitty, Mr. Tubbles. He wanted to check on a few things, but he thought his surprise should be ready tonight.

I had no idea of what it could be, and Tyler hadn't given me any hints. Whatever it was, I was sure I'd like it. Meanwhile, I had a lot of stuff to catch up on.

Taking a shower felt nice. It felt good to be clean and fresh again. Bermuda knocked off the toilet paper and sat on the back of the toilet like always. It occurred to me I needed to remodel the bathroom and come up with a different way to handle the bowel towels. I'd get right on that after finishing the bedroom, getting Sandy and Annabeth back to full health, and cleaning up the park. I guess Bermuda would just have to clear off his perch a while longer.

After breakfast, I headed back to Sandy's bedroom to check on my patients. John hadn't moved, of course, and Sandy was doing incrementally better. The real difference was Annabeth. Her matrix was almost done. There were still a few ragged edges around her toes, but the rest of it looked solid.

I was finally going to have Annabeth back! At least, I hoped she would be back. Surely she would return to consciousness when her matrix was finished? I certainly hoped so. I was still so new to all this, and it would be nice to have someone confirm I was doing the right thing. I guess if her matrix finished and she didn't wake up, I'd figure out something else.

While I waited in nervous anticipation, I fixed up all the Octopuses and Grannies that needed my attention. I'd taken a much longer break than normal with Tyler, so there were a lot of them to fix. When I finished, I started working on Penny. I pushed magic into her until the world seemed empty and gray. Then I pulled magic from her until I felt like I was going to pop. Then I held it until the magic inside me was fully saturated with my colors of sapphire blue and emerald green, and I'd start the process all over again. Penny was still sleeping, and I didn't know how much more I needed to do. I could feel her magic, though, and it felt like the size of a small lake. It was a lot.

The process was rhythmic and soothing, and helped me stay calm as an hour went by, and then two more. Annabeth's toes filled in, but still she didn't wake up. I took a really close look and discovered less obvious parts of the matrix that weren't fully filled in yet. It was happening, though, and it was almost done. I breathed and waited.

In the fourth hour, it finally happened. I felt a click, as the last of the matrix fell into place, and Annabeth's pink magic suddenly dimmed. Her magic was much more stable now, and as a result, it didn't shine outside her aura as much. It would look like she had less magic to a regular supernatural, but I could see inside her, and the color was dense and rich.

Most importantly, she woke up. Her eyes snapped open, and she looked around in confusion.

"Take it easy," I said soothingly. "Just take a moment. You are alright."

She sat up abruptly, then collapsed back with a groan. For a moment, I thought she was going to hurl. She tried to talk, but all that came out was a grunt.

Water. She needed water. I ran to the kitchen to get some. When I returned, she was trying to sit up again, but this time much slower. I put the water down and helped her. For a while she just sat on the edge of the bed, taking deep breaths. Then she started drinking a bit, and gradually her color started coming back. She took a look around.

"Where am I?" she asked.

"You're in Sandy's bedroom," I said a little surprised. She should know where this was. Then it hit me. John had asked the House to make all the changes to the room after she was unconscious. So I kept going and started filling her in on everything that had happened since she sang her matrix into existence. I'd just caught Tyler up on all the events, so this was feeling a bit like déjà vu.

"Bathroom," she croaked. I helped her to her feet and held her hand as we shuffled towards the bathroom. She was very unsteady on her feet and would have probably fallen over if I hadn't been there. She was in the bathroom for a long time. When she finally emerged, she looked a bit more awake and refreshed. She'd washed her face and tamed her hair a bit.

"I know you just told me a bunch of stuff that has been going on, but I really only caught about half of that," she said. She gave me a trademark happy smile. It was just a small smile, nowhere near her normal wattage, but it was the best sign yet that she was coming back to life.

I helped her back over to the bed again. This time she moved a lot better.

"How do you feel?" I asked.

"I'm stiff and sore," she replied. "It's been a good while since I felt this creaky and old." She paused for a moment, evaluating. "Other than that, I feel different. I'm not sure how to explain it." She paused. "I feel brighter? That seems weird to say." She was tentative. "I don't know if it is because I've been asleep for this long or not, but everything seems brighter. More vibrant. And I feel substantial. Like I'm more solid somehow."

"You have your matrix now," I said. "You're packing a lot more magic than what you had before. You are probably feeling the effects of that."

"Is this how you felt?" she asked.

"There was so much going on at the time I don't have a good feeling of how the matrix felt," I said. "I was just trying to hang on. I hadn't slept in a long time, I was in a lot of pain, and I was trying to heal my broken bones. I know that things got a lot easier after I'd made my matrix. Hopefully, that will happen with you too. It's going to be exciting to see how it all develops."

She sniffed the air. Then sniffed herself. "I think the first exciting thing that needs to happen is a shower. Help me up. I'm ready to head home."

I helped her to her feet. She seemed stronger and steadier already. I held her hand anyway. No sense in tempting fate and having a fall. As we slowly tottered off to her apartment, I again told her the story of what had happened while she was out. This time it seemed to really sink in, and she asked a few questions. She seemed especially interested in the surprise from Tyler. I promised to keep her updated.

By the time we got to her place, she was walking pretty well and seemed to have it together. She said she would be fine, but I decided to stay just in case she needed me. Her Tuscan courtyard was a beautiful place to work on magic, so I settled in and worked on Penny for a while. I was glad I stayed because taking a shower wore her out. She'd been unconscious for almost two weeks. You can't just bounce back from that in a few hours.

She collapsed on the couch for a little bit, and I made her some soup. That seemed to wake up her appetite, so I made her a sandwich, and then another sandwich, and then another one. The girl was hungry!

We were chatting again, and she fell asleep right in the middle of my story. I let her nap and went back to working on Penny. I felt like I could hear the tiniest echo from her. Like maybe I was starting to get through to her a bit. I'd woken Penny up before, and I'd do it again. This time was taking a lot longer, but she had absorbed a lot more magic too.

Annabeth woke up a few hours later, looking a lot more refreshed. Her eyes were clear and the color was back in her cheeks. She got up to make some coffee and I didn't even need to hold her hand. She moved like she was still a little sore, but the unsteadiness was gone. We were just starting to settle back down on the couch again, when there was a knock at the door. It was Tyler, and he was grinning from ear to ear.

"It's ready," he said. "I just checked, and everything is good to go." He was practically bouncing in excitement. Whatever this was, he couldn't wait to show me.

I glanced at Annabeth just as she glanced at me. Her glance said she didn't want to be alone right now. We both looked back at Tyler. I wasn't sure what type of surprise this was. It could be a surprise that was just for the two of us. In which case, Annabeth would feel like a third wheel. I didn't want that to happen. On the other hand, it could be something like a gift, in which case, it didn't matter who was there. I tried to compact all that into the look I was sending.

"Annabeth, if you are feeling up to it, you can use this too," he said. I guess he got my transmission. Tyler is smart like that. Although, I was now wondering what two people could use. I was pretty sure it wasn't a toothbrush. Or toilet paper.

My Analytical Side, who is very British, just rolled his eyes. He gets my humor, but he doesn't think I'm very funny. I think I'm hysterical! It's probably a good thing this was all on the inside, or people would think I was crazy.

"I'm game," Annabeth hopped up off the couch, or at least she tried to. It was more like a fast wobble with a side of old-lady-creak, but she made it. I hopped up too, and we were on our way. Tyler took us down a couple floors to the basement. The only things I knew that were down there were the magic charging room and John's apartment. We went past John's massive Hobbit door, past the sparkly charging room door, and stopped at an empty section of wall.

"Wave your hand over the wall," Tyler said mysteriously. I gave him an odd look, but gave a big wave with my hand, sort of like I was finger painting a giant arch.

Nothing happened.

"Try waving your hand like you are trying to find a hidden switch," he said.

Oh. That was different. This time I put my hand on the wall and moved it all around, feeling for a hidden bump or trigger. It was about chest level and a little to the right of me. It wasn't anything physical. Instead, the glowing outline of a hand appeared. I could see an incredibly complex rune etched inside it. I moved my hand away, and it disappeared. If I hadn't known to look for it, I'd have never found it. There was no indication to my physical or magical sight that anything was different. Since I could actually see through walls with my magic sight, I could also see there wasn't any sort of door or room here. This really was strange.

I gave Tyler a questioning look.

"Go ahead," he said. "Use the portal."

I moved my hand close again, and the handprint lit up. Feeling apprehensive, but trusting Tyler, I put my hand in the middle of the print.

Immediately, I was somewhere else.

7

A New Journey

I was on a beach. A beautiful, empty stretch of beach. I wasn't sure where this was, but it certainly wasn't in Louisville. It was like I had stepped into a perfect postcard. The day was beautiful with a cool breeze. The sand was smooth and white. The shoreline was shallow with water so clear and luminous that it was a mesmerizing aqua color rather than just blue. The beach covered a wide expanse that eventually ended at a line of tropical trees.

I was just starting to take it all in when there was a faint pop, and Annabeth suddenly appeared beside me. She gasped and stared. There was another pop, and Tyler showed up.

"Wow, Tyler," I said. "This is just beautiful! Is this our new vacation spot?" I could get used to this. Almost getting killed a few times was really stressful. Coming here to relax and unwind would be wonderful. Now I just needed a lounge chair and a cute cabana boy to bring me piña coladas.

"Oh, no," he laughed. "This isn't for relaxing. This is your new gym."

Huh? I looked at Annabeth to see if she was as confused as I was. This place was amazing. Why ruin it with exercise?

"Walk this way," he said. "I'll give you the grand tour." Ignoring our looks, he started off down the beach. After a moment, we followed.

"Back there is the landing spot." He gestured to where we had started. "It's a good idea to look around, as there is always an indicator pointing towards the return spot." He pointed up towards the trees. I hadn't noticed it before, but there was a faded wooden sign on a stake with a red arrow pointing down the beach in the direction we were going.

"You will always have to travel from the landing spot to the return spot. I have no idea why they can't both be in the same area, but it is something the House enforces. In this case, since Sleeping Beauty has just woken from her nap, the House has made the return point as close as possible." He gestured ahead where something was coming into view.

It was a door. And only a door. Nothing else.

No walls, no house, no pathway. Just a door. It was all very Alice in Wonderland.

"The door you see coming up is actually a full bathroom and locker room. It's an extra feature I added to my own gym. There is nothing worse than going through the portal, traveling all the way to the workout point, and then realizing you need to do a number two."

"That is very thoughtful of you," Annabeth said. "I'm not really sure what all this is yet, but I'm very glad I don't have to go squatting in the woods."

We walked up to the door and opened it. I expected it to be something like a port-a-potty, but it was actually a really nice bathroom and lounge. There were two stalls, dual sinks with nice mirrors, and two walk-in showers. There was also a spot that one might find in a mudroom for hanging up clothes and storing shoes. On the other side of the space was a huge couch, which seemed out of place for a bathroom setting. It looked puffy and comfortable, and big enough for several people to sit on and chat. Part of one wall had lots of extra drawers and shelving. It was all lined with fancy tiles and recessed lighting. This place was high class! There was even a pot of coffee with some coffee cups on the counter. The coffee was already made, ready to go.

This wasn't like a high school locker room at all. It was more like a posh place at a fancy country club.

"Before we begin, go ahead and change into your workout gear and meet me outside." Tyler opened up the lockers, showing us the clothes inside. For me, there were a simple pair of gray shorts and a gray shirt. Nothing fancy, which was perfect for working out.

"Grab a cup of coffee if you want, too," he said. "We need to have a chat before we actually have our first training session."

I realized he didn't need to get changed as he already had on a pair of gray shorts and a gray t-shirt. He was going barefoot, which made sense as we were on a beach. The sand would probably feel very nice between my toes. I grabbed my clothes and changed in one of the big shower stalls while Annabeth did the same. Then I got a cup of coffee, cream and sugar of course, and headed outside. Annabeth was right behind me.

"Before I forget, here is the return marker." Tyler pointed out an outline of a hand in the sand. It was right by the locker room door so it was easy to find. "Just use it the same way as you did the other marker, and you will appear back in the House again."

That seemed simple enough. "One thing to keep in mind is you will probably want to change back into your normal clothes before you return."

"Speaking of workout clothes, we will probably need more than one set," Annabeth said. "Otherwise, it will be hard to have them cleaned and ready for the next day."

"Ahh. Good thinking," Tyler said. "And it's already been taken care of. Just leave your workout clothes in the locker when you leave. When you come back again, a clean set will be waiting."

"Really?" Annabeth asked. Tyler nodded. "Like, really?" Tyler just laughed and nodded again. She sounded so happy. And shocked. "I love that! Magic laundry! I could get used to this."

I found this amusing. "We've seen all kinds of magic stuff, you even do magic yourself, and what makes you jump for joy is clean laundry?" I asked.

I was teasing her a bit. Don't get me wrong, I was happy about that too. I hated doing laundry myself. I usually waited until I had nothing clean to wear. Then I stuffed everything into the washer and got it done in one load. Sure, technically, you are supposed to break things down into whites and colors and all that stuff, but I just figured if it wasn't strong enough to make it through the wash, then I didn't need to wear it.

Annabeth just looked at me. "You know how much laundry I've done in my lifetime? Of course I'm excited about this. Sweaty workout clothes I don't have to wash? Yes, please!" She was lit up and smiling. It was so nice to have her back.

"Okay, training time." Tyler was ready for business. I did a quick look around. I didn't see stepping machines or treadmills or dumbbells. This didn't look like any gym I'd ever been to. What was Tyler going to have us do? Run up and down the beach?

"Part of training is knowing what the goal is. Then you break it down into smaller steps and actually do the work," Tyler said. "Since this is Annabeth's first day back from the Land of Nod, this is the perfect time to start off easy and talk about what we are going to get up to."

We walked down to the water's edge and sat in the sand with our coffee. The waves tickled our feet while unseen birds provided background music.

"I've had an idea for a while now," Tyler said, settling into story mode. "I've been all over the world solving problems for the House. I've helped mages, naturals, and some strange creatures that didn't seem to fit either one of those. I've trained in all kinds of martial styles, and I've watched hundreds of magic duels. I've fought in large battles, and sometimes it's only been one person trying to kill me." He stopped, searching for the right words.

"I know I'm not saying this well. One day, I saw a mage, who was really good, lose a fight over something very simple. He didn't know how to dodge. His shield wore down. His magic ran out, and he had nothing left. Something that was so simple for me was not something he even thought of. He thought in terms of how to attack and defend with magic. And only magic. The world is so much bigger than that. It is sort of like the old saying that if you are a hammer, then everything starts to look like a nail.

"It got me thinking. What if a mage trained like a natural? What if they trained their bodies and minds just as much as they trained their magical powers? What if magic was just one of many tools in their toolbelt, rather than the only thing they knew? How amazing would that be?"

Annabeth was listening intently and nodding a bit. She was taking in what he was saying.

"When I saw you, Jason, I thought this might be the right time to test my theory. You have a powerful magical talent, but your first instinct isn't to use magic. You run from a golem, or you swing a shillelagh, or you dodge and punch. It seems like mages get magic, and then they think that is the only thing they can use to solve a problem. Sometimes there is another, better way."

"Well, it helps that I can't use charms yet," I said. "So there is no shield to rely on. Also, my magic isn't the kind that lets me throw fireballs or force bolts. I have to find a way to stay alive until my small magic can make a difference. You're preaching to the choir with me. I already know this is something I want to work on."

"So what are we talking about, exactly?" Annabeth asked. "Being able to use charms is wonderful, but there are many times they haven't been able to help me. Take the first golem incident. I did exactly what you talked about, Tyler. I went straight to my charms and tried to find one that could take it down. Nothing I did seemed to stop it. I remember feeling so helpless, right before it kicked me. If Jason hadn't distracted it and led it away, it would have stomped me into the ground. I would not be here right now. I still have nightmares about that," she shuddered.

"Naturals usually only have one talent and that can show up years after their Waker Moment," Tyler said. "Their only hope is to develop their physical skills. They learn to run, punch, block, and dodge. They only have strength and speed to rely on to keep them alive. This is what I want to do with you two. I'm hoping to train you, so if you get in a fight and run out of magic, you are just as deadly as before."

"That sounds great to me," I said. "I'm in. One hundred percent." If I'd been better physically, I'd have been able to take out Mustard in our first encounter, and the park would have been okay. And maybe I would not have busted up my hand punching him in our second fight. If I'd been faster and more powerful, I might have been able to keep him from exploding. Or, maybe found a way to contain it. There were going to be other fights. I needed to be better, and Tyler was going to help me get there.

"This makes sense to me," Annabeth said. "I'm in too. Quick question, though, what about John and Sandy?"

"I'm not sure," Tyler replied. "I know I'm supposed to be doing more for your House than simply helping with the Remnants. Your House gave me a permanent room and a door home. That has never happened before. I feel like I should be training you two. It just seems right to me." He paused for a moment. "The thing is, creating all this takes a lot of magic. I didn't do the actual work. I just gathered the magic and gave it to the House, telling it what I needed." A twinkle came to his eyes. "Trust me, you haven't even seen anything yet. There are lots of surprises in store for you."

He laughed. "You're going to hate it sometimes. And sometimes you're going to love it. But hopefully what you learn here keeps you alive. Anyway, back to your question. You and Jason aren't powerful yet, so it doesn't take a lot to challenge you. Sandy and John, on the other hand, can do some real damage. Sandy, even as weak as she is right now, is a prodigy. And John, well, he is part freakin' mountain. It takes a lot to challenge a mountain. It would require more magic than I can gather to provide a real training space for them. I'm sure there are some things the gym can help them with and they are welcome to use it, but the gym isn't going to go all out for them."

That made sense. This was a newbie experience, which was perfect for Annabeth and me. I'd take what I could get.

"Any other questions?" Tyler asked.

"Are you going to teach us Martial Arts?" Annabeth asked. "Will we call you Master and do all that bowing?" she said in a playful tone.

What an idea! Would I have to call him Master Tyler? My body warmed at the idea. Hmmm. That meant I would be sleeping with the teacher. I lost myself in the fantasy for a moment, but was jolted back to reality when Annabeth pinched my arm.

"Ouch," I said, giving her a hurt look.

"I don't know where you went, but it must have been fun," she replied. "You clearly weren't listening, and you had a peculiar look on your face."

Well, crap. This was not the right time for those thoughts. Bad Jason! Behave.

"Sorry," I said. "I just started thinking about finally being able to kick some ass." Time to change the subject. "So, how long will it take to train us to fight?"

"That really depends on you," Tyler replied. "I've worked with naturals before, and it takes at least six months to get good. It takes a couple years to become really good. Mastery can take a lifetime. The good news is that you are a supernatural now. Theoretically, you are immortal, so you have the time to develop your skills to the highest levels if you wish."

"Theoretically I'm immortal, but in actuality, I've almost died a couple times," I said. "I've had an actual, real sword rammed through me. That was no joke. I've had my face punched in by a golem and had the crap kicked out of me by a power-hungry witch. The battle for Louisville isn't over yet, either. I need to get good at fighting, and I need to do it now."

Annabeth was nodding as I talked. She knew we had more battles coming up, and they were going to happen sooner rather than later. Six months really wasn't a long period of time, but I felt that we didn't have six months. Our fight with the Louisville Mages was far from over.

"I agree with you," Tyler said. "I don't think you have that long either. What I'm hoping is that you will learn the natural side of training, and then use your mage abilities to enhance it. You are both creative, and you both have unique talents. Learn what I have to teach first, and then figure out how to make it even better for your talents.

"First, though, you have to start learning how to fight, and that starts with the deceptively simple art of the punch. Break time is over. Let's put the coffee away and get to your first lesson." Tyler hopped to his feet, gathered up the cups, and headed back to the door.

Unsure of what we should do, Annabeth and I got to our feet and followed. He took the coffee cups back inside and led us a little ways down the beach to a clear area of sand.

"Before we begin, let's see where you are starting from. Who would like to go first?"

"I will." Annabeth jumped in before I could. The girl was quick.

Tyler nodded, "Just tell the House you are ready to begin."

It seemed strange, but Annabeth spoke confidently into the air. "House, I'm ready to begin."

The sand in front of her started moving. Annabeth jumped back in surprise. It started piling on itself, growing higher and higher, until it was as tall as she was. The mound stopped growing, and then started forming into the shape of a man. In only a few seconds, there stood a sturdy mannequin in front of her. It kind of looked like one of those Under Armor mannequins with muscular legs, broad shoulders, and defined abs. It had a mannequin type face, with basic features, but no real expression.

"This is your training companion," Tyler said. "He's made of sand so you can't hurt him, and he has a basic human shape so you can get used to landing blows on a real person.

"Let's begin. Annabeth, I want you to punch him."

She looked unsure of herself. "Where do you want me to hit?"

"Anywhere you want."

She made a fist with her right hand and approached the figure. She stopped, and hesitated. "I'm not used to doing this," she said.

Tyler nodded and stood patiently. She looked at me. I shrugged. I've punched people before, but it was usually in the middle of a fight. I wasn't used to punching a mannequin either.

Finally, Annabeth hauled back and let her fist fly at the sand face. It landed with a faint sound, disturbing a few grains of sand. Other than that, nothing happened.

"Try it again," Tyler said. "Try to get the trainer to move back a step."

Annabeth balled up her fist. This time aiming for his chest. Once again, she only made the tiniest of dents in the sand. The grains shifted slightly, and any record of her effort was erased. She hadn't come anywhere close to making the guy move.

With a determined look, she whacked him a few more times with the same result. Finally, she stepped back and relaxed. She rubbed her hand, grimacing. It looked red and sore.

"How did that feel?" Tyler asked.

"It felt confusing," Annabeth said. "I wasn't sure where to hit or how to hit it. My hand is sore now, and I don't feel like I threatened him at all. If he had been a real person,

I don't think my punches would have bothered him in the slightest."

"Good," Tyler said. "Make a memory of exactly how you are feeling right now. Feel the confusion. Feel the lack of power. Feel how sore your hand is.

"This is your beginning. You're only going to get better from here. Remembering this moment is important. There will be times when you feel frustrated with your progress. It will feel like nothing is happening and you aren't getting anywhere. When that happens, all you need to do is remember this moment, and it will be very obvious how much you have improved."

He smiled at her, and she nodded back. Then Tyler and Annabeth both looked at me. It was time for my beginner moment. I felt nervous, like I was on stage and it was time to perform.

I had punched before, so I knew the basics. It was just different this time. This wasn't a real fight, and they were both looking at me, judging me.

"House, I'm ready to begin," I said, and a mound of sand started growing before me. It reached my height and then formed into my own training dummy. He seemed a lot more muscular and solid than Annabeth's guy.

Before I could psych myself out, I made my fists and let them fly. One, Two. A right and left hook connected with his head. They landed with a bit more sound and force than Annabeth's punches. They still didn't make much of an impact, though, and the sand quickly shifted to remove any damage.

My hands stung. Punching sand was softer than hitting a brick wall, but it was still a very solid surface. This wasn't going to be like hitting a softer punching bag. My training partner felt massive, which he probably was. All the sand had to weigh three or four hundred pounds. Moving him was not going to be easy.

The bright side was that if I could get used to hitting him, then a real person was going to feel much easier by comparison.

I looked at Tyler, and he nodded for me to keep going. So I did. I punched the dummy in his perfect chest a few times. I barely made a dent. It only took a second for sand to flow, and he looked perfect again. In fact, he looked too perfect. His sandy muscles looked strong, solid, and powerful. He stood there, with his chest out, daring me to do my worst, knowing I couldn't bother him at all.

Something changed, and suddenly he was every guy that had ever bullied me. He was the guy at school that had slapped me around and called me 'that little queer'. He was the guy in the locker room that had hit me for looking at him a little too long.

I yelled and punched him again. Then I really lit into him. I pounded him as hard as I could over and over again.

Finally, I ran out of steam. I stepped back exhausted, shaking with emotion. Where the heck had that come from? I hadn't even known all that anger was inside me. It felt good to let it out.

I looked at my training mannequin. He stood there, powerful, solid, just like before. I had a feeling I was going to both hate and love his salty ass before all this was over.

I looked over at Tyler and Annabeth. She was a little wide-eyed, but Tyler just seemed patient. He looked like he had done this himself before, many times, and it was no big deal. Somehow, that made it a bit better.

"How do you feel?" Tyler asked.

"I feel weak," I said. "Like I'm too light and not strong enough." I held up my hands and looked at them. "And now my hands really hurt."

"Good," Tyler said. "That is a great beginning. You have the same directions as I gave Annabeth. Get in touch with how you feel right now and make a memory of it. Someday you will look back on this moment and marvel at just how far you've come.

"Here's the good news." Tyler took in both me and Annabeth. "Those were the last unstructured punches you will throw. After today, you will know how to make a fist and how to really hit someone. It will feel awkward and strange at first, but with time and practice, you will start to gain some real power."

8

Hit Like Moose

"Now, let's talk a bit about punching and the overall style of fighting that you are going to learn." Tyler settled into lecture mode. "Most people think a punch is just a punch. You clench your fist and let it fly. Bam! You hit someone and hope they fall. If not, you do it again.

"The reality is, there are lots of ways to hit someone. Take boxing, for example. It's a nice blend of speed and power. It favors those with mass and strength." He demonstrated by throwing some quick jabs into the air, followed by a powerful right hook.

"You could also go for a power style that uses your feet as well as your hands like taekwondo." He settled into a low stance, feet wide apart, and threw some powerful punches that looked like they would really hurt. I know he said the focus was power, but they seemed very fast too. Then he threw some kicks that, again, seemed both fast and powerful.

"What I am going to teach you is called Wing Chun. It was created by a woman, and is designed for a physically weaker opponent to quickly overpower someone larger and stronger. It relies on trapping, redirection, and most of all, speed." He shifted slightly.

I waited for him to punch. Then I realized he already had. He'd moved so fast I hadn't seen it! I looked at Annabeth, and she just looked expectant. I'm pretty sure she had missed it too.

"Can you do that again?" I asked.

"Sure," Tyler said. "Let me do it so you can feel it this time." Before I could protest, he'd already shot a punch right in front of my face. I still didn't see it, but the wind blew my hair and I jumped back in shock. Thank goodness he wasn't trying to land it for real! There was no way I could dodge that.

"Do it to me," Annabeth requested, and Tyler complied. This was my third time seeing that style of punch, and I was still no closer to actually seeing it. Tyler was quick. Damn quick. Lightning quick. I didn't know it was possible to move that fast, and I got excited that maybe I could be that fast too. If I'd been that quick, my last two fights with Mustard would have turned out very differently. I didn't have a shield and I couldn't use charms, but this would be a nice substitute.

"That is incredible," Annabeth said. "Like, just incredible! You said this was all about speed, so what is the power like?"

"I was thinking the same thing," I said. "You're quick, like rabbit. But do you hit like moose?"

They both stopped and looked at me.

"Hit like moose?" Annabeth said with a raised eyebrow.

I waved it off. "It was all I could think of at the moment. Moose are big. I bet they hit really hard. I was just trying to get into the spirit of the old kung fu movies."

Annabeth raised her eyebrow even further, if that was possible.

"You know—they do stuff like 'Mantis Splits the Sun' and 'Bear Squats in the Woods'. Stuff like that," I continued.

"How exactly does a bear squat in the woods?" Tyler jumped in. Clearly, I was amusing the hell out of him.

"I don't know," I replied. "You're the martial arts master. You tell me."

"Maybe it goes like this." Tyler squatted down and started shaking his ass. The whole time he was making constipated faces. It was hysterical, and we started laughing. Tyler had been so serious and teacher-like. Now the whole process seemed fun and a whole lot less intimidating.

I put my hands on my head and made antlers with my fingers. "Mooo," I said, and charged.

Tyler fell over laughing. "Moo?" he said. "What the hell was that?"

"I was a moose," I said. "And I was charging."

He started laughing all over again. Annabeth shook her head, but she was laughing too.

"Mooooo," I hollered, and charged her.

It felt so good to have some fun, and for a while that is all we did. I kept on trying to moose them, and Tyler did a bigger and even more constipated version of squatting bear. Annabeth was having a good time, but she finally called an end to the amusement and got us back on track again.

"As I was saying, before Kung Fu Theater came to town." She got serious again. "This style of fighting seems to be very fast, but I would like to see just how powerful it is." She gestured at the sand mannequins. "I'm a small person, so I can't put a lot of weight or strength behind a blow. If I'm fast, I could hit someone a lot of times, but it needs to be able to hurt them too. The reality is, almost everyone I fight is going to be bigger than me. I would like to know what I'm learning really works."

"That's fair," Tyler said. "I'll give you part of your answer now and part later. For the first part, you both have punched your training partners, so you know just how solid and heavy they are."

We nodded.

He walked over to my sandy dummy, and with no warning, he punched it.

I heard a boom, like when John was throwing his powered rocks, and the entire back of the dummy blew apart. Sand flew for ten feet at least. There was a fist-sized hole in the front of the dummy, but the shock wave had passed through it, getting bigger as it went. The force had exited the back, taking most of the sand with it. My training partner staggered back, and then collapsed.

I stood staring at the sand pile in shock.

"Wow," Annabeth said.

"Wow," she said again.

Tyler turned back to us. "Satisfied?" he asked.

We nodded.

If I could hit like that… Wow, indeed.

"You said there were two parts to your answer?" Annabeth inquired.

"When you are ready, we'll add some extra protection, and I'll let you feel what it is like to be hit like that," Tyler said. "Experiencing the power for yourself takes your belief to a whole new level. I still remember getting hit by my first punch." He seemed lost in thought for a moment.

I couldn't imagine getting hit like that. I genuinely thought it might kill me.

"So, is this worth learning?" he asked Annabeth.

"Oh, yes!" she said, her eyes shining. She was a believer now.

I nodded too, caught up in the moment.

"Okay," he said. "Let's get started. The first thing you need to learn is how to form a fist."

For the next several minutes we learned the art of making a fist. It was an art, too. I had no idea there was so much to it.

First, curl the fingers around the top, meaty part of the hand, with the fingertips resting in the natural bend of the palm. Then wrap the thumb along the front of the fist so it reinforces the fingers and doesn't get in the way. Then make the fist tight and keep the knuckles straight. Don't squeeze too hard, or it will curl the fist around and throw off the striking area. The striking area was the last three knuckles of the hand. The whole effect was to create a solid, compact surface, like a hammer.

We practiced making a fist over and over again, with both hands. It was much harder than I thought it would be. I couldn't get my thumb right and Tyler kept adjusting it. Annabeth kept squeezing her fist too hard, throwing off her knuckle alignment. Tyler said we better learn the right way now, because when we started actually hitting something, it would quickly reinforce just how essential a good fist was. We spent at least an hour making fists before Tyler moved on.

"The next thing to learn is your centerline. This is an invisible line that goes from the top of your head to your feet and splits your body in half. It's easy to visualize because it goes down your nose, down the center of your chest, through your belly button, and down to the floor. This is your place of power. All of your blocks and strikes begin from the centerline.

"Let's begin by putting your palm at your centerline. Keep your hand open and your fingers together. It's almost like you are making a half of praying hands." He showed us what he wanted, and it was pretty easy to figure out. "Now, slowly extend your hand in front of you and form it into a fist." He demonstrated, making it look easy.

It wasn't. Adding a movement on top of making the right kind of fist brought the difficulty level way up.

We practiced that for a while before he added the next part. This time he wanted us to stand a certain way while slowly punching. He had us start with our feet together, standing up straight. Then we bent our knees, settled on our heels, and pointed our feet outward. Then we'd switch our weight to our toes and rotate our feet so that our heels were pointing outward. It was like doing a weird dance move.

Regardless of how we got there, we ended up with our feet about shoulder width apart, with our feet slightly pointed in. It was like we were pigeon toed, and it felt awkward as hell. I had no idea how this was supposed to help us fight. I called it "The Pigeon has to Pee". We drilled getting into the strange stance over and over again.

It felt so awkward that I finally called a timeout.

"I trust you that this strange "Pigeon has to Pee" thing is what we need to learn," I said to Tyler. He just shook his head at the name but let me keep going. "But it feels very wobbly right now, and I don't know how we are eventually supposed to fight like this. Maybe a demo would be helpful? You showed us what a punch of this type can do once we get good. I think seeing how we can eventually use this would let us know what we are aiming for."

Annabeth nodded in agreement. She was picking this up faster than I was, but she still looked unsteady.

"Sure," Tyler said. "That's fair." He faced me and did his little knee bend, foot swivel move, and settled into the Pigeon. "Try and push me over."

I'd seen enough Kung Fu Theater to know this never ended well for the student. I was more than ready to give it a try, though. I felt like a stiff breeze would blow me over. I intended to be a lot more than a breeze to him.

I walked up to him, put my hand on his chest, and pushed. Nothing. He didn't budge. I settled a bit lower and pushed again, harder this time. I felt like I was pushing a brick wall. He was solid, immovable.

I braced my back leg, put both hands on his chest, and pushed with all my might. Tyler shifted slightly, his body rotated, and now I was pushing at an angle. I was giving it all I had, and I wasn't fast enough to stop myself. My hands slid off his chest, and my forward momentum sent me right by him. I tripped over his leg and ended up face down on the beach.

I spit out the sand, got to my feet, and tried again. Nobody could be that good.

It turns out, he was.

I quickly found out that he was way too solid for any half measures to work. It would take everything I had to budge him. If I gave it everything, though, I was committed to a direction, and he would just shift and let me fly right by.

After a few minutes, I stopped and let Annabeth have a try. She didn't fare any better than I had. When she stopped, Tyler suggested we both try at the same time. This time, though, he was going to use the stepping that came with this style of movement. Again, all we had to do was knock him over.

Even though there were two of us, we fared even worse because Tyler was now moving. He would move in unexpected directions, and our perfect attack was suddenly aimed at open air. Sometimes, he would just lean slightly, and that was enough to throw us off. He never seemed to hurry, or exert any real effort. In contrast, Annabeth and I were sweating and puffing as we rushed and pushed and tugged and did everything we could to force him off his game.

It wasn't happening.

Finally, we stopped and admitted defeat. Tyler had certainly made his point. What he was teaching us worked. He hadn't been trying to hurt us at all, but if this had been a real fight, we wouldn't have been able to touch him.

"I know I'm throwing a lot at you right now," Tyler said. "When I learned this, we spent a whole week on just making a fist. Then another whole week getting into our stance. Today, we've covered almost four weeks of material.

"When I was learning, though, I had all the time in the world. Nobody was trying to kill me or destroy my home. You both don't have that sort of time, so my goal today is to get you to where you can do basic punches on your training partners."

In kung fu movies the wise, old teacher always made the padawan do stupid training stuff while the student was desperate to learn something more useful. Then, the student eventually finds out the stupid stuff was really training after all. Sort of like the "Karate Kid" 'wax on' and 'wax off'. It looked like Tyler was going to have us skip that stage and go directly to the training part.

We'd been making fists and getting into Pigeon stance for a few hours now, so we took a quick break. I used the restroom and drank some water, but I was actually starting to feel a bit hungry. I mentioned that to Tyler just as my stomach growled.

"I've already got that covered," Tyler said, motioning to another set of drawers by the sinks. "You are going to find that all this extra activity will use up a lot of energy. Fueling your body so it can develop and grow will be very important."

I went over and opened up the top drawer. It was filled with neat rows of what looked like candy bars. I picked one up.

"Mashed potatoes and brown gravy?" I said in surprise. It felt like a Snickers bar.

"Those are nutrition bars," Tyler said. "They have protein, fat, carbs, vitamins, and several other things all crammed in that little bar. It has everything you need to restore yourself after a workout. They even have a tiny bit of healing magic in there to promote energy levels and make sure you don't get too sore."

"That sounds good to me," I said, peeling off the wrapper.

The bar was white with streaks of brown throughout. It looked like a solid version of mashed potatoes and gravy. I was trying to be cheerful, and I certainly wanted the benefits of eating the bar, but usually meal replacements like this were awful. They usually taste like sawdust stuffed with chalk disguised under a layer of chocolate. Oh, well. This was part of training, so I might as well get it over with. With a slight grimace, I took a healthy bite out of the bar.

The texture was—not bad. I'd even go so far as to say it was good. It was smooth, like the mashed potatoes had been made with lots of milk and butter. There were also little solid bits in it, just like you get when you use real potatoes instead of an instant mix. The gravy part was dark and packed with flavor, just like real gravy. I took another bite. Wow!

Tyler was watching me with an amused look on his face. "You thought they would suck, didn't you?" I nodded sheepishly. "You've probably had mundane health bars from a grocery store. These are supernatural bars made by Tillman and Tiddles Haus of Confectionary. They are the Willy Wonka of the magic world, and everything they make tastes delicious. They used to just make sweets and candies, but now they've expanded into savory snacks as well. There are other, cheaper versions of these bars, but they just don't taste as good."

"How much are these?" I asked. "And how do we get more of them?" I hadn't really thought about money up to this point. I'd just been taking it all for granted. But really, this was all being funded by Tyler. I'm sure magic doors into bathrooms, training dummies made out of sand, self-cleaning laundry, and tasty power bars don't come cheap.

"Don't worry about it for now," Tyler said. "I stocked enough magic with the House to pay for all of this for a long time. There are only two of you, and your training won't take much from the system for now. When the training system runs out of magic, you will be powerful enough to fill it back up again."

"What's going on?" Annabeth inquired. She started washing her hands as I filled her in on the meal replacement bars and everything Tyler was doing for us.

"I don't know that I've thanked you for all this," she said gratefully. Then she gave him a big hug. I joined in too, and we made it a hug sandwich.

"All this is very nice, but there must be some way to pay you back," she said.

"You can pay me back by learning fast and training hard," Tyler said. "It's really nice to have a place to hang out where I don't need to fix anyone. Usually, by the time the House calls me, problems have gotten out of control. Being a troubleshooter is alright, but I get tired of going from one problem to another. This time, with this House, I get to fix a problem and then stick around afterwards to enjoy the solution. I know this House is still in danger, and Sandy and John aren't back to normal yet, but my part is mostly done.

I don't have to run around having sex with everyone to restore the peace.

"I've learned a lot, and I'm enjoying passing on that knowledge for the first time. This is a new project for me, and it feels good. So you can thank me by growing stronger and keeping this House safe."

"That works for me," Annabeth said brightly. "Now I'm ready for one of those tasty bars."

I pulled one out of the drawer at random. Southern Fried Chicken. Really? Even Willie Wonka would be hard pressed to get fried chicken into a bar. I handed it to Annabeth and pulled another Fried Chicken out of the drawer. I had to taste this for myself. I unwrapped it and took a bite.

OMG! It was so good. Like Kentucky Fried Chicken good. The outside was crunchy, salty, and loaded with spices, just like the crispy skin on fried chicken. The inside had a nice texture with a light savory taste. It wasn't real fried chicken, of course, but it was much closer than I ever thought they could get. I was now an official fan of Tillman and Tiddles.

"Damn! This is good!" Annabeth was having the same reaction as I was. I wanted to slow down and really appreciate it, but before I knew it, I had eaten the whole thing.

"One more and I'm good to go," I said to the group.

Tyler just looked amused at how much we were loving his stash. He picked out a few for himself and started munching on them while he waited.

My next bar was Cucumber Salad in Ranch Dressing. Hmmmm. I'm not a big salad person. Sometimes it's nice to have something lighter, and a side salad doesn't hurt. I'd enjoyed everything the Haus of Tillman and Tiddles had made so far. Maybe I would like this too. I opened it up and took a bite.

It was light, crispy, and fresh, with a touch of ranch dressing. It wasn't my favorite, but it was way better than I'd thought it would be. As I kept munching on it, though, I started to like it more. By the time I finished the bar, I'd decided it was way better than a real cucumber salad.

Inspired by the lightness of the cucumber, I decided to try a watermelon bar. It was also refreshing, with just a hint of sweetness. Somehow, it also seemed to be juicy, just like a slice of watermelon. These bars were awesome!

With our hunger banished and feeling refreshed, we headed back out again to continue our training. Over the last few hours, we'd learned how to stand, how to form a fist, and how to punch from our centerline. Now it was time to put it all together.

"Okay, House. I'm ready," I said.

My training partner, that Tyler had destroyed with one punch, reformed from its sandy base. I stood in front of it and got into my "Pigeon Needs to Pee" stance. I put my palm on my centerline, like I was doing half a prayer, and threw my first real punch. It landed on his chest with a faint 'putttt' and dislodged a few grains of sand.

Okay. This was a very humble beginning. I recentered and tried again. 'Putttt.' Same result. There was one big difference, though. I wasn't just practicing in the air anymore. I had a real target, and it was solid as hell. I quickly realized that making the correct fist was very important. When a good fist landed, it felt solid. If I didn't get something right, though, like not aligning my knuckles correctly or not tucking my thumb in tight, then it felt like my fist was fragile and going to break.

It wasn't just my fist, either. My Pigeon stance was still very new and wobbly. When I did get a good punch in, my base was shaky. So the force of the blow pushed me back, rather than being transferred into my training partner. In addition, I discovered that hitting on my centerline was a lot more important than I thought. If my elbow was out too far or if I landed off center, the force had a tendency to twist me.

I worked at it for hours, and it just wasn't coming together. Tyler stepped in often and demonstrated the proper technique over and over again. Towards the end, Annabeth started to get somewhere. A few of her blows had a different sound when they landed. They sounded a bit more solid. Not a lot, but a bit.

I was frustrated, but I wasn't discouraged. I'd figure this out. I was really good at feeling the patterns in things. I hadn't found the base of all this yet, but I would. In the meantime, my body was taking a beating. It wasn't just my hands, although they were the worst. All that intensity and jarring was showing up in my elbows, shoulders, and back. Even my knees were sore. I had no idea punching could be so hard. It certainly looked easy in the movies.

The sun was starting to set when we decided to call it a day. We showered and changed back into our regular clothes, leaving our dirty ones in the lockers. Annabeth was still excited about coming back and having fresh workout gear.

"There is still one more technique I need to show you," Tyler said mysteriously. "It is the secret to the Wing Chun style and is the basis for all its power and speed. Without this technique, you will be limited to your normal speed and power. Once you learn it, however, you can apply it to any physical style of combat and massively enhance its effectiveness."

This totally caught me off guard. We were already dressed and ready to leave. Why was he bringing this up now? We both looked at him expectantly, waiting for him to continue.

"I'm sure you're wondering what it is," he said, and we both nodded. "This is only something you can learn after you have good form, both with how you stand and how you attack. This secret enhances what you are doing. If you don't have good form, then it will magnify your faults and tear your body apart."

Given how sore I felt, I was very aware I needed better form. The whole idea of a secret sauce in physical combat intrigued me. I'd been thinking that there had to be more to this style. The punches were short and fast, but there didn't seem to be anything that gave them power. With boxing, the power seemed to come from your core and your shoulder. With karate, you were kicking so that obviously used stronger muscles and more of your body. These little straight punches didn't have any of that. No wind-up, no shoulder, no momentum behind them. Where was the power coming from? I was itching to find out.

"I think having a goal is both fun and motivational," Tyler continued. "With that in mind, I'm setting a goal for both of you for ten thousand punches. That should take long enough for you to get through the newness of all this and hopefully have developed a good basic form. Once you reach ten thousand, we'll do an evaluation. If you are good enough, then I'll teach you the final piece. If not, we'll set another ten thousand goal."

"Does this mean you'll be evaluating us separately?" Annabeth asked.

"Yes," Tyler said. "I'm training you both together, so your martial arts journeys will be similar. In this case, though, it's something you have to achieve individually. Jason can't fight for you, and you can't fight for him."

That made sense. It also made it a bit of a competition. There was no way I was going to let Annabeth get to ten thousand punches and learn the secret while I was still struggling on basic form. I was going to figure this out.

"How will we know when we've hit the goal?" I asked. I hadn't been counting punches so far, and there was no way Tyler had been able to count for both of us.

"Just ask the House," Tyler replied. "I've already set the goal for you, so everything you have done today counts towards it."

Really? The House was our own personal fitness monitor? That was cool!

"Just say something like 'House, show my punching stats' and you'll get the information," Tyler said. "You can choose to tell your stats, or not, but you are the only person that can see them. Well, except for me. I know your stats because I'm your trainer."

I was curious to see just what my stats were. Ten thousand seemed like a lot, but on the other hand, it didn't take long to throw a punch.

"House, show my punching stats," I said. A scroll popped up in the air in front of me. I don't know what I was expecting, but it was close enough to make me jump. It just floated in the air, waiting for me to read it.

Low Novice Jason Punch Stats

Level = 1

Punches = 678

Notes: You hit like falling snow. Try working on— everything. The good news is you can only get better from here.

I laughed and read it out to the group.

"That is too funny!" Tyler started chuckling. "I have training notes too, and the House has a sense of humor. I like it, so I've encouraged it, and I guess that carried over to you. I'm sure you can tell it to be nicer if you want."

I don't mind a little snark every now and then. It keeps things fun and interesting. Annabeth went next and showed us her stats.

Low Novice Annabeth Punch Stats

Level = 1.1

Punches = 704

Notes: Fantastic first day of effort. Keep it up and you'll soon be punching as well as you sing. Try working on listening. Everything has a sound.

That was a much better review than mine. I think the House was biased. It certainly loved her pink singing.

Because Annabeth is such a kind person, she was concerned that I'd be upset that she had a better training note. I just laughed it off. It didn't bother me at all. I'm glad the House was sweet to her. I think everyone should be sweet to Annabeth.

Because it was Annabeth, we also ended on a round of hugs. Just because we were training how to smash someone's face in was no reason not to show love and support. Tyler said he was heading home to spend time with Mr. Tubbles and we would meet up tomorrow. He palmed the return marker and disappeared.

Annabeth reminded me this was her first day after waking up from her matrix-building coma. It had been a full day and much more active than she ever thought it would be. She needed some time to sleep and recharge. I told her that I thought she was doing very well and I'd see her tomorrow. She put her hand on the portal and vanished too.

I took a moment to look around and just take it all in. The sun was setting in the ocean, and the sky was painted in oranges and reds. The calls of the birds mingled with the sounds of the waves rolling in on the sand. It was peaceful and beautiful.

This was my life now. I hopped through magic portals, trained in martial arts on the beach, and had a sand dummy as my partner. This new life was good. It was really good. I was alive and having a thrilling adventure. Sure there were people trying to kill me and destroy my home, but life wasn't perfect, right?

I watched the sunset for a few more minutes, absorbing the peace and harmony all around me. I needed moments like this to keep me sane. Finally, the sun dropped below the horizon and a chill settled in the air. My body reminded me just how sore and tired it was. It was time to return home.

Reluctantly, I put my hand on the return portal, and the beach vanished.

9

Physician, Heal Thyself

I appeared in the hallway in the basement of the House, right back where I started. Appearing suddenly indoors in a hallway felt strange after being outside by the big ocean. I took a moment to adjust, and then decided to head up to see John and Sandy. I might have been training all day, but I still had all my home chores to take care of.

I'd only gone a few steps, when a stream of Octopuses and Fairy Godmothers rounded the corner, flying towards me. They circled around me in a cloud, and a cacophony of voices exclaimed how much they had missed me and how glad they were I was back. Apparently, my creations had lost their connection to me once I'd gone through the portal.

I told them I was fine and there was nothing to worry about. Once I settled down, I'd take time and fix all of them. The Octopuses landed across my shoulders for a free ride as I made my way upstairs. I'd just arrived at the main floor, when I heard Bermuda.

I was greeted by a yowl and the scamper of little feet. He shot out of Sandy's apartment, flying to me as fast as his tiny paws could carry him. He jumped up and I caught him, giving him a big hug. It was so nice to see my furry baby again. He was glad to see me too, as he started frantically licking my face.

I carried him into Sandy's bedroom, holding him with one hand as I used the other to arrange the pillows on John's lap. Then I settled in for some kitten and magic time. I thought everyone would settle down quickly, but that wasn't the case.

Bermuda appeared upset. He jumped down off my lap, fuzzed up, and paced for a bit. Then he hissed, swatted at me, and then climbed back up into my lap once more.

I got the message. I had been a very bad human by not letting him know where I was going. I tried to make it up to him as much as I could. I loved him and told him I was sorry. He wasn't the only one that was upset.

Octa and the head Granny gave me an earful too. They hadn't been able to sense me after I'd gone through the portal, and that had freaked everyone out. I could have been lying hurt in a ditch, or been kidnapped, or any number of horrible things.

I assured them all I was okay. I told them that I had been training to learn how to protect myself and the House better. I'd been trying to make sure I didn't end up dead in a ditch. No ditches. Bad ditches. Okay me. Happy me, but tired me.

Everyone seemed to need to touch me to make sure I was really alright. So for a good while, I was covered in Octopuses and Granny Godmothers, Flying Miners and Ass Blasters. Even the ones outside cleaning the park swarmed in for a look-see. It was touching and sweet to see just how much everyone cared. It was also a little overwhelming to see just how many creations I had. There were thousands of them. I healed them, filled them up with magic if they needed it, and generally tried to spread around as much love and cheer as possible.

Finally, everyone settled down. All my creations were healed and happy again. Bermuda was now settled in my lap, although he kept looking at me every time I moved. Clearly, I was on cat probation, and he was keeping an eye on me. Sandy was back to being covered in magic-giving Octopuses. Her magic seemed a bit more solid than before. Something else was different, but I couldn't place it for a moment. Then it hit me. She was sleeping on her side!

Before, she'd been lying on her back and had been very still, like she was in a coma. Now she was on her side, like she was sleeping and had just rolled over. I didn't want to get too excited. Maybe John had woken up for a bit and moved her, or maybe the House had done it. I'd have to keep an eye on her to see if more movement happened. But I hoped it was a sign that she was going to wake up soon.

John was still lost in the earth. The Miners and Ass Blaster 2000s had cleared off all the rock they could reach, so I absorbed them for the time being. John appeared a bit smaller, but not by much. When he woke up again, I would need to find another reason for him to expel magic. For now, I was exhausted and ready to head back to my place.

Once in my apartment, I realized I still needed to spend some time with Eggy, so I took him off his stand and curled up with him in bed. I worked on him and Penny while continuing to pay attention to Bermuda on the pillow. At some point, the day caught up with me, and I fell asleep.

I woke up to a full bed. Eggy was still next to me. I could feel his sleepy awareness. Penny was there too, also sleeping, wrapped around my finger. Bermuda was snuggled up to my face, and Tyler was cuddled at my back. Normally, I would spend a long time appreciating this, but I was excited. This was day two of training. I needed ten thousand punches. Time to go!

I kissed Tyler good morning and then rolled out of bed. My whole body ached. I had to shake my hands in the air just to stretch them out and get them working again. I picked up Eggy and headed over to his stand. Every muscle felt tight, and I walked like an old man. I'd meant to spend time healing last night, but everything else had needed my attention. When I'd finally had a moment to concentrate, I'd fallen asleep. Oh, well. I'd make it work.

I put Eggy on his stand and turned around to head towards the bathroom. Bermuda was already awake, keeping an eye on me. Clearly, I was still on probation. The morning light fell across Tyler's sleeping form. My God, he looked good. Even relaxed as he was, he had muscular ripples in all the right places. His nut brown skin seemed to glow with light and life. I wanted to run my fingers through his dark hair and kiss his curved lips.

If I did that, though, I wouldn't want to stop, and this morning I wanted to get an early start. Well, early for me. That almost got derailed when Tyler rolled over and saw me standing there, checking him out.

"Liking what you see?" He gave me a cheeky grin.

"It's alright," I said, trying to be all nonchalant-like.

He just laughed, rolled out of bed, and sauntered over to give me a big naked hug. It felt so good. He was warm, like fresh bread, and sexy, like only a naked man can be. I felt like I belonged. I was accepted.

We stood there in the morning sunlight for a while, just holding each other and feeling right. I had to remind myself I was up early for a reason. It would be so easy to take him back to bed, do naughty things to this magnificent man, and then spend the rest of the day snuggling. Instead, I gave him an extra squeeze, a kiss on the cheek, and headed to the bathroom.

A nice hot shower eased away some of the ache in my muscles, and I ended up feeling fresh and ready for the day. Bermuda followed me into the bathroom, knocked the toilet paper to the floor, and then settled down on the back of the toilet. He was still tired from his day of worry yesterday, so he stretched out and took a nap. Sleeping eighteen hours a day must be rough.

I exited the bathroom to find Tyler in a classy pair of PJs on the couch. He looked like a GQ model displaying the latest line of gentlemen's nightwear.

"I was going to make a nice breakfast, but all you have in your kitchen is cereal," he said. "And you are almost out of milk. If you are going to work out like this, then you're going to need more food with protein in it."

"You're right. But at least I have lots of fiber," I tried to joke.

We settled down to a nice crunchy breakfast, watched an episode on Netflix, and then I was ready. This time I stopped by Sandy's bedroom first to check in with Octa and Granny. It took about twenty minutes to heal and refill the creations that needed attention, and then I was finally, really ready to go.

"You have a lot to do around here," Tyler noted.

I nodded and told him about everything that happened last night. I really wanted to train, but I couldn't ignore John, Sandy, or the park. They needed the help that only I could give.

Once we got to the portal, I gave Bermuda a big hug and kiss. I told him I'd be back later and not to worry as I set him down on the floor. Then I put my hand on the portal, and suddenly I was enjoying a beautiful morning on the beach. I heard a pop from behind as Tyler joined me. Then I heard a little meow.

Bermuda was right beside me, checking out this whole new space. His nose twitched with all the new smells.

"How did you get here?" I asked.

He just gave me a look like, 'I'm a cat, duh,' and then cautiously started moving around. He kept picking his paws up and shaking them. Walking on sand was a whole new experience for him. Tyler and I both had a chuckle about it, and then I looked around for the gym area. It was nowhere to be seen.

"Where is the training area?" I asked Tyler. He gestured at a faded wooden sign with an arrow.

"Usually the House drops me a good distance from the exit. I guess it thinks we need a bit of a warm up before we get started. Yesterday was unusual because it was your first time and Annabeth had just woken up. I think the House made a special allowance for that. Normally, you just gotta follow the arrows and get some running in."

A small run sounded good to me. I was still sore, so maybe this would help.

Tyler started off with a light jog. Well, it was a light jog for him. It was a full sprint for me. I quickly called a breathless halt, declaring we could either go at my pace or he could go on ahead. Tyler said he was in the mood to stretch his legs and he'd see me there. He took off and soon was almost out of sight. He made it look so easy.

I took off again with Bermuda by my side, this time setting a much easier pace. It didn't take long to discover that running on sand is very different from running on a road. The sand isn't solid, so it's much harder to push off on the back part of your stride. I'd run from a golem, so I didn't consider myself slow, but on sand it took a whole lot more work to set a good pace. I ended up getting winded and had to slow down to a walk.

That worked out much better for Bermuda. The sand didn't seem to slow him down at all. He spent a lot of energy chasing smells and interesting things only he could see. We'd gone almost two miles, when he finally ran out of energy and just sat down.

I tried to get him to move, but he was having none of it. Then I threatened to leave his furry ass. He cried and wailed as I walked away. So I came back and plopped down beside him to have a nice talk.

"It's not all fun and games, is it?" I said sternly.

He looked at me with his big round eyes. 'I love you.'

"I have to go and train how to fight. I have to get stronger and faster."

'You're sitting. I'm sitting. This is good.'

"I have to be able to take better care of me and you."

'I'll take care of you, silly. Now scratch me under the chin.'

"I'm going to be here for hours. So maybe you can ask the House to take you home again."

'What's that? Did you smell that? Oh. It's nothing. You can scratch me again.'

"Otherwise, what am I going to do? Carry you?"

'Now that is a good idea! Carry me!'

"I'm not carrying you."

'Carry me! Carry me! Carry me!'

"I'm NOT carrying you. You silly cat. You've got four legs."

'Don't you love me?????'

He looked at me with those big, beautiful eyes, one paw stretched out to touch me. So the only thing left to do, of course, was to pick him up and carry him. Now I was trying to run and hold a cat at the same time.

I called him a lot of names as I struggled down the beach. None of them good. He didn't mind, though. He was smelling the wind, looking around, and having a good old time. I was his very own cat chauffeur.

I was feeling hot and sweaty when we finally made it. Annabeth was already there, working on her punches. I wondered what her count was now? I gave her a wave, but she was in the zone, so I didn't bother her any further.

Tyler was working on some advanced blocks with his own sand partner, which made sense. He might as well work on his techniques while keeping an eye on us.

I changed into some swimming trunks I found in my locker, and then went for a dip in the ocean. I was hot, and all that cool water was right there. The morning ocean felt amazing, and it wasn't long before I was refreshed and ready to go. I toweled off, changed into my workout gear, and summoned my training partner.

I practiced a few times in the air first. I'd only learned this yesterday, so I wanted to review my technique before pounding on the hard sand. Once I felt good, I started punching my partner. He was just as solid as I remembered.

The bright morning sun lit him up, and the grains of sand started twinkling with light. He looked as pretty as a Christmas tree. A powerful, natural, and stoic Christmas tree. I couldn't keep calling him 'training partner' or 'dummy'. That just felt too impersonal for all the time we were going to spend together. He needed a name, so I dubbed him Sparkles.

I did the whole routine too. I asked him to kneel. Then I tapped his left shoulder, his right shoulder, and his head.

"Rise, Sir Sparkles," I intoned. "May you be strong and fast. May you teach me your ways. May your sand always gather for the greater good."

Tyler and Annabeth had stopped to watch. I think they were both amused.

"All hail, Sir Sparkles. First of his name. Defender of the beach and partner to the padawans." He got back to his feet, and I gave him a bow.

"All hail!" I yelled.

"Hail, Sir Sparkles," Annabeth and Tyler yelled back, and then bowed as well.

It was a fun moment, and then I was back to punching. Once again, I just couldn't seem to get the hang of it. Tyler corrected me over and over again. He corrected my hands, my centerline, my elbows, my shoulders, my stance, my feet—everything.

Finally, I took a break, and Annabeth came with me. I needed water and some Tillman and Tiddles bars.

"How's it going?" I asked.

"It's going well," she said. "It still feels weird, but I'm getting the hang of it."

"I can hear the difference when you hit," I said. "It sounds much more solid than yesterday."

"That has been the secret for me," she said. "I've been listening. I was feeling restless and excited last night. Everything I learned was swirling around in my head. Something the House said in its evaluation stuck with me. Everything has a sound. Anyway, I came out here early this morning and started practicing again. It was just me, so I had a chance to experiment on my own without anyone else around. And you know what I found out?"

Her eyes sparkled. She had gotten some sort of breakthrough, and she couldn't wait to tell me.

"What?" I asked. I needed a breakthrough myself, so I was all ears.

"Punching has a sound," she said and looked at me expectantly, like my head was going to explode with the wisdom she imparted.

Instead, I just looked confused. Of course punching had a sound. I'd just told her she sounded a lot better. She shook her head.

"What I meant to say is *movement* has a sound. Actually, it doesn't even have to be movement. Just standing in our stance has a sound."

"Really?" I said. I hadn't heard anything. I hadn't been listening either.

"Yep," she said. "I was standing in the Pigeon stance, watching the sunrise this morning, just listening. I focused on being solid and grounded. I shifted slightly, and I heard this tone. It was a bit like when an orchestra warms up and everyone is playing the same note, just on different instruments. Then I moved a bit, and the tone went away. I kept experimenting, and I discovered that when I align everything up just right, I can hear it. It's like the different parts of my body are in harmony."

"Wow," I said. "That's pretty amazing."

"It's not just standing, either," she continued. "When I punch, I can hear the motion. It's more a melody at that point, rather than a single tone. If the melody sounds right, then the punch is good. If it sounds all jangled up, then the punch sucks. I've gotten so I can hear what part of my punch is wrong, and I can work on fixing it."

"You've created your own feedback loop," I said.

"Yes! And it's made a huge difference. Knowing what I'm doing right has changed everything. I can feel and hear when everything comes together. What's interesting is that even though I know what is correct, and I'm concentrating on making it happen, it still goes wrong so easily. I can see how this is something that would take a lifetime to master."

"That's what I'm missing at the moment," I said. "I don't have a good feedback loop. I can tell I'm getting slightly better, but right now I'm just doing different degrees of wrong. I can't seem to find what's right."

"You'll get it." Annabeth gave me her trademark happy smile. "You'll figure something out that works for you. You are the most creative person I know. Just have faith in yourself and keep trying." She gave me a hug, and for a moment, everything seemed okay with the world. She was right. I'd figure this out. Somehow.

"Speaking of trying, how are your hands doing?" I asked. "I left off last night feeling rough. Today started out okay, but now I'm starting to feel really sore again."

"I know what you mean," Annabeth said. "We aren't supposed to wear multiple healing charms, but I'm wearing three of them right now." She showed me one on each wrist and one on a chain around her neck. "They have been helping me a lot. If I don't punch too fast, it seems like they can keep up with the damage. The healing charms have a melody, and I've been humming it back to them. I like to hum anyways, so it is easy for me. When I do that, it seems like it's keeping their melodies in sync. They aren't fighting each other, and the difference they make is huge."

She gave me a concerned look. "I don't know how you've been able to keep going for so long. I'm sure we could find more healing charms in Sandy's workshop, but they just don't seem to work for you. Are you taking time out to heal?"

I shook my head, and then told her about last night. All my time had been taken up with maintenance for Sandy, John, my little creations, and the park. I hadn't spent time healing last night, and I hadn't spent time yet today.

"The thing is, it takes a lot of time to get centered, zoom in to the cellular level, and then wake a few cells at a time. The whole process is effective, but it's not fast. I've been working on waking up new cell clusters every night. I think that's the reason I've been able to keep going so far."

"Probably another reason is your matrix," Annabeth added. "I can't believe the difference it has made for me. I don't know that I'd be able to listen and react like this without the matrix you started for me." She paused for a moment. "I don't know if I've ever said thank you. I think I just woke up, recovered, and started training."

She held my hand and looked me full on. "Thank you." She squeezed my hand. "Thank you. Thank you. Thank you." Then she gave me another big hug. She's a hugger, and I liked it.

"This matrix is everything I hoped it would be. It's helping me train. It's helping me heal. It's helping me listen. I'm safer today because of you, and I'll keep getting better because of your gift to me."

I was a little embarrassed. I don't know if I'd ever been really deeply appreciated like this before. It was very nice, and I was really glad I'd made such a difference for her. All the attention was making me squirm a bit, though.

"You are more than welcome," I said. Then I sighed. "Time to get back to work."

The next round of training wasn't any better. If anything, it was worse. Everything started hurting again, even worse than yesterday. I kept going, though. I didn't want to fall behind.

Finally, I had to stop. I realized I was hurting so bad I was flinching before I punched. It felt like my hands and arms had developed hairline fractures. That wasn't good. My form had gone from bad to terrible. I couldn't keep doing this.

I felt frustrated and upset. My bad technique was breaking my body down fast. I needed to stop, regroup, and find another way. I turned to my Analytical Side. 'Any suggestions?'

Well, first, you just need to get over yourself, he said in his proper British accent.

You aren't going to learn everything quickly. That is just life. Some things will take longer to learn. Accept that. Just like you accepted your smashed face and broken bones. This process is what it is. Be grateful that you even have the opportunity.

That was certainly good advice. I took a deep breath in, held it, and let it out. I made a conscious effort to release the frustration. It felt good, so I did it a few more times.

I needed to regroup and come up with a game plan. I needed a good think, and the best way to do that was to spend time loving my best little buddy, Bermuda. I spotted him sunning over by the bathroom door, so I hobbled over and lay down beside him.

I must be doing something wrong, because now it hurt to walk. I pulled him close and started gently rubbing his belly. He liked that. Soon the air was filled with purrs, and I was getting slow, sleepy blinks of happiness. We snuggled and loved for a while, and gradually I settled down even more.

I accepted my fear of falling behind. I accepted the fear that I wasn't good enough for this, that I would be an average martial artist at best. I accepted all that, and just let it go.

Before I started working on a plan, I thought I would check my stats. It's always good to know where you're starting from.

"House, show my punching stats," I said, and a scroll popped up in the air in front of me.

Low Low Novice Jason Punch Stats
Level = 0.52
Punches = 1159
Notes: It's okay to fight hurt, but it's the height of stupidity to train hurt. As a wise man once said: Physician, heal thyself.

I didn't know it was possible to go below the absolute lowest level of beginner punching, but somehow I'd done it. Yay for me. My title had changed too. I was a Low Low Novice now. Not just low, but looooowwww. It kind of hurt my feelings. It was right, though. Training hurt probably meant I was just reinforcing bad technique. The last thing I needed was more bad technique.

I needed to at least get back to punching at a 1 again. To do that, I needed to heal. I'd recovered from some serious injuries before, so I knew I could do it. The problem was, it was slow. I could heal, but only in one area at a time. Also, I wasn't the best at targeting exactly where the problem was. When I was dealing with broken bones, it was pretty easy. Follow the big solid bone to the break, then start waking cells. When it was a problem with muscles or other soft tissue, though, it wasn't that simple. Things looked really strange at the microscopic level, and I wasn't always sure where the problem was.

Breaking this down into its smallest parts, I needed to solve two problems. The first was I needed a better way to target injuries for healing. The second was I needed a way to heal more than one injury at a time. Both of these problems could be solved by making a little creation that was specific to healing.

The only problem with that was my creations couldn't directly affect me. I loved on Bermuda and considered the problem for a while, but another solution didn't show up. Then I remembered something Annabeth had said. She'd said her powers worked so much better now that she had a matrix. I could make much more powerful creations now I'd had my Waker Moment and a matrix. Maybe it would work now? Only one way to find out.

I needed a good base to start with. What about a submarine? I could add a scanner that searched for problems. Then I could add torpedoes that shot balls of magic into my cells to awaken them, sort of like the movie "Innerspace". I visualized that in my head for a moment. It just didn't feel right. It felt too violent, like I was going to war and shooting myself.

What I wanted was something natural. Something that listened to what was wrong and then worked with my body to fix itself.

Hmmmm. What was the most natural thing I could think of?

A tree. I liked trees.

I liked the way they felt. I liked the way they looked. I liked the sound of the wind moving through their leaves. I felt peaceful around trees. That's why I liked the park so much. It just felt right.

Okay, so a tree was good, but it needed to move. Let's see… Trees that can move are called Ents, like in "Lord of the Rings". They are really big and really slow, though. I needed something a bit more agile. Then it hit me. How about Groot? The lovable character from "Guardians of the Galaxy" would be almost perfect. I liked the way he moved and the way he grew what he needed. Baby Groot was a little too playful, though. I needed an older, more thoughtful type creation.

With that in mind, I started forming the creation on my palm. He had a solid trunk head with kind eyes and an easy smile. I made his body out of a twisty mesh of wood so it would be easy to move and grow as needed. I added arms and legs, of course, but I added special roots on his feet and hands. They would be able to gently grow into cells, listen for injuries, and deliver the right amount of magic to the problem areas.

I took a moment to look at my new Ent. He looked good! He looked wise and yet capable. I still needed a good healing delivery system, though. How was he going to actually fix the cells?

I thought about it for a bit, and then remembered how I'd recovered from the very first time I'd been injured. After Thing One had almost killed me, I'd been covered in a thick moss. It had felt soft, peaceful, and quiet, like I was wrapped in the coziest blanket in the world. It had flowered a few times, grown some mushrooms, and then finished with some beautiful lavender. At the time, I thought I'd hallucinated all of it. Now I wasn't so sure. Magic was very creative, and it didn't follow conventional rules. I had a warm, positive reaction to the thought, so I decided to go with it.

I covered the main trunk of the tree in a thick moss. I tried to make it just like I remembered, with little flowers and the sweet smell of lavender. Then I decided to do different levels of healing. For areas that were hurt badly and needed maximum attention, the Ent could take the moss directly off his body and apply it. Then it would quickly grow back and be ready for when he needed it again. For areas that simply needed a gentle touch, he could drop spores out of his fingers. They would grow into the healing moss as he moved on to the next location. For areas with widespread problems, he could spray a fountain of spores out of his head. They would shoot into the air and scatter all around him, covering a wide area with healing moss.

Awakening cells takes a lot of magic. Hopefully, I could conserve how much power he used by giving him different levels of healing. It was worth a try.

Let's see. Was there anything I was missing? Oh, a duplicator ring! Once I had a good working model, I'd need to make several of him. A duplicator ring or belt didn't really fit the image. Instead, I made a beautiful ruby and embedded it in his trunk where a necklace would lie. My healer Ent was going to be a stylish dude.

I now had a way for him to duplicate, a way to move, a way to find the problems, and a way to fix them. I think that was everything. I took a while to really go over him and fill in all the fine details. The more real he seemed, the better he would be.

I'd made him about an inch high, so I could make him as detailed as possible. For him to work, he needed to be microscopic, so I started to shrink him down. Then I stopped. Instead, I added a second gem, an orange garnet, that let him control his own size. I needed to fill him with magic, and that would be easier when he was larger. Then, he could shrink down on his own and get to work. Also, if he had control over his own size, then he could switch between small problems and much larger ones.

Time for a test run. I filled him full of magic and turned him loose. For a moment, nothing happened. Then the roots on his feet grew into my hand. It tickled a little bit, but I held still, letting him work. I heard the faint rustle of leaves as his head turned back and forth slightly. He seemed to be feeling for something as I felt his roots sink deeper and deeper into my hand. Finally he stopped. Nothing happened. I waited, and still nothing happened.

I'd never had this problem before. Usually my little creations just hopped to and started working right away. I was asking him to actually find the problem areas this time, so maybe I just needed to be patient. I enjoyed the sun, ruffled Bermuda's fur with my other hand, and waited.

I was just about to give up and start over, when the Ent suddenly flowed into action. He gave me a cheerful wave as he retracted his roots. Then he touched his orange garnet and started to shrink. I followed him with my magic sight as he became smaller and smaller. Soon he was at the cellular level, and he started moving through my hand.

The way he moved was cool. He would shoot a vine out of his hand, let it latch onto something, and then swing forward. As he caught up, his other arm would throw a vine, and the process would repeat. His feet had changed to a surfboard, and if he wasn't swinging through space, he was sliding along my cells. It was almost like he was part Tarzan and part surfer. My little Tree Ent was rad!

As he got close to what he was looking for, he slowed down and started testing cells with the roots in his hands. Finally, he stopped by a long, purple row of cells. I wasn't sure what they were. Nerves? Ligaments? Either way, they looked bloated and sore, like they were inflamed or something. It was times like these when I wished I'd paid more attention in biology class.

The Ent spread his hands over the first group of cells, and green spores started falling. They were filled with so much magic, they sparkled as they fell. It was very pretty. I just hoped it was also effective. The Ent moved quickly down the line as he worked.

A bed of green moss started growing up behind him. The moss was thick and soft, and completely covered the purple cells. I thought it would do its thing and quickly fade away, but the moss stuck around. After a little bit, small white flowers sprang up. The Tree Ent finished the line of purple cells and surfed over to a nearby area of red cells.

This time it wasn't just a line of hurt cells, it was a whole field of them. The Ent slid out to the middle of the field, then started using his mass dispersion system. Twinkling green spores fountained out of his head and rained down to cover a much larger area. Again, the Ent moved quickly, and soon a large carpet of moss was growing to cover the redness.

So far, so good. It looked like my plan was working. I watched my little sprinkler cover two more areas, and I was just thinking about starting a second one, when he stopped, bowed to me, and faded away. I hadn't been expecting that at all. The only time this had happened before was when my little Cyborg Sculptor had run out of magic. I'd used him to make a copy of some of the runes from the golem core in wax.

My Sculptor had slowed down and faded a bit before he ran out of magic. Had the Ent done the same thing? If so, I hadn't noticed it.

I made a second Ent, filled him with magic, and turned him loose again. This time he didn't spend any time growing roots. Instead he gave me a twiggy thumbs up and started shrinking right away. Before long, he was back to where he finished last time. This time I told him to stop when he was almost out of magic. He worked for a few minutes before he stopped, turned to me, and bowed. This time he didn't fade away, although he did look a bit peaked. I pumped him full of magic and sent him off again.

This wasn't exactly what I was hoping for. The Ent was doing a great job laying down healing magic, but he was running out of power way too quickly. I'd solved part of my problem, in that he was finding and fixing problems faster than I could on my own. What I really wanted, though, was a hundred of these little things running through me and repairing me all the time. I needed stronger bones, stronger muscles, faster recovery, and I wanted it now. I could probably run five to ten Ents if I gave it my full attention, but then I wouldn't have anything left over to train.

I filled my little Ent up again as I was thinking. Then it hit me. I needed a rune. And I knew just where to get one.

10

Making Tea

"Annabeth, can I borrow you for a moment?" I asked. She took a break and came over. I quickly caught her up on how I was feeling and what I was working on.

"I got hung up on thinking that charms don't work for me," I said. "But charms are based on runes, and runes work for me in a big way."

"Let me guess. You want to put the rune from the healing charm in your Tree Ent," she said.

"You got it in one," I smiled. Annabeth was a sharp woman.

My Flasher construct could make a pretty bright light on its own. But a light rune amplified its output to epic proportions. Annabeth said her healing charms were working wonders for her. Hopefully, the healing rune at the base of the charm would do the same for my Ent.

"I've been training more than I'm healing anyway, so a break will do me good," she said and settled down in the sand beside me.

I told the Ent to come back to full size on my palm. I didn't want to take the healing charm off of Annabeth as she needed to keep recovering. Fortunately, I didn't need her to take her charm off to see what was inside.

She held out her right wrist, and I took the small charm between my forefinger and thumb. I concentrated on it, zooming in with my magic sight. The complexity I saw surprised me.

I was expecting something simple, like my light charm, which looked like a number four with a few extra squiggles. Sandy had told me light was simple. I just didn't realize how simple. Compared to that, Annabeth's healing charm was on a whole new level.

It had three runes inside a circle, followed by more squiggles on the outside, followed by another circle with some hash lines that appeared to modify the outermost circle in some way. Sandy had said that she had to burn charms in one shot. I couldn't imagine holding all this in my head at once. That would be overwhelming. Fortunately, I didn't need all that. I just needed the healing rune, and I figured that it should be somewhere in the center.

I concentrated on the three runes in the middle. One of them sort of looked like a person with an arrow through them. I'm guessing that wasn't healing. The next one looked like a set of wavy lines, like on an oven or a diagram that shows something was hot. That might be it, but it didn't scream healing. The third one looked like a flower, with a center part, two rows of petals, and what looked like sparks or fireworks coming off of it. I felt pretty sure that was the one I needed. It was also the largest and most complex of the three.

I told Annabeth what I was seeing, and then got to work putting the rune on Ent. I'd made his body a mass of branches and vines so he could grow and bend as needed. That was great for moving, but it wasn't a nice surface for a rune. I modified his belly so it was covered in smooth, silver bark. Then I added dark lines and ridges to form the rune. The whole effect was actually quite pretty.

I took my time making the rune. I'd learned from the light rune just how important it was to get everything correct. Sandy had said that making charms incorrectly could cause them to blow up. I was making one rune, not a whole charm, but I still didn't want that to happen to my Ent.

The rune itself was beautiful. It had some lines in the middle, almost like a Roman number three. There were lines on the tops and bottoms of these three columns, and the whole thing was surrounded with looping lines. It was like the seedy middle of a flower surrounded by petals. Then there was another line of petals followed by lines coming out from that—almost like it was a kid's drawing of the rays coming off of the sun. Each ray went out to a little dot with tiny rays shooting off it.

I was putting the last little rays on the rune as it powered up, when Annabeth grabbed my hand.

"Stop, Jason!" she said. "Shut it down. Whatever you are doing, don't put any power in it."

I quickly told Ent to pull any power out of the rune. He rubbed the bark with his hands, and it changed from silver to black. The lines were still there, but they didn't stand out anymore.

"Okay. It's done," I said. I zoomed back out to real life and gave Annabeth a questioning look. "What happened? What did you hear?"

"Oh, my. It was just awful," she said. "I've been humming for the healing charms for a long time now, so I know what it should sound like, and that wasn't it. Well, it was, but it sounded tortured." She stopped for a moment, trying to gather her thoughts. I'm sure it wasn't easy trying to explain sounds to someone who couldn't hear them.

"Normally, healing charms sound like a spring day. There is a touch of wind, the patter of rain, and a kind of sigh like a plant growing. This was nothing like that. It sounded like rocks growing and grinding against each other, like someone scraping a knife down a chalkboard. There was wind, but it shrieked like a winter gale. I think some of your charm is right, but some of it is way off. It certainly won't give you the effect you are looking for."

"I'm glad you stopped me," I said. I certainly did not want tortured rocks and cold winter winds loose in my body. No thanks. "I thought I had it right, but I'll go back and double check everything." I gave her hand a squeeze and zoomed back in again.

It was hard zooming into two places. I needed to see inside her charm, but I also needed to see the belly of the Ent. It hit me that I could do something about that, so I asked Ent to change his size so his belly rune was on the same scale as the charm. Then I moved my hand so they were both very close together. After that, I had him change the bark from black to a dark gray.

I could now see the rune, but it wasn't vibrant and alive like before. Having both runes together made comparing them a lot easier. It also showed the problem. I didn't have the same number of petals as the healing charm, I had one extra in the first row and two extra in the second row. I erased the petals I didn't need and looked everything over again.

I zoomed back out. "Does that sound better?" I asked.

She nodded. "It sounds better, but it still sounds flat. It's not tortured like before, but this time it sounds like a day at the end of summer, when the grass is dry and the air is too hot. I think what you've done will help a bit, but it's not going to give you the boost like you'd hoped."

Well, that sucked. I was sure I had all the lines in the right places. I'd checked everything. The center had three columns, the lines were there at the tops and bottoms of the columns, I had the right number of petals, and I had the right number of 'rays' coming off the pods. Everything looked as good as I could make it. What was I missing? I told Annabeth everything I'd seen and how I was sure I had it all correct.

"Why don't you try a different healing charm?" she suggested. "The one you are currently using as a template was made by Sandy. So is the one on my left wrist. The one I have on the necklace was not made by her. It's much older. Sandy said she quit using it as it got damaged and stopped working. I can still hear it, though. It's working, but it isn't as loud as the other two. However, it does sound a lot richer."

I gave her a questioning look. "Richer?"

"The sound it gives out has more layers." Once again she struggled to convey what she sensed. "It's like the two charms on my wrists have a strong, clear instrument playing their tunes. It almost sounds a bit like a flute playing something inspired by a butterfly. It's strong, beautiful, and complex. But it's still one melody. The charm on the necklace sounds like it has three instruments—flute, cello, and violin." She waved her hand to clear the image.

"Okay, that's not a perfect description of what I'm hearing. I don't know my instruments that well. And this magic may not fit an instrument anyway. Let's just say it has the same main tone and melody as the two charms Sandy made, but it also has a base melody and another supporting melody. The three melodies layer each other and sound much richer."

"That makes sense to me," I said. "Let's take a look and see what we have."

I released the charm on her wrist and gently held the charm on her necklace. It certainly looked older. The charm on her wrist was in the shape of a leaf, and it looked like it had been sculpted by John. It was thick, which a charm needed to be, but it had fantastic detail. He'd even added a little ladybug crawling up the top. Even though John looked like a mountain man, he had the soul of an artist.

The charm that Annabeth was wearing as a necklace looked like an old battered piece of metal. There was nothing artistic about it at all. If it hadn't been for the glow of magic about it, I would have thought it was just a scrap of junk and would have thrown it away.

I took a deep breath and let it out. I still felt a little nervous and anxious. I needed this rune to work. Hopefully, this charm would have some answers. I took another deep breath and zoomed in.

I could immediately see a difference. This charm had been used for a long time, and the magic had soaked into it. Sandy's charm had clean lines and clean channels for magic. This charm had the glow of magic everywhere. I could also see why it wasn't working as well. The charm had been impacted on the bottom half, and it had seriously messed with the lines of the rune. The second row of petals on the bottom were almost wiped out, and none of the 'rays' that came off of them could be seen. This charm was limping along on only half power. If the magic hadn't already soaked into the charm so much, I'd say it shouldn't be working at all. How was this wreck of a charm still functioning and my rune wasn't? Something else was at work here.

I took my time and went over all the lines that were still there, comparing them to what I'd done. All the basics were there. It had the same inner Roman number three, petals, and rays. One difference was the lines were not uniform. They weren't nice clean curves or straight lines. Instead, they seemed more organic. They were fatter in some spots and narrower in others. The charm was so old, though, and it looked like the magic had melted the walls over time. Did the difference in lines matter, or was it just a function of age? I picked out one of the main columns, zooming in even more to investigate. That's when I saw something shocking.

The magic was moving.

It wasn't just filling the lines and forming the rune. It was actually flowing in the channel, like water. Well, not like water. It was something thicker, like lava. I quickly checked the other lines. Magic was flowing in them too. This had to be the secret. This had to be the difference that Annabeth was hearing.

I zoomed out a bit so I could see the whole rune. Now I knew what I was looking for, it was easy to see. The whole rune was one giant flow diagram. I watched it flow for a minute, just taking it all in. I started mentally tracing the flow around, seeing how it moved from line to line, and then it hit me. The lines! The irregular shaped lines were determining the direction of the flow!

They were like calligraphy. Or like those Japanese letters that are made with brush strokes. You can tell just by looking at the line that it had a flow. The brush started out fat and strong, and then tapered down to a narrower point as it moved along. The magic followed the path of the stroke. Now I could see it, the rune took on a whole new level of meaning. It was like looking at an old painting. The flow was beautiful. This rune was more than just lines in metal. It was a piece of art. No wonder Annabeth said it had a richer sound.

That didn't answer all my questions, though. Now I knew it had flow, I wanted to know exactly how it worked. Where did it flow from? Where did it flow to? Some of the lines were not connected, and yet they had magic. How was that happening?

I wasn't sure where the magic entered, so I decided to start at the exit. On the final row of petals, there were lines, like sun rays, coming off of them. Each ray then ended at a dot, which then had even tinier rays coming off of it.

It looked like magic was filling up the dot, which would then overflow to the surrounding tiny rays. These didn't fill up with magic so much as guide the effect. Each dot was like a tiny sun, sending out healing energy to the world. This was the end of the process.

Each dot was getting filled up with magic flowing down the line from the second set of petals. The line wasn't actually connected to the petals, so how were they getting their magic? I zoomed in for a closer look.

It took a while to figure it out, but it looked like the magic was flowing around the shape of the petals. Some of the magic was faster, and it didn't make the curve. Instead, it splashed out of the petal shape and hit the ray. It was like cars making a sharp curve in the road. Most of the cars made the curve, but any cars going too fast would fly off the road.

This same process applied to the inner petals feeding the outer ones. The faster, more liquid, magic made the jump to the next level. The slower magic stayed on the path.

So that was the secret? The rune moved magic through a path which I'm guessing charged it in some way. When it was changed or charged enough, it would jump to the next level of the rune. When it had enough energy to make it up all the levels, it made it to the end of the rune, and then jumped off into the world. Or, thinking of the flow in the opposite direction, it was like a series of waterfalls, with only the purest water reaching the bottom.

This was so cool! I wondered who else knew about this? Sandy hadn't said anything about this at all when I was working on my light rune. Actually, I wonder if my light rune had flow? Part of me wanted to jump over and check out my Flasher to see if it could be improved.

Focus, Jason. Focus. You are here for healing. There would be plenty of time later to compare runes and figure out flows. The first priority was to get stronger. Get faster. Get safer.

With my new knowledge, I went back to the Ent and started working the bark again. This time I brushed in the lines, giving them flow and texture. The magic basically entered in the middle, and then flowed around in circles from there. So it was easy to figure out the direction of the lines, even though I went back to the charm again and again to check myself. Once I was done, and before I made the lines bright and distinct, I asked Annabeth how it was sounding.

"It sounds really faint, but I think it's good," she said. "Add a bit more magic so I can hear it better."

I changed the bark so it was a bit brighter, and the rune stood out more. "Oh, yes," she said. "You've got it this time. Be careful, but keep turning up the power. I'll holler if I hear a problem."

I kept lightening the bark until it was back to silver again. The lines of the rune stood out clearly. Annabeth hadn't called out a warning. This should work!

It still didn't seem perfect, though. The rune was only lines on a piece of bark. It didn't seem alive and flowing like the charm.

"Any suggestions?" I asked Ent.

He seemed to think about it for a minute, and then started pulling on me for more magic. I fed him whatever he needed. Ever since the first Granny creation had helped me make Penny, I realized there was more to them than I'd thought. I was making them up, but they seemed to take on a life of their own and become real sentient beings. I loved the way the Tree Ent moved and healed, and I trusted him.

If he could integrate the healing rune even more, that would be perfect.

The Ent stood there for a while, seemingly hard at work on something. Then the first white flower grew on his shoulder. It was the exact outline of the rune, but in true flower form. The edges of the flower rune glowed with power as the magic flowed around it. It was beautiful. The bark crumbled and fell off, disintegrating the original rune. It was replaced by little white glowing flowers that sprouted up all over him.

I heard Annabeth coo in delight. That could only mean we were on the right track! Whatever she was hearing, she loved it.

'You are just beautiful,' I told my little creation. I've never seen a tree blush before, but he tried.

'Awww, shucks. Thank you,' he said with a bow. He had a deep voice with a bit of a southern drawl. For some reason it made me think of walking through a misty morning.

I needed to give him a name. I couldn't keep calling him Ent. Ent is what he was, not his name. It would be like calling a dog "Dog".

Heally? No, that was just bad. Henry the Healer? No, that was too human. Maybe I could go with something like the word tree… Trevor? Maybe...

He was a Tree Ent, so how about "TE"? Actually, he looked beautiful, and he moved like poetry in motion. So Art! Tree Ent Art. Or "TEA" for short. Okay, the Art was a bit of a stretch, but I liked tea. It's warm, soothing, and just the right thing for a cold winter day. It's healing and relaxing, and that is what this was all about.

'Your name is now Tea,' I told him. 'May you find happiness in healing, and I shall treasure you always.'

He bowed again, smiling. 'Thank you. I like it.'

His body, which had mostly been plain wood before, broke out in tea leaves. I was pretty sure real tea leaves came from a plant, not a tree, but this was all magic and imagination anyway, so it worked.

Now everything was set up, I turned Tea loose again. He listened for only a moment, did a surf and swing over to a sore spot, and started dropping spores. The difference was huge. Before, the spores had been super tiny with a bit of twinkle. Now they were as big as soccer balls. They glowed too, like they were filled with lots and lots of green lightning bugs.

The effect the spores had was also increased. Before, the moss would grow at a leisurely pace and gradually fill into a thick carpet. Now, the moss grew almost immediately, and one spore covered almost ten times the previous area.

The healing rune had been a success. This process was a lot more powerful than before. I watched Tea work for a few minutes. He was almost flying through my system, and the moss growth was keeping up. I was just about ready to duplicate him and create a whole grove of healers, when he stopped and bowed. He was out of juice. Again.

Damn it! I was so close. I had a wonderful healer, and his effectiveness was through the roof. Healing was a power hog, though, and he just didn't have the juice to go for any length of time. I told Tea to stay put for the moment, then I zoomed out, frustrated. Telling Annabeth what happened helped a bit. Just talking through the problem got me out of feeling stuck and back into problem solving mode.

"Thanks again for sitting with me and letting me borrow your healing charms," I said. "I'm sorry I sound frustrated. I shouldn't be. We've already discovered so much today. I now have a little creation that can work inside me. Something I didn't think was possible before. He's now enhanced with a healing rune, and we've discovered that runes have flow. This is all really good stuff, and it will certainly help." I paused for a moment, thinking things through. Why was I so upset? These were some big discoveries. Normally, I would have been jumping over the moon with excitement.

"I think the frustration is from falling behind. I finally have a path to defending myself, and I feel like I'm not succeeding at it. Getting hurt by Isobel and her golem was so scary. Getting stabbed through the chest with a sword was no joke either. I never want to get hurt like that again, yet I feel like the clock is ticking until our next big fight. When it happens, I want to be able to dodge and hit back. There's a limited amount of time to learn what Tyler knows, and I feel like I'm wasting it." I looked up to find Annabeth smiling at me.

"I think it's even more basic than that," she said. "I think you just don't like to lose. You're competitive, and you like to be first. Or at least in the top of the pack."

I had to admit, she was right. I did like to win. That's what made me a good poker player.

"I think what's making you frustrated is you want to win, and you're willing to put in the time and effort, but you're missing your strategy," she continued. "You're missing your feedback loop. You haven't figured out how to fix what you're doing wrong." She beamed at me with all her trademark sunshine and hope.

"You just need to cut yourself some slack. You're trying too hard, injuring yourself, and delaying your training time. Instead, just relax a bit. Have faith in yourself. You will get the right idea. You are used to being good at things, but I've noticed that most of what you like is mental. You like books, Sudoku, and poker. What you're learning now is physical. It takes a different skill set. You'll have to learn to be physically smart, not just mentally smart."

She gave me a big hug and a big smile. "You might not listen to me, but the best thing you can do right now is to go home and rest. Even if you can only power a few Tree Ents, you are still healing faster and better than before. Let them work on you, and then come back rested and fresh to try again."

She gave me a pat on the cheek, and then headed back to her sandy partner to continue her training. Or, as my Analytical Side noted, she headed off to get even farther ahead of me on her punch count. Bermuda hopped up to play for a while, which left me on my own, thinking about what she'd said.

It occurred to me that she'd done her version of the Cher Slap. "Snap Out Of It!" She'd done it in such a nice way that I wasn't mad at her at all. Instead, it left me thinking she was right. This was a physical skill I was trying to learn. If I was trying to learn something else, like football or basketball, I wouldn't expect to be very good. I'd never done any sports in high school. Not even the solitary sports like running or skiing had held my interest. Annabeth was right, I did like mental challenges. Well, I'm in a physical world now. Enjoying books or being good at poker wasn't going to stop an enemy mage from cleaning my clock.

I sighed and stood up. I hated to admit it, but she was also right about heading home and resting. I wasn't going to accomplish anything here. I told Tyler what I was up to, and he agreed with Annabeth. I needed to go home and heal.

I showered first, letting the last of the frustration flow down the drain with the dirty water. I was amazed at how much I ached. Who knew martial arts training would be so rough?

The bath towels were thick, fluffy, and oh so soft. They were so much better than what I had back at the apartment. I wondered if Tyler would mind if I took a couple home with me? I was lost in the feeling of how wonderful the towels felt, when I had an idea. Tea was working inside me. My magic was inside me. Why couldn't he just fill up with magic on his own?

11

Gem Cells

Annabeth was right again! I just needed to relax, and the ideas would come. I finished toweling off, got dressed, and sat on the couch. The couch had seemed out of place when I'd first seen this magical locker room. Now it made perfect sense. It was a comfortable place to relax and zoom in for a conversation with my Tree Ent. He was where I'd left him, still low on magic.

'Tea, I have an idea, but I don't know if it will work,' I said. 'There is magic all around you. My magic. Can you use that as your source since you are my creation?'

Tea thought about it for a minute, then shook his head. 'That is a good idea, but it won't work. You need to actively give me your magic. I can't just take it.'

'Well, crap,' I said. It was such a good idea too.

'Look on the bright side,' Tea said. 'It protects you from doing something that would harm yourself. Imagine if you made one of us and gave it orders to do something, but didn't put a limit on it. If it could just pull your magic any time it wanted, then it might do what you asked, but leave you an empty shell. At least this way, you know how much magic you are giving away.'

I hadn't thought about that. It was easy to make mistakes, and this was a protection of sorts. I'd gotten really low on magic when I'd made Penny. The world had felt gray, dull, and painfully flat. I never wanted to get that low again if I could help it. Thinking about Penny gave me another thought.

'Can you pull magic from Penny?' I asked. When I had first been in the magic circle and failed at collecting my magic, the idea for Penny had been to create a charm that was all storage—a magical battery. This sounded like the perfect use for a battery. It also seemed like so long ago. Had it really only been a couple of months? Looking back on that day, I seemed so young and naive.

Tea thought about it, then shook his head. 'She's also a permanently awake being. She's not the same as you, as you are the Source, but I still can't pull from her without her permission.' He gave an apologetic shrug that made his white flowers dance.

So this might be an idea for the future, but it wouldn't work for now. Penny was still sleeping off her big meal of neutral magic.

I thought about what Tea had said. He hadn't said no to everything, just to permanently awake beings. How about an awake being that wasn't permanent? Like my little creations? They had shown they could work together before. The Grannies had done a prewash when I'd been fighting off the spirits attacking the House. Come to think of it, when I'd beaten the park golem, the Miners had cleared off their purple contamination by banging their pick axes together. This wasn't exactly the same thing, but it was worth a shot.

'Can you transfer magic between creations like yourself?' I asked Tea.

He looked surprised at the idea, then thoughtful. Finally he shrugged. 'I don't know for sure, but I'm going to give it an optimistic yes?' he said tentatively.

'I'm not sure I could exchange energy with another Soul Fragment like myself. It might work, though, if you created something from the ground up with that purpose.' He shuffled his roots, looking confused. 'I'm not sure why you would want to do this, as you would have to spend even more magic powering the second Soul Fragment.'

Soul Fragment? That was the first time I was hearing about this.

'We have something in the mundane world called a battery,' I said. 'It's used to power all kinds of things. Usually the battery is big enough to power a device, like a phone, for a whole day. I'm hoping to do something like that here. You could then heal wherever you needed, and when you got low on power, you could go to the magic battery and fill up.'

'Ah!' Tea said. 'Like an oasis.' He nodded sagely.

'Um, sure. Like an oasis,' I replied. I wanted to say it wasn't like an oasis at all. It was like a battery. But I'm not sure a magical being would get technology.

'Head back to your starting point while I start working on something,' I said.

Now, what was this battery going to look like? The picture of a car battery popped into my head, but I rejected it. Too literal. Also too boring.

How about an oasis? Tea seemed to like the idea. I tried a couple concepts, but it just didn't feel right. I could see the idea of getting refreshed and taking a drink in the oasis, but where was the power? The water? Maybe the water level could rise when there was plenty of power and fall when it was running dry? I'd keep it in mind, but maybe there was something else.

The problem with the idea was how to scale it. One battery creation would probably only hold enough magic to fully refill one Tree Ent. So I needed a lot of batteries. The batteries also needed to sit right on my skin so I wasn't losing any magic with distance. The thought of being covered in spots of water didn't seem appealing. Also, if I was creating an oasis, didn't that mean the rest of me was a desert? I didn't want to be a desert. I wanted to be alive, healthy, and full of life. That's why I was doing all this healing in the first place.

What if I switched the idea of a battery to the idea of a power up? Like it was a game, and the power up held the energy for the next level? Immediately an image popped into my head of a glowing gem gently spinning in the air. That felt right! It was beautiful, vivid, and would feel at home in Candy Crush. It's power up time!

I took that idea and modified it a bit. I went with a red gem, hexagon shape, and laid it flat against my palm. I liked the idea of it spinning in space, but distance mattered. It was only about half an inch long, but I wasn't worried about the size. If this worked, I wanted space to make a lot more of these.

I'd read an article a couple years ago about phones and battery life. It said that the batteries we think of are actually made up of a bunch of smaller batteries called cells. Battery makers group a bunch of cells together, depending on how much power they want the battery to have, and then wrap it up together in a nice package. I thought that idea would work in this situation. There was a limit to how much magic I could stuff into one creation, but if I linked a bunch of them together, then that could contain enough power to keep some Tree Ents going for hours.

I wasn't sure what else to do to the gem at this point. Normally, I was making something shaped like a person, so I would give them clothes, tools, and stuff like that. This was going to be just a battery cell.

It needed personality, though, or at least detail. Without that, it wouldn't hold much power. Then I had an idea: gem cutting.

I'd seen this guy on Instagram that cut intricate shapes into gems. It gave them depth and focus that went way beyond a traditional sparkly gemstone. That was perfect for what I needed.

I started with the sides, adding a bit of bevel detail to the edges of the hexagon, leaving the center blank. What would be a good shape for the middle? This was going to hold energy, and hopefully a lot of it. Maybe a coil? That seemed like potential energy to me, like winding an old watch. Or a spring. I decided to give it a shot.

I put a coil with about three loops in the middle of the gem. It filled up the space nicely, but it kind of looked like a snake. I thought of the circle I'd made with Penny and how energy flowed around it. That's what I wanted to emulate. Not a snake. Maybe it needed a bit of flow to it, like the healing rune. The coil had originally been a line that had the same width throughout. I modified it so the line was thick on the bottom and tapered to a point at the top. Now it had flow! It needed something more, though. I started adding tiny sparkle shapes to it. I made them outside the thick line at the base, and then let them merge with the coil as it went up. Finally, at the tip of the coil, I added a large, brilliant sparkle. I zoomed back to take it all in.

It looked beautiful. It had enough glitz for a drag queen, and yet the coil added an element of physics and sophistication. Perfect!

I filled it up with magic, and it came to life. To my delight, the little sparkles I'd added to the coil started moving. They flowed up to the top, gave a final twinkle, and reappeared at the bottom. This was even better than I'd hoped. Since it was supposed to be a battery, I decided to push it and see how much it could hold.

Turns out, it could hold a lot, like way more than it needed to fill Tea. Had I stumbled on some sort of power rune with the coil? I didn't have any way to truly compare their capacities. I wished I had something like the amulet that Sandy had used during my assessment. It had fifty bars that lit up as I used my power. The more bars that lit, the more power I was using. I'm sure I could make something like that myself. It would be nice to actually know how much magic I was throwing around. Could my battery gem hold twice as much as Tea? Three times as much?

Once my life wasn't in danger anymore, it would be nice to come back and explore this idea. I could make a little diagnostic helper that would be able to measure magic. For now, I needed to finish this and get my healing on. The battery looked pretty, and it held a lot of power, but could Tea actually use it? Time to find out.

My Tree Ent had reached the surface of my palm and was standing by.

'Okay,' I said. 'Time to see if this works. Try and refill your magic from the battery.'

Tea waved and moved over to the gem. He put his hand on it cautiously and stood that way for a moment, testing it. Then I saw the roots on his hand grow into the gem. They didn't grow far before the sparkles at the top of the coil started drifting towards him. They merged with his roots, and he started to laugh.

'It tickles!' he said, but he didn't pull back. Instead, he firmed up and started looking more solid. The magic filled him, and he disengaged.

'How do you feel?' I asked. I looked closely, but he looked fine, and so did the gem battery. I was afraid his roots might have cracked the gem or something like that, but its edge looked healthy.

'I feel good,' Tea drawled.

He flexed his arms and legs, then popped a couple of spores. 'It isn't quite as good as when I get power from you, but it's close. I think this is going to work. Let's find out!'

He gave me a wave and headed off again. Soon, he was at a problem spot and dropping spores. He surfed along for a few minutes, doing his healing thing, and then headed back to the battery for a refill. It didn't take long, and he was off again.

This was going to work! Now, I just needed to expand my battery capacity. I wanted more battery cells, and to make them, I needed to include a duplicator. I added a tiny hexagonal shape to the bottom of the coil, making that its copy device.

Hmmm. I didn't want all the battery gems to be the same color. It would be a lot more fun to have a whole mix of gem tones. I added a touch of amber to the duplicator. It looked nice, so I followed that with sapphire blue and emerald green. I had to represent my signature colors! I didn't want two gemstones with the same colors right next to each other, so I'd need more than four colors. I had all the primary colors now: red, green, and blue. What other colors were there?

Purple. I liked purple. I wasn't sure if there was a purple gem in real life, but there was going to be one here. How about a pearly, opal, kind of gem? Amber was covering orange, so I decided to add a nice buttery yellow. I wanted to stop there as I already had enough colors, but a final beautiful image popped into my head. It was overkill, but I added turquoise. Its cool blue-green color would mellow out the warmer tones and balance the look of the whole battery.

I told my primary gem to randomize the colors, keeping in mind two similar gems couldn't be touching, and turned it loose. I filled it with magic and then pushed a bit more. A new yellow gem appeared at the top of the red one. I started to fill yellow up and then stopped. I didn't want to have to fill up lots and lots of individual gems. That would be time consuming. What I wanted was to just have one main point that I filled up, and then that the energy spilled over to all the other cells. I zoomed in to the side where the gems touched, and it looked like I might already have my wish. They weren't just touching; they were interlocking, like a puzzle. Brilliant. Now to test it out.

I pushed energy into the first red gem, keeping an eye on the second yellow one. There was a small delay, but the yellow gem gradually filled up. Once they were both at capacity, the red primary gem duplicated again. This time it added a sapphire blue on the bottom. I kept filling up the red gem, and soon the sapphire one was at capacity as well. I continued adding power, and the gem cell network kept growing. I filled in all the sides of the red gem, and then gem cells started appearing around that.

Tea came back for a refill and then took off again. This had taken a while to figure out, but it was going to perform just like I'd hoped. I didn't want to duplicate Tea yet. I wanted to have the battery cells set up first. Actually, I needed two batteries. My hands were damaged more than the rest of me, and I wanted healing going on with both of them at the same time.

I put my palms together, duplicated the main red gem, and then kept it with my left hand as I took my hands apart again. I used that as the base for my left hand, pouring on the magic. I slowed down my right hand so my left could catch up. Once they both had about the same amount of gem cells, I evened out the flow again. I started to run a bit low on magic myself, so I pulled in power from Penny. Once I was filled to capacity, I went back to growing the cells again.

The whole process was beautiful and slightly hypnotic. It was fascinating to watch the pattern form, and the colors meshed gracefully. I found it wasn't any problem to push power out of both hands at the same time. I'd always been ambidextrous, and I could draw pictures or deal cards equally well with both hands. I just usually defaulted to being right-handed because it seemed like the whole world was set up for right-handed people. Now I was pushing magic, it might be a real advantage.

When I had my magic assessment, Sandy had said my magic flow was a bit lower than normal. I'd been pushing magic into a cube and trying to make a turbine spin. The cube had only been in my right hand, though. If I could push magic out of both hands, wouldn't that make my output double? Maybe I wasn't so bad in the flow department after all.

I didn't move on to the next step until both my hands were covered in a colorful array of battery gems. I took a moment to admire them. It looked like my hands were Christmas trees, and they were covered in lights. A less charitable person would say I was the victim of a bedazzler at a twelve-year-old's sleepover party. Either way, the little gay boy in me cooed with delight, mesmerized by the rainbow of glimmering colors. I'm a 'More Is More' kind of person, and this was 'More' in the best possible way.

Now I had the batteries, it was time to turn on the healing. I called Tea to the surface, duplicated him, and moved his twin to my left hand.

'Boys,' I said, 'it's healing time. You have your runes and lots of power to work with. I'm sucking on this whole training thing, and I need all the vitality and stamina I can get. I'm not sure what all is injured, but it feels like a lot. Go and fix me. Make me as strong and fast as you can.

Duplicate as much as you need to, but don't pull more power than the Gem Cells can give.

'I'm depending on you. I have faith in you. Now let's turn this glowing into growing! Go, Team!'

Okay, that last part was a bit cheesy, but they seemed to love it. They gave a 'Woot! Woot!' and danced happy shimmies. Then they duplicated and got to work. They seemed to like my little speech as there were now lots of Tree Ents pulling magic, skating through my system, and dropping spores.

It was everything I hoped it would be. I just needed to keep it going.

I spent a few minutes watching the action and pushing magic. Now that I had everything in place, I needed to head back to the House and get some rest. I took a few minutes to practice walking around the locker room and pushing magic at the same time. It was a bit like trying to text while talking. It was doable, but it would take some practice.

Once I had the hang of it, I left the bathroom to say goodbye and head back to the House. Annabeth was in the zone, punching at a speed that was obviously faster than before. They sounded good too—landing with nice solid bass thumps. This was not the timid Annabeth that had started training only a day ago.

Tyler was training too. He had three sand people coming after him at the same time, and he was somehow blocking and dodging everything coming at him. I took a moment to just watch. He was poetry in motion, both as a martial artist and as a perfect specimen of manhood. He had on gray shorts and a gray t-shirt, simple workout gear, but he made it look good—really good. Muhammad Ali said he danced like a butterfly and stung like a bee. I'd say Tyler flowed like water and struck like a panther.

Annabeth saw me first and paused her workout.

"There you are," she said with a grin. "You were in the bathroom for a long time. We were starting to get worried. Did everything come out okay? Tyler thought maybe something got stuck up there." That was really racy for Annabeth. She usually didn't stoop to doing potty humor.

"My plumbing is just fine," I said a bit more primly than I'd intended. "I just had a couple ideas, and I was sitting on the couch testing them out."

Tyler saw us and stopped his training to wander over and give me a quick kiss. He smelled of sweat—manly sweat.

"You were gone so long I thought maybe something else was going on," he said teasingly, dropping his eyes down to my package. "Annabeth was getting worried, and I thought you might need a helping hand." He put extra emphasis on 'hand', and I knew exactly what he was talking about.

Annabeth just looked on smiling and concerned, completely clueless to the subtext going on. He was just playing around, but I was suddenly very aware of how everything was lying down there, and I flushed. Then I felt all the blood going somewhere other than my face. My third arm was waking up.

The only problem with being well-endowed was when my happy stick was ready to play, the whole world became well aware of that fact. I was wearing a nice fitting, light pair of shorts. They weren't going to hold anything back, and I was about ready to give Annabeth a show.

I was so embarrassed. This hadn't happened for a long time. Damn Tyler. Damn his man sweat and damn his weighted gaze. I needed to get out of there now.

"I think I had a breakthrough on healing," I said quickly, "but I want to see if it works before I talk about it." I spun around quickly and headed towards the exit marker. "See you later," I tossed over my shoulder as I hurried off.

The only problem with my quick exit was that I couldn't find the marker. It should be right by the door. My third arm was stretching and flexing, making a huge bulge in my shorts. There was no way I could turn around now. Where the heck was the exit?

Then it hit me. Bermuda was lying on it. Of course he was. Cats lie on everything. I scooped him up, palmed the marker, and appeared back in the hallway in the House.

I breathed a sigh of relief and took a moment to adjust everything. It still looked like I was carrying my shillelagh around, but at least I wasn't tenting like before. Bermuda looked miffed at being hoisted up so quickly. He decided I could make it up to him by carrying him around for a while. I scratched his head and gave him some kisses while I headed up to see John and Sandy. At least they wouldn't be making comments about my upstanding member.

The thought made me feel a bit sad. John would have teased me for days if this had happened before. Then he would have found a way to turn it into a drinking game. I missed him. Hopefully, he and Sandy would be awake soon.

I got to her bedroom and was greeted by a chorus of little voices. My Grannies and Octopuses were glad to see me. John was in the same spot, but Sandy had moved. I checked her magic levels, and they didn't look bad.

Some of my creations needed repair, which caused a bit of a problem for a moment. I had a cat in my arms, and both hands were covered in Gem Cells. I solved the problem by having them land on my shoulders. Then I connected to them one at a time and sent them all the health and healing they needed.

It felt very strange sending magic out of my shoulders. I had to juggle that while still pushing magic to the batteries on my hands. I didn't want to fall behind with my healing.

It occurred to me that I could push magic from any part of me. It didn't have to be my hands. Because of my matrix, my whole body was a locus of control. I could probably heal my creations with my big toe. The only thing holding me back was how many individual streams I could focus on. Right now, with two hands and one creation, three was my max.

The focus took my mind off of other things, and soon my shorts fit like normal. My energy settled out, and a meditative peace settled over me. I'd pushed so much magic over the last month that now it just felt calm and easy. Healing the Grannies and Octopuses had gotten simple too. I got into a groove and just did my thing for far longer than I'd planned on. Finally, I was all caught up with my cleaners and that jolted me back to reality.

I was tired. Actually, I was very tired. I felt peaceful, and yet heavy, like I was under a weighted blanket on a cold winter night. I just wanted to curl up and sleep. I had enough presence of mind to realize this wasn't normal. What the heck?

I looked down. My arms and chest were covered in a thick, warm blanket of moss. While I'd been healing my peeps, my peeps had been healing me. Bermuda was still in my arms, fast asleep. That didn't help my wakefulness either. He looked so damn cute, like a fairy creature of the forest, napping in a loving nook.

I staggered out of Sandy's bedroom. I wanted to get to my own bed before I collapsed. This healing moss was serious stuff. I made it up the stairs and wobbled down my hallway. I got the door open without disturbing Bermuda and pushed it shut behind me. My knees gave way just as I made it to the bed. Bermuda crawled up to his spot on my pillow, and I crawled the rest of the way onto the mattress. I'd made it. Now all I had to do was sleep and heal. I closed my eyes.

Wake up, you wanker, my Analytical Side hollered in his dry British voice. *You can't go to sleep yet. You're only half covered in moss. If you crash, the cells will run out of power, and you'll only be half done. You haven't come this far to half-ass it.* To drive his point home, he mooned me with a saggy bottom. Ugh.

Damn. I wanted to sleep so badly. He was right, though. I wanted all of me to be vibrant and healthy. Not just the top half. Damn. Damn. Damn. Damn. I groaned aloud and propped myself up in bed. It felt like I weighed a thousand pounds, but I made it.

I checked out my moss blanket. It was shocking just how dense it was. I thought I'd only had moss on my upper half, but I actually had it throughout my whole system. It looked like the Tree Ents had spore bombed the worst of my injuries first. Now, some of them were doing a second pass, and they were almost down to my feet. The bulk of the Tree Ents were hard at work on the third pass. This time it looked like they were fixing just about everything. That's where the real heaviness and density was coming from. They were gliding and swinging through my system so quickly it was hard to get a fix on just how many of them there were. There had to be at least a couple hundred, though. What was the term for a group of trees? A grove? I guess my Grove was getting its groove on! I was too tired to laugh, but it was still damn funny.

The moss had little white flowers growing in it. They were so pretty, waving in the breeze. Actually, it looked like they sparkled a bit. That was strange. I zoomed in for a closer look. The white flowers were healing runes! That was just crazy. How much healing was going to happen? I'd just wanted to get back to normal so I could train again. This was going way beyond that. I guess the Grove had taken my pep talk to heart. There wasn't anything to do at this point except ride it through, and see how it all turned out. I still wanted an even level of healing, so I pushed magic into my Gem Cells and let Tea and his Grove do their thing.

The fresh smell of lavender was soothing as I settled in and found my own supporting rhythm. I pulled in power from Penny until I was buzzing with energy, and then I pushed it out to the Gem Cells. When I got low in magic, I repeated the cycle. It was like magical breathing. In and out. Once again, I was so grateful to Penny and her magical capacity. Without her store of magic, none of this would be possible. She had made my matrix feasible, and now she was making this healing happen. I needed to do something special for her when she woke up again.

In.

Out.

In.

Out.

The trance was real.

At some point I relaxed my focus on the two primary red gems. In a passive way, I could feel all of them, and once I had that connection, I could send them power. My hands lit up with magic, and I started pouring energy into the Gem Cells. They loved it and started duplicating down my arm. I was beating the Tree Ents in the race for power. I guess you could say I was handily beating them. Hehehe. My puns live on, even in a trance.

I stopped the massive power expenditure when the lattice of cells covered my forearms. I'd grown way beyond power gloves. I now had power gauntlets! Eat your heart out, Thanos. My gauntlets looked way prettier than yours.

I checked out Tea's progress. His Grove was almost done with the third pass.

It was time. I settled down in the bed and snuggled up to my furry baby. This had been a good day. I hadn't planned on doing all this, but life in the magical world was never boring. I kissed Bermuda and let myself slide into a peaceful sleep.

12

Anna Lykit

I woke up ravenous. Like "Day of the Dead", I-will-eat-your-brains ravenous. Even Bermuda shied away from my look, like 'Whoa there, Daddy. Tiny morsel here. Stop looking at me that way cause you're scaring me.'

I gave him a quick rub with a moss-covered hand. I wasn't going to eat him, but I was going to eat something!

Tea and his Grove had finished their work, and all was quiet. I was completely covered in a thick carpet of moss and white flowers. Actually, I wasn't just covered, I was stuffed with moss. I was a scarecrow, and moss was my straw. It felt like everything inside me had been spore bombed. It wasn't just my muscles and bones, my organs were getting healed too. I even had moss growing out my ears.

My stomach gave a hearty grumble reminding me of how much I needed food. I rolled out of bed and staggered to the kitchen. I was clumsy, barely awake. The walls were doing weird things too. They kept growing and flexing in strange ways. I made it to the kitchen and fumbled the refrigerator door open.

Gah. Only milk. But I had some cereal!

I didn't even bother to put it in a bowl. Instead, I tore open the box and shoveled Frosted Flakes in my mouth. When my mouth became too dry to continue, I chugged some milk right out of the carton. I felt like a caveman devouring his kill before the other predators arrived.

Just the thought made the room around me change. The floor turned dusty as a harsh sun shone overhead. The landscape of my kitchen changed to show stunted trees and big rocks thrusting up through the ground. This was weird, man. Like really strange. I could see my refrigerator, but now there were a couple jackals circling. What the heck happened to my kitchen? I probably should have been scared, but I just rolled with it. The strangeness was not enough to stop me from shoveling more cereal into my mouth.

Western music started playing in the background, like in the movies when the cowboy rides his horse out on the range. Out in the distance the heat shimmers danced. The sun bounced off the dry, dusty earth, distorting everything, including the figure coming towards me. As it got closer, the silhouette looked interesting. This was no cowboy.

Faster than I thought possible, the figure arrived and struck a pose—a very dramatic pose. It was a fantastically tall and larger-than-life drag queen. She had on gold thigh-high stiletto boots, a tiny pair of gold panties, and a blue and gold studded jacket. Blue hair swept up into a beehive, then fell to gracefully cascade down her shoulders. That wasn't the best part, though. The best part were the giant wings with blue feathers and gold highlights. It was a look to end all looks.

It's time to teach the children! she announced. *Mother has arrived.*

She glowered at the jackals, and they decided they didn't want any part of her. They whimpered and slunk away.

She looked at me, and I felt the full force of her personality.

As for you, My Fine Little Muncher, I say spread 'em. And with that she flexed her wings and spread them wide. She was impressive. My jaw dropped. Or it would have if I hadn't still been shoveling in food. She held the pose, eyeing me. I got the feeling I was supposed to say something.

'Nice to meet you,' I said politely, and held out my hand for a shake.

I'm sure I looked ridiculous, sitting on the ground, covered in crumbs and a few stray dribbles of milk. Her nails were bright blue and at least three inches long, so a proper shake was out of the question. Instead, she took my hand between her thumb and finger and squeezed lightly. Her look said I had been judged and found wanting.

'You look lovely,' I said. That was apparently the right thing to say as she started preening. 'Might I ask your name?'

My name, Darling, is Anna Lykit. She struck another pose, then gave me a bit of side eye. I guess I didn't have the right look of comprehension, so she broke it down for me again. *Anna Lick-It.* She said it slowly, like talking to a dim-witted child.

I was still lost. This whole thing was weird, and I wasn't at my best. I just shrugged, smiling helplessly.

It's a play on "analytic", My Dear Boy, she said. *With emphasis on the "Lick It" to give it a touch of class.* She said it with a lot less sass this time, and I perked up. I knew that voice! It was my dry British Analytical Side. Holy cow! This must be his alter ego.

Seeing my look of surprise and shock, she smirked, touching my forehead with her finger. *You have been taught,* she declared.

'I can't believe this is you,' I sputtered. 'I had no idea.'

I clean up well, she said proudly, followed by a manly chuckle. *Besides, this is your messed up world.*

'About that,' I said. 'What the heck is going on?'

You haven't guessed? she asked. I shook my head. *You're stoned, Dear Boy.* She gestured to the moss. *Hallucinating.*

Floating in cloud cuckoo land.
Riding the pink elephant.
Going on the naked spirit quest.

I looked closer at the moss. There were mushrooms growing on me. OMG. I really was stoned. Well that certainly explained a lot. Come to think of it, this had happened last time. I guess it wasn't so weird after all.

'So, if I'm having a spirit quest, shouldn't I be looking for my spirit animal?' I said playfully.

She struck a pose. That wasn't an answer, so I looked around. Irritated, she struck another pose. I was confused.

She threw up her hands. *Let's change the scene before we talk. "Mad Max" meets "The Magnificent Seven" is not my favorite backdrop.*

She gave a tongue pop, and the world shifted. Now we were in a beautiful woodland glade with soft grass and dappled light. She popped again, making a giant, golden throne appear behind her. She folded her wings and sat down demurely. Everything was so over the top that this gentle move was perfect.

I'm your guide, Boo, she said. *I know you better than anyone. Sometimes I know you better than you know yourself,* she sniffed. *I certainly know you better than some spirit animal would.* Bermuda wandered into the scene and started eyeing my crumbs. *Present company excluded, of course,* she said to my baby.

He gave her a look like, 'Of course, Sugar. No offense taken.'

My stoned world was strange and over the top. I liked it, though.

'So, you're here to guide me?' I prompted.

I'm just here to keep you company and amuse myself while you stuff your face, she replied.

She pulled a bright red fan out of the air, opened it with a loud pop, and began fanning her face and huge electric blue hair. It was built to the heavens, with artful folds and loops. It was way more hair than any one person should have. She was fantastic. And she was my spirit guide.

I'd read about this in books, of course. Usually the main character gains some sort of insight, or a new direction in life. So, what did I want to know?

'Will I ever be safe?' I asked. The question just seemed to pop out on its own. Was this really what I wanted to know? Out of everything I could ask, was this it?

She snapped her fan closed, leaned forward, and gazed at me. I felt pinned to the ground—the look was that intense. I also realized that her eyes were deep blue with little flecks of gold. It didn't keep me from eating, though. I was on autopilot, shoveling it in.

Whatever she'd seen was enough, as she leaned back, popped her fan, and went back to cooling herself.

That's a good question, she said. She pointed at me with a three-inch nail. *A good question for someone who's a little boy and has just lost his mother. That is not a good question for a man.* She leaned forward for emphasis. *You are no longer a boy. You are now a man.*

So let me answer your question, both to the boy, and to the man.

No.

There was a long pause. She regarded me, and I gazed back.

No. That was so… abrupt. And harsh. It took a while to sink in.

'Care to sugar coat that a bit?' I said. I was squirming a bit at the naked truth. I needed more words to wash down the realness.

Of course, My Little Muncher, she said fondly, then tapped her chest to show where I'd dropped a particularly big piece of cereal. I popped it in my mouth, took a swig of milk, and kept going.

When you were little, your mother was the source of your safety. She was everything to you. She provided food, a home, and love. When she died, you were no longer safe. Your father blamed you for her loss, and you never felt safe at home again. Getting kicked out years later was just the conclusion to your boyhood story. So was the boy safe? No.

Now, let's talk safety as a man. You can't look to someone else to shelter you, feed you, and give you a home. You have to create value in this world to get that on your own. You started from almost nothing and learned how to trade your looks and body for what you needed. Then you learned a skill, poker, and started earning your own money. Money meant safety, and you had the start of something good. Now you've become a supernatural, and the illusion of safety has been stripped away yet again. One more time, you are starting over from almost nothing and trying to find security in a much more brutal world. So can the man be safe? No.

What she said made sense. I just didn't want to hear it. Surely there had to be some point at which I could relax. There had to be some space in time where I could just be me and not worry about survival.

Let's analyze safety and see why it's the wrong question, she said. *Power will not bring safety. No matter how powerful you get, there will always be someone more powerful than you. Even if you become the most powerful person left alive, multiple supers could gang up on you and take you down. You would have to be more powerful than everyone else combined before you could say you were safe.*

The chance of that happening is very small, and it still doesn't protect you from other avenues of attack.

Location won't give you safety. Let's say you built a fortress at the bottom of the ocean and closed it off to everyone. You'd still need food, water, and other resources. Something might happen to cut off your supply. Plus, you'd be so bored you might become a danger to yourself.

So, no, you are not safe. You will never be safe. Wrong question.

Dang. That was a lot to process. Actually, I was really talking to myself, so I guess I had processed this already, just not on a conscious level.

'If safety is so unattainable, then what use is it? And why do I want it so much?' I asked. I sounded a bit whiny. I didn't want to, but I was feeling a bit lost.

Safety is useful, Anna said. *It's just not a good final goal.*

She tongue-popped again, and a scantily clad pool boy walked up with a fruity drink on a tray. It had an umbrella, a straw, a slice of pineapple on the rim, and smelled strongly of liquor. She picked it up carefully, gave the lad a wink, and took a long drag.

Ahhhhh, she sighed. *Teaching the children is such thirsty work.* She dropped some solid gold coins on his tray as a tip. *Keep 'em comin', Love.*

A drink did sound nice. I chugged some more milk. My cereal was almost out, so I looked around for more. Anna pointed out there was another bag nearby, so I pulled it over and started eating. It was dry and crunchy as hell. This cereal must be really old. Oh, well. I was still hungry, so it would have to do. For some reason, this really amused her and intrigued Bermuda. He came over, sniffed the bag, and started eating too. This seemed to amuse her even more. I wasn't aware Bermuda ate human food, but even if he did, it wasn't that funny. The cereal tasted strange, like someone had mixed tuna and turkey together. This was such a bizarre world.

How're your teeth? she asked and started snickering. I didn't get it. My teeth were just fine. *It's supposed to help clean your teeth as you eat and provide healthy gums.* She laughed again.

I didn't get why that was funny. All that sounded good to me.

'You were talking about safety?' I said to get her back on track.

Ah, yes. She took another sip of her cocktail. *The concept of safety is useful. Think of it like a direction.*

Huh? That made no sense.

It's like West. No matter how far West you go, there will always be more West. You will always be more West of the person behind you and less West than the person in front of you.

That made sense, in a very weird, mind-bending sort of way.

Gaining more power makes you safer. Learning how to fight makes you safer. Having turbo healing provided by Tea and his Grove makes you safer. Being better gives you options. If you fight, you might win. If you run, you might get away. Being safer means you might not have to fight at all.

Safe is a journey. You've been thinking of it as a destination. She summed it all up nicely.

But that still isn't the best question for you. She gave a long pull on her straw and hit the bottom. A few slurps later it was empty, and the pool boy came over with a refill. This time the drink was a dark red and full of cherries. It looked delicious.

What was the best question? I'd just blurted out safety, and once I'd said it, I knew it was the right one. It was what had been driving me for years now. I got what she was saying about it being a journey. I'd had a fear for a long time that I would never be safe. Now I had my answer. No, I would never hit a point where I was completely safe. But I could be safer. I could be better.

It was a tweak in the way of looking at it, but it was everything. I could let the fear go. I could accept the journey.

My goals were still the same. Learn everything I could from Tyler about fighting. Learn everything I could from Sandy about magic. Use my own creativity to figure out everything else. It's just that now they seemed like healthier goals. They were driven by growth, rather than fear.

So if safety wasn't the question, what did I really want?

'Belonging,' I said softly. 'I want to belong somewhere. I want a home.'

Bingo. Anna tapped her nose, giving me a wink. *You got it on the first try. You want a home. You want to find your tribe. You want a space to laugh, to cry, to relax, to follow your joy. When your mom died, you lost your home, and you've been searching for it ever since. You just got "belonging" mixed up with "being safe".*

She stood up on her impossibly high stiletto platform boots, and the gold throne vanished. She flexed her wings, throwing a shower of gold sparks into the sky.

You want what every human on this planet wants. You want to belong in a space that lets you dance like no one is watching, sing like no one is listening, and most of all love. She started spinning, throwing blue and gold sparks from her hands. *Love and Love and Love and Love. Just find your peace. But most of all, Love.*

She stopped spinning and smiled with all the heart and drama that only a drag queen could, then sashayed towards me.

The best news is... she started.

'I've found my place,' I finished.

'I've found a place to belong.'

Yes, you have, My Little Muncher, she said as she towered over me. *Now don't fuck it up!* I felt like I was on RuPaul's Drag Race and Mama Ru had just blessed me. She leaned down, giving me air kisses.

Then, she spread her wings and lifted off. I heard her exclaim, as she flew out of sight, *Remember. If you can't love yourself, how in the hell are you gonna love somebody else? Can I get an "Amen!"*

'Amen,' I whispered.

I realized tears were trickling down my face. The moment felt profound. I was like Dorothy. What I most wanted in the world was here all along. I belonged.

I loved this House. I loved my tribe. I loved my little kitten.

Bermuda started licking my face. Somehow in this whole lucid dream world, he still looked the same. I snuggled him and kissed him back.

I was covered in crumbs and milk stains, but I didn't care. I thought about crawling back to bed, but it seemed like too much effort and the floor felt nice. So I curled up right where I was and went to sleep.

13

Watering the Flowers

That was where Tyler found me. Curled up on the floor with an empty milk jug and empty cereal boxes.

"What the heck?" he said. He knelt down beside me, giving me a shake. "Are you okay?"

I tried to say something, but it was so hard to focus. It was so much easier to just talk with my mind, like I did with Anna. Real world talking was hard. I didn't even open my eyes, relying on my magic sight instead.

"Healing," I croaked out.

"Oh, Jason. What have you done?" He sounded worried. "I'm guessing you overdid your healing somehow. You were supposed to just rest and recover. Not do whatever this is," he sighed.

"And what's with the cat food all over the floor?" He looked at Bermuda who was snuggled up with me. "Did you do this?"

Cat food? I don't remember there being any cat food.

Bermuda just yawned and gave him the sleepy eye. 'Bitch, please. I'm cute. If I want to make a mess, I will. And you'll like it and rub my belly afterward.'

Tyler just sighed again. He had a cat himself, so I'm sure he knew how to interpret that look. He didn't say anything, just started picking up the cereal boxes, folding them up, and stuffing them in the trash. Then he got my dustpan from under the sink and started cleaning up the mess.

I was too tired to help. Plus the floor kept tilting beneath me. I was afraid to move in case I started sliding around. If I did that, then I might throw up, and we'd have a real mess. Bermuda was happy to join in, though. He started batting the brush and chasing the food around. This was a great game!

Once Tyler was done with the floor, he started picking the crumbs off me. I had a lot of crumbs. Bermuda helped by eating them. Together they cleaned me up until I was good as new. Well, not new. Maybe gently used. Okay, even that was probably generous. I'm sure I looked like shit, like I had gone on a bender and passed out on the floor in my own mess. Ugh. This was not an attractive look for me.

Tyler gently rolled me over. "Are you ready?" he asked.

For what? God, it was so hard to think. I opened my eyes and tried to form words. That's when I saw it. Tyler's aura.

I'd sensed it before, of course, but he held his aura tight against his skin. I don't know if it was because of the mushrooms, or maybe he was unguarded for a moment, but I saw it in the soul realm. I saw him. Who he really was.

He was covered in scars—lots and lots of deep scars. It looked like he had gotten in a fight with razor wire and lost, then went back to fight the razor wire over and over again. Actually, it looked worse than that. The scars were too regular for them to be an accident. It looked like a sadistic torturer had cut his soul again and again and again.

My heart ached for him. Who the fuck does that to a person?

"Scars," I said, reaching up to touch his face.

He jerked away, like I'd slapped him.

"Shhhhh," I said, touching him gently.

His eyes were wide. He looked a bit wild.

I took his hand trying to tell him it was okay. I wasn't holding a hand. It was a claw, with powerful nails dipped in red. I looked up again. He had fangs. His eyes were slits.

He was a predator.

An apex predator.

I wasn't scared, though. At that moment, I could read him. He was like an old bear, heavily scarred from a rough life, who just wanted to eat berries and sit in the sun. Sure he was a predator. He had to be to survive whatever had happened to him.

No wonder he was so secretive. No wonder he had walls up. No wonder he felt isolated.

It hit me. He was probably looking for safety too. I had to tell him the secret. I took a deep breath and forced it out.

"Safety. It's a direction," I said wisely, nodding at him.

He just looked confused. Of course he did. He didn't have Anna to explain it to him. I looked around, but she wasn't here. Maybe I could just skip to the ending revelation. I had to tell him. I might never see him like this again. I might forget all this when I really woke up.

He was a human being—a badly hurt and defensive human being. And he deserved to hear this. I took another deep breath.

"Belonging," I said, tapping my chest. "I see you." When I said that, something clicked. I was glowing. His eyes got wide.

"You can belong with me." I pushed out the words, wanting him to understand. Willing him to see this universal truth. He didn't have to be alone. I was here. We clicked. He could belong with me.

"Home," I said. "Mr. Tubbles. Me." Bermuda wandered over. "Us."

I had enough energy for one last word.

"Home," I said, and tapped my chest again.

I felt it. To the core of my being, I felt it. Tears ran down my face. I wanted to say so much more, but there was nothing left. I hope he heard me.

The moss pulled me under, and I closed my eyes. As I faded, I felt him pick me up and carry me away. I fell asleep in his arms. And that was okay.

***

I woke up ravenous. Again.

I was back in bed, but this time Tyler was with me. I was being naked snuggled, just the way I liked. Normally, I would have stayed that way, not moving and enjoying the moment.

Now, though, I just wondered what Tyler would taste like. Were brains really that delicious?

My look must have said volumes because Tyler quickly grabbed a Tillman and Tiddles bar and thrust it at me. My hands were shaking, and I couldn't get the wrapper off fast enough. Tyler saw that and started unwrapping a second bar to have it ready. Like my mom used to say, Tyler is good people.

I ate the bar so fast I didn't even taste it. I'm sure it was delicious, but I had no time for that. I was famished. I tossed the wrapper over the side of the bed and reached for the next one. That was the start of our little assembly line. Tyler prepped the bars, I ate them, and the floor got the wrappers.

I don't know how many I ate. At least thirty. Probably more.

"Water," I wheezed.

Tyler handed me a glass of Louisville's finest H2O. I gulped it down and asked for more. Tyler was way ahead of me. He already had another glass ready.

Louisville always brags about its water. They were the first to do some sort of filtration or something on their water, and it was so successful it spread to all the other major cities. I don't remember all the details. I just knew the water tasted good. It tasted like life.

With food and water taken care of, I started feeling sleepy again.

"Thank you, Tyler," I said as I blinked at him in gratitude. I didn't have the energy for much more than that.

"It's all good," he said, kissing my cheek. "Go back to sleep. I'll see you on the flip side."

Before I completely faded, I checked out my progress. I was almost completely covered in white flowers now. The smell of lavender was so strong it was almost overpowering, and I still had plenty of mushrooms on me. Basically, I was still a horticultural healing ground.

I marveled again at how thorough the Tree Ents had been. It seemed like they had touched just about everything. Even my brain was mossy and covered in flowers. As the moss smothered me with lethargy, I wondered if Captain Winky and his two mates had been visited by the Grove. If so, I probably had fuzzy balls right now.

'Anna is going to have something snarky to say about that,' I thought with a chuckle, and fell asleep.

***

Pee! I had to pee! Like right the hell now. I was already on the move before my brain caught up. I burst into the bathroom, but Anna was blocking my way. She'd traded her angel wings for fairy wings, and she was now wearing a huge hoop skirt bejeweled within an inch of its life.

'Move!' I yelled, bursting right through her. Thank goodness I was naked and didn't have to deal with zippers or underwear. I flipped up the lid on the commode and let the river run. Ahh, the relief!

Well, aren't you a right pisser this morning, Anna said sarcastically. *Busting all up in here like a wanker while I'm putting my face on.* She waved her makeup brush in the air for emphasis. *The least you can do for all that is water my flowers.*

I looked around, realizing the bathroom was now a greenhouse. There were beautiful exotic flowers everywhere. I had barged in on her after all and I still had plenty of stream left in my hose, so it seemed like the right thing to do as I whipped my joystick around and shared the love.

The flowers reacted right away too, which was kinda cool. Sometimes the plants grew taller and fuller. Sometimes the flowers changed color. Anna was having a blast, pointing out plants I'd missed. Boys have been peeing on flowers since the beginning of time, and I felt like a little kid again. It was way too much fun, and I felt like it went on forever, but eventually the tank ran dry.

You are really going to hate yourself tomorrow. Anna was in a great mood.

'Why?' I asked innocently. I hadn't done anything wrong. I'd only been helping her out, after all.

Oh, My Dear Boy. Anna patted my head. *You are just too precious for words.*

Just a bit of advice, she continued. *These look good on me.* She held up her tapered three-inch-long nails. They were painted electric blue and highlighted her dramatic motions nicely. She was right. They did look good on her.

However, they do not look good on you. She tapped my hand with her fan, then popped it open and gave herself a quick breeze. I looked down to see what she was talking about and just about jumped out of my skin.

I had claws! Okay, they weren't real claws, but they were really long fingernails. Like six-inch-long nails at least.

I was shocked. I'd thought it had felt strange holding my firehose.

'What the fuck?!' I exclaimed. 'How the heck did this happen?'

You're changing, Dear Boy, Anna replied. *If I had to guess, the healing process is pushing impurities out of your body at a much higher rate than normal. One of the ways it does that is through your nails.*

I looked down at my feet. I had talons at the ends of my toes. Gross. Tyler could *not* see me like this. I had the hands and feet of an old crone in a fairy tale. This would not do. I grabbed the nail clippers out of the drawer in the vanity and went to work. I was still stoned, so my depth perception was horrible, but I was getting the job done. Speaking of Tyler, where was he?

He's not here, Anna said. *And thank goodness he's gone. You need work. There are several ways the body expels waste. None of them are cute. Let's start with your hair. You look like an adult version of a troll doll.*

Oh, God. I did. I wasn't naturally hairy, but what I had was on Miracle Grow. I grabbed the scissors next and started trimming.

Let's see, Anna said. She fluttered her wings in thought. *There is always number one and number two. We know number one is good.* She snickered. *How about number two?* She cocked a painted eyebrow at me.

I thought for a sec. 'I'm fine,' I replied. That seemed strange. I'd eaten so much, all that cereal and all those meal bars, and I didn't need to dump a load? Apparently not.

Anna cocked both eyebrows at me in disbelief, but I just shrugged. It was strange, but it was what it was.

Continuing on then. She gave a tongue pop, and the scantily clad pool boy showed up again. This time he had an orange, frozen concoction on his tray. It looked delicious. She took the drink, dropped a few gold coins on his tray, and we both watched his perky butt as it sauntered out of the scene.

Your breath, Anna said. *Every time you breathe out, your body gets rid of impurities. I bet you have the breath of a dragon, all nasty and smelling like a sheep's ass.*

I was afraid to do the sniff test, so I just went straight to brushing my teeth. I finished up, then decided to brush them again.

Finally, your skin. Your body flushes oil and salt out through your sweat. It's shower time for you, My Little Muncher, and I'm going to sit right here and enjoy the show. She tongue-popped again, and her impossibly large gold throne appeared. My bathroom wasn't that big, so I had no idea how we all fit.

Showering was quite the challenge. The water fell sideways, the soap glowed, and the tub was filled with snap dragon plants that wanted to chew on my legs. Anna Lykit didn't help things either. She made snarky comments about dropping the soap and making sure I cleaned all the crevices. She was having a grand old time, and I must admit it felt good to get clean again.

The moss was hitting me hard, though, and I knew I couldn't stay upright much longer. I grabbed a towel and made it back to the bedroom, but I was too tired to dry off and get into the bed. Instead, I laid the towel on the floor and curled up on it. The floor felt nice and cool. Soon, I was asleep.

***

"What the hell happened here?" I woke up. That was Tyler, and he sounded mad. Oh, he was in the bathroom.

"Who the hell pissed everywhere?" He stomped out of the bathroom, furious. I pretended I was still sleeping. I didn't want any part of this. Bermuda kept sleeping too. I'm sure Tyler wanted to smack both of us awake and do some more yelling. Instead, he glared at us, then stormed out of the apartment in a huff.

A few minutes later he stomped back in with cleaning supplies and started scrubbing the bathroom. I pretended to be sleeping the whole time. And, soon enough, I was.

***

I woke up several times after that, now back in my bed. Sometimes Tyler was with me, and sometimes he wasn't. Annabeth stopped by a few times. Between them, they always had plenty of the meal bars available and at least two glasses of water. During my awake moments, I tried to stay as presentable as possible. Hacking off my claws, showering, and trimming as needed. Sometimes I made it back to the bed; sometimes I didn't. Time was weird. But I still had lots of fun with Anna Lykit keeping me company. She tried to play a few more tricks on me, but I was getting wise to her. She tried to pull some shit with Bermuda, but he just popped his claws and smacked her magical ass back to oblivion. Hehehe. I teased her to no end about that the next time I woke up.

All good things must come to an end, and I finally woke up with a clear head. The moss, the mushrooms, and the little white flowers had all faded away. The only thing left was a faint whiff of lavender in the air to let me know it hadn't all been some sort of crazy dream. Morning sunlight streamed in the window, putting a fresh clean touch to the day. I was alone in bed, and I was okay with that. I wanted to get fully cleaned up before Tyler came back again.

I checked out my nails. They were scary long again. Hopefully, they would go back to growing at a regular pace now the moss was gone. Time for a shower and some manscaping.

I stretched and hopped out of bed. Whoa. Something was off. I looked around. Everything looked normal. The walls were white and just looked like walls. They weren't changing colors or fading away to reveal mountains on the horizon. The floor looked like my regular floor. It wasn't covered in grass, or strange plants, or lava. It was just a floor. Maybe everything was normal, and that's what felt off?

My toenails were super long and clicked against the floor. Maybe that was it. I shook my head and let it go. Time to get cleaned up. I walked to the bathroom, but something was still feeling different. Once there, I trimmed my nails back to regular length. That felt like such a relief. I could smell my own breath—never a good sign, so I cleaned my teeth. Twice. My skin felt icky, so I decided to shower first, then trim all my hair, then shower again.

The warm water felt wonderful. I love a good shower. As I was soaping down, I realized something else. I felt different. Like a lot different. I felt muscles. Like defined, powerful muscles. I ran my hands over my stomach. I had abs? I flexed. I had abs! Damn!

Don't get me wrong. I hadn't been chubby before. I weighed about one hundred and sixty pounds, and I wasn't horribly out of shape or anything like that. I just wasn't athletic. As Annabeth had pointed out, I'm more of a mental type of guy. The things I liked to do all involved thinking, not running or jumping or playing sports. I liked athletic guys. I just wasn't one of them. Until today.

I ran my hands over my body. I felt good! Damn good! I felt my legs. They were solid, powerful. I flexed my chest. I had actual man pecs. Big ones. I flexed my arms. Wow!

I finished showering, getting all the grime and sleepy sweats off me. I finally felt clean! Such a relief. Then I toweled off and got to trimming. My hair was long. Like, everywhere was long. My pubes looked like they were doing a Bob Ross imitation. My arm hair was long and just nasty. I trimmed and snipped and pruned myself like I was a wild hedge. I stayed away from the mirror, though. I didn't want to see myself until I was done. I cut the hair on my head as short as possible. I'm sure it would make a professional hairdresser faint dead away, but it was good to feel light and free with all the hair gone. Finally, I was ready. I stepped in front of the mirror.

I stared for a long time. I almost couldn't believe what I was seeing was really me. My face had sharpened somehow. I had a lot less fat now. My jaw was defined. My cheek bones belonged to a model. My eyes were still the same, but my lashes had gotten longer. Even my hair looked good, in a short, natural kind of way. Somehow I looked more manly, and yet prettier at the same time. I wasn't bad looking before, but I'd never thought of myself as good-looking. The guy looking back at me in the mirror was hot.

I looked down a bit farther. I looked powerful. Not in a Dwayne Johnson kind of way. I still had a smaller frame, after all. It was a Bruce Lee kind of way. I looked fast. I looked sexy. Especially when I looked farther down.

I had defined abs—the kind of abs that just look good and don't have to try too hard. I even had the nice V that led my eyes down farther. Unfortunately, I just had a mirror over the bathroom sink, so it didn't show all of me. Well, crap. I wanted to check out my legs too. I did check out my package. It looked normal. No changes there. I breathed a sigh of relief.

I took my second shower and came out feeling brand new. I felt energized, ready to move. I cleaned the bathroom. Then I changed the sheets on the bed. I felt new. I wanted everything else to feel new too.

I wandered over to Eggy and said hello as the morning sun warmed my naked body. I felt so freakin' good. I didn't know it was even possible to feel this excellent. I realized what was different. I felt lighter. I don't know if I was physically lighter, or if I just felt that way now I had more powerful muscles. I don't have bathroom scales, so there wasn't any way to tell. I was ripped, though. Like seriously defined. If anything, I was too shredded. I needed to eat and get some weight back. I'd already eaten everything in my kitchen, including the cat food. I was going to miss Anna Lykit, but her pranks were a bitch. What had Bermuda been eating?

I went to the kitchen and found there was still a bit of cat food left at the bottom of the bag. It would only last for a day, though. A run to the grocery store was high on the list of priorities.

The door opened, and Tyler walked in. It was so sudden I jumped. Seeing me in the kitchen startled him too.

"Oh. You're out of bed," he said. Then I could see him take a second look and really take me in.

"You've cleaned up." He gave me a slower third look, taking in all the changes.

"You look skinny." Well, that was honest. Maybe a little too honest. He saw my face fall, so he hurriedly added, "You look nice too! Really nice. Actually, I think you just look skinny because your healing has sucked up all the fat in your body. You probably weigh the same, but it's all muscle now."

"I'm not sure about that," I replied. "I feel so light, like I barely touch the ground." I shifted awkwardly. I wasn't comfortable with myself yet, and here I was naked, being evaluated by Tyler, the one person I wanted to look good for.

"Awwww. Jason." He covered the distance between us and swept me into a hug. I buried my face in his neck and just held on. "You're okay. This is all going to be okay." His soothing voice and warm touch grounded me.

I would be okay. It just all felt a bit much right now. He kept murmuring sweet nothings in my ear, holding me tight. I could feel his magic surrounding me, hugging me too. When I first met him, it had felt invasive. Now it just felt normal. It felt nice. It plucked at me, like it wanted a treat. Without really thinking about it, I gave it some of my magic. I was in the moment, and it just seemed like the thing to do.

I wondered if anyone had just given him magic before? He's usually eating bad feelings, and his magic is doing all the driving. This was my personal magic, and it was a gift. It hit his system and pulled past his aura. I could still feel it though. I felt it like it was one of my little creations. Then it cycled through his magic, and suddenly, I could feel him—like feel him on a magical level. His magic was sky blue, which shocked me. I thought it would be red for lust, or maybe orange for passion. I certainly never thought it would be a cool color. Maybe that was how he could eat darkness, because he was lighter?

I could feel him. Maybe if I ate a bit of his magic, he could feel me? Still just acting on instinct, I reached out to part of his magic resting against me and invited it inside. It felt cool, just like when I pulled neutral magic from Penny. I breathed, swirling it through my system.

I pulled back and looked into his chocolate eyes. His soul scars were almost transparent on his perfect skin. I kissed him gently. Softly. It felt like a dream, but I'd meant what I said. He could belong with me.

His magic surged, and suddenly it crashed over me. One moment I was awkward and normal. The next moment I exploded in life and lust. I felt so alive, I tingled. Then all that energy hit my groin, and my one-eyed monster surged to life. I've never gotten so hard so fast before.

What was shocking was it hit Tyler too. Somehow, it set up a feedback loop, and all that sex magic bounced back to him. His clothes melted off of him, and suddenly he was naked, hard, and vibrating with lust. Our kiss went from gentle to frantic, and I picked him up. He wrapped his legs around me, and I bolted for the bed.

Damn, you've gotten stronger. My Analytical Side noted. *You never could have done that before.* I didn't reply. I was too busy falling on the bed, with Tyler on the bottom.

I am not a top. I like being the one that gets all the love and attention. But today, I was on fire. Tyler gasped and held on for dear life as I slid my joymaker home. I was too crazy anxious to slow down and take it easy. He was a supernatural; he could handle it.

His gasping turned to moans, and then outright cries of pleasure as I loved the fuck out of him. The feedback loop was still happening. I was feeling a bit of what he was feeling, and it was driving me wild. He must have been feeling the same, as we both came together at the same time. It wasn't a normal climax either. My whole body shook like a rag doll as the passion rolled through me. Tyler hung onto me and shook too. Even counting my other night with Tyler, this was the most intense moment I'd ever had in my young life.

This feedback thing was extreme, because right after I had the first orgasm, the feedback from Tyler started a second one. Which started his second one. Which started my third one. The wave rolled back to him and finally stopped. My supernatural body, even freshly healed and motivated as it was, couldn't keep doing this forever.

I realized I'd been screaming his name like a preacher's daughter in a hay barn. I felt slightly embarrassed. Then I threw that out the window. This was an incubus I was with. My incubus. My Tyler. And he was a badass. Or good ass. Very good ass.

Whatever. I wasn't worried about semantics. Instead, I just collapsed on top of Tyler, who still had his arms and legs wrapped around me. He held me tight. Not saying anything—just letting the amazing moment linger.

We cuddled. I top cuddled. That had never happened before. I'd made Tyler my boy. Sure, it was very unusual circumstances, but I felt oddly proud of that for some reason. I'd ridden the stallion. Brought the hose to the fireman. Been the anaconda in the jungle.

Okay, that last one made no sense, but somehow it was funny. I gave a silent chuckle.

God, Tyler smelled good. Even sweaty and totally surprised as he'd been, he still pulled off an intoxicating, manly scent. He could totally be the guy on the horse in those Old Spice commercials. I got lost in that thought for a moment.

I could still feel feedback from Tyler. He felt content, like he was purring. I kissed his neck.

"Feeling happy?" I asked.

It was hard talking into a pillow, so I propped myself up on my elbows. That didn't give me a whole lot of clearance, so his face was close. Really close. Thank God I'd already brushed my teeth. If we hadn't just made love, it would have been way too intimate. Personal space is not a bad thing.

"Very happy," he said. "It was nice to just lay back and enjoy the ride for a change." His arms and legs were still wrapped around me, and he gave me a nice squeeze. I'm pretty sure I'd never had a hug quite like this before. Was there a Kama Sutra for hugging? There should be.

"So what the heck was that?" I asked. "Am I multiorgasmic now? I thought that was only for women."

He chuckled. "It's called a serial orgasm. That's when you have one right after the other. And obviously, men can have it too." As he talked, I discovered his lips. They were so cute. He could talk to me all day.

"It's rare," he continued. "I've only experienced it a few times myself. My magic got away from me somehow." His gaze sharpened. "Did you do something?"

"Maybe?" I replied. "I'm not sure exactly what I did. We traded magic somehow. Then we could both feel a bit of what the other person was feeling."

"You gave me your magic?" Tyler said sharply. I nodded. Was something wrong?

"Hang on," Tyler said, and his eyes lost focus. He seemed to be searching internally for something. Then he was back, and he looked normal. The intensity was gone. He shifted slightly, and one hand started running through my hair. It felt nice.

"I think I'm okay," he said. "I can feel your magic, but there isn't a lot of it. It will break up in a week or so and get absorbed. I just have to be really careful. I had nothing but contamination at the beginning of my supernatural life, and it has taken me forever to get back to normal. Contamination is no joke. I never want to go through that again."

My ears perked up at the mention of his history. He's usually so reserved about his background. I filed the tidbit away for future thought and was ready for a follow-up question when he beat me to it.

"You said we shared magic. Did you get some of mine?"

I nodded. "I just took a nibble. I've already swirled it around my system like I do neutral magic from Penny."

"And you feel okay?" he asked cautiously. "My magic is much older and denser than yours. Even a little sip could knock you for a loop."

"I think I'm okay," I said. I checked my magic, but everything seemed fine. It was still in matrix form, still emerald green and sapphire blue. I could see bits of Tyler's sky blue in my system, but they didn't seem to be interfering with anything. I refocused on Tyler, and his beautiful brown eyes were filled with concern.

"It obviously had a bit of an effect, because I was able to reflect some of your incubus magic back on you. I'm guessing my magic in you then reflected it back to me. Other than turning my sex pistol into a six-shooter, I think I'm normal.

"The whole thing is interesting. A tiny bit of each other's magic opened us both up to each other. You can't normally affect me directly, and I have no idea of how to affect you. This whole thing could be useful to know."

"Hmmm." Tyler sounded thoughtful. "Usually, the power only flows one way. A student will give some of their power on a regular basis to a master in exchange for teaching. Based on your theory, that lets the master have a lot of influence over the student. The master would never give some of their power away to the student. It might overwhelm them, and it is counterproductive to the arrangement. The whole idea of the student-master relationship is for the student to learn and the master to gain more power."

"Have you ever been a student before?" I asked.

He shook his head.

"Not magically, no. I've had regular martial arts teachers before, of course, but never one that required magical oaths. I would never put myself in that situation. Ever." He looked fierce. "Nobody is going to have control over me ever again."

There was certainly a story there. This was a nice moment, though. I didn't want to ask probing questions and destroy the mood.

I'd already been probing enough. Hehehe. I was so funny. Anna would have enjoyed that one. Tyler snapped out of his thoughts and caught me smiling.

"What are you grinning at?"

"Just thoughts," I said, trying to brush it off. It wasn't that funny, but now that I was trying to ignore it, I couldn't help but chuckle.

"Tell me," he demanded. Looking all mock fierce.

"Nope," I said. So he poked me in the side. I jumped like a goosed rabbit. I am so ticklish sometimes.

"Nooooo." I tried to get away, but he was still wrapped around me and it was easy for him to hang on. The tickle war was on. Well, it wasn't a war. He was doing all the tickling, and I was laughing so hard I thought I would choke.

His magic wrapped around me again. I think it was more reflex than anything else, but suddenly I was aware of just how sexy my tormenter was. His own power bounced back to him, and I saw his eyes fill with lust. His power slammed back into me, and suddenly I couldn't get enough. We kissed with passion and a crazy desperation. I didn't have enough hands to hold him and explore this god under me. He growled at me, and I growled back.

We fucked like fiends. I had no words. I couldn't get enough of him. He couldn't get enough of me. We tore the sheets and wrecked the bed, but it wasn't enough. I lost track of who did what to whom.

Even with a freshly healed body, I could barely keep up. My Gem Cells flared, and my Tree Ents flowed to life. They danced through my system keeping me in tip-top shape. I barely noticed, caught up in a fervor for Tyler, his power, and how he felt about me. Somehow, in the middle of all the pounding and flexing and moaning, I got my basic idea across. I accepted him. I accepted his scars. I accepted his power. He could have a home with me. I felt him get all that, and let it in. And I felt him accept me too. He didn't know what we were yet. He didn't know what we would become. But he accepted what we were building right now.

We would have gone on until one of us passed out, except that his power ate all the negative emotions and settled down a bit. Since we were reflecting, it not only pulled them from me, but also from him. Once his power calmed down, Tyler was able to rein it in the rest of the way, and we collapsed.

For a long while, we just gasped for air. I felt so light. I had no troubles in the world. I felt peaceful, happy. I looked at Tyler, and we started laughing. No reason. Just because. I hadn't felt this content, this satisfied, ever before. It felt like heaven on earth.

Finally, we curled up together again, spooning. I was the little spoon, just the way I liked it. I probably should have gotten away from him while his magic was quiet. This feedback loop with his powers was no joke. I didn't want to, though. I just wanted to snuggle with my man and have a quiet moment.

I didn't want to sleep. I'd been sleeping for who knows how long, and even after having sex like a race horse, I still was wide awake.

"How is Annabeth?" I asked.

"She's doing good," he said. "She's doing real good. Her form is excellent. You can hear it in the way her punches land. She's definitely ready for the next level, and she's almost done with her ten thousand goal."

Good for her. Annabeth was the little engine that could. She just kept going and doing great.

"How long was I out?" I asked. This was the big question.

"About three days," he replied.

Three days. That seemed like a long time. I was behind by three days. If I hadn't just had every negative emotion sucked out of me, I'd have been really upset. As it was, I just breathed, accepted, moved on.

What's done is done. I had a healed body now, and it was much more capable than before. I had a whole new method of healing, so I'd never get in that bad of a shape training again. I was going to be able to train faster and harder than before. It was going to be okay.

Tyler was holding me gently, his supporting arm tunneling under my pillow and coming up to wrap around my chest. This wasn't the first time we had been like this, and he used to be able to reach up and hold onto my shoulder for support. I'd grown, though, and now my shoulders were broader. Now he just wrapped his arm around my chest and tucked his hand under my arm. His other arm was around my waist. His fingers absentmindedly traced the dimples in my abs. My waist felt small, and my shoulders felt broad. It was a gay man's best dream—the lean yet muscular look.

I certainly appreciated looking fine, but I needed to be able to fight too. More muscles would certainly help with that, right? I wasn't used to this new body yet. I knew it should be better at punching and fighting, but how much better? Enough to make a difference? Enough to keep my ass from being hammered? I was both excited and nervous about getting to our beach gym and finding out.

I knew Tyler could fight. I'd seen him take out mages like a honey badger in a pissy mood. I let my magic sight roam over his fine form. Then I compared it to my new body. I was still smaller and skinnier, but I held up my end okay. He was a mountain lion. I was something smaller, like a leopard or cheetah. I didn't mind being a cheetah. I wasn't as big or as strong, but I could be fast. I liked that idea. It would be very hard to hit someone that fast.

We lay there for a while. Tyler was dozing. My mind was wandering, and then my Analytical Side suddenly jumped up.

Eureka! he shouted, and started running around naked. What the heck?

Eureka! Eureka! Eureka!

14

My First Star

'**D**ude!' I said severely. 'Why are you yelling 'Eureka'? And why are you running around without any pants on? Anna would never approve.'

He stopped, giving me the hairy eyeball. *Like you are one to talk, Mr. Walks Around His Kitchen Naked. And what were you doing just now, might I ask? Bumping Uglies in a three piece suit? I think not. The clothing has to fit the moment, thank you very much.*

'So your birthday suit fits this moment?' I thought sarcastically.

It certainly does, he replied snidely. *There was this ancient Greek guy who was tasked by the king to find out if his new crown was made of pure gold. He couldn't harm the crown in any way, but he had to figure it out or the king was going to cut his nuts off. He was taking a bath when he realized he could test the volume of the crown against its weight in gold and see if they were the same. If they were, then it was gold. If not, then the king had been cheated. He ran around the streets naked yelling 'Eureka, Eureka!' which means 'I get to keep my balls', or something like that.*

'So now you are running around my head, naked, yelling "Eureka",' I finished for him. 'Does that mean you are happy we get to keep our balls?'

I don't really know about that part, he said. *It just added some extra flair to the story. Anyway, I've figured it out.* He looked very satisfied.

'Figured out what?' I asked curiously.

He whispered in my ear.

"Eureka!" I yelled, and jumped out of bed. "Eureka! Eureka!" I danced around the bedroom naked.

Tyler sat bolt upright in bed with surprise, and then watched me dance. He shook his head in amusement.

"So what are we doing the Eureka dance for?" he asked.

"I think I've figured it out," I said. "I've figured out my training feedback loop."

I was so excited. I waved at him to join me. He got out of bed at a much slower pace than I had. Clearly, he had been enjoying his light snooze and snuggle. He was willing to humor me, though, and soon he was standing beside me.

"Okay. Now do the Pigeon stance," I said. He bent at the knees, rotated on his heels so his toes pointed out, then rotated on his toes so his heels were pointed out. I did the same.

We had done this together before, at least a hundred times. This time, though, I looked with my magic sight, not my natural sight. And I looked at not just him, I looked at myself too. That's what I'd been missing before. I'd been looking with just my eyes. With my magic sight I could see everything, all at once, in 3D. I could compare us both and make changes to what I was doing. This was brilliant. This was my feedback loop.

Immediately, I could see several problems. My knees were bent a bit more than his, my toes weren't pointed inward enough, my hips were back too far, and all of that was throwing off my balance. I made adjustments that immediately felt better. I kept going. My shoulders were too rounded; I needed to pull them back. My head wasn't centered over my body; I was leaning into the form too much.

I got in and out of the stance over and over again, each time making adjustments. I went from feeling awkward and unbalanced to feeling solid. Finally, it just clicked, and I actually felt comfortable. This was it! This was what I'd been missing. I finally had a way to see and correct what I was doing.

I discovered a bonus too. I could still feel Tyler's magic, and that meant I could feel what he was doing in the stance. He wasn't just standing there, like a human on the floor. He was sending his awareness down, like roots into the ground. He was literally grounding himself. He was also letting his magic flow up his spine and into the sky. He was more than just a form, he was an intention.

I told him all this, and he seemed startled I'd figured it out. He said that I was right, but that was something for me to learn after I'd mastered the basics. Right now, I needed to learn how to stand, how to move, and how to block. Once that was second nature, then there was a whole new level of intention and energy to master.

I knew what he meant. Poker started with the basics. What are hands, and how do you bet? Then there was the next level, where you learn how to apply pressure to get someone to fold. Or, conversely, how to get someone to bet against you when you have the better hand. Then there is a level beyond that. It's where you get in touch with the flow of the game, and it becomes more than probabilities and the actual cards. The game seems to come alive, and you ride the flow until you're one of the last players left. When it happens, it almost feels like you're surfing. It's exciting, yet peaceful. It's being in the zone.

I felt some of that through Tyler. He felt the flow of the martial arts. When he settled into his Pigeon stance, he settled into the zone. He was still. He was ready. I couldn't do any of that myself. Not yet. But now I knew what I was shooting for, and I felt a world of possibility open up. Eureka, indeed!

We finally stopped and went our separate ways. I needed to shower again, and I didn't dare do it with Tyler. He needed to head to his apartment anyway, and I needed to catch up on my House chores first and then start training. I didn't need another hour of amazing sex on the bathroom floor.

I paused for a moment to let it sink in that I'd really just thought that. I didn't need another hour of hot damn, oh God, totally orgasmic sex. OMG. I was growing up.

After my third shower of the day, I dressed and headed down to Sandy's bedroom. John hadn't moved, although Bermuda was passed out on a pile of pillows on his lap. I wandered over to give him some love and deal with three days of repair and refills on my Grannies and Octopuses. They were happy to see me, and I was happy to be in my right mind and see them. I had three days of backlog, so it took a couple hours, but finally the last Octopus swam away.

Bermuda was paws to the sky, making blissful scrunching motions as I rubbed his belly. I took several minutes to just spend time with him and give him my full attention. I'm sure it wasn't easy watching Daddy wig out for three days. Life was busy, but there was always time for love.

He gave me slow blinky eyes, and I snuck in a few kisses. This was heaven. Pure heaven. This whole supernatural thing was scary as hell sometimes. But it also had moments like this to balance it all out.

Finally, I sighed and stood up. I couldn't stay here all day. I took a moment to check on Sandy. She had moved some more, and she had as much magic as I'd had before my matrix. But she still wasn't awake yet. What the heck was taking so long?

I checked out Snowy and Biscuit's food supply. They were running low as well. We needed to make a food run very soon. A hungry cat is a scary cat.

My chores were done for now. Time to train. Bermuda decided he wanted to go with me, but he wanted to be carried. I told him no. He held out his paw, like if I was just a bit closer he'd climb me himself. I told him no, firmly this time. He gave a little yowl. More like a sleepy yawn with sound and held out his paw again. I called him a sad sack of lazy fur, but he won. I picked him up and carried him to the portal.

The beach was just beautiful. The sun was warm, but not hot, and there was a cool breeze blowing. Bermuda decided he wanted to get his smell on, so I put him down, checked the arrow on the sign to make sure I was headed in the right direction, and started out in a slow jog. Bermuda kept up easily, and for a mile or so we just traveled together. It was great being outside. Seagulls called out to each other. The waves crashed and threw the scent of the sea into the air. The wind played with the tropical trees on the shoreline. I was running in paradise.

Bermuda got tired, of course, so I picked him up and carried him. I also increased the pace. I felt warmed up and ready to move. The sand still slowed me down, but I ran easily. My body felt good. I wasn't panting or out of breath. Instead, I felt quick and powerful. I felt like a cheetah.

I was enjoying my run so much, I almost felt a bit sad when I made it to our workout spot. I put Bermuda down so he could run and play, took a quick dip in the ocean to cool off, and then changed into my workout clothes.

Annabeth and Tyler were already there. She stopped her training and pulled me in for a nice hug. Then she stepped back and looked at me in surprise.

"What happened to you?" she exclaimed. "Look at your shoulders!" She started patting me down and sizing me up. I felt like a prize pony in a show.

"Look what I have now," I said proudly, lifting up my shirt. I flexed my abs, and Annabeth mock-fainted.

"Land sakes," she said playfully. "Warn a girl before you bring out the big guns."

"Speaking of guns." I made the classic bicep flex pose.

This was so much fun, and we just played for a while. I showed off all my muscles, and she felt how strong I was and oohed and aahed in all the right places. It was such an enjoyable moment before the work started.

"I just figured you were lying around for three days," she said. "I didn't realize you were going to go all butterfly on me and show up like this." She got serious for a moment. "So how do you feel now? You were three sheets to the wind and zonked out of your mind the last time I saw you."

"I'm good," I said. "My head is clear. My body feels ready. I'm healed and excited to get started.

"Oh. I did meet a really interesting person." I filled her in about Anna Lykit, her outrageous outfits, and her crazy pranks. She laughed when I told her about eating cat food, but she gasped in dismay when I told her about watering the flowers.

"Oh, no you didn't!" She smacked my arm. "You did not!"

"I did," I said, laughing. "It seemed so logical at the time. The flowers even grew and changed colors for me."

"I'm sure they did," she chuckled. "I bet that was a bitch to clean up, though."

"I wouldn't know," I replied and gestured towards Tyler. "He cleaned it up for me while I was passed out on the floor."

"Well, he is a saint," she declared. She yelled a bit louder to Tyler to make sure he heard her. "You are a blessed saint!"

He just waved it off and kept training. I'm sure he'd cleaned up much worse before, but still, it was a very nice thing for him to do. I was so grateful to him that I hadn't had to deal with a pissy bathroom while I was healing. That would have sucked.

"So how is the training going?" I asked.

"It's going well," she said. "Although I haven't been able to hit the goal yet. I had planned on doing more, but I found I needed time to heal too. Ironically, I'm hitting harder now, so when I don't land right, I'm doing more damage and it takes longer to repair. I've been taking extra rest time, sitting with Sandy, and watching you sometimes when Tyler needed a break."

"Sorry about that," I replied. "I hadn't planned on trippin' for three days. It just sort of happened."

She waved it off like it was no big deal. I was grateful, though. This was the third time she'd sat with me when I needed it. Annabeth was a great friend. She was not only fun to be around, but she was also someone you could count on.

"So how are your stats doing?" I asked.

The huge grin on her face told me they must be good.

"I'm still a low novice, but…" She was drawing it out.

I waved my hands like 'Come on! Tell me!'

"My level is 5.6."

My jaw dropped open as she gave a happy dance.

"5.6?!" I did a happy dance with her. "That's insane! That is awesome! I'm so proud of you."

We hugged and danced some more.

"That is a crazy good number. You've made all that progress from listening?"

She nodded proudly. "Listening to my body and my magic has been the key. My technique has really improved, and that lets me hit harder and get injured a lot less. It's a lot of practice, though. I know what to do, but it is still hard to do it perfectly.

"It's like shooting a bow. Even though you know what to do, it's still hard to make the arrow go exactly where you want."

"You know how to shoot a bow and arrow?" I was getting sidetracked, but it was hard to imagine Little Miss Sunshine as an archer.

"Believe it or not, that was a perfectly good sport for a lady back in the day," she said. "My high school had a pretty good archery program, and I got to do that instead of the regular P.E. class. I hated dodgeball, so I was happy to do just about anything else. I rather enjoyed the bow, and I got pretty good at it too."

"That is too cool," I said.

"So when was this? Back in 1908?" I teased her.

She gave me a look of mock horror.

"I'm surprised they even had bows back then. Was wood invented yet?"

She smacked me on the arm, then started laughing. She couldn't help herself. "I'll have you know it was nowhere near 1908. And comments like that will get you shot in the butt."

She punched me in the chest. Ouch! "The next time I get my bow you better watch out." She punched me again. Double ouch! I took a step back. I was feeling her 5.6 rating.

"I wonder what the numbers mean?" I said, switching to a more thoughtful note. "We both started at 1, and we both have different strength levels, so a 5.6 for you wouldn't feel the same as a 5.6 for me."

"I had the same question," Annabeth replied. "Tyler says it's a measure of how much force you can apply over a hundred punches compared to your first attempt. He gave me a formula, but it's basically a number of how much I've improved. My first attempt was pretty pathetic, so improving on that wasn't hard. Still, 560 percent improvement is nothing to sneeze at."

"For real!" I replied. "So how far are you away from the ten thousand punch goal?"

"I'm not sure," she said. "I'm close, though." I gave her a disbelieving look, so she explained a bit more. "I haven't been looking because I want every punch to count. I found I was focusing too much on the number and not enough on improving my technique. I want to hit ten thousand, but my main focus has been developing the best form I can before I go to the next level."

"That makes sense," I replied. "After all, it really is about fighting better, not just getting to a number.

"Speaking of that, I've been thinking about starting over." I looked at her to see what she thought. She looked interested, so I kept going. "I'm thinking of starting over from zero on my punch count, as well as pretending I haven't learned anything yet, and have Tyler retrain me on everything."

"I think it's a good idea," Annabeth said. "You were training injured for a while, so you might have picked up some bad habits. Starting over lets you make sure you are doing it right."

I was glad she liked the idea. I hated losing my current punch count, but it just felt right. We hugged it out, and I let her get back to training. I moved to my section of the beach, and Tyler came over to get me started.

"Did I hear you were starting over?" he asked. I nodded. "Good. I was going to suggest that myself. Let's do a quick mental exercise. Imagine you are holding a cup. Now fill it with all the knowledge you have learned so far."

I imagined myself holding a coffee cup. It had the words 'Kung Fu Fighting' on it, and I added a few of the old batman Pow! Zam! graphics. Then I filled it with my knowledge so far. It barely covered the bottom of the cup.

"Got the image?" Tyler asked. I nodded. "Okay. Now dump it out and watch it sink into the ground."

I did that. It felt surprisingly freeing.

"How do you feel?" Tyler asked.

"I feel good," I replied. "It's such a simple idea, but it somehow makes everything feel fresh and new again. I like it."

"Add this to your bag of tricks to use in life," Tyler said. "I've found it to be surprisingly useful. It helps you learn faster, as you are mentally letting go of your preconceived notions of what you think you know. I've also found it is great for brainstorming. It lets me start fresh and come up with new ideas when I'm stuck.

"Now, let's start at the beginning. This is a punch."

"One sec," I said and pulled out a blindfold.

I wasn't going to make the same mistake and learn with my physical sight. I put it on, and the world shrank down to the twenty foot radius I had with my magic sight. Although it was a smaller view, it felt comfortable. I'd spent so long like this when I'd lost my normal vision. My magic sight might have a smaller area, but it had a lot more detail. I could see all the grains of sand around me. I could even see the dust in the air if I wanted to focus on it. Most importantly, I could see every part of Tyler's body as well as my own. That's how I was going to learn.

Tyler started over at the very beginning, explaining how to make a fist. Now I was seeing it in full 3D, I quickly discovered I had lots of room for improvement. I wasn't placing my fingers quite right, and my fist wasn't perfectly straight. I could also see Tyler's intention and energy—the way it flowed down his wrist and pooled in the last three knuckles of his hand.

I couldn't get to Tyler's level, yet, but I now knew what I was striving for. From there, we went back over moving into the Pigeon stance. I'd already practiced this in the bedroom, and I quickly found my comfort level again. This time I went beyond comfort and basic stability. I was starting to feel solid. I had a base. This was going to make all the difference when punching. Before, I'd felt like my punching was pushing me backwards. It was throwing me off balance, rather than the force of the blow being transmitted into the target.

Next we practiced punching the air. Once again, going from an open prayer palm to a fist was difficult. That's what repetition was for. Tyler was so fluid. He made it look easy. I had him do it in super slow motion while I paid attention to every part of him. I saw how his shoulder dropped and moved forward slightly, how his elbow tucked in as his arm extended, and how his intention continued beyond the fist. Using magic sight and having a temporary affinity with Tyler was the key. This level of learning was well beyond anything I'd experienced before. I was only a novice level, but this was a master class.

It wasn't long before I was ready to actually start training with Sparkles, my sand dummy. This was it. This was where it had all fallen apart before. I was nervous, but I breathed through it and let it go. I'd poured my cup out. This was starting over. I was going to fail for a while, and that was fine. Mastery comes from failure, and I was going to master this.

"Okay, House," I said. "Let's do this." Sand flowed and Sparkles, my training partner, formed in front of me. I thought he would just look like sand, but he sparkled even in my magic sight. That was cool.

At that moment, I heard the sound of a loud gong and saw flashes of light. I looked over, and Annabeth's training partner was shooting stars into the air like fireworks. They were all different colors, and they twinkled and exploded into even smaller stars before fading out. Then, he started doing a happy dance, which looked totally cool. Who knew sand guys could dance?

"Perfect timing," Tyler said. "Looks like Annabeth has hit her goal. I'm going to work with her for a while on getting her to the next level." He gave me a hug and kiss. "I'll check back in with you later. You know what to work on, so just enjoy your practice while I'm gone."

He headed over to Annabeth and joined in her happy dance. Then he pulled her off down the beach to talk about whatever the big secret was. I was glad they were out of range. I didn't want to learn anything else yet. I needed to master the basics first. I wished her happiness and good luck, and then got back to business.

Before I started, I pulled up my stats.

Low Novice Jason Punch Stats
Level = 1
Punches = 0

Notes: Congratulations on a fresh start. It's a new dawn. It's a new day. And you are looking good. Now get to punching!

And that's what I did. I got to punching. I started out slow. I wasn't ready for speed. I needed technique.

Over and over, I punched, searching for the right method. Sometimes I focused on something small, like my hands, making sure they formed right. Sometimes I focused on the big picture, stance, shoulders, arms, making sure nothing big was out of line. Sometimes I focused on the feeling. What felt right?

I lost myself in the rhythm of the practice, so it was a surprise to me when I heard a chime and Sparkles suddenly flashed gold and shot a single star into the air. What the heck? There was no way I was at ten thousand yet. I called up my stats.

Low Novice Jason Punch Stats
Level = 1.1
Punches = 215

Notes: Congratulations! You used to hit like freshly fallen snow. Now you hit like WET falling snow. You are improving!

Looked like my level had moved up a bit. It wasn't much, but I'd take it. It was certainly better than going in the other direction and ending up at 0.5!

I was also surprised I had over two hundred punches. It seemed like I'd just started.

"Thank you, House," I said. It felt a bit strange talking into the air, but hopefully the House heard me. "And thank you, Sparkles." I gave him an affectionate pat. He nodded.

That was cool. Other than forming out of beach sand, Sparkles had just been standing there in his power pose and not moving. He seemed so patient and stoic while I beat on his chest. It felt nice that he knew I appreciated what he was doing for me.

I dismissed the notification and got back to work. Once again, I lost myself in the flow. I was starting to feel comfortable, when Sparkles flashed gold again. This time I got two stars flying into the sky. They flashed up and then split into lots of little stars. It wasn't anything like the celebration when Annabeth hit her goal, but it was still pretty.

Low Novice Jason Punch Stats

Level = 1.2

Punches = 352

Notes: Like the scriptures say: If thy eye offends thee, pluck it out. Oh, wait, a golem already did that for you! Snark! In other words, excellent idea on using a blindfold.

I can't believe the House just went there. Getting punched by a golem was no joke! Well, I guess it was a bit of a joke, since the House just went all snarky on me. Being without my natural sight for so long was turning out to be useful. I was much more comfortable using my supernatural sight now.

It was nice the House agreed with me on using a blindfold, and it was nice I went up a level, but that wasn't going to stop the bad guys. Time to pound some sand!

Annabeth and Tyler came back from their talk and started on her training. After a few minutes, Tyler came over to check on me again. I was doing fine. I had my own feedback loop, and I was gradually honing in on what worked. I had him demonstrate everything for me again, just to make sure I wasn't missing anything. I had him punch from slow speed all the way up to the fastest he could do. His top speed was faster than my natural sight, but not faster than my magical sight. It was so quick I couldn't process the details, but I could at least see it.

Confident I was on the right track and hadn't missed anything, I got back to work. Soon I had another star.

Level = 1.3

Punches = 479

Notes: Nice form. Now maybe you can go a bit harder.

And soon after, another one.

Level = 1.4

Punches = 596

Notes: Turtle, Turtle, on the wall, who's the slowest of them all?

The House was suggesting that I ramp it up a bit, give my punches more power and speed. I was gradually adding a bit of both, but I wasn't sure what this body could handle. I didn't want to go back into a healing coma again. I was focusing on technique, and I could feel it all coming together.

Annabeth was having her own problems. Whatever Tyler had told her had messed up her flow, and she was having to relearn her form. Her punches sounded much weaker, and I winced a few times when I heard her hit the sand wrong. She was persevering, though, and I was sure she would figure it out. I thought about going over and giving her a supportive hug, but I didn't want her to think I was watching her. Having an audience while you fail sucks.

So I let her work it out on her own for a while, and I went back to practicing. I kept waiting for the pain to start. I was hitting Sparkles fairly hard. I wasn't at full power, but they weren't love taps either. My fists were good, so I wasn't landing punches wrong and messing up my hands. My overall form was also good, so I was staying grounded and the vibrations weren't tearing me apart. I kept waiting for the deep aches and pains to start, but they never did. I kept on ramping it up, slowly.

Level = 1.5

Punches = 722

Notes: I guess you are just going to be cautious. There are worse things in the world. Like walking around in underwear that is way too tight. And having a big gravy stain on it. And not having pants. And your whole family is watching. That's worse.

That one cracked me up. Then I did a quick mental check of my nether regions. Was my underwear too tight? I did a quick wiggle and shimmy. Nope. It was just right. And I had shorts on. So all was good.

Level = 1.6

Punches = 906

Notes: Rolling, Rolling, Rolling, keep those punches rolling. Rawhide! Actually, maybe you shouldn't roll them together so much. Make every punch distinct.

The House was back to giving me real advice again. It was right. I'd started rolling my punches together. They were getting a bit jumbled up. I started putting the slightest pause in between my hits. That let me reset and fully focus on each cycle.

Level = 1.7

Punches = 1049

Notes: OMG—you can read! And you can actually follow advice. Hallelujah! I was beginning to think you'd been dropped on your head as a child. Nothing wrong with that, of course. We all have our stories. It's just that this will be so much easier if you aren't an imbecile. Or a drooling idiot. Or stupid stubborn.

I think the House just called me slow. Or stubborn. Or maybe both. That's okay. I was setting the pace here. I was learning how to fight, and I was building a solid base. I'd start speeding up even more when I saw my technique could handle it. I could see my problems, and a few times I'd landed a punch that felt almost perfect. But right now the muscle memory wasn't there. I wanted to do better, but I just wasn't used to this level of physical activity yet.

My respect for those who played sports went way up. I'd never thought it would be so hard to learn a physical skill. Now all the coaching, practice, eating right, recovery time, it all made sense. I planned on being a world class martial artist, and I was just now starting to get a glimpse of how long that journey was going to be.

That's okay. I could heal. I had an amazing coach. I had a great friend to learn with, and the House had provided an exceptional place to train. I was going to be okay.

I saw Annabeth take a break, so I took one too. Now seemed like the right time to show some support.

"How's it going?" I asked.

"It's going good!" she said. She was all bright and perky. This was not what I expected at all. "I learned the 'Big Secret'." She threw up some air quotes. "And it's throwing off my game right now. It's certainly worth learning, though. Once I get it, my level will go much higher than it is now."

"That sounds great," I said. I gave her a big, enthusiastic hug. I wanted to support her in her positive attitude. I'm not sure I'd be as happy about having my form messed up when it was my turn.

We ate some bars, drank some water, and headed back out again. Annabeth was anxious to keep going and master her new knowledge. I was anxious to keep going too. I was certainly hitting a lot harder than when I first started. I felt like I had a lot of potential left.

I couldn't believe how good my body felt. Tea and his Grove were doing a bit of work, but it wasn't crazy moss-ageddon like before. Or would that be a moss-ocalypse? Either way, my fifteen minute break felt like it had been an hour. I felt both rested, and yet, warmed up too.

Tyler came over and watched me pound on Sparkles for a bit.

"You're doing great," he said. "I don't have anything to add or suggest. Your form looks good. I saw a few things that needed tweaking, but you are already working on correcting them on your own. You're at the point where you know what to do. Now it's just fine tuning the way your body moves so you get a consistent result. What level are you at now?"

"I've made it to 1.7," I said proudly. It felt so nice to be able to say that. This was much better than the aching results I'd had last time.

"That sounds right," he said. "Try for 2.0 by the end of the day. That will be double the power and technique you started with. I'm going to go back to working with Annabeth since she could use me the most. You're on the right track. Just keep working on it." He gave me a big smile and a light kiss before heading off.

Keeping it light was great with me. The last thing I wanted was another batch of feedback from his incubus powers. I needed to be training, not dealing with sand in my crack and shocking the heck out of Annabeth.

It seemed like I had hardly started up again, when I got my next level.

Level = 1.8

Punches = 1163

Notes: Your hands are made for knocking. And that's just what they'll do. They'll rock'em sock'em knock'em through. In other words, you're doing well.

I think the House just mixed 'These Boots Are Made for Walking' and a toy robots table game. It must be feeling really proud of itself right about now. Still, it was nice to hear I was doing well. I got back to punching again.

Tyler vastly underestimated how far I could go in a day. By the time the sun was setting, I'd made it to level 2.6. I'd jumped 1.6 levels in one day! I could feel the difference too. My punches were hard and fast. My base was solid, and the force of the blow was sinking into Sparkles rather than turning back on me. When I'd first started, I barely disturbed his sand at all. I'd knock a few grains out of place, but that was it. Now, every punch made a dent. It wasn't a huge dent, but it forced him to constantly reform his chest.

The real star of the day, though, was my new powerful body. Even though it was the end of the day and I'd been training hard all day, I was still fresh. I felt strong, quick, full of energy. If the sun hadn't been setting and everyone ready to go, I still could have kept training. I felt like I could have trained for another twelve hours. Maybe the House was right. Maybe I was ramping up too slowly.

I shook my head. Nope. My body might be able to handle more, but this was the first day of learning good technique. I'd needed to learn what I was doing at the physical level before I really ramped it up. I felt like I had a good foundation on my form now. Tomorrow I'd keep pushing it and see what this body could do. In the meantime, it was time to say goodbye to the beach and hello to the grocery store. The cats weren't going to feed themselves.

I didn't want to go to Kroger on my own. Sandy had gotten kidnapped there, so I wanted to be aware, alert, and have a partner to help me out if trouble started. Unfortunately, Tyler said he couldn't go. He could feel the House pulling at him to run a mission. Then he needed to spend time at home with Mr. Tubbles for a bit. Annabeth said she could if I gave her a few minutes to put her list together.

Tyler went through the portal but didn't end up in the hallway. It seemed like the House had pulled him away already. I guess abruptly losing him like this was just something I was going to have to get used to. Annabeth and I arrived back, and we agreed to meet at Sandy's apartment and head out from there.

When I shopped for groceries for myself, I usually just did a round of the store and picked up whatever I wanted. Since we were shopping for more than one person, I needed to be more organized, so I made a list of my own. It was pretty simple. I liked sandwiches, so I needed lots of bread, lots of meat, and all the fixings. Other than sandwiches, I lived on cereal, so I needed all the stuff to make bowls of crunchy goodness.

My basic list completed, I headed down to Sandy's to see what she needed. Her refrigerator was pretty much bare. She liked fresh foods, and they had all either gone bad, or we'd eaten them while she was sleeping. I had no idea how to shop for her, so I figured sandwiches would work for her too. We also needed lots of cat food and lots of cat treats.

I checked on Sandy and John while I was waiting on Annabeth. Sandy had moved again. Her magic was filled in now, and the color was a nice, saturated orange. She had to wake up soon. She just had to. I didn't have any other ideas of what could be keeping her sleeping. If something else was broken, I couldn't see what it was, and I had no idea how to fix it.

She was a lot older than us, though, and had been a supernatural for a lot longer. Maybe she just needed more power to work. That's all I could hope for. John didn't look like he had moved at all. Whatever his earth cycle was, it wasn't quick.

I said hello to Octa, her Tangle, and all the Grannies. They were just doing their thing and seemed happy. Annabeth showed up, and we headed toward the back of the House. I followed her, but I was a bit surprised. We usually walked to Kroger, which meant we left out the front. Maybe she thought we were being watched and wanted to sneak out the back?

I knew the House had a back door and a back yard. I just never went out that way. I'd checked it out once, but it didn't seem to be anything special. This time, though, I saw something I hadn't noticed before. A section of the yard was paved, and parked on it was a car! Actually, it was an SUV––a Hyundai Santa Fe. I looked at Annabeth in shock.

"You have a car!" I said. She nodded like it was no big deal. Of course she had a car. "We've been walking to get groceries and lugging all the stuff back, and you've had a car the whole time?!" My voice was rising a bit. This was crazy.

"Of course I have a car," Annabeth said. "That's how I got here. I don't drive it much, but I'm not about to get rid of it."

"But why don't you use it for shopping? It's a real pain carrying all that stuff back to the House."

She just shrugged. "I like walking, and Kroger isn't far away. I offered to use my car when I first got here, but Sandy likes all her food fresh. She was going every other day, so the amount of trips made for light loads. Plus, I think she liked loading up John just to see how much he could carry."

That sounded like Sandy. She probably liked seeing his muscles flex. For that matter, I liked seeing his muscles flex.

"Well, I'm glad we are taking the car this time," I said. "This is going to be a monster shopping run."

We threw all our reusable bags in the back seat and headed out. We both agreed we needed to be on high alert and that we should stick together. Annabeth had brought her battle charms along. She didn't have a lot, but they had won the day before. I had my shillelagh that John had given me. It was tied to the string of my sweatpants and hung down inside my leg. I looked like I had a porn-sized trouser snake in my pants, but I didn't care. If we ended up in a pitched battle in the middle of Kroger, I wanted my weapon.

15

Her Darkness

Once in Kroger, we got to work. With everything on our list, it didn't take long to fill up the cart. We got three of those giant, thirty-five pound bags of cat food, so that took up a lot of room right there. Annabeth suggested we do multiple passes as the car could hold a lot more than just one cart's worth of groceries. We thought about filling two carts at the same time, but Annabeth vetoed that idea. We needed to be mobile in case we were attacked. Our first pass was for dry goods, stuff that could sit in the car and wouldn't spoil while we went back for more.

    Everything felt normal. I didn't see or feel any magic other than ours. Annabeth was listening for anything, and she said we were all clear. The only thing off about our first run was the size of our cart. It was stuffed. We had crap on the bottom rack, stuff hanging on the sides, and mounded up on the top. It was so embarrassing.

We loaded it all into the car and went back for more. This time we happened to go by the section with clothing. It was a bit strange having clothing and other stuff in a grocery store, but this was one of the new Kroger stores where they were trying to be more like Walmart. The clothing didn't interest me, but I happened to notice a nice cloth backpack and thought of Bermuda. He wanted to come through the portal with me and hang out during training, but there wasn't any way he could run the distance on his own. So I carried him, but it was awkward for both of us. Maybe he could sit in a backpack and enjoy looking around while I did all the running? It was worth a shot, so I added it to the cart.

We were halfway through our second pass, when I felt something. I stopped, switched over to magic sight, and scanned for trouble. Nothing. Annabeth listened, but didn't hear anything out of the ordinary. We kept going, but at a more cautious pace. We finished our second pass, and thankfully, checked out with no problems.

We still had room in the car and stuff on our list, so we headed back for the third and final pass. That's when I felt it again. There was a touch of magic in the air. Annabeth tilted her head to listen, and this time she heard something. She said it sounded like a murmur of voices, like there were several people talking in another room. It wasn't loud, but she certainly heard it.

On high alert now, we started rushing to get the final items on our list. These were the perishable items, like milk, cheese, and ice cream. I suggested we just abandon the cart and head to the car, but Annabeth wanted to get everything.

She said we didn't know for sure there was danger yet, and we really needed some of the stuff.

We were in the ice cream aisle when I saw her, the lady with the black aura. She had a few items in her cart and appeared to be shopping just like us. She knew we were there, though, as she was looking right at me and slowly pushed her cart in our direction. I nudged Annabeth and pointed. She didn't look alarmed, although she was alert and ready for action. Did she not recognize her?

Then it hit me. I'd seen the whole battle from the House's perspective, so I'd watched the whole fight unfold and I could recognize all the players. Annabeth had been working the shield in the basement, so she probably hadn't seen everything going on. She also couldn't see magic, so she had no idea about the black aura.

"It's the mage with the black aura," I hissed. Then Annabeth seemed to understand.

"Didn't you say she didn't actually fight in the House battle?" Annabeth asked. "I thought you said she just gathered up all the fallen mages at the end."

I nodded.

"Yes. That's right. But she still makes me nervous. She's powerful—much more powerful than us. And why is her aura black? I think that makes me the most nervous. That can't be good."

I didn't get a chance to say anything more as the mage stopped her cart in front of ours. I buzzed with adrenaline, ready to fight or flight. Maybe both. My mind was already running through possible battle plans. I liked the idea of ramming her with the cart, then grabbing Annabeth and running. Hopefully, she could get a shield up in time to protect us both.

"I come in the spirit of Parley," the mage said softly.

I looked at Annabeth. She looked at me. Miss Dark and Scary wanted to talk? Did we trust this?

I scanned around quickly, but didn't see anything else. Annabeth appeared to be listening for a moment, then nodded to me. I guess the coast was clear. It looked like it was just her. I scanned her aura, and this time I really focused on it.

Her aura was dense and thick. And there was a lot of it. Her magic felt older, and I didn't sense anything rotten. She felt a lot more like Sandy than Isobel. Other than her aura being black, and the fact she had been with Isobel, she didn't seem to scream "bad guy".

One other strange thing was that she held her aura close. It was tightly compacted next to her skin, like she didn't want it to actually touch anything. Maybe she was the magical equivalent of a germaphobe?

She was looking at us expectantly. I guess we were supposed to say something. I'd been scanning and looking around, and Annabeth hadn't said anything yet, so she sighed and continued.

"I swear on my power that I will do you no harm, either through action or inaction, so long as you do the same for me. This oath will expire in one hour, or sooner, if harm is done to either one of us."

"I accept your oath," I replied. "But I don't know enough about how all this works yet to feel comfortable swearing anything to you."

Annabeth could swear if she wanted to, but I wasn't doing anything like that. It might be a trap. It didn't seem like a ruse, of course, but that was the very definition of a good trap. You don't know what you're getting into until it is too late.

Miss Darkness didn't like that at all. She frowned, clearly unsure of how to continue. For all her power, she seemed hesitant. Was she afraid of something?

"That doesn't mean we still can't talk," I said. "We'll listen to what you have to say. You have plenty of power, so I'm pretty sure you are safe from us anyway. It's just that you've attacked us and done your best to wipe us out. Swearing anything to you does not seem like a good idea."

She paused, considering, then nodded. "That is acceptable. You should know, however, that I have never attacked you. Not at the park, and not at the House. I would never attack another mage. I only live in peace."

Do what? I looked at Annabeth, and she looked as surprised as I was.

"For being peaceful, you sure have some bloodthirsty friends," I retorted.

"I didn't want anything to do with you, or your House," she replied. "The fight was not my doing. I was only there to protect those I could, and rescue as many of my brothers and sisters as possible. People that your House smashed into the ground." The last was said with some heat. She was clearly angry about it. "You did not have to be so savage and cruel."

Okay, that was just way off base. They had attacked us. Anything they got was their own fault. I opened my mouth to bite back, but Annabeth spoke up first.

"How many died in the battle?" she asked.

"Thirty-eight," Her Darkness replied. Her hands gripped the cart so hard her knuckles turned white.

"Were they your friends?" Annabeth asked.

Her Darkness nodded. "Some of them."

"I'm sorry you lost friends," Annabeth said. She was being much more sympathetic than I could ever be. They had shown up ready to burn the House to the ground, and either kill us or enslave us. They were not innocent.

"Losing people you know and like is never easy. I'm very surprised they didn't use the 180 strategy, though. That would have solved all our problems."

"The 180 strategy?" Her Darkness questioned.

"Yes," Annabeth continued. "It's when you think 'what the heck am I doing attacking innocent people who have done nothing to me? I think I'll turn 180 degrees and just walk away'."

Ohhhh. Burn! Annabeth had gotten her point across perfectly. If you don't want to die in battle, then don't show up and fight someone who doesn't want to fight you.

The burn went completely over Her Darkness's head. Instead, she took it seriously.

"That is what I would have preferred. Nothing is solved by fighting. So much of the supernatural world is hostile. Everyone is fighting someone else for students or power or space. I wish there were supernatural laws that were enforced, just like in the mundane world. Laws that limited how aggressive supers could be. Laws that regulate power. Laws that make our world a better place.

"That is something the mundane world has improved upon. It's not perfect by any means, but it is far better than its supernatural counterpart. We are still in the dark ages, where might makes right. Whoever has the most power can do what they want, until someone with more power comes along and takes everything away from them."

She sounded bitter. I guess she had been on the losing end of that power struggle more than once.

"There is a big difference between defending and attacking," I chimed in. "If we had not defended ourselves, then we would have been homeless and enslaved. Or dead. Defending ourselves was the right thing to do. That is why we are able to be here talking to you today. If there is anyone to blame for your friend's death, it would be Isobel. This was her vendetta, and she used the mages like pawns. She didn't show up for the battle until it was obvious they needed help. The mages were just disposable pieces for her to throw at the House and hope they wore our defenses down. Then, when it was safest for her to show up, she did. When her own attack didn't work, she quickly retreated before she could get hurt. If you want someone to blame, blame her."

"I am well aware of what she did," Her Darkness said stiffly. "The other schools were also critical of her battle strategy. The Louisville Mages lost much that day. The others have declared their debts paid, their favors honored, and have cut all ties with us. Isobel has put us in a situation where we are now completely alone. Why else do you think I'm coming to you?"

That was a good question. Why was she coming to us? I'd love to dive into that right now, but then the conversation might end. She seemed willing to talk, and I had lots of questions.

"So it wasn't just your group attacking us?" I asked.

It had seemed like an awful lot of mages fighting. Of course, Louisville was a big city, the biggest in Kentucky. Not that that is saying a lot. We don't exactly have the population of California or New York.

"Oh, goodness no," she replied. "Most of the Louisville Mages had gone into hiding as soon as Isobel tried to recruit them. Only the ones who were seeking power or fame joined the battle. There were a few who just felt like they needed to represent their hometown and participated out of pride. They were my friends. And they never thought it would get so bloody. Isobel seemed to have everything she needed for a quick victory, and they thought it would just be a quick smash and grab.

"There were too few of our own fighters for Isobel's liking, so she called in all our favors from the surrounding schools. She made it seem like an adventure, something that would be easy and fun. That's why we had so many join us, and why the other schools are so mad at us now. It will be many years before our school can recover."

I was learning all kinds of things today. Now it made sense why we had faced so much opposition.

"So where did Isobel get all her stuff from? We were hit by catapults throwing these glowing rocks, as well as each mage packing a wand or two. This had to be coordinated, because the catapults were spelled to break down and reassemble into the battering ram."

"I don't know," she replied. "I know they weren't from a common enchanter, and I know she didn't make them herself. She had plenty of power, and she was good at casting spells on the fly, but she didn't have the skill to make a charm, much less a wand. If she had gotten them through a regular transaction and paid for it with money, I would have known about it, as I'm the treasurer. I'm guessing she made some sort of deal for the golems and all the battle gear, and I have no idea what that would be, or who it could be with. Maybe it was someone she knew before she came here?"

I would be very interested to know who gave all that stuff to Isobel. Clearly, the House had another enemy lurking in the shadows. When she had been kicking the crap out of me, she'd said the golem wasn't actually hers. She'd borrowed it, and she was going to have to find a way to pay it back now that it was destroyed. That's why she was so mad.

Or, maybe the person she'd borrowed the golems and siege equipment from wasn't an enemy. Maybe he was like an arms dealer, selling weapons to whoever wanted to fight. Either way, it was something we needed to find out. And it looked like Her Darkness couldn't tell us.

"So how can you say you are peaceful when you have such a black aura?" I asked.

She was still willing to talk, and Annabeth was letting me lead the show, so it was time for more questions. This query sounded a bit ignorant. I knew that darkness did not automatically mean bad. How else were you going to see the beauty of the stars without the night? Or an even better example: Dark Chocolate. Enough said. Anyway, I'm sure she'd heard variations of this question many times before. Hopefully, her automatic response would give away more than she intended.

"I'm peaceful by nature," she replied softly. "I don't like conflict. My black aura helps a lot with that. My black magic is worthless as other supers don't want to touch it, trade for it, or have anything to do with it. So I don't have anyone trying to defeat me to gain power."

"Why is your magic worthless?" I asked.

I was puzzled. I'd have thought having a black aura would be more intimidating, and she could use that to her advantage.

She gave me a sharp look. "Are you mocking me, boy?"

I held up my hands, surprised at her heated response.

"No! Not at all. I'm new to everything, and I'm learning as I go. I certainly didn't mean to offend you, and I apologize if I did."

Her sharp look melted. Now she just looked sad—and a little bitter.

"A black aura is not a naturally occurring color for mages. It's a sign that I'm highly contaminated. Because of that, nobody wants my magic. I can make pearls, but nobody wants them, not even the Bank. Nobody wants me as a student because nobody wants my tithe of power.

"It goes the other way too. Not only do I have to be careful not to let my magic touch anyone else, but I also have to be careful not to let any other magic in. Accepting colors of magic might throw off my equilibrium. I'm alive, but it is a balancing act to stay that way."

"I know your magic is dark," I replied. "But it doesn't seem rotten. It looks stable —even healthy. You don't seem like Isobel or any of the mages that followed her around."

"I look stable?" She seemed surprised. "It's hard for me to see my own magic, so I wasn't sure. I knew that someday I'd start to get better. Maybe it's finally happening." She looked cautiously hopeful. "It has been so long since I've talked with someone who can see auras. Can you tell me exactly what you are seeing?"

"Sure!" I said.

This wasn't how I thought the conversation would go. The more we talked, the more she seemed like a regular person. I was expecting something of a Disney villain or someone worse, like Isobel.

We talked for a bit about her aura. I told her what I'd seen about how she kept it close and how it wasn't rolling around like Isobel's had been. She was curious to know the exact shade of black I saw. I'd never thought of black as having levels. It was just black.

We used the packaging on the frozen goods to talk about how dark her aura was. We found a bag of frozen peas that had writing that was almost her exact shade. Her aura wasn't midnight black; it was more of a dark gray. She seemed very happy about this.

"So how did you get contaminated?" I asked. Now we were actually talking, she didn't seem like the type of person to rip the magic from someone else.

"It was long ago, and I was just stupid," she sighed. "Apparently, I have an unfortunate set of attributes. I can see and absorb magic very easily. On the flip side, I have a very weak ability to actually process the magic and turn it into my own. I also have a high magic capacity, so it's easy for me to absorb a lot of magic and hold onto it. That ended up being my curse as well as my salvation.

"As a new supernatural, I sampled all the magic around me. There is magic in just about everything, and most of it is free for the taking as long as you don't pull too much.

I quickly grew in power, and it seemed like a normal and natural thing to do. I pulled too much, though, and I started becoming affected by whatever I was pulling from. If a mage was angry, they'd emit angry magic into the air, and I'd automatically pull it. Then I'd be angry too. If someone was sad, I'd start crying. It wasn't just mages either. I once wandered into a group of geese and thought I could fly.

"Then it got really bad, and I ended up in the wild, running with a herd of deer. I was that way for a long time, just going with whatever was the most powerful thing near me, until one day I came back to myself. I'd grown enough in power to become more stable. Every little whiff of magic didn't move me like before. Somehow, my large capacity was grounding me, and I was able to slowly claw my way back to sanity.

"That's when I met Jeb. He was so sweet and kind. Even if I accidently absorbed some of his magic, it just made me sweet and kind too. He had very little power, but he'd learned to work with what he had. He showed me how to pull in my power and how to shield myself from the rest of the world." She stopped and stared off into space, lost in her memories. She looked so sad. Supernaturals had long lives, but it seemed like our beginnings were really rough. I had a feeling this story did not have a happy ending.

"What happened then?" I prompted.

"We lived happily together for many years," she whispered. "Those were the best years of my life. Then one day he was killed, harvested by another supernatural. Jeb was barely a snack for him. We fought, but I never had a chance. The super didn't want my black magic, and so I was allowed to live. I wandered for a while and finally came to

Louisville. Nobody wanted me, and nobody wanted to be around me, until I met John. He had just started the Louisville Mages, but it was a social club, not a school. He had this crazy idea that mages could just live together and not dominate each other. Because he didn't require the student bond, I was able to join, and I've been here ever since. We aren't a powerful school, and we've been through a lot of changes, but I try to keep John's original idea alive."

"Wow," I said. That was quite the story. She wasn't a villain. She was a survivor. I could identify with that. I was a survivor too.

"What happened to John?" Annabeth asked. She'd been leaning forward, caught up in the tale, and clearly she wanted to hear more.

"He was strong enough to keep the club going for a long time. We kept on attracting new mages, though, and eventually we were too tempting of a target. Henry came into town, dueled John, and took over. I think that was around 1901. John's former family had a shipping company. Once he recovered enough, he booked passage and sailed away. I've not seen him since.

"Henry got rid of the club idea and turned us into a school, although he was a terrible teacher. My aura kept me safe, as he never wanted to gain any magic from me. He also knew I'd never battle him, so instead he kept me on as the secretary, treasurer, and general assistant. I've discovered that teachers like glory and power, but they don't want to actually do the work.

"Henry got tired of being in one place. He always had a bit of wanderlust in him. One day, not long after the airport opened up, he took a few students, got on a plane, and just flew away. We had a rough few years after that. It seemed like we had a new master every few months, until Harb showed up. He was deadly, but fair. He was our first real combat teacher, and several of my friends finally learned how to fight.

"He lasted until Isobel showed up. Her power just rolled over him and that was that. She made us more like a sorority. She brought the club idea back, although she was always promoting an inner circle of mages. Those are the ones she actually taught. I just thought it was all a lot of fluff. She had passwords, secret handshakes, even tattoos. It all seemed a bit much. I had no idea it would go this far." Her Darkness shook her head in disgust. Actually, that didn't seem like a good label anymore. I guess Annabeth was thinking along the same lines.

"I don't think we have been properly introduced," Annabeth said kindly. "My name is Annabeth, and this is Jason."

She held out her hand to shake, but the mage just leaned away. "I don't touch anyone," she said a bit stiffly.

Oh, right! Of course. Annabeth hastily pulled her hand back and started to apologize.

"No harm intended. No harm done," the mage said. "My name is Josette."

Josette, that certainly wasn't a current sounding name. She had to be old—older than Sandy. She'd mentioned 1901, but she'd been a supernatural many years before that. She'd transitioned, gone crazy, got sane, lived in peace, and helped start the club. That was fifty years at least. So that would mean she'd been a supernatural for at least one hundred and seventy years. That was a long time.

"Can you tell me more about contamination and absorbing magic?" I asked. Maybe I'd learn something that would help Sandy. "I think this relates to why you are talking to us now. So the more we know, the more we can help." She narrowed her eyes at me.

"I can," she replied. "But first, I want to hear the story of how you got contaminated. If you guessed I'm here about Isobel's mages, then you will also understand why I'm leery of anyone with a polluted aura." She shifted back, looking defensive.

Annabeth and I looked at each other in shock. "I don't know what you mean," I said. "I'm not contaminated."

"Don't play with me, boy," Josette snapped. She let go of the cart and raised her hands, palms out, like she was going to blast us. I think it was instinctive, but it showed she was ready to fight or defend herself. We'd had a good talk up to this point, but this was a pivotal moment. She'd opened up a bit, but she wasn't sure she could trust me.

"I'm serious," I replied. "I am not contaminated, and I don't know why you would think that." Annabeth was nodding emphatically, backing me up.

"I can see auras too," she said. "You're hiding your power, both of you are, but I'm very sensitive to magic and its hues. I can see you have more than one color. Before we continue with this Parley and I give you my trust, I would know what you are hiding." She looked upset, defensive, and a bit angry.

I looked back at Annabeth, mystified. Then it hit me.

She was referring to our matrices. Before the matrix, my magic would shine out for everyone to see. When the final piece of the matrix had snapped into place, I'd stopped shining. The glow of magic was denser, and it stopped just outside my skin. I checked out Josette's magic again. Her power surface, even with all her years of practice, wasn't as tight and clean as ours were. She was forcing it to stay in place with her will, but sometimes it would ripple and flux. Ours was solid and didn't waver at all. No wonder she thought we were hiding something. I really didn't want to go into detail about our matrices, though. That was our ace in the hole. I wasn't about to tell anyone about them who wasn't one of my trusted friends.

"I'm not hiding my power," I said. "We learned a process at the House that helps us compact our magic. As part of that, our magic is stable and doesn't shine like before. As for my colors, I've always had two colors of magic: sapphire blue and emerald green. This isn't contamination. These are my normal, natural colors."

She looked me over, and it was a hard look. She wasn't calling me a liar yet, but clearly it wasn't adding up for her.

"I'll choose to believe you about the process you described, although I've never heard anything like that before. You both are young mages, and there is no way you could control your leakage as cleanly and consistently as you are both doing without some sort of help. How old are you anyway?"

"I've been a mage for about two months," I said, then I looked over at Annabeth. It was up to her if she wanted to share that info or not.

"About nine months for me," she said. She didn't elaborate more than that. How old we were supernaturally felt like personal information somehow. I wanted to build trust with Josette, but I didn't want to tell her my life story. I guess Annabeth felt the same.

"I would be very interested to hear how you learned to reduce your leakage so drastically," she said. Then she sighed. "I'm sure that will have to wait till a different time. We have much more serious things to discuss. Just know that this process the House has gifted you is very valuable. I think you both are so new you have no clue how important it is," she sighed again. "Just know that determining magic growth is simple. It's magic you absorb versus magic you expend. If you absorb more magic than you expel, then your power goes up. If you lose more power than you gain, then your power level goes down. Simple, right?"

We both nodded. This was good stuff! If I had to guess, Josette was lonely. Her black aura kept everyone away. Her sharp personality didn't help either. Now she had two people actually listening and learning from her. That had to feel good on some level.

"You can gain power in many different ways. You can absorb it from your environment. You can create more internally, although that doesn't become a real source until you are a few hundred years old. You can gain it from pearls and objects, and you can take it from other magical beings. Almost all of it will not be your color, though, so it will muddy your aura. That is a whole different discussion. We are talking about the value in your current process. You want to know the number one way mages lose power?"

We both nodded. I figured it would be spells. Spells take power, and mages love to use spells.

"The way you lose power the most is through leakage." She nodded at us wisely, like she was imparting a precious secret to us. "Most mages think it is spells, but I can see auras, and the leakage some people have is astonishing. They leak magic when they are emotional. They leak magic when they touch things. They leak magic just paying attention to something. I was aware of that when I was a young super, and that's what I plucked out of the air and absorbed.

"You two don't leak any magic at all. There isn't a trace of your magic on the cart handle or anything in the cart. No magic is traded when you look at each other. You haven't leaked any magic towards me. Since power growth is magic in minus magic out, you know what that means, right?"

"It means we will get powerful a lot faster than someone leaking magic," I said softly. This was a very good thing to know. Building the matrix was huge. I already knew it was powerful and very helpful. Now I had learned it was even more helpful than I'd thought.

"Exactly," Josette said. "And now, back to my original question. How did you get contaminated? And don't give me that crap that it's natural. I've been around a very long time, and I've seen many auras. There is always only one primary color. Anything outside of that is foreign magic and must be assimilated by the mage. Too much of another color cripples a mage. You cannot exist with two colors in balance. Even a freak like me uses a multitude of different colors to balance things out."

"Those are my colors," I said stubbornly. "I respect that you have been around for a long time. I respect that you have seen a lot of auras and sampled a lot of magic. I can only tell you these are my colors. They have always been my colors."

"That is not possible," she stated flatly.

"You think it isn't possible. I know myself, it is possible." I was feeling stubborn and angry. I felt like telling her I'd had magic ever since I'd been a little kid, and my magic had always been green and blue. When I pulled in neutral magic, it changed into my green and blue. If blue was a contamination, then neutral magic would only turn into green magic. I'd used blue magic in my matrix. It responded to me, and I could make blue spheres and move them around. It was mine just as much as the green was.

I thought about saying all that, but stopped. This was a lot of information to give away. I wanted to hear her knowledge, not spill my own secrets. Plus, Sandy had said she had never heard of anyone doing magic before their Waker Moment, so Josette might not believe me anyway.

"I'm not lying," I continued. "But I don't know how to convince you I'm telling the truth. Is there some sort of truth spell we can use?"

She nodded slowly.

"Yes, there is. But if you don't want to swear peace on your magic, then you won't like this. The only way to determine truth is to swear on your magic. You have to be very careful to limit what you are swearing, though. You don't want to be stuck telling the truth forever."

"Do you have a format for a truth swear?" I looked at Annabeth, and she just shrugged and patted my shoulder. She supported me, but doing the swear was up to me.

"I do," Josette replied. "It's best to create a simple effect if you are lying, and limit either the time or the number of sentences that the effect pertains to. For example, you could say 'I swear on my power that my face will turn green for one minute and my hair will catch on fire if the following statement is false.' That limits your exposure to just one sentence and the effects are very noticeable and dramatic. There are ways to cheat this, but I doubt you would know how to do it." She got her sharp look again.

"So, are you certain enough to swear?"

16

There Can Be Only One

"Just to be clear," I said, "I swear I am telling the truth that I am not contaminated, and when I prove that I am not, you will believe me and trust me moving forward. I understand you are leery of anyone with excessive pollution, but you will agree that I am not in that category anymore."

She thought for a moment, going over what I'd said.

"Yes. I agree. If you can swear on your magic so it convinces me you are telling the truth, then I will build trust with you. I will then tell you about contamination and how it works with supernaturals, and how it is causing our current problem."

Her phrasing was a bit old-fashioned, but the idea was there. I needed more information, and she had it. It was time to swear.

I took a deep breath and let it out. Suddenly, I was a bit nervous. Annabeth held my hand for support. I gave her a smile and a squeeze. I was alright. I could do this.

"I swear on my power that my face will turn green for one minute and my hair will catch on fire if the following statement is false."

I felt my magic wake up and take notice as I finished speaking. Something clicked inside as it prepared to judge what I was about to say. Swearing on my magic was no joke. I felt a little bit of sweat pool at the small of my back.

"To the best of my knowledge and understanding, both the emerald green magic and the sapphire blue magic are my natural colors, and neither one is a contamination."

Something pinged inside me, and my magic went back to normal. I tried to look confident, when all I really wanted to do was look in a mirror to see if my hair was on fire.

We all looked at each other nervously for a moment. I'm sure Josette was expecting a whoosh as my head went up in flames. Annabeth was trying to project confidence, just like me, but her grip on my hand told me how nervous she was too.

Finally, the moment passed. I wasn't on fire, and based on their expressions, my face hadn't turned green either. I gave a little sigh of relief. But Josette seemed to only become more agitated. She started to speak, then stopped. I felt a little sympathy for her. I knew exactly what it was like to have an impossibility come true.

"Well, that was unexpected," she finally said. "I don't want to believe it, but you clearly do. Plus the evidence suggests you are right." She paused again, gathering her thoughts.

"Here is what I know about contamination. I used to think all of this was true. What I'm about to say is a combination of what I've been told, what I've experienced, and what I've observed. It has stayed consistent, until today. Regardless, you can judge for yourself.

"Mages absorb magic all the time, and this magic can be all the colors of the rainbow. Once magic is pulled in, the mage's natural magic wraps around it and attempts to convert it to the mage's color. This can take days or weeks depending on the volume of magic that needs to be converted. The time also varies among mages. Some mages are very good at assimilating foreign magic. Some, like myself, are very bad at it. This absorption is a natural process. It starts to become real contamination when it's more than the mage can handle.

"A good rule of thumb is it takes three times as much natural magic to convert foreign magic. So if a mage is pulling from their environment normally, they will have about one percent of their magic be foreign. That means it takes another three percent of their natural magic to begin converting this foreign magic. Do you follow me so far?"

"Yes," I replied. "So based on what you said, if a mage fills twenty-five percent of their capacity with magic that isn't theirs, then it will take them three times that, or the remaining seventy-five percent of their magic, to convert it."

"You have the right idea," Josette continued, "but you are missing something. A mage lives on magic. So some of their power is spent just keeping them alive and functioning. For new mages, this can be as high as eighty percent. That means only twenty percent is left over for spells or handling foreign magic. As the mage gets older and more powerful, their capacity goes up, so their life force takes less of their total magic, and they will have more free mana left over. That means they can cast more spells, or assimilate more foreign magic."

"So if a new mage only had twenty percent free, then that means they could only handle a max of five percent different magic," I said thoughtfully. I was used to quickly calculating odds in poker, so I was following this discussion pretty easily.

"I'll take your word for it," Annabeth said. "I was never that great at doing math in my head. I think the question now is, what happens when a mage pulls in more than their limit?"

"That's when it becomes contaminated," Josette replied. "Mages use the word contamination all the time, but absorbing magic is natural and normal. It's only bad when a mage pulls too much. Contamination is bad because it starts to change the basic magic of the mage. The mage then finds themselves becoming influenced by the magic they pulled in. They lose a bit of themselves in the process."

"So that's what happened to you?" I asked. "That's why you went mad and thought you could fly and all that stuff?"

She nodded.

"There has to be another level beyond this, though. Your magic isn't rotten. Your aura is black, but it's healthy, and you have control over it." I hesitated. How much did I tell her about what I saw with Mustard? He might be one of her friends, and I'd killed him.

"You've seen Isobel, so I'm sure you're referring to her magic," Josette said. "I don't know how much you know, but she had an inner circle of mages, and they all had some of the same problems. The rot happens when a mage pulls in over a hundred percent of what they can handle. Because they are over capacity, the magic isn't supported, and it starts to decay.

"I've never been overcapacity myself, but from what I can tell, it just hangs around, like dead energy, until it's used in a spell. Once that happens, it's gone. The mage gets no long-term benefit from the extra magic. There is a long-term penalty, though. The dead magic leaks over into a mage's natural magic and starts to corrupt it. I've seen this happen with mages in Isobel's inner circle. They would start out with normal, healthy magic. Then they'd gain more foreign magic than they could handle. The rot sets in, and even when they use up the extra magic, their aura is still damaged.

"I think it's addictive too. The mages get a taste of more power, and they like it. They start craving even more. Isobel seemed to limit their access to this extra energy, but even so, some of the weaker mages would burn out. The rot got too powerful, and they went mad. I've seen this happen twice with Isobel having to put both of them down."

That was a perfect opening for talking about what was going on today, but I didn't want to go there yet. Josette was still feeling chatty and spilling good information.

"That brings up two questions for me," I said. "The first one is related to spell casting. You said that the mana a mage uses for spell casting comes from their pool of free mana. That's mana that is not being used to keep the mage alive, and it isn't being used to convert foreign mana. Did I get that right?"

Josette nodded, waiting for my real question.

"So what happens if a mage uses too much? What if they are in a battle and its life or death, so they keep casting spells. What happens then?"

"They start drawing on the magic that is keeping them alive. It doesn't mean they die, just that all their functions slow down. They feel sluggish and sleepy. Their wounds don't heal as well. If they keep going, their magic can get so low that they will fall into a coma."

This is what I wanted to get to. This is what happened to Sandy. She had been drained against her will, but she was in the same predicament.

"So if this happens, how do they recover?" I asked.

Annabeth kept a straight face, but she squeezed my hand slightly. She knew what I was after.

"I've seen this happen before and it just takes time," Josette shrugged. She looked restless, like this wasn't really what she wanted to talk about. But she clearly enjoyed having an audience and being the teacher, so she kept going.

"The first time it happened to a fellow mage, I thought she was dead. We actually buried her, put up a grave marker and everything. Then a few years later, she woke up and dug herself out. She was dirty, her clothes had rotted off of her, and she could barely walk or talk. She sort of looked like a zombie. We got her cleaned up, gave her some food and water, and within a month or so, she was back to normal.

"Many years later, it happened again. It was a different mage, of course, but this time I didn't bury him. Instead, I used some blankets to make a bed on the floor of an old shed that nobody used anymore. I got him as comfortable as I could and left him there. It took about two years for him to wake up and another year to get back to full power."

Well, that sucked. We didn't have two years for Sandy to wake up. And we didn't have another year after that for her to get back to full power.

"So what do you think happened to them?" I asked. "How did they get better?"

"I don't know for sure, but I'm guessing they still had a core of personal magic, and that gradually grew over time. All supernaturals generate some magic on their own, so their personal magic gradually grows back. Once their core was big enough, they could start to absorb and process ambient mana, and that would speed up their recovery as well. I know it's a long, slow process, and I hope it's something I never have to go through."

That was in line with what we had theorized. It wasn't what I wanted to hear, but it made sense.

"Talking about ambient magic brings us to my second question," I said. "What about neutral magic? I assume that it is easier to absorb than foreign magic?"

Josette looked at me like I was talking gibberish.

"What are you calling neutral magic?" she asked. She gave me a sharp look like I was stupid, or going to challenge what she knew again. "There is no neutral magic. All magic has a color, and all magic is foreign."

"I'm talking about white magic," I replied. "I don't know exactly what you would call that. I've been calling it neutral magic. It doesn't have a color, and it looks like little sparkles of light."

Josette shook her head.

"There is no pure white magic. I've seen magic for a very long time, and I haven't seen anything that is pure white. I've seen some magic that is close to it. For whatever reason, the magic's saturation level is very low so almost no color is visible, but magic like that just looks like a light gray."

Well, that was interesting. Either Josette couldn't see white magic, or I was just lucky enough to find some. Come to think of it, the first place I'd seen neutral magic was in the Circle Room at the House. Maybe the House was doing something to the magic to make it white? The other place I'd seen it was by the picnic bench in the park. I'd just assumed white magic was everywhere, but now I thought about it, I don't know I'd seen it anywhere else. My Grannies could spin magic in their vacuum cylinders and convert foreign magic to neutral magic, but she didn't need to know that.

"So, if there was pure white magic, what would that do for a mage?" I asked.

"First of all, there isn't any such thing as pure magic," she snapped, "so I can't tell you what it would do for a mage. I can tell you that the color saturation affects how long it takes for a mage to convert magic. So magic that is foreign and very saturated takes a long time to convert. Magic that is mostly gray can convert much quicker, but it's usually weaker in power." She gave me a sharp look. "If there was such a thing as pure white magic, I'd say that it would be both powerful and easy to absorb. Where have you run across this magic?"

"There is a room in the House that has white, sparkly magic in it," I said. I didn't want to tell her about the park or talk about my Grannies. Mentioning the Circle Room in vague terms was the best option. "I guess it must be something the House is doing."

"I guess." Josette didn't look satisfied. This was twice now I'd said something that didn't match her view of the magical world. Clearly, she was not used to that.

"Per our agreement, I've answered your questions," Josette continued. "Now let's talk about why I'm here. I can't spend much more time talking with you." She looked around, furtively.

Suddenly it clicked. I knew what to do for Sandy. I turned to Annabeth.

"Remind me to talk about Sandy on the way home." She nodded. I turned back to Josette.

"Do your Louisville Mages know you're here?"

"No," she said softly. "They have no idea I'm talking to you. Of course, there isn't much leadership left anymore, but there are some people that would be very upset if they knew I was here right now. I'm a peaceful mage, and I've survived because I don't take sides. If the situation weren't so critical…" She trailed off. Her hands shook. She grabbed the cart handle again to hide her anxiety.

"Know this. I'm loyal to the Louisville Mages, and I'm loyal to the ideas of its founding. It has been a difficult realization, but I'm not loyal to any one person in our school, no matter how powerful they are." She took a deep breath, letting it out.

"Let me start at the beginning. When Isobel arrived, she didn't come alone. She had two men with her, Karl and Marius. Their auras were rotten also, but to a lesser degree. They were also a lot less powerful. I didn't pay that much attention to them at first. I was focused on Isobel and how she was taking over the school.

"I got to know Marius first. He's handsome, charming, and loves the ladies. He doesn't seem to be driven by magic, although I think he has a big capacity like myself. Instead, he has an enormous sexual appetite. If you have two legs and a wet spot, he'll chat you up and see if he can charm his way into your pants. He's so damn good-looking it's hard to stay mad at him, though. He's mostly harmless, other than causing a lot of social drama."

Josette was smiling as she talked about him. I'm thinking that Marius didn't mind a little black aura and tried to get into her pants. I'm not sure if he succeeded or not, but Josette clearly liked the attempt.

"The other one, Karl, is anything but harmless." She paused, searching for the right words. "I think there is something wrong with him. It's as if he doesn't know how to react. He only laughs once he sees other people are laughing. He's almost never the center of attention. He just watches and joins in when it seems appropriate. I first thought he was socially awkward, but it's more than that. He's a weird combination of practical and emotionless. I know that doesn't sound like anything really bad, but together they can make him very ruthless.

"Both of those weak mages I told you about, the ones that went mad, he was the one to actually kill them. Isobel gave the order, but he was the executioner. I was at the wrong place at the wrong time, and I saw the first one. Karl strangled her. It took time, but he didn't seem to mind. He overwhelmed her magic, wrapped his hands around her throat, and held on. At first she fought, then she just twitched, and finally she lay still. He was calm the whole time. It was just a job to him, like changing the oil in his car.

"He saw me watching, and that didn't affect him at all either. He didn't appear surprised or guilty. He held her down for several more minutes to make sure she was really dead, watching me the whole time. When he was done, he got up, walked over to me, and mentioned that he needed me to buy something for him with school money. He was just checking things off his to-do list. I've been alive a long time, and that was the creepiest thing I've ever seen.

"I have kept away from him ever since then. He was never mean or threatening, but he scares me. He scares me badly." Josette was gripping her cart tightly. Even so, I still saw her hands shake.

"The three of them were all contaminated and rotten. And it got worse the longer they were here. Somehow, they could handle it. Isobel was driven, but she never went mad. I don't think she was actually that powerful with regular magic, but somehow she could hold and use far more foreign magic than should be possible. Karl tripled in available magic, but it didn't seem to affect him either. Marius' magic seemed to come and go, although I rarely saw him actually do anything with it. It was all strange and a mystery to me until Isobel left. Then we discovered something. Isobel was using a rune."

This is the part we already knew about from our fight in the park. I let her keep talking, though. Maybe Mustard hadn't told us everything.

"Somehow, the rune let the user steal magic and keep it, without going too crazy. It also allows a person to steal magic from someone else that had the rune. It turns out

Isobel had a pretty good con game going. She'd have a circle with her mages, and they would suck a poor creature dry. She let her mages take most of the magic, and they would get the boost of more power. They all loved her for that. It seemed like such a selfless act, giving them most of the power and keeping little for herself. She seemed like the perfect leader.

"What was actually happening, though, was she was gradually draining the free mana from the mages into herself. As I already mentioned, everyone leaks magic to some degree, so losing a little bit of magic wasn't something they would notice. Their magic would fall over time, and that would just increase their appetite for new power. It was a vicious cycle, playing right into her power scheme.

"I don't know the next part for sure, but I think it wasn't just good social manipulation that Isobel was doing. I think she was using her mages as filters for the foreign magic. Let me explain. When a creature dies violently, the magic released at death is saturated with their color. The creature is dead, so the magic is easy to absorb, but the saturation makes it hard to convert to natural magic. I'm thinking her inner circle of mages took the brunt of the damage by absorbing all the saturated magic. Once they had it for a while and had been processing it, the colors would become a lot more muddled. That's when she would pull it from them into herself. It wasn't a perfect system, but it would protect her from the worst of the damage."

"That is diabolical," Annabeth said. "She looked like the good guy, but she was totally using them."

It *was* diabolical. It was also kind of genius. I was scared of Isobel and glad she was gone, but in some ways, she was one smart cookie.

"I don't know that for sure," Josette cautioned. "I'm just extrapolating from what I know about magic and what we found out. It makes sense, though. What I do know is true is that Isobel had some sort of addition to her rune that kept the other runes in line. She could open and close the connection between herself and her mages. She also limited their ability to take magic from each other.

"Isobel concealed the rune in the membership tattoo she had the mages get as part of their initiation into the inner circle. Karl and Marius have the tattoo also, although it is a simpler design. I think even their tattoos have extra markings to hide the parts that are real. What really matters now is that the master rune is gone and the result has been pure chaos."

"What happened?" I asked. I was being all innocent, but I already knew. Josette was filling in a lot of the details, though. It was nice to hear the whole story.

"It started when a few of the mages were in our headquarters. They were lounging around, watching a movie, when one of them started playing with her magic. She said she felt a source of power, like when they were in one of their circles. She pulled some magic, and she said it felt easy. So she pulled some more. Then one of the other mages shrieked and pulled back. Suddenly, they were in a magic battle, and there could only be one winner. The second mage collapsed in a pile of dust. I was at the clubhouse, of course, and saw most of it. The winner was freaking out, but we finally managed to calm her down and found out what happened. The story spread fast, as most stories do, and we had our second battle that night. Those two didn't like each other, so their fight wasn't that unexpected.

"I had hoped that was the end of it. We'd had one accident and one grudge match. Now things would get back to normal. Except they didn't. The next morning, we had a four-way showdown. The sudden influx of magic was too much for the winner, and he went mad. He started attacking things at random, blowing up furniture and punching holes in the walls. It looked like he had gone rabid. His eyes were wild, and he was all hunched over and snarling. He even drooled on the carpet. Finally, he blasted a hole in an outside wall and left the clubhouse. Nobody was sure what to do until Karl showed up. He and Marius went after the mage. They returned an hour later, saying he had been taken care of.

"Karl spoke like he had put the mage down for our benefit, but I could see he and Marius now had a lot more power. They hadn't just killed him. They had fought him and sucked him dry. What was interesting was most of the power stayed with Marius. I know he didn't do any of the fighting, so I'm not sure how he got the power. What's also interesting is both of them seemed to act normally. They had both absorbed the power of four mages, and they didn't seem to be affected. That didn't seem right to me.

"We had two more fights before it really sank in what was happening, and then everyone scattered. The mages without a tattoo didn't want to get caught in the crossfire, so they went into hiding. The mages with tattoos realized they were in the fight of their lives. They had stolen power from many other sources, and now it was their turn. They could either hunt or be hunted."

"This sounds a lot like the movie 'Highlander'," I said. "These immortals fought and killed each other for hundreds of years, knowing there could only be one winner. The last person standing got some sort of ultimate prize, although nobody was sure what it was. They had this quote, 'There can be only one'."

"It also sounds like Fortnite Battle Royale," Annabeth chimed in. "They drop a bunch of people on an island, and they fight until there is only one person left standing."

"You play Fortnite?" I was shocked. Annabeth had never struck me as a gamer.

"I don't play, but I know what's going on," Annabeth said primly. Clearly, I was getting into 'you're old' territory, and I needed to tread lightly.

"I haven't seen either one of those," Josette interjected. This was her conversation, and she wasn't going to let us get sidetracked. "But it sounds something like that. Isobel's former inner circle is going to fight each other until someone holds all the magic. Whoever is left standing will be very powerful."

"How much magic do you think they will have?" Annabeth asked.

"I don't know for sure, but I'd guess they would have five or six times more than Isobel," Josette said.

Annabeth and I just looked at each other in shock. Holy crap! A super-powered Isobel was not what we needed. I think Josette thought we didn't believe her because she hastened to explain.

"I know that sounds like a lot, but here is my reasoning. There were seventy-two mages that got the tattoos. Individually, they were much weaker than Isobel, but together they had many times her power. This isn't a clean process, though. If a mage gets too much power too quickly, they go mad. From what I know, they never recover. Once that happens, they have a tendency to kill themselves from doing something stupid, or the magic gets away from them and they explode.

"The smart mages are picking their targets and only gaining as much as they think they can handle. Then they wait, get a handle on their new power, and then get more. Because there is so much potential for problems, I'm assuming over half of the power will be wasted. That's how I came up with my final analysis."

I didn't have a clue how powerful these inner circle mages were, or how many of them would be smart and survive for a while. So any guess Josette had would be much better than I could do. It still sounded like a whole lot of power, though.

"How do you know all this?" I asked. "You said all the mages scattered, and there has surely been a lot of fighting."

"The Louisville Mages know I'm neutral and my allegiance is to the school. So some of the winners have been contacting me. They want to take over the school when they 'win', and they want my help to do it. We will need a new teacher, so I've been open to talking with them. In exchange, they've told me a lot about how the fights were going.

"From what I can piece together, there are three main challengers. Oliver is tenacious, and he has been with the school for a long time. He's the furthest behind in power of the three, but he seems to be handling it the best. If I had my choice, I'd love for him to be the ultimate winner.

"Perry is smart, but he can be mean sometimes. I would not have thought he would be capable of handling this much contamination, but he's proven me wrong. Either way, he's second in power and has a good chance of winning.

"Karl and Marius are acting as a team. This shouldn't be possible, but somehow they are pulling it off. They are the clear winner in power. Despite also having the most contamination, they don't seem to be affected by it."

This was all good information, and we'd learned a lot. We'd established a measure of trust with Josette, and she would hopefully continue to be a good contact. She wanted something from us, though, and now it was time to find out what that was. I shot Annabeth a questioning look. She nodded.

"It sounds like you have everything in hand," I said. "The winner will work with you, and the school will continue. You are here talking to us for a reason, though. What do you need from us?"

"I need you to find a way to stop Karl," she said flatly. "He cannot win."

"Why?" I asked. "He sounds like he's a bit of a psychopath, but this whole supernatural world is a bit crazy. I get why you wouldn't like him, but why talk to us?"

Josette looked down. She was taking deep breaths and started shaking all over. It hit me that she was scared. Like deep down scared. What was going on? Finally, she looked up.

"Karl will turn us all into his slaves," she said. Her voice quivered, and Annabeth started to head over and give her a hug before she remembered there was a 'No Touch' policy.

"The scariest thing about Karl is he's practical. He isn't worried about what's right or wrong. He isn't worried about protecting the weak or defeating the strong. He doesn't care about looking like a hero or playing any of the normal social games we all use to get along. Instead, he has a goal, and he just goes for it in the most ruthless way possible.

"In this case, he wants to own and direct the Louisville Mages. He doesn't want to lead by example or let people grow in their own way. Instead, he wants the mages to do exactly as he says, when he says it. To make this happen, he's going to force us to swear complete loyalty and obedience to him. He's going to make us swear on our magic. If we don't swear, then we will die. If we do swear, then we will effectively be his slaves.

"With this power he can make us do anything. He can have us attack the House again, but this time it will be with everyone, fighting as hard as we can. We will fight until we die. We will have no choice. He can make us give him everything—our money, our houses, our bodies, our magic. There is nothing we can deny him.

"I would be very afraid of this with a normal human, but I'm even more scared of him. He isn't right. There is no humanity in him—no compassion, no empathy, no spark of grace. He will destroy the school and everything it stands for. He will destroy all my friends. He will destroy me."

She looked at us, with tears streaming down her face. She left herself open, showing in her vulnerability just how honest she was with us. She was seeing her world crash down around her again. She was a survivor that had found a home. Now that home was going to be destroyed. She was going to be destroyed. Just when her magic was starting to get better, her free will was going to be taken from her. She might technically be alive, but it wouldn't be her life anymore.

I knew some of what she was feeling. Isobel had said she was going to crush me and turn me into her slave. She was going to use me and torment me until she was bored with me. Then she would kill me. I knew what it was like to look into the future and see endless pain. I knew what it was like when failure was not an option.

"Why don't you run away?" I asked. "You could come back much later and see how it all turned out. If Karl wins, you could just stay away."

She shook her head.

"He has marked us. No matter how far I run, he can find me. It's the same with the tattoos. Nobody can truly hide. They can find each other. That's why their only option is to stay and fight."

"So telling us what is going on is your way of fighting," Annabeth stated. "You're hoping that we can defeat Karl for you."

Josette nodded. She wiped her tears away, attempting to pull herself together.

"I'm not a fighter. If I fight, I fall out of balance, and my magic will consume me again. All I have is information. And maybe a bit of advice."

"What advice do you have for us?" I asked curiously.

"I heard you had a very intense fight against Isobel and a few of her inner circle. My advice would be to think about ways to limit the power that Karl will get. If you wait until he defeats all the tattooed mages and takes their magic, then you will be too late. What you can do is take out the mages first, then he can't get their potential."

"That is actually a good suggestion," I said. "Is there any other advice?"

"I know he and Marius are a team. If you could catch him by surprise when he is not with Marius, that might be a decisive advantage. I know he has a lair, and it's somewhere near here. I don't know where it is exactly, but if I find out, I'll get a message to you.

"When your House battles him, it would be a good idea to make him use as much magic as possible. Most of the power he has is stolen, but every spell has to have a core of his personal magic in it. If you can get him to use enough of his personal magic, the power ratios will flip, and the contamination will eat him alive."

I knew all about that. When the power ratios flipped on Mustard, he'd exploded. I didn't want to imagine what kind of explosion Karl was going to make if that happened.

"One more thing," Josette said. "I'm telling you this for your own survival, not just mine, and not just for the Louisville School. He sees the House as a threat of the highest order. You took out Isobel, and he thinks it will only be a matter of time before you come after him. So he plans on coming after you first. The House won't have the option of swearing to him. He plans on killing everyone and burning the House to the ground. I know you stopped Isobel last time, but if he has more power and the full backing of all the mages, he might succeed next time."

With those dire words she backed her cart up, looked around carefully, and turned to go.

"I've spent too much time here. Someone may see me. I have to go. Remember what I said. And good luck." With that she hurried off.

Annabeth and I just stood there for a moment. I was feeling overwhelmed. My life was in danger again. The House and the lives of my friends were in danger again.

"Let's get out of here," Annabeth finally said. "We can talk about everything on the way home."

So that is what we did. We grabbed the last of our frozen goods, made it through the checkout, packed the bags in the car, and headed home.

17

Asylum

I thought we would talk the whole way home, but we didn't. It was a short trip, just a few blocks, but we were both quiet, processing what we'd heard. Annabeth parked the car, and we sat there for a moment, looking at the House and the back garden. It was so peaceful.

There were lots of different flowers with bees busy collecting pollen. There were a few sunflowers, one of which a squirrel had climbed and was hanging almost upside down plucking out the seeds. Some birds flew in, poked their heads into the grass for a minute, and then flew away again. This was a regular backyard, full of nature and life. And it would be under attack. Again.

Finally, Annabeth turned to me. "We need to unload the car, but first tell me what you figured out about Sandy. I don't want to wait until later in case you forget something."

I nodded. That was good thinking. I didn't want to forget anything either.

"Josette basically said you need to have a certain amount of your own natural magic to function like a normal person. I think we did the right thing at the beginning by helping her to absorb as much neutral magic as possible. Over time, she's been converting more and more of it to her natural color. I've been feeling frustrated because I feel like she's had enough magic to wake up, but that hasn't happened.

"I think the problem isn't the amount of magic she currently has. The problem is that not enough of it has been converted to her own color. By giving her more and more neutral magic, it's diluting her color and keeping her from waking up. What we need to do now is take the Octopuses away and let her natural magic conversion catch up. Then I think she will come out of her coma."

Annabeth thought about it for a sec. "Based on what Josette said, that would make sense. Let's give it a shot and see if it works. If not, we can always go back to what we were doing." She opened her car door. "Now it's time to get the food inside."

We unloaded her car, taking in the frozen stuff first. It seemed like we had bought a lot at the store, but by the time we had unloaded it into three different kitchens, it didn't seem as excessive. The cats, of course, wanted treats and fresh food right away. So we took the time to make them happy.

We were getting ready to bring in the last load, when I saw a woman running down the alleyway. She saw us at the same time, and picked up the pace.

"Hey!" she yelled. "Hey! Wait up!"

"Incoming," I said to Annabeth, pulling the shillelagh out of my pants. She dropped her bags and checked to make sure she was wearing her charm bracelet.

"She's got a rotten aura," I told her. "It's not the worst I've seen, but it's not the best either. She has more power than Mustard when we first fought him, but less than the second time."

"I'm ready," Annabeth said calmly. She looked ready too. She was no longer the nervous uncertain granny mage of before. Now her feet were solid on the ground, her jaw set, and her eyes clear and ready. Her charms were gripped in one hand, ready for a quick casting. She might be small, but she looked tough.

I was nervous, but a little excited to test out my new abilities. I wasn't as calm as Annabeth, but I was ready too. This wasn't my first battle, and I was much more prepared than before. Whoever this woman was, she was in for a beat down.

"I'm not here to hurt you," she panted. "Wait a minute."

She was running pretty fast, heading straight for us, when she smacked right into the House shield. I guess she couldn't sense it, because she rebounded from it like she'd hit a brick wall. It was painful to watch, but funny too.

I snickered. I don't know why watching people falling down is so funny to me. It just is. It was totally inappropriate, given the situation. But that just made it funnier.

She sat up, glaring at me with her hair all messed up, and I flat out laughed out loud. Annabeth shook her head like, 'You're one crazy boy sometimes.'

Neither one of us moved forward to help her up. She was outside the shield, and we were inside. That's just the way I liked it.

The fallen mage got to her feet and moved forward till she was touching the shield.

"Please let me in," she said. "I need to come in."

"You're one of Isobel's mages," Annabeth stated. "You attacked us."

"I'm sorry about that," she said. "I was just doing what I was told. I don't hate you guys or anything."

Oh, that was nice. I'm glad she didn't hate us. That made everything okay then. Not! I guess she read my look of sarcastic disbelief, because she flounced a bit and smacked her hand on the shield.

"Serious! I'm sorry. Really sorry. I didn't mean anything by it." She looked over her shoulder. "I need asylum. I'm requesting asylum. Please. Let me in." She smacked on the shield again.

"You have a rotten aura," Annabeth said. "I can hear it clearly from here. You have taken power that is not your own and was never meant to be yours."

"I didn't mean to," she said. "Please let me in. I think someone is chasing me."

"You didn't mean to?" Annabeth said in disbelief. "What did you mean to do then?"

"It was just plants and stuff," she wailed. "I didn't mean to do anything wrong." She looked over her shoulder again and then back at us.

"Look, I'd just show up and something was already in the center of the circle. We'd join hands and chant for a bit. Then Isobel would split up the magic. It wasn't a big deal. We all did it. It wasn't like it was me making it happen."

"So you put a plant in the middle and drained it of magic?" Annabeth asked.

The woman nodded impatiently.

I was intrigued. What kind of plant has magic?

"How about animals? Did you take magic from animals too?"

The woman nodded again, although more reluctantly this time.

"Did the animals and plants die?" Annabeth asked.

"I think they were already dead. I didn't kill them."

"How about people? Were the people dead already too?"

"Look, I didn't do anything wrong," the woman sounded defensive and scared. "We stood in a circle and moved magic. That's what everyone did. That's what we needed to do to move up in the school."

"So if everyone jumped off a bridge, would you jump off a bridge too?" Annabeth said sternly.

I turned to her in surprise.

"That is such a mom thing to say!" I said.

"Well, I'm a mom," she replied. "So I get to say mom things." She turned back to the mage.

"And you don't get to hide behind the excuse of 'Everyone was doing it'. You, of your own free will, chose to be part of something that destroyed the lives of magical creatures. Maybe you didn't actually suck the final piece of magic out of them, but you still participated in their destruction. You could have stopped. You could have left. There are other schools and other teachers in this world."

Annabeth sounded furious, and she was picking up steam.

"Instead, you chose to make yourself more powerful at the expense of someone else. It has ruined your magic, and now karma has come back to smack you in the face. Just as you took magic from others, someone is now trying to take magic from you."

The mage stepped back like Annabeth had slapped her.

"I didn't mean to." She started to tear up. "I really didn't. I'm sorry. I need help. That's why I'm here. Isn't that what you do? Isn't that what this whole place is?"

"We aren't a church," Annabeth stated. "You can't just step inside and be safe from the vampires. It doesn't work like that. Especially when you're a vampire yourself."

"This is where all the weird people go to be safe, right?" The mage was not giving up. "I can be weird too. It would just be for a little while. I don't have to stay long. I could even clean, or something."

Wow. She was willing to lower herself and hang out with the weird people for a while. She must be desperate. And she would even clean. Or something. How could we pass up an offer like that? I was letting Annabeth handle this, but I was dying to say something sarcastic.

"It's not up to us," Annabeth said. "It's up to the House. If you don't have a good soul, then you don't qualify to come inside. Maybe if you dumped all your magic and genuinely changed your life around, the House might let you in then. I still don't know."

Annabeth actually sounded sincere. Despite what this mage had done to our House and to innocent creatures, Annabeth still found a measure of kindness and support. She's a much better person than I am.

I was pretty sure this mage was selfish. She wanted power and she took it, regardless of who it killed. She was feeling bad now that it was her own life on the hook, but she still didn't really care for anyone else. I did feel empathetic for her need to survive. I wanted to survive too. I cared deeply about that. But, I wasn't taking power from someone who didn't want to give it. And I wanted power for more than myself. I wanted it so my friends and my House could stay safe too.

The mage looked over her shoulder and shrieked. There was a man coming down the alley. She started to run away, but there was another man coming up the alley from the other direction. She was caught in the middle with nowhere to run.

Both men slowed down as they reached us, and I got a good look at them for the first time. The first guy looked like a dock worker. He had a flat cap, faded blue shirt, and worn jeans. The jeans looked worn from actual work, not because they had been manufactured with a distressed look. He was big, well over six feet, and solid. He didn't have pretty muscles, but he looked strong. His face was weathered, and he looked a bit rough. His jaw was stubborn, and his eyes calculating. He didn't look cute, or like anyone I'd care to know.

The second guy was the exact opposite. He looked like a young Antonio Banderas with long, curly, Latin lover hair and perfect Latin lover skin and dark Latin lover eyes. Did I mention he looked like a Latin lover? He walked with his hips out, like he was stalking a maiden in a romance novel. His shirt was a deep purple and unbuttoned way more than it should be. His jeans were tight and showed off his strong legs. I had to admit, he looked hot.

If I hadn't seen Tyler, I'd have said that on a scale of one to ten, he was a ten. Now, though, I just felt like he was trying way too hard. Tyler looked a bajillion times better, and he did it effortlessly. Of course, I might be biased.

"Mage Cassandra," the dock worker said.

She hissed at him. "Karl." She took a firm stance, hands balled into fists. Since flight was no longer an option, she was prepared to fight.

"Marius." She briefly looked at the Latin lover, before centering on Karl again. Clearly, she thought he was the bigger threat.

So this was the pair Josette had warned us about. I checked out their auras. Karl's aura wasn't what I expected at all. I thought it would be big and powerful, like Isobel's had been. Instead, it was smaller than Cassandra's. It had a lot less rot than I expected too. Marius, on the other hand, was a dense stormcloud of energy. His magic was thick, much thicker than Isobel's had been, but just as rotten.

Karl was checking us out too. He gave me a long look before he switched to studying Annabeth. His face stayed neutral. It didn't betray any hint of how he felt about us, or what he saw of our powers. Then he looked at the House. He took his time, really taking it all in.

Cassandra started cussing him out, but he just ignored her. I looked over at Marius, realizing I was being evaluated in an entirely different way. He undressed me with his eyes and found me worthy. Sort of. I got a faint smile and look of promise. At a different time, under different circumstances, he might let me sleep with him. If I played my cards right.

Then he gave Annabeth the once over and the same look. This guy was a pro. It was just the right kind of 'Yes' that gave a person hope, with just the right amount of 'No' to make it a challenge. A younger me would have fallen for it. I admired his skill, but I'd seen my kitten do better.

Bermuda would sit on the cushions on John's lap, looking so cute, soft, and lovable, and he'd give me that look. It was part 'come over here and love me, big boy' and part 'I'm too damn good looking for my own good, so stay away'. He'd seal the deal with sleepy eyes and a big yawn. Of course, I'd go over and love on him, and he'd just purr away. He'd trained me well.

Marius was trying for that level of skill, but he just didn't have the kitten power to back it up. Annabeth gave him a stern look, then ignored him. Karl got all her focus. I guess granny power trumps Latin lover.

"What do we do?" I asked Annabeth quietly. We were still inside the House shield. This didn't have to be our fight. Although, if Karl was that good, he was going to take Cassandra down and get her power. I didn't want that.

"Let's wait," Annabeth replied softly. "We are the only House defenders. We can't get into an unwinnable fight. If Karl and Marius are as good as Josette says, then we will need Sandy and John to take them down.

"Something is up with the two of them. They don't sound like I think they should. Karl is too weak and Marius is too strong. Let's watch and listen, and see if we can figure out what their secret is."

Cassandra was still cussing, so I felt sure we weren't overheard. Karl was still checking out the House, so I guess she thought this was her chance to attack. She had one hand hanging down and slightly behind her, like she was using it to keep track of where the House shield was. The other hand was finger waving and getting all the attention. I didn't think anything about it until her back hand started to shine with power.

I zoomed in to see she had three small rocks resting in her fist. I couldn't see that clearly through her aura, but it looked like she was wrapping magic around them. It only took about twenty seconds, but soon the rocks were blazing with power. Just when I thought they couldn't possibly hold any more, she flicked her wrist and shot the rocks one after the other at Karl.

The rocks were fast, much faster than I'd seen a regular spell fly. The first rock smacked into his shield, because, of course, he had a shield. It hit with a lot of power. I could see his shield rippling with the impact. The second rock hit and overloaded the shield. The third rock hit Karl.

He'd started to dodge, but he wasn't anywhere near fast enough. The rock smacked into the side of his chest. It hit with a solid, meaty sound and spun him around. It wasn't a killing blow, but I'm sure it really hurt. Cassandra quickly stooped over, grabbed three more rocks, and started charging them.

I was shocked. She was fighting on a level I hadn't seen yet. Within a second, she had taken down his regular shield and struck the first blow. Maybe she didn't need our help after all. Either way, the battle was on.

Karl recovered quickly and started his own preparations. He cupped his left hand, and a basketball-sized sphere of power quickly formed. His right hand flexed, and soon he was gripping a baton made of pure magic. This was new. I'd never seen anyone make a weapon out of pure magic before. This fight was going to be intense. I was glad I wasn't a part of it. I could just stand behind the House shield to watch and learn.

When Karl was making his weapon, I saw a thick band of magic spring up between him and Marius. I tried to get a close look, but Karl had his weapon together quickly, and he dropped the link.

Cassandra shot a rock at Karl. I guess she was hoping for a quick hit, but it wasn't charged up as much, and it didn't fly as fast. Karl was ready this time. He shifted his ball of magic down, absorbing the stone. It wasn't like he blocked the magic and the stone still got through. He absorbed both of them. His ball of magic was a great defense.

Both of them paused for a moment. Karl looked like he was on the defensive. I think he was waiting for Cassandra to run out of ammo. She just used the pause to continue charging her stones. Once again, she super charged one of the stones and let it fly. This time she aimed at Karl's front foot. It was a good strategy. If she could limit his mobility, she could probably take him apart from a distance.

The spell stone was so fast I almost couldn't see it, but Karl was ready.

He used his ball of magic like it was a yoyo. He dropped it down in the path of the stone, while keeping a string of power connected to his hand. I thought the fully charged spell stone might punch through, but his ball of magic was too dense. It ate the spell stone just like the last time.

With a jerk, Karl pulled the ball of magic back to his hand, ready for the next attack. Once again, the battle paused. Cassandra seemed unwilling to use her last stone while Karl was so well prepared. On the other hand, Karl wasn't ready to charge in yet and risk making a mistake.

They sized each other up for a moment. Then Karl jerked toward her in a feint. It was a great move, using her nerves against her. And it worked. She was wound up so tight, she let her last stone fly. Karl stopped it with his magic yoyo, and then charged for real.

Cassandra dropped to the ground to grab more rocks, but Karl was on her like a dog on a bone. He charged and started hammering her with his baton. That would have been the end right there, except her shield charm absorbed the first few blows. She had enough time to throw her hands in the air and generate two thick round shields of magic. I've talked about shield spells before, but these looked like actual shields. When her amulet failed, she started blocking Karl with her shield hands.

This worked for the short term, but since both hands were busy blocking, she didn't have a free hand to grab stones. She tried to drop one shield, but Karl was just too fast. He was constantly varying the angle of his attack, looking for an opening.

I noticed something else too. Every time he hit her shield with his baton, there was a flash of magic, and both his baton and her shield looked a little less substantial. This was a battle of more than just force. It was a battle of magical attrition. Each hit was using up a bit of magic from both of them. Eventually, one of them would fail.

Cassandra was recharging whichever shield Karl wasn't hitting, and then trying to switch shield hands for defense. Karl was recharging another way. The band of magic sprang up between him and Marius again, and this time it stuck around. I zoomed in for a closer look.

Karl was pulling magic from Marius and using it for his battle. The band was thick, and the amount of magic he was pulling was staggering. When I'd had my magical assessment, Sandy had tested me for magic flow. She said I was slightly below average on how fast I could move magic around. Karl did not have that problem. In fact, I'd say he had an affinity for magic flow. He was pulling magic like water blasting through a fire hose.

Despite the amount of power leaving him, Marius didn't look concerned. His aura looked untouched. He seemed just as powerful as when he started.

The power band started from Marius' chest and went to Karl's upper right shoulder. With all the magic flowing and the aura's interference, I couldn't get a closer look. But based on the way their skin was glowing, I'd guess they had matching runes tattooed on them that were creating the connection.

The action was furious, but they were both evenly matched. For the moment. Cassandra was doing a great job of blocking Karl, but she couldn't go on the offensive this way. It also looked like her magic output couldn't keep up with Karl's pounding. He was slowly wearing her shields down with his baton. She had to do something, or she was going to lose.

Cassandra must have thought the same thing because she yelled and launched herself at Karl, shield hands extended. Karl didn't seem surprised and jumped back out of range. Now she had some space, she dove toward the gravel. She rolled and came back to her feet, stones in her hands and a triumphant look upon her face.

It was a great move and would have extended the fight, except Karl had a great move of his own. Instead of using his yoyo ball of energy for defense, he used it for attack. He shot the ball at her, and just as she got to her feet, it hit her solidly in her chest. She didn't have any defense there, and the magical construct hit her hard. The impact lifted her off her feet and slammed her against the House shield. She bounced off, falling face first onto the ground.

Karl jerked his hand, and the ball of energy flew back toward him. It smacked into his hand as he sprinted towards her. Once again, he clubbed her, except this time she didn't have any defense. He laid into her like he was whipping a dog. The end was short, brutal, and shocking. It was right outside the House shield, so they were right in front of us.

Annabeth grabbed my hand and held on. The attack was so savage I felt it in my gut. The supernatural world was merciless. I'd been on the receiving end of a smackdown before, but the shock of broken bones and damaged flesh had made the whole thing seem like a bad dream. This time, though, it wasn't happening to me, and the emotional impact hit me with full force. By the time he stopped, I was shaking.

"Oh, Cassandra," he said. "You could have made this so much easier for me." His voice was flat and factual. It was like he was telling her he was going out to get pizza. Now I knew what Josette had been talking about. He was scary as hell.

Karl straightened up and stepped back. He looked at us, and I felt frozen in place. If the House shield hadn't been there, he'd have taken us apart. We couldn't fight on his level.

He used his foot to flip Cassandra over so she was facing the sky. Then a patch of skin on his chest flared to life, and a ribbon of power reached out to her chest. An answering patch of skin on her chest lit up, and the connection was made. He flexed and started pulling the magic out of her.

It wasn't a fast transfer like it had been between him and Marius. This was slower and more deliberate. He pulled for almost a full minute before Cassandra recovered enough to resist him. I don't think she was even really conscious, but the flow stopped and even reversed back to her again.

Karl's left shoulder came to life, and a new connection was made. Then the inside of both of his thighs flared up, and two more connections were added. Her resistance collapsed as he started sucking magic from her again. He also opened up the link between him and Marius, but this time the magic was flowing out of him.

So that was Karl's secret. He had multiple runes, five in all, so he was winning the battle of wills between himself and other mages with the sucker rune. Then he wasn't keeping the magic, so it wasn't making him crazy. Instead, he was treating Marius like his battery, and somehow Marius could handle it.

It was a great plan, and obviously it worked. Having seen it in action, I was pretty sure he and Marius would be the only people left standing from Isobel's inner circle. Josette was hoping for a win from Oliver or Perry, but unless they had multiple tattoos too, they wouldn't stand a chance.

Time passed, and Karl kept pulling the magic at a deliberate pace. I'm sure he could have inhaled it a lot faster. Why was he going so slowly?

He didn't look concerned and neither did Marius. If anything, they acted like this was normal. Marius wandered over to the alley wall opposite us and leaned up against it. He pulled out a pack of gum, selected a stick, unwrapped it with care, and popped it in his mouth. Then he put the pack and the empty wrapper back into his pocket. At least he hadn't littered.

What kind of thought was that? At least he doesn't litter? I realized I'd stopped shaking, even though I still felt horrible and confused. Should we go inside? Should we stay? It felt so wrong to just stand there and watch the life slowly getting sucked out of her. On the other hand, it felt so wrong to leave her lying there.

I looked at Annabeth. She seemed calmer than I was. She'd lived a lot longer than me, and I'm sure she had seen some terrible things already. She probably had a better perspective on how rough life can be. She stood strong, giving my hand a squeeze. I wanted a big hug, but that would have been really out of place.

We waited a bit more. I started feeling restless, so I decided to tell Annabeth what I'd seen. I leaned down, cupped her ear with my hand, and whispered everything I was seeing. I was hoping she would have a clue of what to do. Or if there was anything that could be done. I wanted to keep it quiet, though. I didn't want them to overhear how much I'd seen about what was going on. I'd started to realize how rare it is for people to see magic like I could, so they probably thought their secrets were still safe.

When I finished, Annabeth just nodded, then spoke up.

"Karl." He gave her a flat look. "That is your name, right? Karl?"

He didn't nod or acknowledge her in any way.

"How long is this going to take?" she inquired.

He said nothing, just watched us.

"I have better things to do with my time than watch you stand there." Annabeth managed to sound haughty. She put her nose in the air, like she was smelling something bad, and turned to march into the House.

"You should stay," Karl said. "The next part is the best. It takes a while to get there safely, but then it happens all at once."

Annabeth turned back to him.

"Why?" she said scornfully. "Why does it take you so long? I would think a man of your power could just pull and be done with it."

Annabeth was putting on quite the act. She looked like an older matron scolding a young boy. Karl was a grown man. He wasn't going to let that stand.

"You think you're smart, don't you," Karl said in an even tone. He just watched us. Annabeth hadn't baited him at all. He was cold. Unnaturally calm. Scary calm. I felt chills.

"Actually, I'll tell you. It won't help you at all as you don't have the mark. At least, for now." A ghost of a smile touched his lips. "I'll tell you, as it will give you something to look forward to. Something to anticipate. Something to dream about at night.

"The reason I pull life so slowly is I want the soul to stay with the body as much as possible. The more life I take, the slower I have to pull. The soul wants to follow the magic, so slow and steady wins the race.

"In your case, that means the agony of death will be that much more real. You will feel your magic slipping away, piece by piece, while your soul screams. Have you heard a soul scream before?"

I shook my head, entranced. I didn't want to listen to him, but I couldn't look away. It was like he was the snake and I was the mouse. I was too scared to move.

"You would be hearing a soul scream now if she wasn't already unconscious. I didn't mean to hit her that hard. But shit happens." He looked over at Marius and jerked his head.

"He's right," Marius chimed in, still chewing his gum. "Soul screams are awful things. Used to keep me up at night, it did. You get used to them though." He shrugged and looked unconcerned.

"Let me rephrase that. YOU won't get used to them. You'll be the one screaming after all. It's never good to be in that spot. I wouldn't know firsthand, of course, but it does seem like losing your divine spark is quite painful." He nodded back towards Karl.

Well, that was an interesting tidbit of information, even if it was delivered in a chilling fashion. Taking magic slowly decreased the contamination.

"What makes you think I would ever get your mark?" Annabeth was still playing the haughty matron.

"You won't have much choice," Karl said flatly. "I'm going to come back to this little place you call home, and I'm going to huff and puff and blow it down." He smiled like he had made a big joke. I think I preferred him when he was stone-faced.

"Then I'm going to take you and break your arms and your legs. That will give you a nice warm up for what is to come in addition to making sure you don't run away. Then I'm going to take you one at a time, put the rune on you, and pull the life right out of you. It's going to be delicious. And I'm going to feast for days." His smile had changed to a leer. His eyes were unfocused. He was living the fantasy in his head right now.

"You two won't last that long, of course. I'll try to go even slower, but you both don't have much to begin with. What I want is that rock man. He's the one that will truly suffer."

"Why?" Annabeth demanded. "What have we ever done to you?"

"Why?" He focused back on Annabeth, and for the first time, I started to see real emotion. "Why?" He started to roar. "You stupid bitch. You dare to ask why? Because you killed her! Your tiny, little, pathetic crew dared to touch her.

You are rats. Sewer rats. And she was everything. You were not worthy to bow before her.

"She found me. She bathed me and sat me at her right hand. She taught me. She loved me!" He was screaming and walking towards us. "I drank her nectar, and she gave me life. You know nothing! You are nothing! And you will suffer!"

He ran into the House shield and started beating on it. He wasn't using power; it was just raw animal emotion. His eyes were crazy big, and he foamed at the mouth. Actual foam and spit.

That was some crazy, religious sounding stuff he was spewing out. It sounded like Isobel was his goddess and his lover, and he was very upset she was gone. He blamed us, with good reason.

I was pretty sure we were never going to be friends, and trying to talk out our differences was a lost cause. Suddenly, all the crazy switched off. He wiped his mouth, adjusted his shirt, and walked back to Cassandra. This guy was psychotic. Like truly unstable.

He stood with his back to us the rest of the time. Even in the middle of his rant, he'd never lost control of his link with Cassandra. And he'd never lost control over his careful, constant flow. He was deliberate, cold-blooded. And he was coming after us.

It took at least ten more minutes before it happened, and then it happened quickly. Cassandra looked dry, like the water was leached out of her. Her hair turned brittle and fell apart. Her skin pulled tight over her bones before it cracked and peeled away. Her insides turned to dust, and all that was left was her skeleton. That lasted a minute longer before it bleached white, and the bones started cracking open. They fell to dust with only her teeth left. Then they were gone too.

All that remained of the mage was a dusty patch in the alley. Without looking at us, Karl just walked off. Marius gave us a cheerful thumbs-up and hurried after.

The sun was still shining. A bird was singing again somewhere. I just felt worn out and cold.

"Let's get inside," Annabeth said. We gathered up the last of the bags and went into the House.

18

The Secret to Power

It felt a bit unreal to do something as mundane as finish putting away groceries after what we had seen, but that is what we did. Afterwards, we regrouped in Sandy's bedroom and discussed what had happened. Annabeth and I didn't really come to any new conclusions, but it helped to fix in my mind what I'd seen. The fight had given us a lot of new information, and I didn't want to forget anything.

I was feeling unsettled and restless. I was safe, but I felt like I should be reacting somehow. Watching a life and death fight was almost as traumatic as being in it, or at least it felt that way to me. My body felt tight, and I could feel myself breathing in short, shallow breaths. My mind felt clear, but I was feeling the effects on a physical level.

Annabeth said she was coming down from the fight too and just wanted time on her own to hum it out. Her words. She hummed little tunes when she was happy, but right now she needed to hum a darker theme and let all the anxiety out.

I needed to do something physical, so I decided to go and punch it out. First, though, I needed to change up Sandy's treatment plan. Octa and her Tangle were collecting magic from the Granny Godmothers and the Circle Room and giving it to Sandy to absorb. I didn't want to take the process completely apart, as I wasn't sure my solution for Sandy was the right one. I just needed to give Sandy a break from any new neutral magic for a while and allow her to catch up on converting what she had into her own magic.

The Granny Godmothers were still cleaning the park and that magic needed to go somewhere, so I decided to send it to the House to fix up my apartment. I still needed some improvements to my place, and so far the only upgrades had been Eggy's stand and the new window. To be fair, I had been too busy healing and training to really work on it. Survival takes precedence over decor any day.

Octa and the Head Granny liked the idea, so we set up a new routine. We stopped taking magic from the Circle Room. It didn't make sense to take magic from a room in the House to put it into another room. The House needed more magic to make changes, not the same magic.

The Grannies started flying up to my apartment instead of going to Sandy's bedroom, and then Octa took it from there. Her Tangle took the magic from the Grannies, and then stuck to the ceiling and walls of my apartment until the House absorbed it. It wasn't personal magic, like

Annabeth gave with her humming, but hopefully the House would still be able to use it.

I watched the process for a few minutes. It didn't take long before my ceiling was covered in purple Octopuses, and they started settling on the walls. I told Octa not to go too far down the walls or Bermuda might decide they were fun to play with. Bermuda had settled down a lot from when he'd chased his first Octopus, but he still popped one every now and then. Octa batted her eyes at me, assuring me she had everything in hand. I grabbed Bermuda and my new backpack and was practically shooed out of the apartment by my little creations.

Now that everything was in good hands, or tentacles, I went down to the basement and through the portal. Once again, it hit me just how beautiful the beach was. Being in nature felt calm and peaceful compared to the violence I'd just seen. I put Bermuda on the sand so he could start out on his own adventure. Then I slipped on the empty backpack and started jogging down the beach.

It felt good to stretch my legs and get the blood flowing. The tension started to leave my body as I settled into the rhythm of the run. I guess I settled into my run a little too quickly, as Bermuda started yowling for me to come back and pick him up.

I introduced him to the backpack. At first, he didn't seem too sure about it. He liked the straps (they were fun to play with), but did he really want to get inside?

Maybe?

Maybe not?

He changed his mind at least ten times before I gave up. I scooped him up and plopped him in the backpack, then put it on as quickly as possible. He hadn't jumped out yet, so I started running. It took a bit, but he finally settled into it, ultimately deciding it wasn't too bad after all. I think he liked the extra height as his head was moving around a lot, taking in the sights. With my magic sight I could see his little nose was flaring too, so it looked like he was getting his smells on. He chirped at me a few times, and I slowed down to rub his head over my shoulder. Finally, he settled down in the backpack with one paw over the edge and a happy look on his face.

Yep, this was acceptable.

It worked better for me too. His weight was on my back in the center, which was much easier to manage. Also, I now had both arms free and could settle into a nice rhythm. I practically flew up the beach, and I marveled at just how good I felt. This upgraded body was amazing. I was running faster than ever before with a lot less effort.

I arrived at the gym, changed into workout clothes, and did some air punches to warm up. I called up my stats to see where I was at.

Low Novice Jason Punch Stats

Level = 2.6

Punches = 2896

Notes: Whatever you have seen, whatever you are feeling, bring it to the mat. Burn it for fuel. Convert anger, worry, and fear to useful power. This is your space. Own it.

I called up Sparkles and got to it. It felt good to pound away at his sandy chest and lose myself in the flow. I hadn't planned on spending a long time here, as I'd already had my main workout for the day. This was just something to help me blow off steam.

Before I knew it, the sun was setting, and I'd spent almost four hours working out. I'd been afraid that the flow wouldn't come back as easily, or that I'd have to relearn the techniques again. Instead, I settled into punching like it was an old glove.

I felt tired, but it was a good kind of tired. My body felt like it had gotten a workout, but I wasn't sore in a way that said there were any injuries. I'd physically processed all the adrenaline in my system from watching Cassandra and Karl fight, and I felt much steadier. I gained several levels because Sparkles had given me lots of stars, but I hadn't stopped. Finally, I let Sparkles fade away as I called up my stats to see how I'd done.

Low Novice Jason Punch Stats
Level = 4.2
Punches = 5910
Notes: Go. Rest. Do something else. Give your muscles and mind time to refresh and lock in all they have learned. You have done well today.

OMG! I'd jumped another 1.6 levels! No wonder Sparkles had been giving me lots of stars. Equally as good was my number of punches. In one day, I'd done over half the number of punches for my goal. That meant I could very well hit ten thousand punches tomorrow! Wow!

Not having to stop and heal all the time was making a huge difference. I sent happy thoughts out to Tea and his Grove. I'd felt them moving around, keeping me in top shape. I did a quick body scan. There were some small, scattered patches of moss, but it was nothing like before. Thank goodness I wasn't going to have to go through another spirit quest delirium.

I changed back to regular clothes and found Bermuda waiting for me to head back to the House. And by waiting, I mean napping like a boss. He was passed out on the huge couch, all four feet in the air and his head stuffed between the pillows. I guess the light was a little too bright for his sensitive eyes. I sat on the couch and lightly rubbed his belly until he woke up. He gave me the sleepy eye, so I scooped him up like a baby and portaled back to the House.

I decided to check on Sandy and Annabeth to see how they were doing. They were both in Sandy's bedroom. It looked like Annabeth had fallen asleep in her temporary bed while keeping an eye on Sandy and doing some reading. I took the book out of her limp hand, putting it on the floor for safekeeping. Then I covered her up and tucked her in. Even asleep, she looked peaceful and happy.

In the middle of all this peacefulness, Bermuda decided he was now awake and ready to play. So I made a Feather Dot for him to chase and sent them both out in the hall. Even through the closed door, I could hear the sounds of frantic dashing. Trusting that Feather Dot would wear out my kitten for me, I turned my attention to Sandy.

I'd previously focused on the quantity of magic she'd absorbed, but this time I was all about the saturation. The House had maintained all the candles in the room. Hopefully, all that flame and orange-yellow light was helping her to convert the neutral magic.

The hue of Sandy's color was right on. It was as orange as orange could get. It was like the beautiful color near the base of a candle flame. Or maybe like a light pumpkin color. The saturation wasn't there, though. It looked too white, like neutral magic.

I took a mental snapshot of how it looked. Hopefully, tomorrow it would be better. I wished there was some way to measure all this. Surely this supernatural world had some way to accurately measure magic, its color and its saturation. I needed one of those medical scanners like they have on Star Trek. I could wave it over Sandy, and it would tell me all about her magic, and what she needed to recover.

I sighed. That was just wishful thinking. Maybe one day I'd find something like it or know enough about magic to make my own. In the meantime, I was tired. I still had a cot down here from when I was keeping an eye on all three of them, and it looked very inviting. I decided to nap for just a minute. I closed my eyes, and when I opened them again, it was morning.

I yawned and started to stretch. That's when I realized my cot was very crowded. I had all the cats with me. They had the whole rest of this huge bedroom to sleep in, but Bermuda, Snowy, and Biscuit had decided that my cot was the place to be. Since I couldn't do a full stretch, I flexed in place, feeling the life flow back into me.

"Good morning, sleepy head," Annabeth said cheerfully.

She was sitting on her bed, munching on a bowl of raisin bran with her book beside her. I guessed she'd been using the quiet morning to catch up on her reading.

"Good morning, Miss Sunshine," I replied happily.

Annabeth grinned at me. She liked her nickname.

"I've been thinking about a plan for the next few days," she said. "Are you awake enough to talk?"

"Sure," I replied. "I'll do some loving and listening." I had two hands, so I started rubbing Bermuda and Biscuit.

Before long, the air was filled with the sound of happy purrs. Snowy gave me 'The Look', then grudgingly forced her way into the cuddle puddle. I made sure Sandy's babies got plenty of love. I knew they were missing their mama.

"Sandy has been a lot more restless recently," Annabeth continued. "I think she is going to wake up soon, and one of us needs to be here when that happens. I know we also need to keep training, so I think we should just trade off. One person stays here, while the other person heads out and does whatever they need to do."

"That sounds good to me," I replied. "How about switching off every eight hours or so? That's a big enough block of time to either sleep, have a good workout, or just get stuff done."

"I like it," Annabeth said. She seemed awake and restless. "If you want, I can take the first watch."

"Nope," I shook my head. "You go first. You're more awake, and you already let me work out last night. I still need breakfast, and I haven't worked on my magic in a good while."

Annabeth must have been ready to get up and move, as she didn't argue too much and quickly left. I had breakfast and then worked on trading energy with Penny. She felt like she was gradually waking up too.

The schedule we'd set up worked out well, and the next two days passed swiftly. Sandy got more restless, and her magic became more saturated. We were on the right track for recovery. Annabeth finished up her second set of ten thousand punches and started on the third level of training: movement and dodging.

She said it was very different and not what she expected at all. She tried to explain it, but it didn't make much sense. I'd just have to wait until I hit that stage and found out for myself. Whatever secret she had learned on punching made a big difference, though. After the first set of ten thousand, she'd been at level 5.6 and feeling like she was maxed out. Now she was at 9.4 and feeling like there was still room for improvement.

I wanted to feel what that was like, so I found an old phone book and held it up to my chest for her to punch. It was pretty thick, so I wasn't sure I'd feel that much. Boy, was I wrong. She punched hard, and the force shook me. It didn't knock me over, but I wouldn't have wanted to take too many of them in a real fight. They would hurt!

I hit my first goal of ten thousand punches at the end of the next gym session. It was too late to learn 'The Secret', so it would have to wait until next time. I switched out with Annabeth and left her and Tyler training together. I got back to Sandy's bedroom feeling restless. Switching off watching Sandy was great, but I was missing my snuggle time with Tyler. I compensated by trading a huge amount of energy with Penny. I pulled out her neutral magic and gave her back my natural magic. At the end of our time together, I could feel her starting to wake up. One more session might just do it.

I switched out with Annabeth again, and now it was just Tyler and I on the beach. I was excited to learn 'The Secret', but I really just wanted to spend time with him.

"What's the matter?" Tyler asked. I guess I must have looked a bit down.

"I miss you," I said.

So he pulled me into a warm hug.

"I miss snuggling with you. I miss our time together." I kissed him lightly.

"I didn't think about this at the time, but I'm sleeping on that cot now." He cocked an eyebrow at me, not following where I was going yet. "I don't think there is enough room for both of us, and if there was, I don't think we could sleep naked together. John and Sandy are there, and Annabeth might show up at any time."

"It's just until Sandy wakes up," he said soothingly. "You said she is going to wake up soon." He gave me a kiss. "Until then, we'll have to be like forbidden lovers." He kissed me again. "Presenting a modest front to the rest of the world." He pulled me in close. "But finding stolen moments for our hot passion." He said it in a playful, sexy tone, and I laughed.

The look in his eyes, though, was firing me up. When he kissed me again, it was all passion, and our desire exploded. I guess the magic we'd given each other still hadn't been assimilated yet. I could feel him, and I could feel him feeling me.

We made it inside our beach locker room, but we didn't make it to the couch. I didn't want sand in bad places, so the floor of the locker room was good enough. Clothes flew off, and soon I had all the Tyler I wanted.

We did it on the floor, then on the couch (much more comfortable). We had some snuggle time, and then did it again in the shower trying to get clean. The problem was the feedback loop. It took us from gentle, romantic touches to full-on explosive hunger for each other in seconds. He couldn't resist me, and I sure couldn't resist him. Add in some incubus magic, and we spent way too much time in heaven when we should have been training. Heaven was nice, though. Very nice.

I finally had to kick him out of the bathroom so I could get cleaned up and get ready. When I got back onto the beach a few minutes later, he was all business. Well, he wasn't *all* business. He saw how happy I was and got a very satisfied smirk on his face. I let him have it. He'd more than earned it.

I'd lost an hour of training time, but it was worth it. I felt whole and happy, and I was now in a good space to learn 'The Secret'.

"You've reached your ten thousand goal," Tyler said in a formal tone. "Show me a punch."

I got into my Pigeon Stance and threw an air punch.

"How does it feel?" Tyler asked.

"It feels good," I replied. "It feels solid. Natural. It is certainly way better than when I started."

"What is your current level?" Tyler asked.

"I'm at level 5.9."

"That's really good. I've only seen students get that high when their first punches are terrible. But you had punched before, so your first ones were not awful. Did Annabeth tell you how the levels were calculated?"

I nodded. "Sort of. She didn't get the math, but she did say it is a measure of how much better you are from when you started."

"That's basically it," Tyler said. "Here's the math side if you are interested. The House looks at your first punching attempt, and it makes a judgment on how much force you would exert over a hundred punches. Over time, it recalculates how much force you could generate with a hundred punches and compares that to your original number. Every whole number you add to your level means you are doing a hundred percent more power than you started out with."

"I think I got that," I said slowly. "Can you give me actual numbers as an example?"

"Sure. Let's say a new student can punch for thirty pounds of force. Chances are, they can only do a few punches against hard sand at that level. It isn't long before their power falls off. They usually stop punching well before they reach a hundred, so there are a bunch of punches that count as zero. Let's say their total amount of force for their first try would be something like five hundred pounds.

"After they have trained for a while, they can hit harder and actually hit for all one hundred punches. So they may now have a total force of two thousand pounds. Two thousand divided by five hundred gives you a level of four. Make sense?"

I nodded. That was a nifty way of comparing power. It factored in endurance as well as raw hitting force. Now I knew how it worked, I was also surprised my level was so high. I hadn't thought my first attempt was that bad. Was I really hitting that much harder?

Of course, now I was punching with my fully healed body. I'd lost three days of practice, but in exchange I had more endurance, more speed, and more power. Even my scar from getting run through with a sword was gone.

"Now you have good form, there is one last technique to teach you." He grinned at me, and I smiled back in anticipation. "That technique is the art of Relax and Tense On Contact."

Huh? The way he said that, you could actually hear the capitals in the sentence. This was good secret stuff. The answer to power itself. This was how he'd demolished Sparkles in one punch.

But I had no idea what he was talking about.

"I'm going to break it down for you. But before I do, I want to talk about the power that comes from this. You'll learn it first with punching, but I've found it can be applied to almost everything. It will feel strange at first, but you'll find the power and speed of your punches will skyrocket. You'll also use this in blocking attacks, dodging, and even absorbing blows. I've even used it with non-martial arts activities like running and chopping vegetables. I'm not a mage, but I'm curious to see if it has applications with spells."

He paused and looked at me to see if I was taking this seriously. I still had no idea what it was, but I was eager to learn.

"The idea of Relax and Tense On Contact is very simple. You get your speed from relaxing through the motion. Then, you take all that speed and turn it into explosive power when you reach your target. Simple, right?"

I nodded. The idea was simple. At least, the way he was saying it was simple. I'm sure it was much harder to execute.

"Let's start with speed. Call up your training dummy."

I called up Sparkles. He formed out of the sand beside us.

"Sparkles, I need you to tell us how fast Jason is punching."

Sparkles just nodded.

"Go ahead." Tyler looked back at me.

I threw a punch in the air and then looked at Sparkles. The numbers 29.4 formed in the sand on his chest.

"Good, that gives us a base to work with. Now this time, I want you to punch hard. As hard as you can with as much force as you can. Imagine there is a wall of ice, and you have to break through."

That was a nice visual. I could work with that. I set myself up and punched hard.

Sparkles showed 20.9. That was almost a third slower.

"Again," Tyler demanded.

I let it fly.

19.8

Damn. That was really slow compared to what I'd started with.

"Sparkles, give us an average after a hundred punches."

Sparkles nodded.

Tyler turned to me. "Now I want you to get both power and speed. Hit as hard as you can as fast as you can."

I set up again and started letting the punches fly.

"Harder!" Tyler barked.

That's what he said, Dearie. I heard Anna Lykit's voice in my head, which almost caused me to lose my concentration. Focus!

I turned up the power even more.

"Come on! Hit it!" Tyler egged me on.

I strained for every ounce of power I had. I gave it my all. And then it was done.

I looked at Sparkles. 22.1.

"Okay. Shake it out," Tyler said.

I took a deep breath and waved my arms around. I could feel fresh oxygen pumping into my limbs.

"Throw a couple of regular punches to reset yourself."

It took more than a few punches to get back into my groove, but I got there. I was a bit slower overall now. About a 28.5.

"This time I don't want you to use any power at all," Tyler said. "Instead, just relax your hand through the whole motion."

I shot a punch. 29.9.

"Relax your shoulders, your chest, your spine. There is no resistance for you to overcome. Your hand just flows."

I tried again. 31.0.

And again. 29.5. I was slowing down. Crap.

Again. 26.2. I'd tensed up. I could feel it. And it showed in my speed. This was harder than I'd expected.

We continued to work on it together. Tyler kept on throwing out different visuals, "strike like a snake", "snap like a rubber band", "spark like electricity". It took almost two hours, but I started to get the hang of it. My punch speed was now consistently in the low to mid-thirties. Who knew relaxing could be so hard? It was fun working on something new, and seeing my speed go up.

"Tension is the enemy of speed," Tyler said. "If you feel yourself slowing down, look for the tension that is blocking you. It doesn't just have to be physical either. It can be mental tensions like worry, fear, or expectations. Let everything go. Just exist in the movement of the moment.

"Intention is good. Especially when it is paired with a lazy peacefulness. You'll find your greatest speed comes from a relaxed flow. It's a bit of a paradox, in that your movement feels so effortless it seems slow to you. To your opponent, it's blindingly fast.

"Now you have a glimmer of where you are headed with relaxed speed, let's talk about Tense On Contact. To help with that, I've brought out a specialized piece of equipment." He reached into the sand beside him and pulled out a rectangular metal object. "A bathroom scale."

Really? A bathroom scale was going to help with punching?

"This isn't just any bathroom scale," he continued. "It has a special reading that shows the max amount of weight the scale registers. Let's start by getting your regular weight."

He put it back on the sand, and I stepped up on it. The needle jumped around a bit before it finally settled on 167. That was a bit higher than I'd expected. My new body felt so light, and it was so much leaner. I was sure I'd lost weight, not gained a few pounds.

Although the main needle was on 167, there was a red needle that pointed to 185. When I had first stepped on the scale, it had jumped around a lot. I guess the max weight it had hit was 185.

"Okay, good," Tyler said. "Now I want you to jump on the scale."

"I'll break it," I protested.

"No, you won't." He shook his head. "It's a heavy-duty scale with a much higher reading than normal. An elephant could stand on it, and it wouldn't break."

It didn't look that sturdy to me, but I'm sure he knew what he was talking about. I carefully jumped on the scale. He just laughed.

"Do it again, but this time, really jump on it. Jump on it hard."

I stepped off and jumped back on. I realized I was still being gentle without Tyler having to say anything, so I stepped off and really jumped on it. This time, when I let the scale settle, the max needle was at 1089 pounds! For a moment, the scale had registered over six times my body weight. Was that for real?

Tyler just smiled at my questioning look. He wasn't ready to explain yet.

"Now stand on the scale and just jump in place. Try to push the max weight as high as possible."

This was fun! I jumped as high as I could and slammed down on the scale. It hit 1126. I jumped again. And again and again. I found that jumping way up high didn't give me the best reading. I got better readings by barely going up at all. Instead, I pulled my knees up and then thrust my heels down hard. My main body didn't move much, but the force I got from the landing was huge. One of my jumps got all the way up to 1745 pounds! That was ten times my body weight.

Finally, I stopped and stepped off the scale. I was a bit winded from all the jumping, and I couldn't think of anything new to try to beat my record.

"You're really smart, Jason," Tyler said. "You have a good head for figuring things out. So you tell me. What is the secret to Tense On Contact?"

I was pretty sure where this was going, but I took a moment to gather my thoughts and put them in order.

"There is a moment in time where you can generate a lot more force than you would normally. Tense On Contact is all about generating that force right when you hit your opponent."

Tyler nodded that I was on the right track and to keep going.

"Standing on the scale generated a certain amount of force. We didn't do this, but I'm guessing that if I had something to brace against and pushed with my muscles, I could double that force. So muscle force is like 2x regular force."

I was feeling good. I was on the right track, and I could feel the theory coming together.

"The next thing I tried was jumping as high as I could and hitting with momentum. That was better than just muscles, and I got about 6x force. The best result, though, was just a fast stomp on the scale. I didn't use much momentum. Instead, I used speed as an explosive force. That got me to 10x."

"You're right on the money," Tyler said. "I'd kiss you right here if that wouldn't lead in a whole different direction." He blew me an air kiss instead. "Now transfer that thinking over to punching."

"Well, a simple punch lands with X amount of force. If I use my muscles to power the punch, then I would get 2x the amount of force. That's nice, but that approach favors the bigger guys with bigger muscles. The next way of attacking would be to use momentum. I'm guessing that is what boxers and kick fighters use to get their power. Following the numbers from the scale, they would be able to get 6x the amount of a regular punch.

"The best, of course, is explosive power. I'm guessing that is the Tense On Contact part of the secret. With that I was able to get 10x the amount of power. I'm guessing that pairing it with the speed from Relaxing, you could get even more power."

Tyler was grinning at me.

"Damn, Jason. That's exactly it. That is the exact theory of Relax and Tense On Contact. It gives you maximum speed followed by maximum power. Your punches are faster, so they are much harder to block or dodge. You can also throw more punches in a fight than your opponent. You're relaxed so you spend less energy, and when your attack lands, it does a lot more damage. Now, let's actually practice what we've learned."

Over the next hour I realized that again, it was a lot harder to do than it sounded. Tyler wanted me to have a loose fist all the way up to first contact. Then, the fist tightened into a rock-hard force as it sank into the target. The rest of my body had to release its power at exactly the right moment too. All that made for a full-body explosion of energy at the best point of impact. Then everything had to instantly relax again so the fist could withdraw at full speed, setting up the next punch with the opposite hand.

It was a lot to handle, and the timing had to be perfect. Tensing too soon took away all the speed and power. Tensing too late meant hitting with a soft hand and might damage my knuckles or wrist. This was going to take a lifetime to master.

I would have felt very discouraged if I hadn't already had my Eureka moment. Regular learning and feeling my way through the techniques on my own would have taken weeks to get down. Even then, it would be at least a year before I could master it.

I didn't have to wait that long, though. I could learn it directly from a master. A master that I had a special feedback loop with.

With that in mind, I had Tyler call up his training dummy next to Sparkles, and we both practiced punching together. I pulled out my blindfold again and sank my awareness into my magic sight. Time went by as I honed in more and more on just mine and Tyler's movement.

I reached a level where I could see intentions, the way our magic moved and flowed. What was fascinating was his magic changed density. Most of the time it flowed like water. His lower half in particular flowed, but it had the weight and power of a body of water.

His upper body changed the most. His punches started like smoke. It rolled out of his core, across his shoulders and down his arms. The smoke was light and fast. His actual strike had elements of lightning. I could see his magic flash. When he struck, it was fire. His whole upper body burned for a split second.

I'd used the word explosive force before as a description, but his magic actually seemed to ignite. It was like the smoke was filled with gasoline vapor and tensing was the spark. All that force slammed into his target, channeled by his arm and fist. Then it vanished back into smoke, and the vacuum of power sucked his arm back again.

The speed and power he generated was beyond human, and I didn't have anywhere near that control over my magic. At least not yet. I knew what I was trying to achieve now, so I started out with baby steps.

I got the flow of the water down. That just felt so natural and easy for me. Relaxing and flowing like smoke was much harder. I kept failing, and that caused me to tense up and fail even more. Tensing at the right moment in the right way was all about timing. When I hit correctly, I could see a spark. It wasn't a rolling explosion of fire like Tyler achieved, but it was affirmation I was on the right track.

It seemed like I had just started to get the hang of it when Tyler stopped and announced our time was up. The eight hours had passed quickly. I'd been up almost twenty-four hours, so when I switched with Annabeth, I used my time to sleep. Tyler had been up even longer than that, so he went home for a while too. Annabeth said she was good to train on her own.

I tried to sleep lightly in case Sandy woke up. Sleeping Beauty did not awake, but her magic color was noticeably richer. I switched out with Annabeth again and had another long training session with Tyler.

Once again, I put on the blindfold, and we punched side by side. The House could pull Tyler away on a mission at any moment, so I needed to learn as much from him as I could. As we worked out, I kept on discovering more of the nuance that went into Relax and Tense On Contact. I thought I was getting it down in the last session, but I discovered I had so much more to learn. We didn't take a break or even talk that much. I just got into the zone and used all the feedback to learn.

We were almost at the end of our time together, when I had Tyler stop, and I punched on my own for a few minutes. Had I learned enough now to practice and improve on my own? It seemed like I had. My flow had elements of water, smoke, and fire. My punches were landing right, and my timing was good. The real test would come after I'd had a break and tried to punch this way again.

"I'm sure Annabeth has already told you, but here is your next assignment," Tyler said. "Your goal is to use the Relax and Tense On Contact method for another ten thousand punches. At the end of that time, we'll both evaluate how you are doing and see if you are ready to go to the next phase."

"That sounds good," I said. "It has taken a lot of pre-practice, but I think I'm ready." I'd been so laser focused on learning the new technique that I hadn't interacted much with Tyler. I mentally relaxed and gave him a warm smile.

"Thank you for all your help and patience. I'm sure it wasn't that exciting for you to just punch over and over again. It sure helped me, though."

"That's okay," he said as he gave me a warm smile back. "I have a request, though."

"Sure! What do you need?"

"We still have a few minutes left. I've missed our snuggle time, and I wondered if you felt like spending it on the couch together?"

Oh, wow. Tyler wanted to snuggle with me? It made me feel all wanted and loved.

"Of course! I'd love to!" Not wasting any time, I grabbed his hand, and we ran to the door. Once inside our locker room, I jumped on the couch, pulling Tyler in after me. It took a few moments to figure out how our arms and legs meshed, but soon we were snuggled up together.

It felt like heaven. I had someone in my arms who wanted to be there. Someone who wanted to be with me. Someone who wanted to spend time with me. I soaked it in like a hot bath. We still had our clothes on, and that was okay. We didn't have that long, and I was trying very hard not to make this sexy. Tyler had sexy all the time. He'd had years and years of sexy. This was snuggle time. This was valuable, and I wanted both of us to appreciate it as much as possible.

I tried to keep the conversation light. I told him about waking up with all three cats on my cot. He laughed and told me a few stories about Mr. Tubbles trying to get around. With only three legs and one eye, he'd had some pretty funny adventures.

Somehow I mentioned Josette, and I got a funny look from Tyler. I realized I hadn't told him about our conversation with the Mage with the Black Aura. I also hadn't told him about the fight between Karl, Marius, and Cassandra. Our time was almost up, so I kept the story as short and concise as possible. As the memories of watching Cassandra die in front of me came back, I started shaking again. Tyler just held me tight and listened. It was exactly the comfort I needed.

All too soon our time was up. Tyler said he wanted to hear it again soon, and this time he wanted all the details. We needed to dissect the fight and learn all we could. We needed to be ready for Karl's strengths and have an idea of what his weaknesses might be.

I reluctantly let Tyler go and headed back to the House. He stayed at the beach to continue training Annabeth. I loved our snuggle time, and I was missing him already. These eight-hour shifts didn't feel as long as I thought they would. It seemed like I had only just settled into an activity, and then time was up.

I got lunch and settled down to work on Penny again. It felt like she had almost woken up last time. I settled into my normal rhythm—pulling magic from her, making the neutral magic mine, pushing it back. The work was repetitive, and soon my mind drifted. I played back over the conversation with Josette. I thought about how she said we are always giving off magic and taking more magic in. I thought about Tea mentioning sharing magic with Soul Fragments. I thought about how Eggy had called me a Source. It all stirred around in my brain, and suddenly I had an idea.

19

Terraforming Penny

When I first made Penny, it had been an accident. I was under the impression I was trying to make a simple charm and attempted to wake it up. But like with most things I do, I went way overboard. Instead of making a penny capable of handling magic like a charm, I'd managed to completely wake her up. Now she was an awake and aware magical creature.

    I'd always thought it was the volume of magic I'd given her that woke her up. If that was true, though, wouldn't all powerful mages have charms like Penny? At full strength, Sandy had a lot more power than I did. She should have been able to make something like Penny before this. Instead, I'd found out that having an awake and aware charm was incredibly rare.

So if it wasn't the volume of magic I gave her, then what was it? I think I stumbled across the answer when Tea called my creations Soul Fragments. This was all just theory, but what if my little creations were powered by pieces of my soul? That would explain why they had personalities and could do all the wonderful things they did. Following that logic, what if Penny came to life because I'd given her enough magic *and* enough of my soul?

She was like one of my little creations, except she had a physical body and was permanently aware. If she was soul born, that would also explain how she could absorb my magic as well as my creations when they were not needed anymore. So it wasn't just my color I was trying to give her to get her back to wakefulness, it was my soul.

Going with this theory, I was giving her soul with my current process of magic transfer. I'd pull magic from her, fill it with soul, push it back. There was only so much magic I could push and pull, so the amount of soul I could give was limited.

Maybe there was a better way.

I realized I'd taken an up-close look at myself, but I'd never really done that with Penny. She had an aura, like all living things, but I'd never tried to see through it. Now was as good a time as any, so I zoomed in for a closer look.

The first thing that jumped out was her physical makeup. She was mainly zinc with a tiny bit of copper. At the micro level, she was just beautiful. So smooth and colorful. I wasn't here for her zinc, though, so I let that go and focused on her magic.

I discovered it was very tightly contained with a clear boundary. Josette would be proud. There was no leakage that

I could see. I zoomed in even further and started to drift through the start of Penny's aura. I thought there might be some resistance, but her energy was welcoming to me. So I drifted right up to the edge of her magic. At this range, Penny's power was impressive.

It was dense, and so compact I thought it was solid. I hadn't seen magic like this before. The most powerful magic I'd seen up to this point was when Tyler cut himself to show the difference between transformation and healing. When he'd done that, I could see the magic inside him. His power had been thick, like lava. This was even more substantial than that.

How much magic was Penny holding? She wasn't very big, so I'd always thought she couldn't store much. Now I wasn't so sure. She had energy left over from the park golem even before she had absorbed all the Granny Godmothers from the Necro Golem attack. That attack had included a wave of ghosts, the saber tooth tiger golem, and the Necro Golem himself. That had to be a crap-ton of magic.

I felt a bit intimidated, but I kept going. Her wall of energy in front of me was mostly white. Now that I was this close, I could make out patches of my emerald green and sapphire blue colors. If this was the ratio of my colors to white, I was only at around one percent. She was going to need a lot more than that.

I called my colors to me. At first nothing happened, so I called again. I felt them answer, but they felt muffled and slow. I zoomed in even more. The very air vibrated with power. I wasn't scared, though. Okay, I was a little bit scared. Actually, let's go with "cautious". That's a better word. I was dealing with a lot of power, and I wasn't entirely sure what I was doing.

I kept calling and pulling until the greens and blues near me condensed into a spot on the wall. I could feel the difference. The rest of the wall was pure power, but it didn't know me or care about me at all.

This little spot, though, it liked me. It knew me. It was part of my soul. I reached out and touched it.

The effect was instantaneous. The colors strengthened and grew. They became more saturated, and I could feel the power of the wall becoming mine. Not the whole wall, of course, just that tiny spot. Still, it was a start.

I switched from pulling my colors to pushing them. They began to spread out from me, converting more and more of the neutral white magic. I didn't push too fast as I didn't want them to become diluted.

I found that all it took to add more color was my attention and a sense of welcoming. It wasn't enough to just notice a spot of magic. I had to give it my full attention and treat it like something that mattered. I had to send out an invitation.

In a weird way, it was like meeting a room full of strangers for the first time. They weren't hostile or upset. They just didn't know me and weren't sure they wanted to be friends. So I smiled and called out to them. I let them know I was safe to be around. I was a nice guy to hang out with.

I introduced myself to the neutral magic and asked if it would be mine. It was as simple as that. A few patches of neutral magic held out. They didn't convert right away, but once the area around them switched to green and blue, they switched too.

Once I got a large enough area of magic converted, it started growing on its own. I realized this was an awful lot like the process to awaken my cells. I'd focus on a few cells, then get a patch converted, and finally the process would keep going on its own.

Now I knew the secret, I started moving around the wall and converting new areas. It took me several minutes, but I got much better at the invitation process. It was almost like I loved the magic, and the magic ended up loving me back.

I still had all the wonderful, warm feelings from snuggling with Tyler, so I let the wall have it. I blanketed it with affection. I zoomed out even more, so I could affect a larger area. It took a bit more attention, but once it converted, it grew like wildfire.

I found there was a limit to how far out I could zoom and still be effective. Once I moved outside of Penny's aura, I could no longer affect her magic. This was strictly an inside job. It took a bit of experimenting, but I finally found the best level of zoom where I could affect the largest area with the least amount of effort.

Once I had that, I just flew above her, like I was Superman on a lazy Sunday outing. I beamed down my welcome, like I was using his heat vision, and the white expanse below me burst out in my rich colors. It was so cool. It was like I was terraforming a planet, or something.

It wasn't long before I heard a familiar chime. Penny was awake again! I took a moment to send her a happy mental hug. As a piece of metal, she hadn't understood hugs at the beginning, but now she knew it was something flesh creatures did to show love and belonging. She trilled happily and started bombarding me with questions. What had happened? Where were we? What was I doing now?

I promised to catch her up on everything that had happened while she was sleeping, but right now I wanted to keep going on shoring up her magic. I don't think she got what I was doing, and I didn't explain it well. But I had good feelings and a good flow, and I didn't want to stop now.

I focused and shut everything else out, including Penny, and went back to sending my soul invitations. I flew and converted for what seemed like a long time. Penny was wrapped around my forefinger in two spirals. I flew all the way to one end, turned around, and flew to the other end, then flew back again, converting all the way. My invitation was strong enough that neutral conversion happened even when I wasn't directly affecting it. On my last pass, most of the surface was converted over to my colors. There were still a few lighter spots, and I took the time to convert all of them.

I'd now converted all of her magic that I could see. I was working at the surface level, though, and there was obviously a lot of magic in her core. I could only imagine that the conversion from neutral to personal magic was continuing on the inside.

With that in mind, I wanted the surface conversion to be as powerful as possible. I checked out the terrain below me, but this time I wasn't looking for white patches. Instead, I was looking at the overall saturation of the colors. The neutral magic had been converted, but was it happy about it? Was it hosting a party and celebrating being part of the Jason Cole Soul? The answer was 'Yes! Mostly'.

Most of the surface was so saturated, the magic sparkled just like emeralds and sapphires. It seemed happy, welcoming, and alive. There were some patches, however, that looked like they were colored with crayons. They were on team Jason, but they weren't that happy about it. I flew over and gave them some extra attention. Soon, they were sparkling just like the rest.

I did a couple more laps but couldn't see any problem areas. Penny was stuffed full of magic, and all of it was personal and ready for her to use. Most importantly, if she absorbed a lot of neutral magic again, I now knew how to convert it much faster and wake her up.

I zoomed out to my normal level and relaxed. Penny was breathlessly happy and full of energy. She was feeling better than she had since the fight with the park golem and was dying to know what I'd done. I curled up on my cot and told her all about it. She was fascinated with the whole process and very happy to hear that any future sleeping would be short lived.

She wanted to know everything that had happened up to this point. As I started to tell her, I realized she had missed so much. She'd missed the fight in the park, Annabeth getting a matrix, Octa, Karl and Marius, Tea and Anna Lykit, and all the training. I told Penny I'd have to gradually fill her in over time. She liked all the images and for me to actually relive the events for her. That takes time.

It was so nice to have her back. When she was asleep, it felt like part of me was missing. I guess that really made sense now. She was an extension of my soul. It was more than that, though. She was fun to talk to. She listened well and was highly amused by all the antics of us "fleshy people".

She told me several times how amazing she felt, like she could finally hear, feel, and see as if she had just been born. I could tell a difference too. She sounded clearer, and her images were sharper. I could also feel her magic on my finger. I'd gotten used to the physical sensation of her as a ring, but now I could feel the power as well. It was nice. It made all the work seem worthwhile.

As I chatted with her, I realized I was feeling a bit weird. I was feeling shaky, like I had low blood sugar. I ignored it and kept going until the room started spinning. It wasn't horrible, but it was definitely a low-grade vertigo. Then I started feeling sick, like I might throw up. I didn't want to do any praying to the porcelain god, so I took deep breaths and told myself to calm down. What the heck was going on?

Well, you did just give away a bunch of your soul, my Analytical Side spoke up.

Oh, right.

You were out there, fighting the good fight, terraforming the land, he continued in his dry British voice.

True.

Boldly going where no man has gone before, he sounded a bit disapproving now.

I didn't think it was fair to use Star Trek against me.

Going forth, with reckless abandon, spraying your soul all over the place like you were watering the flowers.

'Hang on now,' I started sticking up for myself. 'This was for a good cause. I needed to bring Penny back.'

Of course, you did. And to do that you needed to convert all of her magic in one go. He was going all thick with the sarcasm.

'Well, no. I didn't really need to do that in one go,' I replied.

And you needed to not only convert it, but make sure it sparkled when you were done. Like fully converted. Like please take my soul. Just take it. I have lots of it. I have mountains of soul just sitting there wasting away. Now he was sounding a bit like Anna Lykit.

'You know when I like to do things, I like to do them right. I couldn't just leave it half done.'

I know, he sighed. *But a bit of caution wouldn't hurt. You don't need to rush into everything. Sometimes it is okay to start something, and then take a break to see if there are any ill effects first.*

I didn't reply back. I was too busy breathing deeply and trying not to toss my cookies.

My Analytical Side gave me the parental 'I'm not mad, I'm just disappointed' look before throwing up his hands and walking away.

'What is "tossing cookies"?' Penny inquired.

'It's what we humans do when we've done too much partying. Or, in this case, when we've given out too much soul.' I sent her images of what I was feeling right now and what it was like to be bent over the toilet hurling your guts out.

'Oh, wow,' Penny chimed. 'Flesh creatures are so strange. If you throw up, can I watch?'

I guess one person's misery was another person's entertainment.

I was going to answer her, but Annabeth and Tyler chose that moment to show up. It was the end of the eight-hour shift, and it was my turn to train. I was in no condition to move, so I ended up telling them all about my soul adventures with Penny and how I was feeling now.

Tyler snuggled up on the cot beside me and began rubbing my back. His touch grounded me, and it helped. Annabeth was excited. She was almost done with her current course of training and then would learn something new. I told her that was awesome and I was so proud of her. Her steady progress was kicking my ass! I really needed to train for this next eight-hour segment, but that wasn't going to happen. I needed eight hours to just chill and recover, and Annabeth felt like that too.

Annabeth was ready to head up to her apartment for a while when we heard a groan. We all looked at each other. It wasn't any of us. Sandy was awake! Tyler and Annabeth rushed to her side. I figured throwing up on her wouldn't be the best way to welcome her into the land of the living, so I stayed where I was. Sandy was awake, but she wasn't looking good.

"Bathroom," she croaked as she tried to get out of bed on her own, but she could barely manage to lift her head.

Tyler helped her get to the bathroom, then Annabeth took it from there. It seemed like they took a while. When Sandy came out, she looked like she'd been cleaned up a bit. She also looked utterly exhausted. I know when I'd been recovering from my beating in the hotel room, even the simplest things wore me out. She looked like she was going through that.

She made it back to bed and promptly fell back to sleep. Annabeth hung around for a while, but Sandy was out like a light. So Annabeth headed up to her apartment for a little alone time. Tyler and I snuggled and napped on the cot. It felt so nice and peaceful. Tyler was there, Penny was awake, and Sandy was going to be okay. We still needed to figure out John, but for the moment, life was good.

I guess my soul recovered, because the vertigo left, followed by the nausea. I still was a bit shaky, but Tyler's strong arm around me steadied me. I basked in his warm body. It felt so strong, and yet so comfortable. Eventually, Bermuda showed up and lay on my head for a while, purring. Before I knew it, the shakes were gone too, and I felt back to normal.

When Annabeth arrived for the next eight-hour segment, I was feeling ready to go. We spent some time talking about Sandy and how to proceed, and agreed for the next few days to keep up our rotating schedule. Sandy still needed someone keeping an eye on her all the time.

Annabeth said she still wanted some chill time and was fine with me taking the next shift at the gym. I was excited to get back to training. Tyler wanted to head home for a while, so I found myself alone on the beach. This was going to be the first time I was really practicing Relax and Tense On Contact without Tyler beside me, and I was kind of glad I was on my own. If I really screwed it up, nobody would be watching.

20

Second 10k

Before I began, I called up my punching stats.

> *Low Novice Jason Punch Stats*
> *Level = 5.9*
> *Punches = 10000*
> *Notes: You ignored all my stars. You ignored all my notes. I guess you don't need me. <sniff> <walking away> <fading into the distance>*

Oh, crap! I'd managed to upset the House.

"House," I said to the empty air. "I'm so sorry. I didn't mean to offend you. And I certainly didn't mean to hurt your feelings."

I paused. That didn't feel anywhere near enough said. Honesty was the best policy. I just needed to come clean to the House, even though it might make me look stupid.

"I ignored your stars and notes because I felt like I was behind. As you know, we aren't in the clear yet with the Louisville Mages. There is going to be at least one big battle coming up, probably more. I need to be ready.

"I'm getting faster. I'm learning quicker. But I just wanted to push ahead and get through the first ten thousand punches so I could get to the next level. That's why I didn't stop and read the messages. You have lots of personalized coaching to impart, though, and I want to learn from that. I'm very sorry I ignored you. It won't happen again."

I looked around, but nothing changed. There was no sign by the House that it had heard me. I guess I'd just keep going and see if the House reconsidered.

I called up Sparkles, put on my blindfold, and got to work. It was amazing how fast it all came back. The Pigeon Stance felt so comfortable now. The punches flowed easily, and soon my energy lined up right. I felt my watery base, fluid but stable. I felt my smoky arms, relaxed with a touch of lightning. I felt the fire, the spark and power when I struck the target.

All too soon, I heard a ding. I took off my blindfold, only to see one little star listlessly fade away in the breeze. The star didn't shoot into the sky, or burst into other tiny stars and cascade down in a pretty display. This was the 'I'm still mad at you' star.

"Thank you very much," I said with as much enthusiasm as I could muster. "I deserved that. I'll do better. Now, let's see what notes you have for me."

Low Novice Jason Punch Stats
Level = 6.0
Punches = 10121

Notes: none

I guess the House was still mad at me. Oh, well. I put on the blindfold and started again.

Ding.

I'd gone up already? I quickly pulled off my blindfold, and again, I got a little, wimpy star.

Level = 6.1

Punches = 10239

Notes: none

I thanked the House and kept going. Ding. 6.2. No notes. Ding. 6.3. No notes. I just kept going. On one hand, I was worried about the House. On the other hand, I was blown away at how fast I was climbing levels. Was I really punching that much harder?

I didn't want to think about it too much and lose my flow, so I put it out of my mind and just focused on Relaxing and Tensing On Contact. It didn't seem like long before I hit a milestone, 7.0.

This time I got stars—lots of them. And they were the big, bright ones too. I guess the House was coming around. I was a bit nervous, but I called up my stats.

Level = 7.0

Punches = 11310

Notes: I guess you really did learn a lot from Tyler. Your form is good. Your energy is good. You're relaxing well. You're tensing with great timing. I can do one thing for you. I'm turning off the celebration until you reach 8.0. I think you can do it without any more feedback. See you then.

"Thank you, House," I said. "Thank you very much. I'm glad you aren't really mad at me. I love working out here, and I love staying in your House with my friends and

Bermuda. You really are a home to me. I'd give you a hug if I could, but I don't know how."

I thought about it for a moment. "Actually, maybe I do. Sparkles, it's love time."

I stepped up to my training partner and gave him a big hug. I figured the House magic animated Sparkles, so in a way I was hugging the House.

The best part was that Sparkles hugged me back. It was a good hug too, solid and comforting, if a bit gritty. Finally, I stepped back.

"I like the plan of holding off celebrating until I hit the next major level. It will be easier to get in the right mindset and just train for a while. Thank you again for everything, and I'll talk to you at 8.0."

I brushed off a bit of loose sand, put on my blindfold, and went back to work. Now I wasn't stopping so often, I could really sink into the craft of it all. This was more than a skill. It was an art form. I'd modeled my form on what Tyler had taught me, but I also personalized it for myself. I had a different body and different energy than he had. As I kept punching, I took his style and made it mine.

My arms were a bit shorter than his, so my timing needed to be a bit faster. The lightning in his speed appealed to me more than the smoke, so I focused on building that. My sparks of fire got bigger. They were nowhere near the size and intensity of Tyler's explosions, but they were a lot better than I'd started with.

Ding! Ding! Ding! Ding!

I'd made it already? I pulled off my blindfold to enjoy the star display. This time Sparkles didn't hold back. The stars were huge, and they shot hundreds of feet into the air. Then they exploded into lots and lots of little stars. Then those stars exploded into even tinier ones that fell all the way to the ground. It was like being showered with pixie dust.

It was so beautiful and fun. I threw up my hands and just danced through it all. I was at level 8.0. That meant I had eight times more endurance and power than I'd started out with. My fists were becoming weapons!

Level = 8.0

Punches = 12902

Notes: You are making this skill your own. I have nothing to add. See you at 9.0.

I did another happy dance, thanked the House, put on my blindfold, and started again. I punched for a long time. I was in prime shape, so I wasn't getting tired. I was hitting correctly, so my fists weren't getting torn up. There was a certain level of wear happening, but Tea and his Grove were on the job. They weren't just healing—they were strengthening. I was having my workout and recovery at the same time. It was the best of all worlds.

Ding! Ding! Ding! Ding!

Once again the whole beach became showered with tiny, sparkling stars. Bermuda went apeshit crazy. He was out sniffing around the sand instead of sleeping on the couch like normal. I thought he would be scared of the bang when the bigger stars exploded, but he sat and watched in fascination. When they started raining down on the beach, he tried to catch them all. He ran around like a crazy cat, pouncing on the sparkles in the sand and trying to catch them in the air. I'm sure to him it was like a whole Christmas of Sparkle Dots showed up for him to play with.

Once the shower of stars ended, he was still on high alert. He kept looking around, searching for any sparkles he might have missed. My kitten was just too cute for words.

Level = 9.0

Punches = 15898

Notes: Congratulations! You continue to improve and grow into your power. You can't always improve at such a rapid pace, so you will find it harder now to gain levels. I believe in you. See you at 10.0.

What an amazing day! I'd gone from level 5.9 to 9.0 in one workout session. I was ranked over fifty percent stronger than when I'd started. 'The Secret' was an amazing thing. On top of that, I was catching up on my training. I was over halfway to my next goal.

I'd been training this whole time with my blindfold on, so I thought I would throw a few punches with it off. I was curious to see what Sparkles looked like now when I hit. I settled into my stance and let loose.

Bam. The sound was deep. Commanding. It sounded like power. The best part was watching Sparkles' chest. The sand exploded away from the point of contact, leaving a shallow crater behind. Some of the sand flew outward in a fine shower. Some of it rippled away from the point of contact. It was like a small earthquake had shot across Sparkles' chest.

This was so much more reaction than when I'd started. My first punches had only shifted a few grains of sand. Now Sparkles had to work to recover fast enough between punches. This was awesome! So I hit him again. And again.

What would it feel like to hit a mage? How fast could I take a shield down now? If I had a defense to match this offense, I would be set!

The timer went off and my shift was over, so I headed back to the House. Bermuda was still full of energy, so I made three Feather Dots and turned them loose. He wasn't training like I was, but he was getting fast. He wasn't a kitten anymore. He was looking all long and lanky, like a teenager. My little baby was growing up.

Annabeth said Sandy had woken up again, but only for a few minutes. She'd gotten her to drink a bit, but then she'd crashed out. I took over sitting duties, and Annabeth went to train. The bedroom was quiet, and for the first time in a long time, I didn't have to work on Penny. I still needed to work on Eggy, but I wanted to make sure my soul was back up to full strength before I tried that.

So I chilled on my cot, played Sudoku and chatted with Penny. It was so nice to have her back again. I continued to play back memories and update her on what had happened. I had made it to the big fight with Mustard in the park when Sandy woke up again.

I got her propped up in bed and gave her some more water. I also gave her a Tillman and Tiddles bar. Those things are so nutritious with a touch of magic. Even one bar would do her good. I gave her a Cobb Salad with Green Goddess dressing. I wanted to keep it light and fresh for her first snack. We'd get into some fried chicken when she was feeling stronger.

She was so weak it took her awhile to eat it. Girl was looking rough. I had hoped she might bounce back like Annabeth did when she woke up. Annabeth had recovered and been training in the gym by the end of the day. That wasn't going to happen here.

While she was awake, we all sat on the bed with her. I sat beside her with my arm around her. It was half hug / half support so she didn't fall over. I wanted to let her know on a physical level that she was loved and we were here for her.

Snowy and Biscuit rubbed on her and licked her hands and face. I could tell they loved her and missed her so much. With the little energy she had, Sandy loved them back. All too soon, she finished her T&T bar. She scooched down in the bed, gave me a small smile of thanks, and fell asleep again.

Snowy and Biscuit lay down on either side of her, like guardian angels, and I returned to my cot. I took a break from storytelling with Penny and played Sudoku for a while. It felt so nice and normal. Nobody tried to kill me for being a Sudoku master.

Annabeth came back from her training, and I gave her the bars I had. She thought that was a great idea until Sandy could stay awake longer. Then she wanted to give her some hot food, like soup. I asked her how the training was going, and her face lit up like the sun. Training was going great, but she didn't want to tell me too much and spoil my anticipation. She would only say she was becoming more of a complete fighter, but there was still a lot to learn.

I left Sandy in her good care and headed out to the gym. Tyler wasn't around, so I decided to get started. For some reason, it took me longer to warm up this time, but once I did, I felt the power flowing like never before.

Ding! Ding! Ding! Ding!

Mid Novice Jason Punch Stats
Level = 10.0
Punches = 19003
Notes: You are still improving quickly. This is unexpected. For a beginner, your form is excellent. Your timing is excellent. Your energy is excellent. Keep going and let's see how high you can go.

I thought that was excellent advice, and that is what I did. It wasn't long before I hit my second ten thousand goal. The House went overboard on stars this time. I did a happy dance and gave Sparkles another sandy hug.

I pulled up my stats to check everything and noticed something different.

Mid Novice Jason Punch Stats

I'm a Mid Novice now! Woot!! When the heck had that happened? I'd just gotten used to ignoring the first line. I already knew my name and I knew I was a novice, so I usually just glossed over the text, going straight to the level. What was next? High Novice? Advanced Novice? Oh Great and Powerful Master Novice?

There weren't any stars or anything, but I still did a happy dance. I was no longer the lowest of the low!

I still had almost another hour of time left, so I kept punching. I finished at level 10.3. I was still climbing in power. I headed back to the House and told Annabeth the happy news. I got multiple happy hugs as we did a happy dance together.

She wanted to feel how much power I had now, so we pulled out the phone book. She held it against her chest, I got into my stance, and let a fist fly.

I hit her so hard the force knocked her off her feet. Not only that, it also knocked the breath out of her. For a few moments, I thought I'd done some real damage, but once she recovered and got back on her feet again, she started laughing. I chuckled a bit too. It's hard not to join in when she was laughing, but I was still a bit worried. She seemed fine, though, so I guess the phone book took the worst of the blow.

Tyler showed up, and he wanted to feel how I was progressing too. He picked up the phone book, held it to his chest, and I let him have it. The punch rocked him back on his heels a bit, but it didn't knock him over.

I guess I looked a bit disappointed because he hastened to assure me he had really felt it. Then he wanted to feel how Annabeth was doing. She popped him a few times. Her punches looked and sounded great. Then I wanted to feel it too, so I took the phone book.

She hit hard now. It didn't knock me off my feet or anything, but I could feel the shockwave moving through me. Her speed was fast too, and her timing was spot on.

Tyler offered to punch both of us through the phone book, but we both gave a firm 'No'. If Tyler could destroy Sparkles in one punch, he'd leave me a mangled mess on the floor, phone book or not. I had no desire to recover from a broken chest. He just laughed, and said maybe later when we were stronger. I said "Sure!", but what I meant was that's never gonna happen. Tyler was way too powerful for me.

I'd been up a long time, and so had everyone else. We all decided to just take the next eight-hour shift and sleep. Annabeth took to her bed, and Tyler and I curled up on my cot. Bermuda settled on the pillow and decided my nose was dirty. Actually, my whole face was dirty. His tongue wasn't too raspy, so I was good for a while, but finally I had to tell him 'No'. My face had been wonderfully exfoliated, just like I'd been to a spa, only a lot cheaper.

Tyler wrapped his arms around me, and I was in heaven. I wanted to stay awake for a while and just exist in this moment of peace and happiness. Instead, I fell asleep.

21

Pigeon Steps

Sandy woke up twice during that shift. Annabeth got one time, and I got the other. It was so hard to crawl out of my nice warm nest, but I made it. I put my arm around Sandy again to feed her meal bars. This time she ate three of them before crashing. She was getting stronger.

We all slept in the next morning and woke up rested. I was so excited. Today was defense day! Offense was great, but since I couldn't use a shield charm, I needed to learn how to defend myself. The next time a golem threw a punch at my face, I was going to be ready.

We had breakfast together in Sandy's kitchen, and it felt a little bit like normal. We were missing Sandy and John, of course, but it was still nice. Annabeth said she had some orders on Etsy for charms that she needed to fill with happy magic and send on their way. So I was welcome to take the first shift at the gym.

I decided to shower in the locker room, so Tyler and I took off for the training beach. The water felt good and woke me up. Then Tyler joined me and *really* woke me up. I'd been a good boy thus far, being responsible with Sandy and keeping everything platonic. All that went out the window when Tyler decided he had to wash me personally. It took a while, but I can say I was very clean when he was done. I felt very satisfied and happy too. The whole feedback loop we had going on was fading, for which I was grateful. That level of sex was too intense to have all the time.

It was fading, but it wasn't gone yet, so I planned on using the feedback during our next training session. Being able to feel how Tyler moved during combat was invaluable.

"You've learned how to punch, which is wonderful, but nobody is going to line up in front of you at exactly the right distance and wait to get hit," Tyler said. We were on the beach in our workout clothes as he started my new training. "This means the next skill you need to learn is how to move."

"Since we have lots of practice time, I'm going to show you several movement techniques, then you can work on them on your own time. Let's start with the simplest of them, The Shift. Go ahead and get into your resting stance."

It was like second nature at this point. I bent my knees, pointed toes out, then rested on the toes, swiveling my heels out. My feet were now about shoulder width apart with my toes pointing in. This still seemed like a very strange way to rest, but had proved to be remarkably solid for punching.

"What name did you invent for this stance?" Tyler asked.

"I originally called it the Pigeon's Gotta Pee Stance," I replied laughing. "It's pigeon toed, and it kinda looks like you are in the middle of doing the pee-pee dance."

Tyler chuckled. He loved my goofy names.

"Well, I can't wait to see what names you invent for what I'm going to show you today. Just concentrate on your feet for a sec. Notice how the right one is pointing in about thirty degrees to your left, and the left one is pointing about thirty degrees to your right."

I nodded. That was very obvious.

"What that does for you is allow you to move swiftly at an angle. The fastest one is The Shift. To do it, you just shift in place, like so."

He rotated his right foot so it was the same angle as his left. At the same time, he put his weight on his left leg. He was now no longer facing forward, but was at a slight angle. I'll be honest, it didn't look like much.

"I'm sure you are wondering how the heck that is useful," Tyler said.

I smiled and nodded. It looked like a whole lot of nothing.

"Stand in front of me and put your fist on my chest," Tyler said.

He got back into the basic Pigeon Stance. I stood in front of him and put my fist in the middle of his chest, just like I'd punched him. This time, when he rotated, I saw the power of the move.

My fist was no longer in the middle of his chest! In fact, given the angle he was now facing, I wouldn't hit him at all. In one quick shift, he had dodged my blow. It was such a simple move, but a very useful one.

"I can see you've got the idea now," Tyler said. "Let's get Sparkles over here so you can try it for yourself."

I quickly found out it wasn't as simple as Tyler made it look. I kept over shifting, which threw off my balance, or under shifting, which meant I didn't dodge the punch. I got Tyler to do it with me and kicked in my feedback loop. It wasn't long before I got the flow down. I at least knew what I was trying for. I could perfect it later.

"Now you have The Shift down, let's add a step to it."

It was basically the same thing, except I stepped out with my base leg first. It was slower to execute, but instead of dodging the fist by a little bit, I dodged it by a lot.

"Most people are not going to hit at the center of your body," Tyler said. "They are typically going to hit to one side or the other. Usually you can shift the right way and have plenty of room for them to miss. Sometimes, though, they are throwing wild swings, and you need more room. That's where the Step Shift comes in."

"It will also be really useful for dodging spells," I replied. "They are usually a lot bigger than fists, and I'll need to give them more room to miss me."

We practiced that together until I had the feel of it down.

"Normally, I'd stop now and let you practice that first. Today, though, I'm going to keep going. I think you can handle learning more. For practice, I want you to do twenty thousand Shifts while Sparkles is throwing slow punches at your centerline. You need to do ten thousand to the left and ten thousand to the right. Then you need to do twenty thousand Step Shifts, ten thousand to the left and ten thousand to the right."

Tyler sure did like the number ten thousand. The Shift was quick, but that was still going to take some time to get in that much practice. I didn't mind, though. This was the beginning of my defensive skills. If I'd known this, I could have avoided being punched in the face by a golem and just watched its big fist of stone sail right on by.

"Now you have the basics of Shifting, let's talk about actually moving backwards and forwards," Tyler said. "First, let's do it like most people think of moving: straight forwards and backwards. I'll start off and be the defender. You are the attacker. Just use an open hand and try and touch me."

I stepped towards Tyler, trying to put my hand on his chest. He just stepped back. I stepped forward again, a little quicker this time, and he stepped back just as fast. I lunged at him, hand outstretched, and he practically ran backwards.

This was kinda fun, so I kept chasing him until we were outside of our gym area. He called a halt at that point.

"Just to drive this lesson home, let's reverse our roles. I'll be the attacker, you be the defender."

It was much harder being the defender. Tyler was so fast I had to practically sprint backward. We got to the other side of the gym, and only a wild leap back saved me from getting tagged.

"Now, what did you learn from this?"

I thought about it for a sec.

"I'm not sure I learned anything," I said. "We just went back and forth. I guess I learned that I need to be faster." I shrugged. If Tyler was trying to impart a lesson, I wasn't getting it yet.

"Imagine that we were not on a beach with all this open space. Instead, we are in a room with four walls, and it's as big as this gym. What would have happened then?"

"You would have backed into a wall when you were the defender, and I could finally reach you," I said. "And vice versa. I would have run into the wall, and you would have tagged me."

"Correct," Tyler said. "Now imagine I was a mage and I'd thrown two punches, both of which you avoided by backing up. Then, instead of throwing a punch, I threw a spell. How would your movement save you?"

"It wouldn't," I said. "The spell would travel a lot faster than I could back up, and I'd get hit."

"Keep that in mind as we try this again," Tyler said.

We moved back to the center of the gym. This time, Tyler got into the Pigeon Stance. I stepped forward to touch him, and he stepped back. But this time he stepped back at an angle. I'd move forward with my right hand and right foot. In response, he'd step backwards, but at a thirty degree angle to my left.

I'd moved forward pretty quickly, trying to tag him before he got too far out of reach, and now I was way overextended. I was so off balance I had to take another step to recover, which meant that Tyler was now behind me. With one step, Tyler had dodged my punch and used my momentum against me.

It was genius!

I reset and came at him again. This time I didn't go as fast, so I wasn't off balance. He stepped back at an angle again, and I was nowhere near close enough to touch him. I quickly followed it up with another punch. This time he stepped off at a different angle.

We kept this up with me chasing him all over the gym. The whole time he was in complete control of our "fight". I couldn't fully commit to a lunge because I wasn't sure which direction he was going to retreat in. The imaginary walls of the gym didn't bother him at all. By retreating at an angle, he never ran out of space, and I could never pin him up against a wall.

"So, what did you learn?" Tyler asked.

"I've learned angles are an amazing thing," I said. "I was throwing punches, but if I'd been throwing spells, I still wouldn't have been able to hit you. What you're doing is brilliant. Just brilliant."

"You've just seen the defensive side of it," Tyler said. "Let's do this again. You attack me, while I defend. This time, though, I'm going to change the defense into an attack. I'll touch you lightly, and when I do, step back slightly like I'd actually hit you with force. Got it?"

I nodded. I couldn't wait to see what Tyler was going to do now.

We set up in the center of the gym again, and I stepped in to punch. He angled back. So far it was the same thing. My first few attempts were cautious, but soon I put some speed into my punches. That's when he switched it up. Instead of stepping back, he stepped forward at an angle. I moved right by him. The whole thing happened so fast I didn't have time to react before I felt a whole series of light touches on my side. He hit me at least four times before I could recover and turn to face him. I moved back a few feet like he had actually hit me with a bit of force.

I was on the defensive now, and he didn't let up. He moved to attack me this time, but again, it wasn't directly at me. Instead, he moved to the side of me and attacked from there. I spun to face him, trying to back up. He just moved in again, this time to the other side.

Again, he completely controlled the fight. He chased me all around the gym, tagging me at will. The only time he actually moved directly at me was when I just turned and ran. Then he ran with me to maintain our distance. As soon as I ran into the "wall" of the gym, he switched back to angle attacks again. Trying to defend against him was maddening.

"So what did you learn this time?" Tyler asked.

"Defending against that was just crazy," I said, shaking my head. "I didn't know how you were going to come at me next. All I could think about was just trying to get out of the way and not getting hit. Your offense was so fast and consistent, I didn't have any time to figure out how to go on the offensive myself.

"This method of movement reminds me of the knight in chess. It moves up two and over one. Everything else in chess moves in straight lines. The knight is so unpredictable. It is hard to trap it as it has so many places it can move to. It is also hard to defend against, as it can keep coming at you from different angles."

"That's exactly it," Tyler said. "And all that angled movement comes from the way you place your feet. You're pointing your toes inward with the Pigeon Stance so you can shift your weight and move quickly off of one foot."

He demonstrated.

"Once you've stepped, you keep your toes pointed inward. Even with one foot in front of the other, you are still in a modified Pigeon Stance. Now you have two more options of how to move backwards at an angle."

He demonstrated again.

"Or, you have two options of how to move forward."

He demonstrated.

"Or, you can do your Step Shift we learned earlier, then pivot your lead leg, and you're back in the Pigeon Stance again."

Wow. That was a whole lot more options than "forward" or "backward". No wonder Annabeth hadn't been able to explain this to me. It was something I needed to experience for myself before I'd get it.

I spent the whole rest of the time learning how to move around. Once again, Tyler made it look easy, and the concept was easy, but the actual execution was rough. I kept on stepping too wide or too narrow. Or I'd pick a direction, but lead off with the wrong foot.

Once I got the concept down, I put on the blindfold and had Tyler move around with me. I thought maybe his magic in his lower half would switch from water to something else, but it didn't. It stayed water, and it flowed so quick and smooth that it barely rippled. Tyler had it down. He didn't think about it anymore. He just did it.

One session wasn't going to do it for me, but at least I knew how it should feel. This feedback loop I had with Tyler was amazing for training. I was so far ahead of where I would be if I was just trying to learn this with sight alone.

All too soon, our training session had to end.

"Okay, you already have your Shift and Step Shift homework," Tyler said. "Now it's time for your next assignment. I want you to practice your Pigeon Steps with Sparkles. Have him start out punching towards you very slowly. Pick a direction and step out of the way. He'll come after you, and you step out of the way again. Don't rely on one direction. Mix them up and master them all. The House will assign you a level again.

"Your goal is to get to level ten. This is a fundamental skill you need to master. The best offense and defense come from movement. I don't want to start you on blocking until your stepping is automatic."

"Got it," I said. Then I smiled at him. "Pigeon Steps?"

"I thought you would like that," he smiled back. "You've got Annabeth calling it a Pigeon Stance too, so I thought I would just roll with it."

"That's called a Pigeon Roll," I said playfully.

"And this is called a Pigeon Swat," Tyler said as he gave me a light smack on my ass.

"Well, this is called a Pigeon Peck," I said, giving him a little kiss.

"That was too easy," he laughed. "It's already called a "Peck on the Lips". How about a new one, the Pigeon Tickles?" He flexed his fingers, lunging for me.

"No!" I squealed and ran. Tyler had some serious tickle power. He'd almost made me pee my pants before.

I called a truce in the locker room, and we showered and changed like regular adults. Then we headed back to the House to meet up with Annabeth. When we got to Sandy's bedroom, I was shocked. Sandy was sitting up eating soup!

22

What About John

For the first time, Sandy's eyes were clear, and it seemed like she knew who and where she was. Being careful not to jostle her too much and spill the soup, I settled on the bed beside her.

"Hi, Jason," she said. Her voice was rough.

"Hi, Sandy," I said. "I've missed you."

She leaned her head towards me, and I gave her a gentle half hug. Then she went back to eating soup.

"Annabeth tells me this is my bedroom?" she asked.

"Yep. John made most of the changes for us when he was awake. Annabeth was unconscious too for a while, so it was just me taking care of everyone. I needed everyone to be in the same room to keep an eye on you all. So the House expanded your bedroom, added more beds, and increased the height so John could stand up if he wanted."

"What happened to you?" Sandy asked Annabeth.

Annabeth got through most of her story before Sandy finished the soup and started nodding off. We quickly ended story time, tucking Sandy in for her next nap.

"I'm not sure she will remember any of that," I told Annabeth.

"That's okay," she said. "She's at least looking around and getting curious. That's a big step forward. I didn't remember everything you told me after waking up the first time either. There will be plenty of time to catch her up on what's been happening."

"Switching subjects," I said, "I learned about Pigeon Stepping today."

She lit up. "Isn't it wild? I can't believe how much power there is in simply moving. I also can't believe how hard it is." She made a face.

"I haven't started practicing it yet. I've just learned the technique. Where are you at with your goals?"

"I've finished the Shifting and the Step Shifting. Now I'm just practicing with Mr. Pebbles on my actual stepping. So far the House has rated me at 2.6. Which really means I get a few good steps in before I end up going the wrong way. I either trip over my own feet, or he tags me and the round is over."

"Mr. Pebbles?" I asked.

"It's my name for my training partner," she said. "You have Sparkles. I have Mr. Pebbles." She sounded a bit stern, like she was thinking I'd laugh at it.

"I think it's a great name! How did you come up with it?"

"Well, I felt like I needed something nice. He's already very big and intimidating. He didn't need an intimidating name too. I tried a few names, but they just didn't fit. Then one time I was hitting his chest, and I noticed that he wasn't only made up of sand. He's actually got lots of little tiny rocks in there too. So that's how I came up with Pebbles. I added Mr., because I like Mr. Rogers, who's always so nice and sweet and wouldn't hurt anyone. And there you have it, Mr. Pebbles."

"It sounds perfect to me," I said, smiling. "It's very you."

We talked a bit more about training. It was nice to finally be working on the same thing again. Even though she was still ahead of me, we could talk about the same developments together.

Tyler headed home for a while, and Annabeth headed out to train. Sandy had just fallen asleep, so she would be good for a few hours at least. For the first time in what felt like a long time, I was actually free to do what I wanted.

It felt a bit strange. I wasn't sure what to do with myself. I decided to head up to my apartment, get changed, and spend some time there. I hadn't seen my apartment in days. I'd either been sleeping in Sandy's bedroom or training at the gym. The showers in the locker room at the beach were nice, so I'd been using them to stay clean. I had a few clothes stashed under my cot, but I'd already worn everything at least twice, so it was time to switch them out. I didn't want to start smelling too ripe.

I gathered up my small pile of dirty laundry and headed upstairs. I walked into my apartment, stopping in surprise. Purple Octopuses were everywhere. In my head, my apartment was still very sparse and mostly white. I'd forgotten I'd shifted the whole neutral magic absorption system upstairs. Once I got over my surprise, I felt bad. I'd been so focused on training and watching Sandy that I hadn't taken the time to visit Octa and her Tangle.

I would do better. Starting right now. I said 'Hi' to Octa and spent time going to every Octopus making sure each one was okay. The word got out to the Granny Godmothers that I was around, so they all flocked in to say 'Hi' as well. I hadn't been outside in a long time, so I asked the head Granny how the park was doing.

I got a very detailed report, which basically boiled down to the fact that they were about half done. The worst of the damage had been cleaned up, but there was still a long way to go. I thanked her for all her hard work managing all the Grannies. The park was going to recover so much faster because of their work. I got a kiss on the cheek and a few happy twirls in the air in response.

I then asked Octa how things were going with her Tangle. She said she had duplicated to match the power the Grannies were bringing back. So far everything was in balance and working well. I gave her a big 'Thank You' too.

It looked like everything was going smoothly, so I stepped into the bedroom. This time I really stopped in shock.

My bedroom had been transformed into a tropical paradise.

Everything was different. Like, everything.

The floor was now made up of strips of some light-colored wood. My issue with hardwood floors were they felt so rigid under my feet. But this wasn't like that at all. This floor felt soft and springy, and all the wood texture gave it an organic feel. Usually a floor was just a floor to me, but this was beautiful.

Looking up, my ceiling was now super tall. It had an A-frame, with a very high peak in the middle. The ceiling itself was some sort of thatch now. In the middle of this A-frame was a long pole with fan blades on it. The whole thing turned softly, creating a light breeze.

The only part of the room that remained unchanged was Eggy's area, but it flowed well with the rest of the space, with its light weathered wood walls and flowing linen curtains. The only place that didn't have the curtains was the wall behind the bed. It had tall wooden shutters running the entire length. What was even better was I could see the deep blue ocean peeking through them. There is no ocean in Louisville, Kentucky! Somehow, my bedroom was now looking out onto a whole new place in the world. Amazing!

The bed itself had changed too. I had been very happy with my mattress on the floor, but now there was a huge four-poster bed with white linen curtains pulled back and tied to the posts. A quilt of different shades of ocean blue covered the bed. And I had to admit that it went quite well with Eggy's glass water stand.

I stepped further into the bedroom in awe. It was so much bigger now. Some of that extra space was taken up with plants. There were some ferns, tropical flowers, a vine climbing up one wall, and even a small palm tree. What a paradise!

My eyes roamed around my glorious new space soaking it all up, when I stopped to gaze upon the two little bed dressers. They were the short ones that sit by the bed. Are they called night stands? I needed to ask Annabeth. Either way, they had three drawers each and a blue lamp on top. It occurred to me that I had two night stands, and the bed was definitely big enough for two people. Was the House hinting at something?

But the surprises didn't end there! On the opposite wall from Eggy, there was an archway. Curious, I stepped through. I was now in a walk-in closet. It wasn't a tiny thing either. This space was just as big as the main bedroom.

It was divided into two parts, so I guess it was designed to be shared. The closet looked like it had been put together by a designer. It had hangers up high and hangers down low. They were the nice wooden hangers too. There was also a section with drawers that opened smoothly, and then did a soft close. Some of them were shallow. Perhaps for jewelry? And yep, there was a rack for shoes as well.

It was all so nice, and maybe a little overwhelming. My clothes certainly looked out of place, and there wasn't much to fill the colossal closet either. I never owned a lot of anything, as I always traveled light. I ran a hand across my t-shirts. They were neatly folded, taking up one drawer. Socks and underwear were likewise folded, each in their own drawer. I chuckled a little at the decadence. I was used to everything lumped in together.

I did have one nice outfit which I used for playing poker. It was nice, but not too nice. Some of the guys I played with had thousand dollar suits that were tailored just for them. This was more like "JCPenney off the rack" nice.

I didn't want to give the impression I was great at the game. I wanted to be accepted, but also underestimated. The outfit belonged here a lot more than my well-worn clothes.

Another reason the closet looked so luxe was all the under-cabinet lighting. It modeled my clothes and presented them like they were the crown jewels, even my old tattered jeans.

Both sides of the walk-in closet were identical. In the middle sat a full length mirror with a beautiful wicker chair. I guess it was so that one person could sit and chat while the other person got ready.

Once again, I took a moment to just take it all in. I'd gone from Goodwill chic, with one beat-up dresser and a mattress on the floor, to a luxury suite. It was almost too much. Almost. A part of me giggled with delight.

I remembered that I still needed to switch out clothes, but I couldn't just pile the dirty ones in a corner anymore. This place was too good for that. Instead, I discovered I had a pull out hamper. It even had sections in it so I could split up my shirts, pants, and underwear. I decided to go with the flow and sectioned out my clothes.

What I had on was dirty, so I changed into fresh clothes and took a few extra shirts and underwear for the stay downstairs. I was looking forward to getting to know my new bedroom, but right now Sandy came first. I needed to stay downstairs on the cot for now, but I certainly anticipated coming back here soon.

I left the walk-in closet and went back to the bedroom. I took a moment to look out the window at the ocean, and then rolled around on the bed for a while. It was just the right amount of soft and firm. It was so freakin' big. I wasn't used to anything this huge.

That's what he said, Anna Lykit chuckled wickedly.

'For once, I may actually want to downsize,' I laughed. 'I want Tyler to snuggle me, not get all sprawled out on his side of the bed.'

Just give it a chance, My Little Muncher, she replied. *After a while you might find it fits after all.*

Anna does love her naughty double entendres.

I looked over at Eggy, and it gave me an idea. I got up to see Octa.

'Can you divert some of your Tangle to spend time with Eggy and give him neutral magic?' I asked. 'I've discovered how to change neutral magic to my personal magic in a charm. So rather than push all my magic into him over and over, I could take what you put in there and just convert it. That might be much quicker.'

She batted her eyes at me, then gave a little twirl in the air. She was so pretty, and I told her so.

I poked my nose into the kitchen and the bathroom to see if there was anything new. So far, they were the same. I sat on my old, comfortable couch for a while and played Sudoku. I found the process of figuring out the numbers soothing and relaxing. It was nice to just chill with my creations and spend some time with them. All too soon, it was time to head down to Sandy's bedroom. I said goodbye to all my little peeps and promised to stop by again soon.

The next three days passed quickly. I got my training in when I could and finished off my Shift and Step Shift goals. Sandy continued getting stronger. Her naps became shorter, and she stayed awake longer. Her magic also became more saturated.

She'd been out a long time, so we gradually caught her up on what had happened. Her focus wasn't that good yet, so we had to tell some stories multiple times.

At one point, Tyler was called away on a mission by the House. I found myself missing him and hoping he was okay.

On the third day, Sandy called a meeting. She said she was tired of being in bed and being watched over. She still felt rough, but that's life. It was time to plan for the next step. I wasn't exactly sure where she was going with that. Did she mean the next step for dealing with the mages? The next step on learning how to fight? The next step for her recovery? Either way I was very glad she was feeling motivated and ready to move on.

Sandy, Annabeth, and I got together in her kitchen and settled in around the kitchen table. I had a nice cup of coffee. That always helped me think, and it just felt warm and comforting too. Annabeth and Sandy opted for tea. Sandy looked much better. She'd cleaned up, fixed her hair, and added a touch of makeup. She was wearing regular clothes too—jeans and a red t-shirt that said "I Love My Peeps" with a drawing of baby chickens. It was cute.

Sandy looked serious, and I waited for her to begin.

"I've called this meeting today to discuss John. I think he is in danger."

I looked over at Annabeth in shock. I knew John needed help. He was still a nine-foot rock giant after all. But I didn't think he was in danger.

"Oh, no!" Annabeth exclaimed, reaching over to hold Sandy's hand. "Tell us what is going on."

"I think he is in danger of fading into the earth and never coming back again," Sandy continued. I reached over and held her other hand tightly. Sandy was trying to keep it together, but tears started running down her face. "I can't lose John. I just can't."

She straightened up, gripped our hands hard, and pulled herself together. "I will not lose John." She let us go, wiping her eyes.

"I will NOT let that happen," she said with steel in her voice. "WE will not let that happen." She clasped her hands carefully in front of her on the table.

"Now, let's pool together what we know and figure out a way to help him."

She took a deep breath and a sip of her tea. "I'll go first."

"John's father started out as a human. Somehow, he bonded with the spirit of a mountain. John said his father used to eat rocks, and he gradually started changing into a mountain troll. As you can imagine, that didn't sit too well with his wife. They had ten children and a little plot of land, and she was furious that he was leaving her to become an earth spirit. He was about to leave and become one with the mountain, when she tried one last time to remind him of the joy of being a human. It didn't work and he left, never to be seen again. What did happen, though, is she became pregnant and nine months later John was born. None of his brothers and sisters had powers, but John was part mountain troll from the beginning. John said that even though he never met his dad, he could always feel his presence.

"John said there was always a lot of fighting between the clans in Scotland at that time, and one day he ended up on the wrong end of a sword and had his Waker Moment. That unlocked his powers, and he's been working with the earth ever since."

Sandy looked at us to make sure we were following along. We both nodded to keep going.

"I think the story of his father has haunted John. He hears the earth all the time to some degree, and he's always thought that one day he would just walk into the earth and leave humanity and the supernatural world behind. When I first met him, he was close to doing that. I was a new supernatural and going through all the emotional adjustment that comes from your Waker Moment. I became part of House Chicago and started learning magic. They had a garden that had an amazingly lifelike statue of a man. He seemed kind, and yet so sad. When life got overwhelming, I spent a lot of time in the garden talking to the statue. It helped me to process my thoughts and handle my emotions. It was just a statue and nobody else seemed to come to the garden, so it seemed safe to tell him everything.

"Imagine my surprise when one day the statue talked back! I was beyond shocked, and at first, I was mortified. I'd told him so many personal things. Over time, we became good friends. He was such a great listener, and eventually he opened up and told me some of his stories too. After a time, I became strong enough that the House started sending me on missions. To my surprise, John joined me, and we've been together ever since."

She stopped talking for a moment, lost in her memories. I had questions, though. I'd been trying to figure out how to fix John for a while now, and I needed more info.

"So, when you first met John, was he made up of stones like he is now?"

"Yes," Sandy said. "Although it wasn't exactly the same. He was only a little bit taller than his normal seven feet. It's so hard to estimate height. Maybe he was like seven-and-a-half feet tall? But it wasn't anything like his current height. That's why I'm so worried about this. He's been rocky before, but never as rocky as this."

"Do you remember anything else about last time? Anything that is different from how he is now?"

Sandy sipped her tea, searching her memories.

"It feels like so long ago. It's hard to remember. I think he was more statue-like last time. This time, he's made up of a bunch of rocks. I remember him having a more clearly defined face, even if it was stone. This time he's more like a golem. He was also covered in moss and lichen last time from being in one place for so long. I know because I'd spent a couple hours scrubbing him down and cleaning him up."

"So this time, he's much bigger and rockier," I summarized. "Do you know if he came to life and moved around at all when you weren't there? Did anyone at House Chicago mention that he moved around, or talked to them?"

"Nope," Sandy said. "Not that I know of."

"Well, this time we know for sure he's coming back every now and then. Let's plot a timeline and see if there is a pattern."

Annabeth got a piece of paper, marked it up for the days, and then we started figuring out when we'd had contact with John. It looked like we'd had daily contact with him right after the fight. Then it started skipping days. I was the last person to talk to John, and that was way back when he'd powered the changes to Sandy's bedroom. That had been twenty-one days ago!

I hadn't realized how much time had passed. Now I was really worried too. Three weeks was a long time to go with no movement and no contact.

"I'll agree the pattern looks really bad," Annabeth said. "But before we get too upset, I just want to note that we haven't had full time, twenty-four-hour, awake coverage of Sandy's bedroom. Over the last few days, we've really made an effort to make sure Sandy had full coverage, but even then, we were all sleeping for part of the time. Plus, we would shower, eat, get stuff from our apartments, things like that. It's possible that John has awakened more than once, seen Sandy was still the same, and went back to the earth again."

"That is true," I nodded. "When I last talked to John, he was only awake for about fifteen minutes. I had to talk fast and keep his attention. If I hadn't been sitting on his lap at that moment, I'd never have known he was back."

Sandy took a few deep breaths. None of this was changing her mind that John was in trouble.

"So, it sounds like we need to keep a closer eye on John. There are three of us now, instead of two, so it should be easier. The big question is, how do we fix him?"

"The solution, I think, is to get him to expend a massive amount of magic," I said.

I told them about how John had given a lot of his magic to the House. It had kept the candles lit, added more beds, and added a lot more space. Afterwards, the Miners had been able to remove about two inches of stone. It wasn't much, but it was a start.

"The only problem with getting him to push out a lot of magic is we have to convince him fast. There needs to be some sort of need that makes him focus and really push his magic. Last time Sandy and Annabeth were in trouble, so I was able to convey that and get him to do something about it. He kept wanting to fade away again. He said the earth was strong, and he would talk to me on the next cycle."

"The problem with that is his cycle is twenty-one days late," Sandy said severely.

I really wanted to say that maybe we should check if he was pregnant, but I managed to keep my mouth shut. This was not the time for humor.

"Is there any way to pull magic from him without having to wake him up?" Annabeth asked.

That was a good thought, and one we'd hashed out before. I'd already tried with my little guys. John's aura was just too strong. They couldn't mess with his magic at all. Sandy didn't have any new insights.

You could get magic through blood, but John was a big pile of rocks right now. You could also exchange magic with sex, but, again, pile of rocks. You could kill someone and take their magic, but that would be the exact opposite of what we wanted.

One thing we hadn't tried yet was getting a sledgehammer and a crowbar and trying to take his rocks, one chunk at a time. Technically, every rock should have magic in it, so that would reduce his size and reduce his power. It was worth a shot.

We talked about the problem from every angle we could think of. We even thought about trying to get the sucker rune and seeing if we could put it on John. Then one of us would have to have another rune, and that person would have to be strong enough to pull the magic out of John. That would cause a whole lot of other problems. Whoever won the power war with the Louisville Mages would come here, and if they could get through the House shields, maybe they could drain John of all his magic. It was a terrible idea and quickly dropped, but at least we were trying to think of every possibility.

We ended the meeting with the sledgehammer idea, and finding a reason for John to spend his magic next time he was awake. That's all we had. It didn't seem like much.

We found some hammers and a crowbar in John's apartment and tried that. It didn't work. The rocks refused to come out. His magic was just too strong for us. When Tyler came back, we had him try. He was the strongest of all of us, but he couldn't get any stones out either. He did bend the crowbar, though, so he had really used a lot of force. We'd have to lower John's magic first, and then get rid of the stone.

The only true reason we could think of that would take a huge amount of magic was getting the House shields back to full strength. I wasn't sure that was urgent enough to keep John focused. I felt like it needed to affect Sandy. She was always his first priority.

***

The next five days passed quickly. Between the three of us, we made sure that John had full coverage. When he woke up, we were going to be ready. We decided to go with the emergency that the mages were going to attack soon and the House shields needed to be back at full power. This was a great story as it was all true. Hopefully, it would be enough.

Sandy didn't leave John's side. She stopped getting into her own bed and started sleeping on the pillows in his lap. She would talk to him and remind him of the adventures they had been through together. She even sang to him sometimes.

It was like John was on life support in the hospital, and Sandy was trying to pull him out of his coma through sheer force of will. It was intense, and I loved her for it. If anyone could save John, it would be her. Annabeth and I supported her however we could. We brought her food and talked to John while she had bathroom breaks and took a shower. When Sandy fell asleep on his lap, we'd take over telling stories.

I had a theory, but I kept it to myself. I didn't want to offer any sort of false hope. Time for the earth wasn't like time for us. Mountains form and erode over millions of years. If John was talking to the earth, then time was probably passing very slowly for him. Hopefully, these stories and songs would filter down to him. If he listened, he would have to speed up his time perception by paying more attention to us than the earth. Hopefully, everything we were doing would bring John back to us.

The one break from this deathbed intensity was our training. For a while, we were both doing our Pigeon Step practice, although Annabeth was at a much higher level than I. When I started out, it seemed like Sparkles hit me a lot. I was either stepping too early, or too late, or in the wrong direction. He didn't hold back either. His hits were solid and would knock me off my feet. It wasn't enough to really hurt me, but it was a very clear indicator I'd messed up. Once I got the timing down, the process became more like a puzzle.

It was better to step away from the hand punching you. So if Sparkles punched with his right hand, I'd step back to his left. I couldn't do this all the time, though, as it made me predictable. I had to mix it up. If I was stepping back the same way as the punching hand, I needed to take bigger steps, and they needed to be faster. The timing had to be just right.

Once I got the skill down, the puzzle part was easy. I'm great at puzzles, and I shot up the levels quickly. Sparkles increased to medium speed, and it would take him about thirty or forty punches before he'd tag me. It was a lot of fun making him chase me all over the beach.

I hit level ten on Pigeon Stepping a day after Annabeth. I was catching up. The next thing to learn was blocking. In a strange way, it was a bit of a letdown. Everything I'd learned up to this point had been weird and wonderful. The Pigeon Stance had been so weird, but once I learned to move, it had become a wonderful defense. Relax and Tense On Contact was weird, but once I had it down, my power shot through the roof.

I expected something similar with blocking, like I would have a Wax On and Wax Off moment from the Karate Kid. That didn't happen. The blocks were just blocks. Well, I wasn't really *blocking* a blow, I was *redirecting* it. Trying to actually block, or stop, a punch from Sparkles would be an exercise in frustration. He weighed a lot, and his punches were powerful. Trying to stop them would tear me apart. Instead, I learned to redirect his punches. As Tyler was fond of saying, "It doesn't matter how much their punch misses you, just as long as it misses you." The blocks were open palm slaps, designed to shift the aim of the blow and make it slide right on by. Of course, Relax and Tense On Contact was a big part of it. Relaxing made my blocks lightning quick, and the Tense On Contact provided the power.

Once I added blocking to Pigeon Stepping, it took my defensive ability to a whole new level. Sparkles increased his attack speed from medium to fast, and I was still able to defend against thirty plus attacks. One time, I was in the zone and ran up the score to one hundred and twelve punches.

It felt amazing. I was the wind, flowing around Sparkles' aggressive strikes. He couldn't touch me. When we finally broke apart, I got a round of applause from both Tyler and Annabeth. I was so happy. I finally had a defense. Sure, there was more to learn, but I finally had something I could apply in a fight. I wasn't invincible, but I could now get out of the way of a lot of damage headed towards me.

I decided to end my day on that note and leave Annabeth and Tyler to train together, when the House alarm went off. Either John was awake, or the House was under attack. We ran to the exit portal and raced upstairs.

I made it to the bedroom first, to see Sandy screaming at John and hurling weak fireballs at him.

23

Oath and Vow

I ran first to the pillows, as they were starting to catch fire.

I wasn't sure what had happened, but the last thing we needed was to have a major fire in the House. Tyler joined me as Annabeth rushed over to Sandy. Thank goodness her fireballs were weak right now. Her full-strength fireballs would have had the whole bedroom in flames. We got the pillows out of the way, and the flames stamped out as Annabeth grabbed Sandy and shook her.

"What happened?" Annabeth demanded in her no-nonsense grandmother voice.

"He came back," Sandy sobbed. "He came back, and then he left."

"Did you tell him about the House shield?" Annabeth asked. She shook Sandy again. "The shield. What did he say?"

Sandy stopped throwing fireballs and swayed on her feet. It looked like she was going to collapse. Tears streamed down her face.

"He said he's not coming back," she whispered. "He said he heard us and was checking in one last time to make sure we were okay. He said he couldn't fight it anymore."

She took a deep, painful breath as her body shook.

"He said goodbye."

We looked at each other in dismay. This was not supposed to happen. John couldn't leave us.

John was my friend. John was Sandy's lover. John was the maker of ale and the player of jokes.

He was an artist, the kindness in this world, a gentle giant that kept us safe.

He was my inspiration. I looked up to him. I hoped that when I'd lived hundreds of years, I would end up like him.

He was my family.

This was not okay.

If I felt that way, Sandy felt all that, and so much more.

She gathered herself and stood tall. Her eyes flashed as her voice grew strong.

"Hear me," she demanded.

"Hear me, John. I will NOT let you go."

"Hear me, EARTH. You may not have him."

"Hear me, HOUSE. Hear me all POWERS, all RUNES, all BEINGS both above and below."

"HEAR ME!"

"I, Sandy Marie Felton, head of House Louisville, hereby bind myself to Lain Rankin MacRae, of the clan MacRae, for all eternity."

"Where you go, I go. Where I go, you go."

"What you swear, I swear. What I swear, you swear."

"Your magic is my magic. My magic is your magic."

A wind suddenly sprang up around us, scattering the pillows and making the bed sheets flap.

"DEATH shall not part us."

The floor started shaking under our feet like a small earthquake.

"EARTH shall not part us."

Then I felt them all around us. A weight, a presence like ancient beings standing all around.

"John is the missing half of my soul."

The candles in the room flared up brightly.

"I am half of HIS soul."

I smelled lavender and jasmine.

"As of now, we are joined. WE speak with ONE VOICE."

She threw out her arms as if commanding the foundation of the world.

"I DECLARE it so. On my Magic. On John's Magic. On all that is right and good in the world."

"I DECLARE IT SO!"

There was a bass rumble. I felt it in my bones.

It grew louder and louder until I shook with the intensity. The whole room shook too. In fact, the beds shook so much, they started moving around the room. And I watched in amazement as the candles rose up and began floating in the air.

John opened his eyes. He tried to speak, but couldn't.

He looked at Sandy with such love, such compassion, such hope, it took my breath away.

He stirred and slowly held out his hand. It seemed like it was difficult for him to move. Sandy held out her hand too.

They touched, and everything focused on that moment.

Their hands glowed. I heard a single, deep toll of a bell.

"Accepted." It sounded like an earthquake speaking.

"Accepted." It was a woman's voice this time. She sounded amused.

"Accepted." It was a man's voice, and he sounded like Gandalf.

Then everything stopped.

The weight disappeared. The candles settled back down again. The floor stopped shaking. And the bell faded away .

OMG! I was vibrating from all the intensity.

"Get me a chair," Sandy demanded.

Tyler raced to comply. He slid it under her, and she sat down without releasing John's hand or losing his gaze.

"Jason, Annabeth, build me a matrix. Now."

I looked at Annabeth. Oh, boy. I wasn't saying no, but that was a tall order. It would solve the problem, though. Sandy needed magic, and John had too much.

"Um, that takes a lot of magic," I said. "Annabeth collapsed when we made her matrix. Are you sure you can use John's magic?"

"Yes," Sandy replied calmly. She never broke eye contact with John, and she suddenly seemed serene and peaceful.

"One last thing," I continued. I don't know how I was so bold, but I felt like this needed to be said. "If we build the matrix with John's magic, then it will be mostly his power inside you. You could lose your orange color. Or his magic might be considered contamination. You could really hurt yourself."

"John won't allow that to happen," she said. "And if it does, I've made my choice. Now begin."

"Tyler, can we get two more chairs?" I asked. "Annabeth, join me at her other hand."

Tyler got the chairs, and we both took her left hand.

"Sandy, I need you to swear to let us into your aura and your magic."

I gave her the wording we'd used with Annabeth. Sandy swore on her magic and amended the agreement to include both me and Annabeth. She also swore for John so we could use his magic too. We were ready to go.

"I'll start the matrix," I said to Annabeth. "Once you can hear it, then sing it into existence, like you did with your matrix. Give me a heads-up before you do that so I'm prepared for it."

Annabeth gave me a tight smile in agreement. I zoomed in on Sandy's hand and got started.

I quickly found out just how weak Sandy's magic was. I'd thought she was up to Annabeth's pre-matrix level, but she wasn't even close. Her magic was faint and wispy, and it took a lot of calling before I had enough of a cloud to split it apart. Just like before, the strands of magic broke apart from each other and formed small capsules of magic. I stacked the capsules together, and soon I had my first sphere.

Like with Annabeth, it took fewer capsules of magic to form a sphere. Sandy took about twenty capsules before they snapped together into a magic ball. Annabeth had taken around fifteen. Mine had been sixty capsules for green and thirty-five for blue. I wondered why mine was so much higher?

I pushed that thought aside and just focused on the matrix. It was slow going, but mainly because her magic was so sparse. Finally, though, I had a fairly stable matrix of fifty spheres on each side. I tapped Annabeth's hand to let her know it was time to do her thing. I stayed zoomed in to see how things were going.

I saw Annabeth's pink magic trickle over the baby matrix and start to hum. All the balls of magic started vibrating and then appeared to hum back. More pink magic flooded the area, and soon all of it was vibrating at the same frequency. Orange magic flew into the area, breaking down into magic spheres. Then they flew up to an empty spot in the pattern to join the chorus.

This was so much faster than my method! When I'd built mine, I'd placed most of the spheres by hand. My matrix had finally started building itself, but it had been so much bigger before that had happened. This was fascinating.

It wasn't long before Sandy ran out of magic. I felt her start to shake, and her breath grew ragged. Her magic had only filled up her fingers and part of her hand. This is where Annabeth had collapsed before. This time, though, a flood of power poured in from John. It flowed in from her other hand, across her body, and joined the structure we were building.

This was the moment of truth. Would John's magic fight with Sandy's? Would he make different size spheres and throw off the balance?

It turned out John's magic didn't fight with Sandy's, but it didn't join the party either. It just bunched up around the matrix, trying to do something, but unsure of what.

"Stop, Annabeth," I said. "John's magic has changed the song. What we've been doing isn't working anymore."

"Sandy, fill up on John's magic. Pull everything you can, and keep pulling until you feel like you are going to burst. That will keep your body going, and you'll have all that magic ready for when we start up again."

I didn't get a verbal reply from Sandy, but she started doing what I asked. That was good enough.

I scanned the divide between Sandy and John's colors. I had to find a way to merge their magic somehow. Sandy had so little of her own pure orange. Maybe I could rebuild the matrix, but this time do it with John's magic? Then, I could substitute about one in twenty of John's spheres with one of Sandy's. Maybe that would work. It was basically the idea I'd used for myself. My main matrix was made up of emerald green, but the center of each "box" in the matrix held a sapphire blue sphere.

I gathered John's magic and found he took nineteen capsules to make one sphere. Sandy was at twenty. Close enough. I made a bunch of spheres, cleared a space in the center of her hand, and started the new matrix.

It didn't take long before I discovered this wouldn't work. John and Sandy's magic did not want to be in a matrix together. I tried different ratios of spheres for the matrix, as well as putting Sandy's spheres in different locations, but it just didn't work. Once I got the matrix to a certain point, about twenty spheres per side, both magics started actively repelling each other. That tore the structure apart.

I took a deep breath. This had to work. Somehow, I had to make this happen. This was the solution to John and Sandy's magical problems. I just had to figure out how to do it.

My mind drifted, trying to think up alternate combinations. Nothing new came to mind as I let my focus wander over the divide between the two magics. The divide was pretty consistent. Sandy's magic pushed John's back by exactly the same amount.

Except for one area.

I flew over for a closer look. The area was so small, only a few spheres wide, but John's spheres weren't being repelled by Sandy's. Hmmm.

I examined them closely, but didn't see anything that really stuck out as different. Except, maybe there was a touch of orange to them? It was so faint. John's magic was gray, like stone. It had lighter and darker shades, and it twinkled a bit. It didn't have color, so even the tiniest hue stood out.

I couldn't figure anything else out by looking at it, so I decided to take one of the spheres apart. As soon as I did, I could see what had happened. One capsule of Sandy's magic had gotten trapped in the center. Was that the secret?

I was very surprised to see this. When I'd been making my own matrix, I'd tried to combine my green and blue magic together. It hadn't worked, and I'd given up on the idea. That seemed like so long ago. Maybe there was a way to combine my colors after all? Now that I thought about it, I'd tried to combine roughly the same amount of capsules. What I was seeing here was a much different ratio.

I counted the capsules that had come from the sphere and got another surprise. There were twenty-five of John's capsules with one of Sandy's capsules. So twenty-six capsules total. I put the sphere back together and compared it to a neighbor that was just John's magic. They were the same size. Somehow, combining both magics made for a denser sphere.

This was all fascinating stuff, but now I needed to see if I could scale this knowledge into a working matrix. There were three of the anomaly spheres, and I'd already fully examined one of them. I broke the other two apart to see if they were any different. They weren't. They both had one of Sandy's capsules as the core and then twenty-five of John's magic to go with it. So the idea and the ratio were the same. Now I needed to make more of them. A lot more.

I started splitting up John and Sandy's spheres down to their component capsules, when I had another idea. Annabeth could listen to a matrix and then sing the rest of it into existence. Could I do the same thing?

I tried to listen to the new sphere. It wasn't talking to me. Or, if it was, I couldn't hear it. What I could do was feel. And taste. I took a moment to appreciate just how versatile my magic senses were. The new sphere felt different. It felt denser and seemed to have a harder "skin". Spheres that were pure Sandy or John felt like a water balloon. They were a bit squishy and felt like they would pop if I squeezed hard enough. Spheres that had the new mixture of both felt like a balloon had been stuffed inside of a balloon, and then stuffed inside another balloon before being filled with water. They felt weightier and more solid.

As for taste, I could certainly taste a difference.

Just how do John's balls taste? Hmm? Anna Lykit's voice popped into my head.

'Ewww. Go away,' I replied.

And does Sandy even have balls, I wonder?

'That's just gross, stop talking about my friends' equipment. Now go away. I'm trying to save lives here.' Anna wandered away, but not without a parting shot.

You could open a fusion restaurant. Have different magic balls on the menu. Call it Bowl of Balls. All the supernaturals would love it!

That was a funny thought. Anna Lykit was a clever queen, but I couldn't tell her that or she'd never shut up.

Okay. Now time to focus.

I concentrated on the mixture of capsules floating before me. I kept the feel and taste of the new fusion ball in my mind, and projected. At first, nothing happened. Then a few capsules came together. Then a few more. Pop. I had my first sphere.

Pop. I had another one.

Pop. Then another one.

Pop. Pop. Pop.

Suddenly it was like popcorn. In the space of a few moments, I created over a hundred fusion spheres. That sure was a lot faster than trying to make them by hand.

I discovered something else too. *Pushing* the magic worked, but it wasn't as effective as *inviting* the magic. This reminded me of when I'd converted the neutral magic in Penny. The magic seemed friendly. It wanted to help. It just didn't know how.

Now I had lots of fusion spheres, it was time to form the matrix. Before, I would have pulled the spheres into place one by one. This time, I just invited them to line up.

And they did.

They were like toy soldiers, lining up for playtime. It was both fast and fun.

I told them they were amazing and wonderful, and invited all the magic around them to join in. I was trying to affect a bigger area, so it took a lot more intensity in my invitation, but the results were spectacular.

Both magics sphered up and zoomed into place. It was awesome. A cube fifty spheres to each side might not sound like much. But that's fifty times fifty times fifty, or one hundred and twenty-five thousand spheres. That's a lot to do by hand.

This time, it only took a few minutes of invitation, and the baby matrix was ready.

"Okay. Annabeth, do your thing," I said.

Once again, I saw her pink magic swirl around the pattern, and then everything started humming together. The humming attracted more magic, both John and Sandy's, and soon the fusion matrix was growing at a rapid pace.

I stayed zoomed in to watch it happen. It was like watching a time lapse video as it grew to cover her whole hand, and then moved up her arm. I zoomed out at that point, happy with the results.

I returned to regular awareness, only to find Tyler frantically beating on John and pulling rocks off of him.

"Help me!" he shouted. "As John's magic is receding, his rock is changing to regular stone. He's becoming more human, and he's going to get buried. That can't happen!"

With no time to waste, I grabbed the sledgehammer and started beating on John. I had to be careful. I didn't want to hit him so hard it would injure him when he became human. On the other hand, I needed to break the rocks up.

This was working! We were getting huge slabs of stone off of him. When he finally shrunk below eight feet, I switched out the sledgehammer for the crowbar. It was bent, but it still worked.

John and Sandy stayed still the whole time. Never losing sight of each other. Never losing contact. I was very careful when breaking the rock off of John's hand. I didn't want to accidently smash Sandy's fingers. But the magic kept flowing, and they appeared to be alright.

Sandy's matrix finished up when John was almost done. It was such a relief pulling off the last of the rock and seeing skin underneath. Some of the rock still clung to him in patches, so Sandy kept pulling magic. She didn't stop until it was gone.

She glowed with magic. I knew what it was like to pull magic until you thought you would explode, and she looked like that. She took her other hand out of Annabeth's grasp and held it up. John's human hand reached up and held it, and Sandy pushed some of that extra magic back into John.

I was afraid rocks might start sprouting off of John again, but thankfully that didn't happen. Finally, it was really finished. Sandy looked powerful, but okay. John looked okay too.

They both stood up. John was naked. He towered over her, but somehow Sandy looked stronger, bigger.

She wrapped her arms around him, buried her face in his hairy chest, and started bawling. John wrapped his arms carefully around her and held her tight.

He looked stunned, like he had just woken up from a long sleep and had no idea where he was or what had happened. Which was basically true. Then big, wet tears started rolling down his face.

For a long while, they just held each other and cried. Tyler came over and put his arms around me. I was surprised to find I was crying too. Then Annabeth came over, and we had a three-way hug. And a cry.

They were happy tears. I felt such relief. The weight of worry had been a constant companion for weeks now. For the first time, I could breathe. Sandy and John were going to be alright.

We stayed that way for a long while, until Sandy let John go and stepped back.

"John." Uh-oh. She was sounding formal again. "I know we are now sworn to each other. And that should be enough. But I'm an old-fashioned girl. The heart wants what the heart wants."

She got down on one knee. We all gasped.

"John, I've loved you for a long time, and I want to spend the rest of my very long supernatural life together with you.

"Will you marry me?"

Time stopped. I couldn't breathe.

John tried to speak, but nothing came out. He hadn't spoken in a long time. Maybe he'd forgotten how?

He tried again, but all that came out was a bass rumble.

Sandy stayed on one knee, waiting.

He pulled his shoulders back. He faced her tall and proud.

"Sandy, I too am an old-fashioned guy.

"Yes! With all my heart, yes!"

We burst into cheers, and he swept her off her feet and into a long kiss.

They kissed like famished lovers. Like two people that desperately needed the love in each other. They soaked it in like the desert drinks the rain. It was a beautiful thing to see. It was like a Hallmark movie, only in real life.

Finally, they parted again. John looked happy, if a little breathless.

"Annabeth, will you stand with me?" Sandy was sounding formal again. The surprises for the night weren't over yet.

"Of course!" Annabeth gushed, running over to hug her.

"Jason, will you stand with me?" John rumbled. He sounded formal also.

"Of course!" I ran over and hugged him too.

He was still naked and hairy and dusty, but that didn't stop me. In my own way, I loved this big mountain man. I wanted him and Sandy to be so very happy together. I would do anything for them.

Then, they both looked at Tyler.

"As a representative of the House and a good friend, will you marry us?" Sandy asked.

"Of course!" he said and ran over to hug them both.

"Are we doing this tonight?" Annabeth asked.

Sandy looked at John.

He nodded.

"Yes," Sandy replied. "I won't wait any longer."

Everyone nodded. We were doing this.

"Might I suggest that John gets dressed and maybe takes a shower?" Annabeth said. "Taking an hour to get ready won't hurt anything."

This was such an important moment that we really should take more time. Weddings usually take months to plan. They weren't going to wait, though. They had almost lost everything. Even as long as they had lived, time was precious. Annabeth was probably pushing it just asking for an hour.

They both agreed, so we split up. Annabeth took Sandy, and Tyler said something about getting the House ready. I grabbed John's hand, and we headed downstairs. I got him in the shower, talking to him the whole time. He looked fine and moved well, but I was scared that if I slowed down, he might go back to the earth again. He'd lost his excess magic and Sandy was grounding him now, so he was probably fine. This was the biggest night of his life, though, and I didn't want to take any chances.

I went through his clothes while he was cleaning up. He didn't have anything formal looking. He didn't even have a proper shirt. John was a very casual dresser.

That wouldn't do, but I didn't have anything else to work with.

I thought about running upstairs to change into my one good outfit, but I didn't want to leave John alone. I finally decided that John would look casual and so would I.

Finally, he emerged from the shower, looking cleaner and much more awake. He looked rough, though. He needed some manscaping. An hour wasn't much time, so we settled for a shave, and I quickly trimmed his wild hair. I'm no hairstylist, but it looked much better once I was finished.

I toweled the loose hair off of him, and it was finally time to get dressed. I'd found a black pair of pants for him to wear. They were work pants, but they were clean. Then I went with a white t-shirt and layered it with a plain blue t-shirt. It wasn't much, but the white undershirt made the blue shirt look more formal. He didn't have a tie or a hat, so this would have to do.

We needed one more thing. Actually, two more things.

A pair of rings.

You can't get married without rings.

"John, we need wedding bands," I said. "Have you been working on something for a customer? Or got anything mostly finished?"

He just shook his head slowly. He still seemed to be adjusting to being human again. It was probably going to take time to get the old John back.

"I know you can do something, John. Even if it is a placeholder for something better later."

He just looked around, lost.

"What does Sandy like?" I asked. I needed to get him thinking. "Does she have a certain type of stone, or a certain shape she's attracted to?

"She isn't a fancy girl," John said. "I'm pretty sure I like sparkly things more than she does. I've offered to make her rings before, but she's always said no. She likes what I make for others, but she wouldn't want them for herself."

I thought for a moment. We needed something simple. Something that represented their love for each other. They had joined their magic together for all eternity. There had to be a ring for that.

"Magic!" I said excitedly. "You joined your magic together. That is how you saved each other. That is the basis for all your happy moments from here on out. You need something that shows your gray magic together with her orange magic."

John's eyes lit up. We were on the right track. He went over to his workbench and began sorting through his metals and stones. He quickly found what he was looking for. When he turned around, he had copper, gold, silver, and another metal that was a bit darker than silver in his hand. I don't know metals by sight, so they might have been different, but that is what it looked like.

John started pinching the metals together. Even though they should have been rock hard, he squeezed them together like they were playdough. Once he had them mixed, he rolled them between his hands to form a thin line of metal. He looped it around and joined the edges together. The shape of the ring was there, but it didn't look like much yet.

He started humming to it, and the ring slowly changed in front of my eyes. The copper and gold intertwined and became a light orange color representing Sandy's magic. The dark and light silver intertwined and became John's magic. The orange flowed up one side of the ring and swirled at the top to form a thicker circle of metal. It looked sort of like a comma. John's gray metal flowed up the other side, and it formed a comma too—just the opposite direction from the orange. It looked like an organic yin yang, with both magics in harmony and balancing each other. He kept humming, and the metal changed from a smooth flow to more of a fractured surface. When he was done, there must have been thousands of little flat facets on the surface of the ring. They reflected the light, and the whole thing sparkled like it was covered in gemstones.

Finally, he stopped and held up the ring for me to see. It was breathtaking, and just perfect. It represented the joining of their magic and their new life together. It was all metal, which suited Sandy the battle mage. It also had lots of sparkle, which suited John the artist.

It was John and Sandy and their love, in a ring.

"It's perfect, John," I told him. "She is going to love it. Now make one for you too."

John repeated the process, but with a lot more metal. His ring was much wider and thicker as his hands were huge.

Their rings had almost identical designs, except the colors were switched. Sandy's magic came up on the right on her ring, but on John's ring it came up on the left. It was a small thing, but I felt it made the two rings even more perfect.

Once John was finished, our time was up. I took his giant hand in mine and led him upstairs. He seemed to be speeding up a bit more and shaking off some of the lethargy of the earth. I wasn't taking any chances, though, so I talked to him the whole way. He seemed a bit amused that I was leading him around, but he went with it.

We reached Sandy's bedroom, but there was no sign of the bride or Annabeth. I was pretty sure the groom was supposed to enter first and be waiting, so we went inside. Sandy's bedroom still looked grand, with its tall ceiling and all the candles, except now it had a runner of pure white leading to an arch in the back wall. That certainly hadn't been there before. Red rose petals were sprinkled on the white runner, and their scent filled the air. Still holding hands, we walked down the runner and stepped through the arch.

We walked into another world. We were in a clearing in a forest, surrounded by flowering trees. I don't know my trees so I wasn't sure what they were, but it reminded me of how it looked during the cherry blossom festival. It was a stunning vista of color and beauty. There was a light wind blowing, so a snow of white and pink petals floated through the air.

The sky was filled with stars, and the scene was lit by a full moon. The white runner continued into the center of the clearing, ending on a low slab of rock. Alongside the runner were flaming torches, and they continued all around the rock. We had lots of ambience and yet plenty of light to see by. I also liked that Sandy's fire and John's rock were represented in the scene.

On the rock at the end of the runner was Tyler. He was dressed in a full black tuxedo, because of course he was. Tyler always looked perfect for every occasion. He smiled and waved us forward. Still holding John's hand, I led him onward. When we reached Tyler, he gestured to his left. I pulled John over to the grass beside Tyler, and then stood beside him. Tyler was on the rock, but it was only a little over a foot high. It was just enough to give him a sense of presence as the master of the ceremony.

"You look wonderful," he told John, giving him a clap on the shoulder.

"Thank you," John said simply. Then we both turned and looked back towards the arch.

We waited.

The night was beautiful. I don't know how Tyler and the House pulled off such a romantic setting so fast, but kudos to them.

Annabeth appeared next. She was wearing a light blue summer dress with yellow shoes and a pearl necklace. It was cheerful. It was spring. It was classic Annabeth.

She was humming as she walked down the white runner, and her pink magic filled the air. It was the perfect complement to the little pink and white petals from the trees.

When she reached the end of the runner, she nodded to each of us, but she didn't stop humming. She stepped to Tyler's right, leaving space for Sandy to stand next to John. She turned back to face the arch, and her voice raised in song.

I'd never heard her sing before. She was always humming around me, but her voice was magical. She sang an old song, "Somewhere Over the Rainbow," and it was stunning. Her voice filled the clearing and called all those who witnessed to celebrate the hope and joy that was present. She changed up some of the words, and I realized she was mixing the song with "What A Wonderful World."

I was already tearing up before Sandy walked through the arch. I was fine with that. I'm such a sensitive gay soul with a soft spot for romance. After all, it's not every day that two soul-kissed lovers declare their eternal devotion to each other.

Sandy was also wearing a blue dress with little yellow flowers. She and Annabeth had coordinated their outfits. That was amazing for only an hour's notice. Thank goodness I'd picked out a blue shirt for John.

Her dress was perfect. It talked of spring and hope. Fresh flowers and new beginnings.

She walked down the white runner, her eyes locked on John's, and his eyes were locked on hers. The affection and hope between them was palpable.

She reached the end of the runner and stood there while Annabeth finished her song. She was so regal, beautiful, and strong.

John was a lucky man. I looked up at him, all seven feet of him, with his handsome features and kind eyes. Sandy was a lucky woman too.

Annabeth finished her song, and the night grew quiet. The only melody was the breeze in the trees. Sandy stepped forward and took John's hand. Then we all turned and faced Tyler.

Somehow, Tyler had changed his outfit. His tuxedo was now blue with yellow trim. It perfectly complemented Sandy's dress. Damn, he was good!

"Today, we are called to witness the joining of Sandy Marie Felton and Lain Rankin MacRae. They have already pledged their magic and their souls to each other. This has been witnessed and approved by the Earth, the Runes, and the Ancient Beings of Magic in the world. This ceremony is to bring them together in more than magic. It is to bring them together with Love. Tonight we give this Love a moment in time. We shape it with our words. We give it a foundation to rest upon. A place to grow from. We call it Marriage. And tonight, Sandy and John will create that foundation together."

He sounded different. His voice was deeper with more of an accent. What he was saying seemed different than a traditional wedding. I'd only been to a few of them, but I'm pretty sure they hadn't begun like this. He gestured around at the clearing.

"We stand in a special place tonight. The All Rune has declared this a place of TRUTH. No falsehood may be uttered here tonight, even unintentionally. You must speak the truth you know, and the truth you don't."

He looked at Annabeth.

"Who stands as Sandy's witness tonight? Who stands as the Champion of her Love?"

"I, Annabeth Sarah Matz, stand as the witness for Sandy," Annabeth said firmly. She tried to look serious, but ended up giving Sandy the biggest smile.

"And who are you, that you could Champion for her?"

That was an odd question. Tyler was still speaking in his weird voice. Was something wrong?

Annabeth looked at us, confused. She obviously didn't know what to say. I just shrugged. I wasn't sure either.

"I am the first born of House Louisville," she said clearly. She sounded good, but she looked a little shocked. She wasn't done yet, either.

"I am the first student of the Head of Household, Sandy. I am the bearer of her charms and the heir of her knowledge"

"I am She Who Listens. I am She Who Sings."

"I am She Who Goes Before. I am a Champion of the Balance."

"I am the Right Hand of God."

The clearing fell quiet. We all waited to see if she would say anything else. She looked stunned, but she stayed quiet. Before we could dwell on what had happened, Tyler looked at me and continued.

"Who stands as John's witness tonight? Who stands as the Champion of his Love?"

"I, Jason David Cole, stand as the witness for John," I said.

I was nervous. I was pretty sure I knew what was coming next. I didn't have any big titles, though. Not like Annabeth.

"And who are you, that you Champion for him?" Tyler asked.

I started to shrug, and then my mouth opened and words started pouring out.

"I am He Who Makes. I am He Who Heals."

"I am a Champion of the All Rune. I am a Champion of the Balance."

"I am the Destroyer. I am the Builder."

"I am..."

Suddenly I couldn't speak. A war raged on me and through me. I felt hot, like I was going to explode. Then it was gone. The House wrapped me in power, and suddenly I was fine. A voice in the wind whispered in my ear.

'Not now, little one.' I steadied myself and took a deep breath.

'Not now. Not here. Tell no one.'

Everyone was staring at me, waiting for me to speak. I just shook my head.

Everyone was still looking at me, so I waved my hand for them to continue. I didn't trust myself to open my mouth.

Tyler looked at me like 'We'll talk later,' but he turned back to Sandy and John and continued.

"The witnesses are present. The champions are acceptable. This is the time. This is the place. Your Marriage begins here.

"Love is most often known as a feeling. It sweeps through you and lifts you up. You thrill at the sound of their voice and you ache for their touch. This is Love like the wind. Sometimes it blows strong. Sometimes it doesn't blow at all. You two already have this Love.

"Love is also an action. It is being there for each other when there is need. It is being there for each other in battle. It is being there for each other first, regardless of your other demands. You two already have this Love.

"Love is also a commitment. It begins with words. They lay the foundation for your life together. They are the soil in which your Love grows. They anchor you when all else fails. This Love you do not have yet. This is the Love you are creating today."

He turned to Sandy.

"Sandy, create the foundation of your Love with John."

She turned to him and took both of his hands in hers. She paused, considering what to say.

"I promise to laugh with you. I promise to listen to you.

"I promise to tell you I love you, and show you I love you in every way I can.

"I promise to let you in when I'm hurt. I promise to be with you when you are hurting.

"I am a mature woman. I've married and loved before. I've laughed and lost and hurt before. I promise a fresh start for us, yet seasoned with experience, so we can have the best life possible. If I have missed anything here, I simply say this.

"I promise."

Her hands were shaking, and tears ran down her face. She was giving John everything. She was committed to him. He was her love, and she was going all in. John had his back to me, but I could see his hands shaking too.

Tyler turned to John.

"John, create the foundation of your Love with Sandy."

"Sandy, I started loving you the first day I heard you in the garden. I knew there was something special about you. I could feel it in my soul. I've been with you ever since, because I love you.

"I don't have all the fancy words. I feel more than I speak. So here is what I have.

"I promise to keep doing what I've been doing. That has created our love today, and it will continue to create our love tomorrow.

"I promise to listen to you, and still tell you when you're daft.

"I promise to make you laugh, even when you pretend to be upset in the moment.

"Most of all, I promise to be good for you, in every way I know how."

The moment caught up with him, and he swept her up in a kiss.

"I think that part is supposed to come later," Annabeth noted. Tyler just grinned and waited.

And waited.

It was a long kiss.

Finally, they broke apart, and Sandy grinned at us.

"Sorry about that," she said. She didn't sound sorry, though. She sounded like she wanted to do it again.

"That's quite alright," Tyler said with a smile. Then he gestured to include us all.

"The foundation has been spoken. And witnessed."

I thought the rings were next, so I pulled them out of my pocket and waved them discreetly at Tyler.

"Bring the rings," he commanded.

Annabeth and Sandy gave me a questioning look as I stepped forward and handed them over. Sandy got a good look at them and gasped.

She turned to John. "They look beautiful!" There was wonder and happiness in her voice.

"Wow. These are stunning," Tyler said in his normal voice. Then he seemed to straighten, and the deeper, accented voice was back.

"Sandy and John, you are My Champions. You hold to the hope I provide. You are the defenders of My House. Your Love resonates with My Foundation. May you live long. May your Love prosper. May you always dwell in My House."

"It is customary to ask for a blessing on the rings. I, the All Rune, will provide that blessing.

"Behold!"

The rings floated off of Tyler's hand and hovered in the air. They started glowing a soft yellow. The light wasn't bright, but the power coming off of them was intense. I felt warm, like I was standing in bright summer sunlight. I tasted strawberries. A yellow rune formed in the air beside them.

Then the light changed to red, and I felt a slight chill. I smelled leaves and tasted apples. I felt the excitement and the loss of heading out on a journey, like it was a quest I might never come back from. A red rune formed beside the yellow one.

The glow on the rings kept changing. The next color was white, and the chill deepened to a frigid cold. I was suddenly so cold I started shivering uncontrollably and my teeth were chattering. I didn't taste anything, but I felt resolute. Like I was grounded, my will was strong, I knew my purpose. It was a calm sort of power, but there was wisdom in it. A white rune formed beside the red one.

The glow changed again to a light green. The chill left, and I just felt normal. I stopped shaking, and now I tasted lemons. I felt strong, healthy, and full of energy. I suddenly felt so much energy, I just wanted to dance and sing and twirl around in a circle. It was a good thing this wasn't a musical, or I'd have burst into song. A green rune formed beside the white one.

Then all my weird tastes and smells disappeared. I went back to just feeling normal. That had been intense! Was I the only one that had felt all that? I looked over at

Annabeth, and she was shooting me the 'What the heck?' look.

The runes were moving, so I quickly focused back on Tyler and the floating rings. The four runes merged together, making one incredibly complex white rune. I'd never seen anything like it. Even in the golem core, there hadn't been anything like this.

It wasn't done yet. Dark clouds appeared on the horizon and rushed towards us. The wind started blowing, like a storm was approaching. The rune rose into the air and grew to at least twelve feet wide. The wind whipped up all the little petals from the trees, and suddenly they started getting sucked into the rune. When the petals got to the rune, they just vanished. It was eating them somehow.

Then the clouds arrived, and lightning started flashing. The rune turned in the air and grew even more. It was now flat over our heads and large enough to cover our little group. The lightning danced among the clouds for a moment, and then arced down to the earth. The thunder was deafening, but the rune ate the lightning bolt. It ate the next three too. I clapped my hands over my ears, but that only helped a little bit. I had never been that close to a lightning strike, and I hope to never be that close again.

When the lightning stopped, the rain started. It wasn't just a few drops either. It felt like a bucket in the sky had tipped over, and the rain lashed down. It hammered the trees and grass all around us, but the rune ate all the rain over our heads too. That was one thirsty rune!

As quickly as they formed, the clouds broke up and blew away. The giant rune over our heads was now so bright it was hard to look at. The energy it was putting off was palpable, and I kind of felt like ducking down. The rings floated higher in the air, merging with the rune and all that power.

At first, I didn't see anything happening. Then I noticed the rune was now a little smaller, a little less bright. It took time, but it slowly shrank down until all that was left were the two rings. Somehow, they had absorbed the rune and all that energy. I thought they should be shining brighter than the sun, but they weren't. Instead, they had a faint magic glow.

The rings floated back down again and settled onto Tyler's hand. I had no clue what all this meant, but they clearly had a lot of magic packed inside them. The All Rune must really like Sandy and John because it had blessed the shit out of their rings!

Tyler looked at the rings and looked at us. He seemed at a loss for what to say next.

"Ummm. I'll be honest here. I've never married anyone before. The All Rune has been helping me so far and right now it's silent." Tyler was speaking in his regular voice.

"Usually the vows go with the giving of the rings," Annabeth spoke up. She probably had the most experience of everyone here, as she had been married and she'd helped plan her son's wedding.

"I think just a simple 'I do' and exchanging the rings would be fine."

"Thank you, Annabeth," Tyler nodded to her. He looked at Sandy and John. "Does that work for you?" They both nodded.

Tyler handed Sandy's ring to John.

John went down on one knee, like he was going to propose to her. It was way too late for that, but we were kind of out of sync anyway and making it up as we went. We'd already had magic vows that saved John, a stunningly beautiful location, and a blessing from the All Rune. It would be impossible to mess up the wedding at this point.

"Sandy." John held her hand gently. "In every way, I Do." He slipped the ring on her finger. There was a world of sincerity and love in that simple statement.

I'm very sure it doesn't go like that at a traditional wedding. It was simple and effective, though, so it worked. He got back to his feet, and Tyler handed John's ring to Sandy. She took his giant hand in hers.

"John." She looked up at him, the moonlight reflecting off the tears in her eyes. "In every way, I Do." She slipped the ring onto his finger.

"By the power invested in me by the All Rune, I pronounce you Husband and Wife!" Tyler proclaimed joyfully.

"You may now kiss the heck out of each other!"

He was a little late. They were already kissing again.

We clapped and cheered and celebrated their moment. They finally broke apart, and then started laughing. We all got hugs and offered our congratulations. John was being careful so my ribs didn't creak too bad when he picked me up, wrapped his arms around me, and gave me a big squeeze.

"Thank you," he said sincerely. He was still holding me close in the air as his head tilted forward and his forehead rested against mine. Somehow, that created our own little intimate space.

"Thank you for taking care of Sandy. Thank you for taking care of Annabeth. Thank you for taking care of the House." He said each sentence slowly and distinctly with full sincerity.

"And thank you for taking care of me.

"You are my little brother," he declared, and then kissed me on each cheek. I started to say something, but he got the feels again and gave me a big squeeze, so I had no air to speak with.

Then he put me down, and the moment was over. I was fine with that. We'd have a few pints of ale later, and I'd say how much he meant to me then.

I had a great moment with Sandy too. Unlike John, I wasn't swept off my feet and crushed with happiness. Instead, I got a normal hug, and I had enough breath left to notice she smelled good.

"Thank you for everything, Jason," she said. "I know this hasn't been easy for you. Taking care of others takes stamina and compassion. It can change your whole world around. You have done a wonderful job, and I'm so grateful."

There were tears in her eyes as she leaned in and kissed me on both cheeks. It seemed like that was the thing to do tonight.

"We will have a long talk later," she continued. "Just know that you have a special place in my heart."

Normally, there would be rice throwing, cake eating, and dancing. But we didn't have any of that here. This moment was perfect, and I didn't want it to end for them. I also didn't really want to go back to the House. That would lead back to Sandy's bedroom, and right now that felt like the sick room. I guess Annabeth was thinking the same thing because she spoke up.

"I wish there was some way for you two to spend some time away for a while. John, I feel like you really need to celebrate life and stay away from the earth as much as possible."

"You mean, like a honeymoon?" Tyler said with a twinkle in his eye. "It's already been taken care of."

"Really?" Sandy sounded so excited. I guess she wasn't looking forward to going back right now either.

This was great! I was still concerned about John's connection to the earth. He needed some good human time. And what would be better than a honeymoon?

"The House said it has a surprise in store for you. I don't know what it is, but I'm sure it's wonderful." He gestured back down the path. "Just go back to the arch, and you'll be on your way."

John and Sandy shared a look. It said they couldn't wait to get started!

"I don't want to just run off and leave you guys here," John rumbled.

"Yes, you do!" I laughed. "Don't worry about us. We'll be just fine. Now, go!"

"Are you sure?" Sandy said. She was both hesitant and excited.

"Yes! Go!" Annabeth chimed in. "Get to celebrating."

"Go test the suspension on your new Husband," Tyler said with a wink.

We didn't need to tell them twice. Sandy and John were already sprinting back up the white runner.

"Thank you!" Sandy yelled over her shoulder, and then they were at the arch. They both turned and waved and blew big kisses. "Thank you, again," they both yelled, and then they stepped through the arch and were gone.

24

Twin Sinks

That night I went to sleep in my own bed. What bliss. Pure heavenly bliss. I thought the bed might be too big, but I found I loved the size. I could lie down in the center, stretch out, and still not touch either side.

The best part were the sheets, not too hot and not too cool. They had a nice weave, allowing easy movement. I've slept in a lot of beds in my life, and I've discovered that having the right mattress was nice, but the icing on the cake was getting the perfect sheets. Silk sheets were too slick, and high thread count sheets were often too hot. Somehow, the House had gotten them just right.

I told Bermuda just how wonderful they were, but he didn't take my word for it. Instead, he sniffed all around the bed, like he was looking for a trap or something. I just stuck my tongue out at him and snuggled in even deeper.

My only gloomy thought was that Tyler wasn't with me. He was spending a bit of time with Mr. Tubbles. Maybe I'd wake up with him in the morning. That was a delicious thought.

I rolled over on my back and gazed up at the ceiling. My eyes traveled to the long bar running the length of the room. Every few feet, fan blades turned slowly. I enjoyed the breeze as I watched the slow hypnotic turn of the blades. Behind the bed, the shutter slats were open, letting in the fresh night air. This must be what living in a home in Key West felt like. Or maybe Hawaii.

I hadn't known how I would like all the greenery in the bedroom. Lying here, with the breeze blowing and plants softly fluttering, it felt perfect. The House had created something wonderful for me. My bedroom wasn't just a place to sleep anymore; it was my own little slice of paradise. My sanctuary.

Bermuda finished sniffing around and hopped up on my leg. Then he walked all the way up my body and sat down with a little sigh on my chest. I cuddled him up, running my fingers through his fur. He closed his eyes in contentment and turned on the purr. It was a strong purr too. I could feel the vibrations bouncing around my chest.

For the first time in a long time, I felt at peace. Sandy and John were okay. They were off celebrating their wedding bliss. Tyler was okay. Annabeth was okay. Bermuda was okay. I was okay.

There was so much more to do, but in this moment, right now, I was happy. I was content. I closed my eyes, basking in Bermuda's love. He rolled over on his back, threw his paws out to the side, and let me get in some good belly snuggles.

I was grateful for moments like this. They recharged my batteries. They reminded me that life was so much more than survival. Life was friends. Life was affection. Life was kittens.

Bermuda was still purring when I drifted off to a restful sleep.

***

I got up in the middle of the night with the urge to pee. After a quick dash into the bathroom, I felt a weird mix of tired and restless, so I stood with Eggy at the window for a while, looking out on the night. I decided to work on my adopted charm. He was the last of my friends that was still sleeping. Now I had a new technique, I was anxious to wake him up. He had a lot more capacity than Penny, though, and I didn't want to overdo it. I figured I'd give him a bit of soul as often as I could, waking him up gradually.

I picked him up and took him back to bed with me. Bermuda settled down on my pillow as I curled up with Eggy. I took a moment to appreciate him. Even as an egg, he looked beautiful.

I zoomed in to see what I had to work with. His power capacity was certainly bigger than Penny's—like vastly bigger. If Penny was a large pond, he was one of the Great Lakes. It was a bit intimidating. I was going to eventually fill him with magic? I couldn't imagine what that would take.

He did have a lot of neutral magic to work with, though. Octa and her Tangle had been giving him a lot of cleaned magic from the park. At least it was going to good use. I could see some of my magic in there too. What was interesting was the other magic he contained. If I had to guess, it was from his original source.

What should have been a deep, earthy brown had faded over time. Now it was a flat gray, with only little dots of color to show what it was supposed to be. This magic hadn't rotted like Isobel's stolen magic, and it hadn't gone back to neutral like the park magic. Instead, it had just faded and died. There was no sparkle and very little life left. Poor Eggy. He hadn't been renewed in a very long time. No wonder he just wanted to sleep.

While Eggy's power capacity was vast, his actual power density was a lot less than Penny's. Her magic seemed solid. I'd felt like I was outside a solid wall, and it had hummed with power. His magic was more like a wall of rain. It reminded me of when it rained so hard you could see it coming down in sheets. Sort of like the rain we had experienced at the wedding. Maybe, someday, when I finally filled him all the way up to capacity, his density would be like Penny's. Until then, this is what I had to work with.

Just like before, I put my hand on his power and called to my colors. They came a lot easier than with Penny. With her, it felt sluggish. But with him, they leapt to obey. Once again, I started from the little circle of soul I'd created. I reinforced it and then added more. I pushed my colors out, extending the invitation to all the magic around. The neutral magic joined pretty easily, but the gray magic just sat there.

Some of it converted, but it wasn't much. Oh well, I'd gradually wake it up.

This time I didn't go overboard. I pushed while I felt strong and stopped as soon as I saw my color intensity dip. I had gotten a lot done, and I was very glad there was all the neutral magic available. Trying to get Eggy going with gray magic alone would have been rough. I put Eggy back on his stand, letting the purple Octopuses settle on him again.

"Thanks, guys," I said to the purple Tangle and took a moment to give them some affection.

"Good night, Eggy," I told him. "You'll be awake soon."

I crawled back into my perfect bed, listened to the ocean, and went to sleep once more.

***

I woke up with Tyler snuggling me. We were spooning, and I was the little spoon. Bermuda was here too. Instead of snoozing on his customary pillow, he was curled up in a ball, spooning with me. A little, furry spoon.

I had fun with the silverware thoughts for a moment. Tyler was the tablespoon. I was the soup spoon. Bermuda, since he was so much smaller, was the tasting spoon. We were a spoon family. I imagined us moving into a new neighborhood and introducing ourselves to the neighbors as "the Spoons".

I chuckled, but only mentally. I didn't want to wake everyone up. Tyler must not have been fooled by my sleep acting because he started gently kissing the back of my neck. I tried to stay in my sleepy zone, but it felt so damn good.

Finally, I rolled over, and we got down to some serious kissing. The feedback loop was over. I'd absorbed his magic, and he'd absorbed mine. It was so nice to just take my time and let the passion build slowly.

I ran my hands over his body, letting my fingers map him out. The Land of Tyler was a beautiful place, and I thoroughly enjoyed my vacation. Then the Land of Tyler started having earthquakes–rolling, powerful earthquakes. We got a disgusted look from Bermuda and he left, but I held on for the ride. And what a ride it was. My tour of the Land ended in a firework display and some more snuggling.

Afterward, we chatted about the wedding and enjoyed our morning together, but finally it was time to get up. I was on my own schedule now. I didn't have to do everything in eight-hour segments, but I still had a lot I wanted to get done.

I got out of bed and headed to the door, only to stop in surprise. There was now a second door in the bedroom. I looked at Tyler. He just shrugged. I opened the first one. That was the one I was used to; it still led to the living room and the kitchen. I closed it and turned to the new one. Where was it going to lead?

Tyler came up beside me. We opened the new door together.

"Wow!" I breathed.

"Wow!" Tyler said. "This is a bathroom?"

We stepped inside. It was a bathroom, but that was like saying the Ritz Carlton was just a hotel. This bathroom was magnificent.

First of all, it had room. Lots of room. I was used to a bathroom where the first step inside was the sink. Take one more step, and it was toilet time. The next step you're in the shower. The three-step bathroom was my normal.

This one had a lot of steps. I don't know how many. But lots.

The House had kept with the sandy, tropical theme, but kicked it up a notch. The floor was made of wide, heated sandstone tiles. The warmth felt good on my toes. No cold floors for me! The walls were tiled with a dark brown color at the bottom that gradually changed to a sandy color at the top. But what really caught my attention were what looked like gemstones in some of the tiles. I'm sure they weren't real gemstones, but they looked like bits of pirate treasure waiting to be picked up.

My eyes traveled up the pirate treasure walls to the vast ceiling above me. It was a light blue, like the sky. And hanging from the sky was a huge crystal chandelier. I gave a little squeal as I took in all the sparkles and rainbows. I had a freakin' chandelier in my bathroom! It was so over the top, but also, so perfect. I sent a silent thank you to the House for making me a very happy gay boy.

I turned to the wall to the right of me and took in the long vanity with His and His sinks. There were lots of drawers and cabinets, and clever lighting. In keeping with the pirate theme, the handles on the drawers were gold doubloons. I couldn't help but smile. It looked like the House was planning on Tyler and I getting ready together in the morning. I could totally get behind that.

But wait, there was more!

Past the double vanity was a huge floor-to-ceiling mirror. It was almost as wide as it was tall. I'd never had a mirror like this before.

After the mirror was the throne. It wasn't just any throne, either. It was a dual flush, and the top of the toilet was extra wide and slightly indented. It was the perfect spot for Bermuda to lie down and survey his bathroom domain.

I'd always put my toilet paper on the back of the commode, but now it had its own special holder. It was a seahorse, just the right height, and looking like he was ready to ride. The main roll went at the top of the saddle, allowing the lower part of the saddle to be loaded with spare rolls. It was cute and functional all in one.

After the toilet, came the shower. I'd seen walk-in showers before. But this was a walk-*through* shower. A person entered on the right side and got rained on by a whole ceiling of shower heads. Then they walked to a drying station with floor to ceiling air jets and exited out the other side. It was like a luxury car wash, but for people.

That took up the whole back wall. Against the left wall was a huge whirlpool tub, big enough for two. Next to that were floor-to-ceiling shelves for spare towels, washcloths, etc.

The whole thing was luxe, yet playful.

Well, I needed to have a shower and get ready, so it was time to try everything out! The House had already stocked everything, including blue towels, toothpaste, and two electric toothbrushes. I hadn't used one of those before, but it was nice. My teeth felt extra clean after I was done.

I also had a fresh razor with lots and lots of replacement heads–like hundreds of them. I'm the type of guy that uses a razor a lot longer than I should, to the point where it's pulling my hair. With this many replacements, I could afford to switch out heads once a week. Heck, I could switch out heads every other day and still have enough for a year. It was such a simple thing, but it felt mind-blowingly decadent. I felt about the razors like Annabeth felt about self-cleaning laundry.

Going through my morning routine with Tyler felt nice. We laughed and joked and pointed out new features of the bathroom as we noticed them. I could get used to this.

After shaving, it was shower time. The shower heads were wonderful! They didn't create hard streams of water. Instead, they issued fat, warm drops of water, like a summer rain. There was a digital readout where I set my water temperature. The shower did the rest.

The House provided body wash instead of soap, and it had a nice lavender scent. I finished the shower feeling clean and invigorated, and moved on to the drying section. There were air jets in the wall that covered my whole body, and again, there was a digital readout for how dry I wanted to be and how fast. Or I could just dry off with a towel like a regular person. I had to try the jets, though. I got it wrong the first time. I selected very dry and very quickly. The air jets lit me up. I felt like I was standing behind a 757 airplane gearing up for takeoff. Tyler laughed so hard that he cried. He tried to stop, but every time he went to describe how I'd looked, it set him off again. I ignored him as much as I could, grabbed a towel, and dried off the old-fashioned way.

"Aw, baby, don't be mad at me," Tyler said after he got himself together. "Here, I'll show you what it looked like."

He cranked the dryer all the way up and turned it loose. I was a little peeved at him, so I didn't really want to look, but I couldn't help myself.

He was right; it was funny as hell. The air blew his mouth open and popped out his cheeks like he was a fish. His skin flattened and rippled, the air was so strong. It kind of looked like he'd been dipped into one of those Dyson hand dryers like they have at airports. His hair went crazy, and when the jets stopped, he looked like a mad scientist.

"Damn!" he said. "That was intense!"

I stopped laughing long enough to go over and smooth his hair down. Then I kissed him. And he kissed me back. It was nice, so we kissed some more. Then things got a little heated.

He pulled me back in the shower, and we made love in the rain. What a tropical heaven.

We used a lot more body wash than two people should ever need, but finally we were clean and happy. Again.

Tyler picked me up, and we moved to the drying station. This time we got the setting right and dried off together. Tyler held my hands and hummed a tune as we slow-danced with each other. It was romantic, playful, and practical all rolled into one. Finally, we were just the right amount of dry and exited the shower.

We headed to the sinks, but I stopped when I saw myself in the full-length mirror. Was that really me? The last time I'd taken a good look at myself, it had been in the old bathroom with half of a mirror. This told me the whole story.

I'd always been skinny, and some guys liked that. Now, though, I looked defined. I had shoulders that looked wide and a rounded chest. My abs were so clear they flexed as I breathed. I had that lovely V that led down to my love maker, and my legs, they looked powerful. I'd never had powerful legs before. Even my feet looked good. I'd always thought my feet were a bit big, but now they fit me.

I flexed. I twirled. I checked out my own ass. My butt was perky now! If I put on a pair of tights, I wasn't too far off of one of those ballet dancers. Tea and his crew had done a brilliant job with me. Just brilliant.

I wandered closer to the mirror, checking out the finer details. My skin was so smooth. My acne scars were gone. Even my battle scars were gone. I had no black heads or imperfections of any kind. I looked like a model, after the model had makeup and a bit of Photoshop. Except this was real life. I was going to look like this all the time. Even my eyelashes were long, dark, and sultry now.

"Liking what you see?" Tyler asked.

I jumped. I'd been so caught up in the new me, I'd zoned out a bit.

"Yeah," I said. "It's cool. But it's strange too."

I backed away from the mirror a bit.

"It's like it's me, but it's not me. I'm not that perfect. Yet, somehow, I am."

"It is you," Tyler said gently. He gave me a side hug. "All supernaturals go through this transition if they live long enough. Usually, it takes years and years of the magic sinking into your cells before any of this starts to happen. When it does, it happens very slowly.

"You just had your system changed in three days. That makes it a lot more noticeable."

I stepped over a bit and pulled Tyler in beside me. We were both in the mirror now. Tyler was still bigger, still stronger, but we didn't look as mismatched now. Tyler was ungodly handsome, but I no longer looked like his second-rate hang-on.

Then I had a moment of panic. What if Tyler liked the "fresh supernatural" way I'd looked before? What if perfect skin and perfect abs were so "normal" at higher levels of power that Tyler wanted something different? Maybe different was better?

Smack! My Analytical Side smacked me.

Smack! He smacked me again.

My God, man, he said in his dry British voice. *Pull yourself together. Is there no pleasing you?*

You had low self-esteem and wondered if Tyler would ever like you when you looked one way. Now you look another, and you're right back at it again!

Grow some self-respect! You are you! You are enough.

He smacked me one more time and left in a huff.

"What's going on in there?" Tyler asked gently.

I guess my mental pep talk had taken a little too long.

"I just..." I shrugged. "I feel uncertain." My fears sounded ridiculous. Even to myself, they sounded ridiculous. How could I tell them to Tyler?

He turned me so I was facing him.

"Let me guess. You suddenly feel and look different. You are wondering how people will feel about you now."

I nodded silently. How had he figured that out so quickly?

"You forget, I've gone through this transformation already. Everyone questions themselves at some point."

He pulled me into him, putting his arms around me. "The truth is, nothing changes. You are still the same person you were before. Some people think it will change their whole life. They work hard for this, and they are so disappointed when nothing shifts for them. They are still the same person.

"Let me put this a different way. Let's say you got in a fight with a big crab and it hacked off your leg at the knee." He put me back at arm's length. "Now, stand on one leg like you're missing a limb.

"That's it. Now would Annabeth like you any less?"

I shook my head. Annabeth would do everything in her power to cheer me up and help me learn to get around on one leg. If anything, she'd probably like me more, because she'd get in some quality mothering time.

"Now, let's say you got in a fight with a magical ugly stick and it gave you a cleft lip. Go ahead and give yourself a cleft lip."

I laughed and tried to contort my face so one side of my lip was higher than it should be. I knew I looked ridiculous.

"Good. Now would John like you any less?"

I shook my head again. No, he would not. He would probably make me a special drinking glass, pour out some of his latest ale, and drink me under the table. Then he'd keep doing that until my liver gave up, or I stopped feeling sorry for myself.

"Now, let's say you went to pick blackberries and you fell into a thorn bush. You came out covered in deep, nasty scars. Do you think I would like you any less?"

He looked deep into my eyes. I was still on one leg. Still pretending I had a cleft lip. Imagining I was covered in scars.

I looked into his eyes and saw the truth. It wouldn't matter to him. He liked me for me.

I realized the opposite was true. I'd seen his true self when I'd been hallucinating. He was covered in magical scars. His hands were claws. He was a predator. It didn't matter to me. I felt the same way towards him. It would be very small of me to think he would do anything less.

"No," I said softly. "You would still like me. Scars and all."

"Exactly," he said, and kissed me.

We held each other for a while. I breathed in his fresh manly scent, feeling happy. Feeling content.

Finally, the moment passed, and we finished getting ready.

Today was already a good day.

25

Arena

"Welcome to the arena!" Tyler gestured at the new addition to our gym.

It was thirty steps long by about twenty steps wide. It had sand walls that went up higher than my head, with an observation area on the side facing the rest of the gym. It seemed pretty big. It stretched from the tree line almost to the water. The whole structure had appeared over a day ago, but he and Annabeth had kept quiet about it until I was ready for it.

"You've been learning how to punch, how to move, and how to block, but up until now you've learned everything separately. In the arena, for the first time, you'll put everything together. I could explain more, but it's a lot more fun to see it in action. Annabeth is getting ready to give it a go, so let's watch."

As I moved closer, I realized the walls were higher than I'd thought. They towered far over my head. I might be able to get a handhold on the top, but I'd have to jump really hard. Tyler and I climbed the sand steps to the observation spot, a room with a ceiling and two walls. It was nice because it provided shade while still being open to a cool breeze. It also had two sand chairs in the center, waiting for us. We were going to watch Annabeth in comfort! Now all I needed was an umbrella drink and a scantily clad cabana boy. If we added in a third chair for Anna Lykit so she could provide some colorful commentary, it would be perfect!

There wasn't a door into the arena, but there were steps leading down into the arena from the observation room. Annabeth was already inside. She gave a cheerful wave as we settled in our firm, but surprisingly comfortable, sandy seats. I waved back. I hoped having spectators wouldn't throw off her game too much.

Tyler gave her a thumbs up to start.

"Arena, begin!" Annabeth commanded.

A circle formed in the sand not far from where we sat. Annabeth jogged over and stood in it. As soon as she did, three human-like figures rose out of the sand on the other side of the arena and started running towards her. They weren't as big as Mr. Pebbles and moved a lot slower. Still, there were three of them, and they were trying to box her in.

Annabeth wasn't about to let that happen. She ran to the sand figure on the right. It took a slow swing, but she Pigeon Stepped past it easily. Then she shifted so her centerline lined up with the sand figure, and punched it in the side. It flinched and staggered back. Not wasting any time, Annabeth followed it, landing three more body blows. It dropped its hands to protect itself, leaving its face open. Two good headshots ended the fight for Opponent Number One. One down, two to go.

The only problem with focusing so much on one opponent was it had allowed the other two to get into position, and now they were after her. It took some fancy footwork and good blocking for Annabeth to get out of range, but she made it happen. She was able to maneuver so that Opponent Two was in the way of Opponent Three, and then used the opportunity to go after Two. She got in some good hits, slowing the sand fighter down, although she didn't get rid of Two entirely. Three moved around Two and then came in swinging, hoping she was distracted, but instead she was quick to switch her focus to him. Three appeared to be stronger and faster than the others, pushing his advantage. Annabeth faded back, and Three came after her. That was a smart move, as it put more distance between them and Two, who was still recovering. This way there was less chance for Two to surprise her as she worked on Three. And work on him she did! She pulled him into her optimal space, stepped around all his punches, and hit him at will. It was a beautiful thing to see.

By the time Two recovered and got back into the fight, Three was on his last legs. She lined Three up, hit him with three good punches, and finished him off. That only left a weakened Two. She was about to complete the fight, when she stepped the wrong way. Instead of stepping away from Two's punch, she stepped into it.

He hit her hard. It hurt just watching. She staggered back, and he came after her. Two never let up as he rained blow after blow onto her. She was able to block a bunch of them and dodge a few more. He clipped her a few times but didn't get in another solid punch. Instead, Annabeth recovered, got her groove back, and finished him off.

I didn't realize how tense I was until Two collapsed into a pile of sand. Then I leapt to my feet and started clapping. Annabeth gave me a bow and a tired smile, then started heading toward the steps to the observation area.

I was so incredibly impressed. My Annabeth had just taken out three attackers in a fair fight. She was short, with a little extra padding, and a grandmother to boot. And yet she kicked ass!

When she reached the top of the stairs and joined us, I gave her a big hug. She still had sand on her, so I helped brush her down, then hugged her again. She was laughing and smiling at how excited I was.

"I am so freakin' proud of you!" I exclaimed.

"Thank you," she said. I think she was a little embarrassed with all the attention.

"I mean it," I said. "We've only had the arena up for a day, and already you are taking on three guys. That is awesome!"

"I couldn't have done any of this without Tyler," she said.

I knew she was deflecting a bit, and that's okay. I'm not that comfortable with being praised myself.

"Yeah. He's alright," I said nonchalantly, giving Tyler a playful glance.

He just poked me in the ribs, making me jump, before giving Annabeth a hug of his own.

"You did well out there," he said. "I'm sure I don't have to tell you what to work on."

"I knew as soon as I moved that I'd gone the wrong way. But it happened so fast I couldn't stop myself."

"You did a great job of recovering, though," Tyler continued. "That's what a real fight is like. You might get hit, but you don't stop. You block, move, attack–whatever you need to do, to recover and regain control of the fight."

He looked at me.

"Are you ready to get started and have your first match?"

"Yes," I nodded. "Tell me about the rules first. You know I like the details."

"Yes, I know you do." Tyler just laughed. "The arena starts you out slowly. You'll begin at level 1. Once you win enough times, your level goes up. That gives the arena more points to create your opponents. The reverse also happens. If you lose too many times, your level will go down."

I opened my mouth to ask about levels and how that translated to opponents, but Tyler was way ahead of me.

"Your most basic opponent is a level 1 sand guy. He doesn't move that fast, and it only takes a moderate amount of damage to take him out. A level 2 sand guy will be faster *or* take more damage. A level 3 sand guy will have *both*– better speed and tougher defense. It just keeps going like that until you get to level 10. Then they start having ranged attacks. At level 20, they get weapons.

"Each level you gain gives the House another point to work with, and it usually mixes up the enemies you will be facing. Take this last battle with Annabeth as an example. She is level 5, so the House has five points to spend. It went with two level 1 guys and one level 3 guy."

Tyler paused, so I jumped in.

"So she could face anywhere from five basic, low-level sand guys up to one really good level 5 opponent."

"Correct," Tyler nodded. "And that's basically it, other than how you start off. When the match first starts, you will see a circle in the sand. You need to stand in it briefly to allow your opponents to form. Sometimes they start close to you, and sometimes they start farther away. You don't need to wait in the circle, though. You are welcome to start moving as soon as you see the sand shifting. Any questions?"

"How do I see my level?" I asked.

"It's almost the same as your punching stats. Just ask the House to show you your arena stats."

"House," I said to the air. "Show me my arena stats."

Low Novice Jason Arena Stats

Level = 1

Matches = 0

Notes: What are you waiting for? A gold plated invitation? Let's get started! Or maybe you need to eat some cat food first...

I laughed out loud. The House really thought it was funny. It was right, though. Time to get started.

Tyler and Annabeth wished me luck as I headed down the steps to the floor of the arena. I felt my adrenaline kick in. I was nervous, but excited.

From the floor, the arena felt a lot bigger. There was plenty of room to move around, and I took a moment to just feel the space. It was larger than the range of my magic sight, but that was okay. My opponents were going to be coming to me. At least they would for the beginner levels. I'd figure something out when I got to a high enough level for ranged attacks. I didn't want to overthink this. It was time to start.

"Arena, begin."

I looked around, and the circle in the sand was right beside me. I stepped inside it and stepped right back out again. I didn't want to get in the habit of just standing there.

A lone opponent formed on the other side of the arena, then started toward me. The House was giving me plenty of time to get adjusted. Looking down from above, I could see how slow these guys were. On the arena floor, they didn't seem so slow. As it lumbered towards me, it seemed downright fast.

The anticipation was killing me, but I forced myself to concentrate and get in the flow. I filled my lower half with water. I filled my upper half with smoke. I called the lightning. I was ready.

My opponent reached me and led with a right hook. All my training with Sparkles kicked in, and I stepped away. He followed me, swinging with his left hand. I stepped again.

For the next few minutes, we danced together. He swung at me, and I gracefully faded away.

I didn't try to hit him yet. I just wanted to learn his rhythm and find my flow in this new place. Now we were actually fighting, I could feel he was a lot slower than Sparkles. The only thing he had going for him was persistence. He didn't stop. If I lost concentration, he was going to hit me.

Once I felt comfortable, I picked my moment and hit back. My fist flashed with lightning, and I felt my fire spark the explosion. I didn't have to consciously think about Relax and Tense On Contact anymore. It just happened.

My opponent was made of sand, just like Sparkles, so he was a solid target. Unlike Sparkles, though, he reacted like he was a real human, and a weak one at that. He staggered back, then collapsed in a pile of sand. I waited on high alert. Surely, he would reform and come back at me again. He just lay there. Had I won the match?

Annabeth started clapping, so I looked up. She gave me a bright smile and a thumbs up. Tyler just smiled and waved.

I'd won the match! And it had only taken one hit. Was I punching that hard now? If so—Wow! I pulled up my Arena stats again.

Low Novice Jason Arena Stats

Level = 1.1

Matches = 1

Notes: Congrats on beating a slow opponent. Next up, another slow opponent. Try to keep up.

It looked like the House had every confidence I'd win. That was nice.

I went up to the observation deck and got congratulations from Annabeth and Tyler. Then Annabeth went again. This time she was facing two opponents. One was a level 3, both tougher and faster, and the other was a level 2, just faster. Despite their extra speed, it was easier to handle two opponents rather than three, and Annabeth stayed in control of the fight the whole time.

Afterwards, she needed a bit of a break, so I went three times in a row. I was still level 1, and there wasn't much the House could do with only one point, so I faced a single slow opponent every time. This time I didn't need to find my rhythm, so I finished them off quickly.

I'd learned my lesson about paying attention to the House, so I called up my stats after every fight to see if it had any good notes for me. Right now, it was just having fun providing colorful commentary.

We continued like that for the rest of the day. Annabeth finished the day at level 7, almost level 8. I climbed the levels quickly and finished the day at level 5. Fighting multiple opponents definitely increased the difficulty. It limited the ways I could Pigeon Step out of a situation. The idea when handling multiple opponents was to find the one guy that was a little outside of the others. Then I maneuvered so that my target was in front of me, and the other opponents were behind him. From there, I had a small window to take him down, or at least damage him. If I couldn't do it quickly, then it was best to disengage and find the next weakest person.

In a weird way, it was like playing billiards, except there was no cue ball. I could hit any ball at any time as I maneuvered around the table. Unlike billiards, the balls were constantly on the move, and they were out to get me.

I also found out I had a huge advantage with my magic sight. It was so useful, it almost felt like a cheat mode. I could see twenty feet around me in all directions without having to take my eyes off my primary opponent. That meant I knew exactly where everyone was all the time, and it let me pull off some incredible dodges. I could see where the holes were, and I just slipped through them to attack from a new angle.

It made me grateful I'd lost my natural sight for so long. It had forced me to become very familiar with my magic sight. There was a time when my magic way of seeing felt overwhelming, and I used to keep it turned off. Now, I had it on all the time, and it felt normal to see both ways.

***

That night I woke up again feeling restless, so I spent time with Eggy working on converting his magic. He wasn't awake yet, but I felt like I was making real progress. The purple Octopuses were giving him more magic, and I was converting it to my colors. The new process was a lot more efficient than just exchanging my magic with him.

I was a bit worried about how much soul I was using. I had lots of my little peeps running around, I'd given Penny a lot to wake her up, and now I was doing the same with Eggy. Was there a limit to my soul? There didn't seem to be. Sometimes, my colors didn't seem quite as bright, but if I waited a few minutes, they went back to normal. When Sandy got back, I needed to have a long discussion with her about this.

My working theory was that my soul was the sum of everything that made up me. It was my interests, my likes, my dislikes, and my projects. It was the moments I looked forward to and the ones I regretted. As long as I was active in the world–growing, learning, doing—I was just fine. We give away bits of our soul all the time. We leave a bit of it behind when we hug or say a kind word. We give it away when we focus on something or spend time somewhere. The arena certainly had some of my soul in it. So did my amazing bedroom. So did Tyler. And I was happy with all that.

I cared about my creations. I cared about my friends. I cared about defending all of them. My soul was going to the right places. Of that much, I felt certain.

***

The next day of training was very productive. Annabeth and I both ended the day at level 10. I had finally caught up with Annabeth. What that really meant was I'd finally caught up to where I would have been if I'd had a more traditional training path. Although my journey had been challenging and strange, I'd ended up with some real advantages. My body was far ahead of where it would have been. I was beginning to suspect it wasn't just my strength that had gotten a boost. My reaction times were incredibly quick, and my mind felt clearer. My recovery time was also insanely good. The arena matches were intense, and fighting took a lot out of me. But by the time I got up to the observation area, I was mostly rested and ready to go again. I felt like I could run the arena over and over again all day without a break.

In addition to a much better body, I had a whole new way of looking at my movement, thanks to my feedback with Tyler. I hadn't just observed how he'd moved, I'd felt it. That was a world of difference. I'd skipped months of bad habits and experimentation. Instead, I'd gone straight for the good stuff. I knew what it felt like to punch like a master, move like a master, and block like a master.

I was caught up in my training level, but the abilities I'd gained were so much better than they would have been. Evaluating where I was at, I could honestly say it was well worth the detours.

That night I worked on Eggy again, and he woke up. I didn't have a deep connection with him like I did with Penny, but it was very nice to have him back. Of course, he wanted to know what had happened while he was out, so I gave him the quick overview. He seemed very concerned by Karl and Marius. I promised to fill in all the details with him later and then fell asleep.

Now that we were level 10, we had a new type of opponent: the ranged fighter. Or maybe it was a mage fighter. Either way, the new guy stood back from the fight, hurling balls of sand at us. The sand balls were compact and fast, and really hurt when they hit. Fortunately, that wasn't too often. Again, my magic sight was invaluable for dealing with this.

My main strategy was to keep the fighters between me and the mage so he wouldn't have an easy shot. A harder strategy, but a lot more fun, was to get between the mage and the fighters. That way when he shot at me and I moved, it ended up hitting his own teammates. There was a lot to keep track of doing it that way, and I got tagged more than once. Still, it was very enjoyable seeing the mage knock one of his own teammates on their ass.

I finished the day at level 15, and Annabeth was a high level 13. That night I worked with Eggy again. Penny had caught him up on everything she knew about, and now he had specific questions for me. We went over the conversation with Josette in detail, as well as the fight between Cassandra and Karl. He thanked me for waking him up and noted it was much sooner than he had hoped it would be.

He also told his first joke. He said I was a good source, like one type of rock to another. We were talking in images, and the two images he sent me were of two different types of rock. I had no frame of reference at all to appreciate the joke, but he clearly thought it was hysterical. Apparently, he'd told it to Penny, and she'd loved it. He was a bit miffed I didn't get his rock humor, but I sent him images of love and belonging, and told him it was a flesh thing. We just had a different frame of reference, and I'd get better at understanding him over time.

He seemed happy with that explanation, and then he said something odd. He said he would have a sit, have a think, and then speak to me again. The words themselves weren't bad—it was just the way he said them. It was like I'd asked Eggy a question and he needed to think about the answer. As far as I knew, I hadn't asked him anything, but I told him that sounded like a great plan.

***

The next four days were wonderful. We spent most of the daylight hours at the arena honing our skills. I advanced up to level 31, which gave the House plenty of points to use for opponents. My matches usually consisted of more than one mage and at least three fast, tough fighters. The mages scaled too. The upgraded ones shot a whole stream of sand, which was a lot harder to dodge. The base mage stayed in one spot and just shot balls of sand. The upgraded mages moved around, looking for a good opening. I got hit a lot more, and sometimes I lost the match. But I also started to get good at going with the force of the hit so it didn't throw me off my game as much. The new fighters were much tougher, and I couldn't destroy them with one punch anymore. They also moved a lot faster, so it was harder to isolate one of them on its own and take it out.

Life wasn't all work, though. Annabeth invited us over to her place for a pajama party, which was a total blast. We drank homemade margaritas and mimosas, and played Chutes and Ladders. That was an old game, but it was all she had. Being adults, we turned it into a drinking game. We gave out drinks when we were going up the ladder, and we had to drink when we fell down a chute. The game was totally random and a whole lot of fun.

After we were nice and toasted, we pulled out sleeping bags and told ghost stories until we fell asleep. I didn't really know any ghost stories, and Annabeth only told stories with happy endings. It was Tyler who told the real scary tales. His stories were sinister and gave me chills. I do not like to be scared. There's enough scary crap in real life.

We also did another grocery run, but this time nothing weird happened. Thank goodness for that. I continued to enjoy my new bedroom and bathroom. Going to sleep at night with a cool breeze while listening to the sounds of the ocean was pure heaven. Nothing else changed in my apartment, although Octa and her Tangle were still putting the cleaned up magic from the park into the walls. They were also putting neutral magic into Eggy, and every night I took time to convert it into my personal magic. He was still in his "sit and think" phase, so I just let him be.

I did a tour of the park to see how it was doing. The Granny Godmothers were doing a wonderful job. Almost two thirds of the park was now contamination free. That included sidewalks, lawns, and houses that surrounded the park too. Even the mundane people could feel the difference. There were more people in the park now, and there were a lot more smiles. The neighborhood was getting cleaned up.

Despite all the good stuff, I began to get a sense of foreboding. Something bad was coming this way. I shrugged it off as nerves, but it kept coming back, like a dark shadow in a lit room. I hadn't planned on doing anything different until Sandy and John came back. Then we could come up with a war plan. Sandy and John had a lot more battle experience than I did. Right now, we were just defending. Annabeth could handle the shields, and I could defend the House. If Tyler was here, he could help too, but it wasn't a guarantee he would be available.

All that changed on the fourth night, when I woke up in my Throne Room.

26

Behold

I was confused at first. The only times I'd been in my Throne Room were when I had intentionally wanted to go there.

I'd found my Throne Room by accident when I was recovering from getting punched in the face by a golem. Apparently, this place was the seat of my power and could be used for all kinds of advanced magic. I'd primarily used it to get a good night's sleep.

My Throne Room once again had a cot in it, and that's where I woke up. It had been a while since I'd been here, so I sat up and took a moment to look around. The walls had tapestries showing some of the major events in my supernatural life, and now there were a few new ones.

One showed Anna Lykit striking a sassy pose in all her winged glory. Tea had his own tapestry too, showing him surfing through the microworld and dropping spore balls. I was a little surprised there wasn't a tapestry about learning how to punch or step. I'd spent so much time working on my fighting skills, I thought there should be something related to it. I guess it wasn't a magical or life-altering event, so it wasn't included.

Other than the tapestries, the room was a little bigger than I remembered. It was clean and nice, not too grand. It was the type of Throne Room that a small, but prosperous kingdom would have. I didn't need anything big and opulent. I preferred a cozy, homey kind of space.

I was also surprised to discover I wasn't alone. Penny, Eggy, and Bermuda were standing by a table, looking at me. Penny looked beautiful as always. She was about six feet tall and built like an Amazon warrior. Her skin was silver, and her eyes and hair copper. Her hair fluttered in an invisible breeze as she smiled at me like the sun rising on a spring morning.

This was my first time seeing Eggy as a whole being. I was surprised to see he was dressed like a soldier. I'd thought he'd left his martial years behind. He looked older, but powerful, with short trimmed hair, plate armor, and a long sword by his side. Of course, he was made completely out of liquid steel.

Bermuda looked like himself. He didn't need any changes. He was perfect just like he was.

Eggy gave a nod and motioned me over to the table. As I came closer, I realized it wasn't just a table. It was a model of all of Louisville and the surrounding area. It was pretty big too, like one of the battle-planning tables on *Game of Thrones*. Clearly, this was not a social visit. We were here to discuss strategy.

The map was made out of silver, with some parts highlighted in copper. Based on the colors, I'd say this was Penny's creation. Bermuda hopped up on the model, but nobody seemed to mind. He sat down on a neighborhood in the south of Louisville and made himself comfortable. Or as comfortable as he could get considering he was laying down on little metal pieces. He gave me a look like 'If I can put my ass on it, it's mine. I own this hood! I am the king! And the king is now resting. Peace out, bitches.'

"You are in danger." Eggy wasn't mincing words. "You must intervene, or you will rest." He didn't mean resting in a nice way, like taking a nap. He meant resting like my bleached bones drying in the sun. When he had been a sword and had been driven right through me into the ground, I'd had to explain that this was not a good thing for us fleshy creatures. We do not rest well. If we rest like that, then we are dead.

"Behold," he nodded at Penny, and the model started moving.

It looked like the little copper highlights were people. They moved and some of them started melding together. Each time they fused together, the copper piece got bigger. Eventually, it was over a foot high and looked exactly like Karl. He walked across Louisville and approached the House, which was only a few inches tall. When he got there, he stomped it flat with a bang. I jumped as his boot came down.

That was pretty self-explanatory and very graphic. The copper pieces were the mages with the sucker rune, Karl was the winner, and he took out the House like he was squashing a bug. I was assuming I was in the House in this scenario. I was now flat as a pancake—resting.

"Are you sure about this?" I asked. "How do you know where all the people are? How do you know how much magic they have?" The visual was nice. But did their power really add up to a twelve-inch tall game piece that could squish the House?

Penny sounded like bells when she moved, and she came around the table to stand beside me.

"I have communicated with the All Rune. It has provided the information. This is its assessment also."

She gave me a hug. She knew I liked hugs, even though it made no sense in her world of metal. I got a gentle hug from Eggy too. Clearly, they had discussed this and decided I needed comfort. My kind of comfort. It felt nice, but left me wondering if they thought we humans were very fragile and squashable.

I was surprised at just how warm they felt because I'd have thought that metal would be cold. I appreciated the effort they were making, but it made me wonder what other bad news they might have for me.

"I have sat," Eggy declared. "I have thought. This is so."

He flashed images to me of him running scenario after scenario, looking for a different outcome. I hadn't thought of Eggy as a strategic resource. He had been a sword for a very long time, though, so I'm sure he'd been present at many battle planning sessions over the years.

"What do you suggest I do?" I asked.

"You must destroy the enemy first," Eggy declared.

"Behold!" He nodded at Penny again.

The model reset, and this time a little figure exited the House and started taking out mages. The mages still fought each other and the winner emerged bigger and stronger, but there weren't as many available targets anymore. This time, the final winner was a lot smaller, only about six inches or so, and it couldn't stomp the House.

"I know you are not happy," Penny chimed in.

She sent images of me rolling around on the floor sobbing my eyes out. Was this how they thought I would react? No wonder I was getting hugs. I was nowhere near that level of upset. I'd been training for something like this. I wasn't feeling sad or angry. Instead, I was feeling determined. I was ready to defend the House and save my friends.

Don't get me wrong, I was nervous too. Fighting sand people was one thing. Fighting a crazy and powerful mage was another.

"This is your chance to temper yourself," Eggy jumped back in.

He sent me images of metal in a forge, sweating out impurities. At least I think that was what he was trying to send.

"You must strike now. The enemy is still fragmented, and some of them are very weak." Penny helpfully pointed out a few copper figures that were smaller than the rest. They were also near the House.

"What about Annabeth?" I asked. I wasn't sure how she was going to feel about all this. Would she be ready for a fight, or would she want to wait for Sandy and John to return from their honeymoon?

"Annabeth must stay and shield the House," Eggy declared.

"You will not be alone," Penny said. "Bermuda and I will be with you."

Penny looked like a strong woman in here, but in the real world she was just a ring. I wasn't sure how much help she could give. As for Bermuda, he gave a big yawn, and then folded himself in half so he could lick his privates.

"Okay," I said. "I'll run this past Annabeth tomorrow, and we'll come up with a plan." I wasn't ready to just rush out into the night right now. I wanted to be prepared.

Penny and Eggy both shook their heads.

"No," Penny said. "It must be now. Tonight."

She sent images to me of their analysis and where the mages were right now. They projected that tonight was the big night. Several of the more powerful mages were out hunting, and they were going to take out a lot of the lesser ones. After tonight, the power would be much more consolidated. And the leading mages would be a lot harder to fight.

This all felt very sudden, but I couldn't argue with their analysis. They had obviously put a lot of thought and effort into it. I had just expected that we wouldn't do anything until Sandy and John came back. They were the heavy hitters in our outfit.

Now all the responsibility had landed on me. I was the one that was going to have to fight and win the next battle. Thank goodness I'd been training!

"Thank you for all your planning and thinking," I told Eggy. "This wasn't what I thought you were thinking about, but hopefully everything will work out."

"Penny, as always, it is wonderful to see you. Thank you for modeling all this and helping Eggy. If you don't mind, I'm going to study your model for a few minutes and get a feel for where the mages are."

Penny tinkled her bells as she stepped out of the way of the model. I'd used Google Maps to get around, so I had a good idea of the layout of Louisville, but still, this model was fantastic. Every house, every tree, even the cars were represented.

The first copper figure was about two blocks north of us on Fourth Street, towards downtown. The figure looked misshapen, almost like a blob, and it wasn't moving. There was another copper figure east of it that looked like it was casually walking around. From there, it looked like there were a few mages at Fourth Street Live.

That was a special section of Louisville that they had turned into a street party. They had blocked off the street, installed a stage, and added lots of neat lighting. There were several nice restaurants and shops down there too. It was a special effort by the city to bring more people downtown and make it a lively, fun place. It was similar to Beale Street in Memphis, Tennessee, or Bourbon Street in New Orleans. The project had been a success, and there were always lots of people enjoying the nightlife and staying out late. Hopefully, it was late enough that all the party people had left.

Other than that, there was another cluster of mages in downtown Louisville by the waterfront. I committed everything to memory as best as I could before I told Penny and Eggy goodbye and woke up.

I opened my eyes and heard someone banging on my apartment door. I quickly threw on some underwear and ran to open it. It was Annabeth, and she looked flustered. Her hair looked a bit wild, and she was still wearing her nightgown.

"I'm so sorry to bother you, Jason," she said. "I'm sure you were sleeping. It's just that I had the strangest dream."

I stepped aside so she could come in.

"I was dreaming that there were all these black blobs of magic rolling around Louisville. They kind of looked like rolling balls of oil. They seemed to be attracted to each other, and when they met, they merged together into a bigger ball of oil. Finally, there was only one giant ball left, and it started rolling towards me. I screamed and ran, but it rolled right over the top of me and picked me up. I started drowning in oil. It was just horrible."

She was shaking, so I gave her a hug to calm her down.

"I would have just chalked it up as a strange dream, except I had this when I woke up." She showed me her hands. They were covered in black, oily marks. That was just freaky. Looks like she'd had her own premonition about what was happening.

She was still shaking, so I held her tight while I told her about my own Throne Room experience and what Eggy had figured out.

"So what are you going to do?" she asked.

"Well, I was going to come and talk to you first, and then probably head out there and see if I could knock their magic down to size."

She'd stopped shaking, so she gave a final squeeze and stepped back. Then she looked at me critically. "You are just too skinny."

"Am not!" I laughed. "This is gay chic. Plus, Bruce Lee was a skinny dude and look what he could do."

"That is just not right." She was shaking her head. "I need to start force-feeding you sandwiches."

Annabeth was having a fun moment and deflecting the conversation with humor. Her eyes told me she was still worried, though.

"Besides, I'm not skinny–I'm aerodynamic. That's where I get my speed from!"

I made zooming noises and pretended I was the Flash. She chuckled, giving my arm a pat. Then we got serious again.

"Where's Tyler?" she asked.

"I don't know," I shrugged.

I really wished he was here and could go with me. I could use a backup.

"So are you heading out now?" she asked.

"I thought I'd get dressed first," I said teasingly. Annabeth just rolled her eyes.

"But after that, yes, I'm headed out. I memorized the map, so I know where they are right now. The longer I wait, the more the situation will change."

"Well then, let's get you dressed." Annabeth was all business now.

We went through the bedroom and into my walk-in closet. I was starting to pick through my t-shirts for a dark one when Annabeth pointed.

"What's that?"

It wasn't any outfit I'd seen before. It was a black, long-sleeved shirt that looked like it was made out of some sort of wicking material. It was a flat black too, so it seemed to soak up the light. The pants were long and skinny and just as black.

"It looks like the House is working some of its magic tonight," I said. "That'll be perfect for running around after dark."

I put the outfit on, and realized it was even more perfect than I'd thought. The shirt had a hidden hood and mask. It was super thin so it tucked away, but if I needed to, I could use it to cover up my head and face. The sleeves also had hidden gloves. The pants were very light and stretchy. The outfit wouldn't slow me down at all. I felt a bit like a superhero. The outfit could pass as regular clothing when I walked along the street, but if I needed to hide in a dark alley, I could just pop on the gloves and hood and practically disappear. It was my very own stealth suit.

The House had also provided a pair of black tennis shoes. There wasn't anything fancy about them, except there wasn't a single part that was shiny or reflective. When I put them on, though, I found out one more thing—they had steel toes. If I had to kick someone in the balls again, it was going to really hurt!

"Going all black is wonderful," Annabeth said. "But you are going to have to be extra careful around traffic. They aren't going to be able to see you crossing the road until it's too late."

That was certainly good advice. Good thing Annabeth was watching out for me.

"You do look handsome in your new gear," Annabeth said fondly.

"I don't look too skinny?" I asked playfully.

"You do look much better with clothes on," Annabeth replied.

I laughed. "Gurl, you are going to give me a complex. I'll have to go to a shrink and undo all this damage you are doing to my psyche."

"I think Tyler will take care of your body image just fine." She gave me a friendly pat on the butt.

Before I did anything else, I took the time to summon some of my battle helpers. I started with the Flashers. Those little guys were awesome. I'd made them so many times, it was easy to create the firefly body, add the trench coat, and add the light rune. I remembered I still wanted to examine the light rune for flow, but it was too late now. The one I was using was plenty bright enough. This time I added a cool pair of sunglasses. My little flyers were going to be bright *and* stylish. Once I had my main Flasher set up, I duplicated him nine more times. That might be overkill, but I'd rather have too many than too few. I could always absorb them later.

Next, I worked on Bob the Basher. I made him tough. He was a basher after all. I included his sucker boots for sticking to shields and his jet pack to fly around with. He had been a huge help with Mustard. I didn't know if any of the mages I'd be fighting tonight had shields or not. If they did,

Bob was going to be very helpful. I duplicated him nine times as well.

I mentally ran down the rest of my little guys to see if I'd missed anything. The League of Flying Miners was only useful against stone golems. The same with the Ass Blaster 2000s. Octa was useful to give magic to someone, but I was on a mission to take magic away.

The Granny Godmothers might be useful if I ran into a contamination problem. They could also be used for finding the mages and keeping an eye out for trouble.

I debated about taking the shillelagh, but decided to leave it. I'd been training without it, and I didn't want it to mess up my timing.

I realized I'd reached the point where I'd done all the preparations I could. Now it was time to actually head out. I felt apprehensive. I really hoped this went okay. I had an image of me lying dead in a ditch, but I pushed it away. There would be no dead-in-ditches for me today. I had to believe that.

"Good luck," Annabeth said a bit sadly. "Be careful out there. Remember, your first priority is to come home safe. You can always recover and try again."

"I will," I said. "I'll see you again soon. If Tyler shows up, be sure and send him after me. I would be much happier if he was taking the lead on this."

Annabeth held my arm as we walked to the front door, and I appreciated her support. I was feeling nervous now. My palms were sweaty, and I could feel my heart racing. I felt hyper aware, like I was ready to step into the arena and have the biggest fight of my life.

"Good Luck!" she said as brightly as she could.

I just nodded, not trusting myself to speak, and stepped outside. Bermuda slipped out the door and ran down the steps ahead. He was ready to go. I wish I could feel his confidence right now.

He gave me a look like 'Come on, Dude!' and started down the sidewalk. I knew Annabeth was watching me, but I didn't look back as I started after him. Ready or not, it was go time. I just hoped my training would keep me alive.

27

Going Mousing

The night was clear and moonless. It was going to be a dark night, but I didn't mind. The night was an old friend. I used to live a large portion of my life at night. In fact, my day hadn't really gotten started until the sun went down. I often played poker into the early morning hours. It also wasn't unusual for me to find my next bed to sleep in by hooking up with a new guy at the nightclubs. So as I walked down the street, an ease settled around me.

The street lights were widely spaced, and the singular spots of illumination cast long, spooky shadows. I was fine. I was accustomed to using both my natural sight and my magic sight together, and my magic sight didn't need light to see by. Actually, I was better than fine. Now that I was out of the House and on my way, I felt the nerves leave me.

It also helped that I wasn't alone. I had thousands of Granny Godmothers flying in the air above me, and Bermuda was confidently leading the way.

He was just a young cat, but in a weird way, I felt like he was taking me mousing for the first time. Hopefully, we could catch many mice tonight. All those mice were going to turn into the Rat King and try to slay my Nutcracker. I wasn't about to let that happen.

I think I just offended all the fans of the Nutcracker ballet, and I'm not sure Tyler would appreciate being called a nutcracker. I thought it was funny, and right now that's all that mattered. I had my skills and my little army of Sugar Plum Fairies, and we were going to dance all over the bad guys.

Now my fun pep talk was done, I asked the Granny Godmothers to scout ahead and find our first target. If my memory of the map was correct, the mage should be about two blocks north of us.

They quickly found him and let me know. I'd never used my creations as scouts before, but I found it very useful that I could feel where they were and communicate with them at a distance. It looked like he hadn't moved at all from where he'd been on the model. That seemed strange.

Two blocks went quickly, and then the dark alley was right there. It wasn't so much an alley, as a small back road that ran behind the businesses facing the main road. It should have been well lit. Louisville was usually pretty good about making sure places were safe at night. But all the lights were blown out, and the alley was dark. I'm not talking street-shadows dark—I'm talking pitch-black dark.

Which was why it was very curious that I could physically see everything. I could see there were lots of those big garbage bins for trash. I could see the lights had been shattered and lots of glass scattered everywhere. I could also see there was a body on the ground and a person standing over it. Whoever they were, they swayed slightly, but otherwise there was no movement.

Moving very softly and carefully, I stepped off of the street and in between the buildings. Once I was fully in the alley, I stepped behind a dumpster and stopped. I needed to figure this out. Could I really see in the dark or had my magic sight grown? I closed my eyes.

Nope. My magic sight was the same, about twenty feet in every direction. That was enough to see the first part of the alley, but not enough to see the figures at the end. I opened my eyes again. I could clearly see the whole alley. The colors were very muted, but the shapes were there. Holy Cow! Not only had my natural eyesight improved in clarity and focus, I could also see in the dark!

I'm not sure you can see in complete darkness, my Analytical Side spoke up. *I think it's more likely that you can see much better than a normal person in low light situations.*

'Like an owl?' I asked.

Probably a bit like that. They can open their pupils really wide and let in a lot of light. If someone could see you right now, they would probably think you had all-black eyes, like those demons from the show "Supernatural".

'That's kinda cool!' I said.

Sure. We'll go with cool, he said in a lecturing voice. *The other reason you can see better in the dark might be that you have a lot more of the receptors that see gray. Colors still look normal to you. If anything, they look more vivid, so maybe you have more color receptors too.*

'That sounds neat,' I said.

I'm sure everything sounds 'neat' to you. I'd prefer to say you are now an ocular wonder.

'That would make a cool superhero name. Look! It's a bird. It's a plane. It's Ocular Wonder!'

My Analytical Side rolled his eyes. He rolled them hard.

'Anyway, now I know what's going on, I need to get back to business. Owl see you later.'

He just groaned and walked away. Sometimes I'm too good for him to handle.

Bermuda was almost halfway to the swaying mage, but then he'd stopped and turned to stare at me. The look said 'Dude! What the heck are you doing?'

I waved at him and started silently making my way down the alley. As I got closer, it was easy to see that the person on the ground used to be a mage. She was now just a dried-out husk with a tiny bit of magic swirling around her. The sucker rune was all shriveled up but still visible on her arm. Obviously, the swaying mage was the winner of their contest of wills. So why wasn't he moving?

His clothes were burnt and barely there, and he was badly misshapen and hunched over. As I got closer, I could hear the raspy sigh of his breathing. It sounded like he was on his deathbed. And maybe he was.

His aura was thick and pulled in tight. It churned and writhed, just like Mustard's had been doing right before he exploded. I needed to proceed with extreme caution.

I told the Grannies to fly very high and keep an eye out for any approaching danger. Once they were out of what I thought would be the blast radius, I continued my cautious approach.

The figure had to have heard me coming, but he just swayed and didn't turn around. I waited for a moment. Nothing happened. I decided to walk around to his front, my body ready to fight and my senses on high alert. I moved until I could see the standing mage's face. It was tight with concentration and effort. His lips quivered and his eyes twitched. His hands were balled in fists by his side. Clearly, he was barely holding it together. By the look of things, my guess was that these two mages had fought and he was the last mage standing. But when he had pulled the magic from the loser, it had been too much for him to handle. He hadn't exploded yet, but he was on the knife-edge of losing it. He couldn't move or cast or do anything, other than breathe in ragged, wet breaths. And watch me.

His black eyes stared at me. I saw fear, and so much anger.

This wasn't how I thought my first encounter would go. I thought there would be spell slinging, dodging, punching, and hopefully I'd win. After a battle, there would be one less mage to join the Rat King.

This was different. This was more like a choice. A deliberate act. The civilized part of me rebelled at what I knew I had to do.

I wanted to show mercy. This mage wasn't threatening me at this moment, so I wanted to walk away. In the mundane world, I could call the police. They could come and deal with this. That world had laws and jails. That world valued life–gave people opportunities to change, to be better. This was not that world.

In this world, there were no police. You took care of your own. You were either the predator, or the prey. You either lived, or died. This mage wasn't threatening me directly right now, but he was ammunition for someone who would. Josette said the mages with the sucker rune could sense each other, so running wasn't an option. But I wasn't so sure.

This mage could have boarded a plane and run somewhere far away. Gone to South America, or even farther. Sure, the winner could have hunted him down, but it would have been a long time in the future. That might have been enough time to become strong enough to offer a good defense. He could have worked on getting rid of the contamination and tried to become a better person. Maybe he could have figured out how to get rid of the rune. Or maybe something would have happened to the winning mage here, and the problem would have been solved that way.

Instead, this mage had chosen to stay. He'd chosen to play the game. He'd made his choice. And I'd made mine too. Way back in the hotel room with the hit squad, I'd chosen to live. When Isobel had kicked the crap out of me, I'd chosen to live. When Thing One had tried to possess me in my Throne Room, I'd chosen to live. This mage wasn't directly attacking me right now, but he was part of the power that was trying to stomp the House flat.

I chose to live.

He saw the decision in my eyes as I stepped towards him, ready to punch. He hissed at me and smiled. A triumphant smile that said, 'I'm gonna take you with me, sucker.' And he let go. His magic finished contracting inside him as he started to shake.

Oh, crap.

He was going to blow!

Bermuda and I both sprinted toward the nearest dumpster. It wasn't great, but at least it was some sort of shelter. We didn't make it before the mage combusted. This time, the blast went straight up instead of outward like it had with Mustard.

The force blew the mage apart. His head and shoulders launched high into the sky as the rest of him collapsed to his knees, falling over. I don't think the blast was as powerful as Mustard's had been, but it was directed entirely upward. High enough to hit the bottom layer of clouds and light them up. High enough to be seen all over Louisville.

Well, that sucked. Mr. Head and Shoulders had just alerted all of Louisville to where a battle had gone down and where more wounded mages might be. This was like throwing chum into the water. The sharks would be circling soon. Time to get out of here.

I didn't want to be in the center of a battle. I wanted to be on the edge. My goal was to take out the easier mages, not go toe to toe with someone like Karl.

Since the blast had gone up, it had destroyed several of my Granny Godmothers. I felt sad and pissed off. I'm pretty sure they didn't get hurt like I did. They were summoned creatures that could be absorbed and then summoned again. But still, nobody wants to get blasted out of the sky.

Some of the Grannies were alive, but injured, so I called them in for some healing. I'd had weeks of healing and refilling my creations, so I was very familiar with the process and could repair them on the move. There were over a thousand of them still left, thankfully, and the ones I already healed spread out again to look for trouble.

I was already heading back up the alley when I got a Granny Alert. Trouble was knocking. She let me know there was a mage on Fourth Street, and he was headed my way.

I didn't want to face him on a well-lit street, so I pulled up my hood, hunched down behind a trash bin, and blended into the darkness. I waited. It was just one mage, so hopefully I could handle him. I finished healing the last of the injured Grannies, and they flew up high in the air again, ready for my next orders. Thank goodness I had my aerial patrol. At least I had been forewarned that someone was coming. I pulled in extra magic from Penny. Better to have too much than too little.

All too soon, the mage was at the mouth of the alley. He stopped and spent a moment, peering into the darkness. I'm sure he was looking for the source of the explosion. The alley was dark, though, and I was behind a dumpster. There was no way he could see me unless he had some sort of magic sight like I did.

Deciding it was safe enough, he started cautiously down the alley. With a gesture, he lit the whole place up. I almost cussed and gave myself away. The damn light had caught me off guard and blinded me. My pupils had been wide open, and now my eyes were completely overloaded.

I felt disoriented and dizzy, as tears streamed down my face. Now I knew what it felt like when someone got blinded by my Flashers.

It wasn't fun. It wasn't fun at all.

I closed my eyes and took a deep breath to steady myself. My natural sight was out of it. All I could see right now was a host of bright spots flashing behind my closed eyelids. Fortunately, my magic sight was still good to go.

Not only had I lost my regular vision, I'd also lost my concealment. The alley was brightly lit now, so he could easily see me behind the dumpster if he just looked. He walked forward into the radius of my magic sight, so I was able to keep an eye on him.

His aura was rotten, of course. I was expecting that now, but it wasn't as bad as some I'd seen. If I had to guess, he'd only won against one other lower-level mage. He didn't have enough stolen magic to account for multiple people.

He should have been keeping an eye out for me, but he wasn't. He only had eyes for the scene at the end of the alley. I know one dried-up husk and one blown-up mage makes for fascinating viewing, but he still should have been keeping an eye out for danger.

I waited until he walked past before making my move. I stood up from my crouch and started after him. I couldn't let him get too far ahead, or he'd walk out of my magic sight.

I thought I was being silent, but obviously not silent enough. He spun around, blasting a fireball as he turned. I guess he was ready for trouble after all.

He'd formed his spell before he'd even really seen what was behind him, so his aim was terrible. I, on the other hand, had been blasted with so many sand balls in the arena that I knew exactly when to dodge and when to just let it fly on by.

I ignored his fireball, settled into my Pigeon Stance, and stepped towards him.

He was fast. I'll give him that. His eyes locked on me, his hand gestured, and a second fireball was on its way.

I Pigeon Stepped. The fireball sailed on by.

He cast again, larger and hotter this time.

I Pigeon Stepped left. The fireball sailed on by.

I was almost to him. He panicked and threw a stream of fire, like a flame thrower.

Step Shift to the right. The flames roasted where I'd been.

Two Pigeon Steps right. I was so close that I could smell him.

He tried to follow me, but my left hand blocked his arm. His side was wide open.

Lightning Punch. I felt something break inside him.

He started to scream and dropped his arm to protect his side. Too slow.

Lightning Punch. More ribs snapped.

Still screaming, he twisted and tried to hunch over. His spells were forgotten. But all the twisting did was open up the front of his body. He invited me, so I obliged.

Lightning Punch.

Lightning Punch.

The blows slammed him against the wall of the alley.

Bermuda jumped in and clawed his leg. The scratches were insignificant, but the personal magic spilling out wasn't.

Just like Mustard, he was now a ticking time bomb. Eventually, he'd lose too much personal magic, and the balance of power would shift. The stolen magic would gain the upper hand and have its revenge.

Boom.

I'm sure with time and attention he could have recovered. He could have fixed his aura and slowly regained his natural magic. But that wasn't going to happen. Not tonight.

This was a game of power. A game of chess. Pigeon takes Mouse. It wouldn't win the match, but the enemy would be down a piece.

I settled into my stance, ready to finish him, when I had a thought. Mr. Head and Shoulders in the Sky had been the bait to bring this fellow along. Maybe he could be the bait for the next mouse?

It was worth a shot. My new Bait was crying and moaning, but he was still on his feet. I grabbed him by the neck and marched him out of the alley. I put him on Fourth Street, pointed him north, and turned him loose.

He staggered like he was drunk, but he slowly made his way up the street. My eyes were still having problems, so I let him go for now and waited. It would be very easy to catch up. Plus, I needed to give him some space. Following right behind would only raise suspicion and get me blasted again if he decided to suddenly blow.

I waited in the alley, and gradually my eyesight cleared up. I peeped out to see how far he had gotten. He was two blocks away, heading for three. I stayed where I was and let him go. The Grannies were keeping a watch, and nothing was headed towards my position, so I could afford to wait.

He was four blocks north when I got the Granny Alert. Three mages were closing in on him fast. I took off after him. The blocks flew by, and once again, I marveled at my new body. Running felt effortless now. Before I would have wanted to pace myself at a slow jog so I wasn't out of breath when I arrived. Now I just ran, and it didn't bother me.

I was close enough to see the three mages grab Bait and hustle him into an alley. Taking on three at once wasn't a good plan, so I told one of my Flashers to go in and light them up. My little fella flared his coat, flexed his wings, and flew on ahead of me. I arrived just as the alley lit up like the sun.

My Flashers were insanely bright. It looked like giant spot lights were shining out of the alley and across the street. The alley was open on top, so once again, the sky was lit up. I wasn't doing a good job of being subtle. Oh well, more chum in the water.

The Flasher turned off his light as I reached the mouth of the alley. I slowed to a stop and peeked around the corner. It looked like one of the mages had already started the battle of wills with Bait through the sucker rune. The second mage was screaming and rubbing his eyes. It seemed like he had been looking right at the Flasher when my creation let loose. It was going to take him a while to recover. That only left one mage who must have been the lookout. He was facing away from Bait, so he hadn't been blinded.

That's okay. I should be able to handle one mage. Lookout saw me as I rounded the corner and started toward him. He flexed his hands and grew two short swords out of pure magic. I stopped for a moment to assess him.

His aura was a bit bigger than Bait's. I'm guessing he was a two-time winner of mage battles. Eggy had been right to push for me to get out tonight. So far I hadn't seen anyone that was just a basic mage. It looked like everyone left had won at least one battle. Of course, my sample size was really small, so that might not be true. Still, it was clear that power was being consolidated in the hands of the better mages. This was the time to cull the herd.

Lookout's short swords were terrible. It looked like they were modeled after a kid's toy. The design was blocky, and the edges were rounded. They were almost clubs that looked like swords. They should have been one color, his natural color, but instead they were made of a nasty mix of purple and brown. I like the color purple. Octa was purple. But this purple wasn't nice. It was like an old bruise that was fading away. As for the brown color, it had a viscous look to it. Like it was dirt that came from an abandoned oil waste facility.

Since I was no longer coming at him, I guess he decided I was scared of his mighty swords, so he charged at me. I thought that was great. It helped pull him away from the other two and made it harder for them to come to his aid.

He slashed at me. I shifted. He slashed with his second sword, and I stepped inside his guard. I wasn't that close to him, when he did something unexpected. He stepped back and slashed again with his extended sword. Without thinking, I blocked it with my hand.

I'd planned on just dodging his swords, getting in close, and finishing him off. It was a fast and simple plan. Those swords gave him lots of reach, though, and he was quick. I was afraid that just touching them would burn me.

Or contaminate my magic. Or give me rabies. They looked that nasty.

Instead, I got a wonderful surprise. My gem gauntlet flared to life and stopped his sword. My fabulously pretty, multi-colored, totally gay battery cells faced down the sludge and muck, and said, 'Not today, Heifer!'

Wow! I got the power!

That changed everything. I effortlessly redirected his swords, stepped in close, and Lightning Punched the crap out of him.

His swords flickered out, and he hit the ground unconscious. Bermuda jumped in, slashed him, and jumped back out, hissing. Lookout's natural magic started leaking out. He was now a ticking time bomb too.

Time to kick this thing into high gear. I took care of "Ahhh! My Eyes!" next. He never saw me coming.

Like, literally, he never saw me coming. Hehehe.

Bermuda and I quickly reduced him to ticking time bomb status and then turned our attention to the third member of their party. He won his battle of wills with Bait. He sucked him dry, leaving a pile of ash and bones. It must have felt good, because he roared and shook his head like he'd just taken a hit of coke.

He turned around, and that's when he got a hit of Lightning. He got a couple hits actually. Now he didn't look like he felt so good anymore. I stuck with body blows, so he was disabled but still on his feet. Bermuda slashed him, and I grabbed him, hustled him out of the alley, and turned him north. With a gentle push, I sent him on his way.

I followed behind him pretty closely for the first block. I wanted to get out of the area as much as possible before everything went kablooey. We were on the second block and I was letting him get farther ahead, when the first mage we'd left behind exploded. It sounded like a cannon. Car alarms up and down the street started going off. Then the second mage exploded, and this time I felt it in the ground. I looked over my shoulder and saw one of the walls of the alley sag, and then fall over. Whatever business that was attached to was going to have a nasty surprise in the morning.

I dropped even farther behind Bait 2, when I noticed his new magic was a bit wild. It was swirling around him like crazy, setting some of the leaves and trash on the sidewalk on fire. As he headed north, it got worse. He was almost to Fourth Street Live when he set a car on fire. It wasn't the whole car, just the tires, but it made an awful stink and created a lot of dirty smoke. Fortunately, there wasn't anyone on the street. That seemed a bit unusual for the part of town we were in. I checked the time. It was two a.m.

Bait 2 staggered across the street and into Fourth Street Live. The music had long since finished, and the restaurants were shut down. There were still a few mundane people hanging around, but they started to sense something was up. His stolen magic started acting up even more. There was a lot of trash in the area. I guess they hadn't cleaned up yet from the crowd, and it all suddenly caught on fire. It flared out quickly, but it still made for a lot of heat, and the last of the mundane stragglers got the heck out of there.

According to Penny's model, there were two rotten mages here. I waited, but they didn't show. Bait 2 made it to the end of the block and kept going. Still nothing. He made it almost all the way to downtown and the waterfront before his new magic became too much for him. He didn't explode, though. Instead, he just kind of melted into a pile of goo. His stolen magic flickered around wildly and finally went away. I hoped that would draw someone out, but again, nothing.

The Grannies weren't seeing any activity either, so I decided to keep going and check the waterfront. According to the model, there should be mages there. Louisville butts up against the Ohio River, and there are a whole series of places that take advantage of the view and the water. The most popular were the Overlook on the Belvedere and the Great Lawn. There were a few romantic couples kissing and talking and a few homeless people sleeping on benches, but nothing in the way of rotten mages. Where the heck was everyone?

I decided to go back to Fourth Street and head south, back towards the House. I'd done some damage tonight. Some of their magic capacity was off the table. It wasn't as much as I'd hoped, but this night had certainly been a success.

I was amazed at how well Tyler's techniques and training had worked. It was one thing to train in the arena against sand people. It was another thing entirely to fight actual mages and win. It had only been a few weeks ago when I'd fought Mustard, and he had been at the very upper end of what I could handle. Tonight, I'd fought several mages at Mustard's level and handled them easily. Tyler's way of hitting and moving had made a huge difference. I wasn't at his level, of course, but I was a lot more capable than I'd been before.

Now it was time to go home and tell Annabeth all about my adventures. Tomorrow I could come out and do it all again. I picked up Bermuda, settled into a light jog, and before I knew it, I was back at Fourth Street Live. There was a bar on the corner that was still open, but other than that, nobody was out and about. I'd been secretly hoping to take out one more mage, but I guess that wasn't happening. Oh, well.

I was in the middle of the block, right by the stage where the bands played, when the Granny Alarms went off. They were shrieking at me to get out, and there were so many alarms, it was hard to think. They were appearing all around me. Was this a trap? Or maybe two rival groups of mages fighting? My first instinct was to make a run for it. I was fast, and it would put all the mages behind me. I could run, dodge any spells coming my way using my magic sight, then circle back and hit them one by one.

It was a great plan until the largest man I've ever seen stepped out of a doorway and blocked my path. I glanced over my shoulder. Two mages were covering the other end of the street. This was a trap!

I had to think fast. Maybe I could dodge around the guy in front of me? He was huge, though. One hit from him would flatten me. I was used to John in his human form, so for me to say a guy was huge was a big deal. This guy would have towered over John. He was not only tall, he was massive. And not in a muscular way. He was like the Kingpin or Juggernaut from the comics. He wasn't a nice, clean version of them either. He was all kinds of twisted. Like Dr. Frankenstein had taken the biggest, ugliest pieces of human he could find and dipped them in acid before stitching them together.

He had large bumps in weird places, as if he had tumors under his skin. He had hair in strange places—long hair sprouting off one elbow and a skunk strip of gray hair up one side of his chest. It didn't help that he was naked, and I could see why. How would he find clothes big enough to fit him? Even something like a bathrobe wouldn't fit around his shoulders, and it wouldn't be long enough anyway.

The stage was to my right, and a rotten mage stepped out of a service doorway right behind it. Of course. That's why the Grannies hadn't seen them—they had been inside. I'd been thinking they could see everything, but they could only sense what was visible from the sky.

I needed to get off the street. Now! I hopped up on the stage and ran towards the service door. It was still shutting slowly and hadn't locked behind him yet. The mages all around the street opened fire. Most of the spells missed with only a few grazing me.

They didn't knock me off my feet or spin me around, so I kept going. The mage by the door saw me coming at him, and he fired point blank. I still had Bermuda in my arms, and he slashed at the spell, breaking it apart. Harmless magic washed over me as I knocked the mage aside, barreling through the door.

I was at the end of a hallway. Not great. The first mage through the door would have a clear shot at me. I couldn't fight with a cat in my arms, so I lobbed Bermuda down the hall. Then I crouched on the ground.

People first look for someone at their own height. They rarely look down or up when they are in a hurry, and I knew the mage I had just knocked aside would be in a rush. Sure enough, he threw open the door and dashed inside, firing blindly down the hall. That would have sucked if I was still running away, but I wasn't. Instead, I punched out both of his knees. He screamed as his legs bent back the wrong way. That lasted for the half second it took me to stand up, and then I really hit him. He collapsed, Bermuda scratched him, and now he was a ticking time bomb.

I was sure the other mages were running towards this door, but they were still out of range of my magic sight. That meant that I had a brief moment, so I ran down the hall. There were a few doors leading off of it, but I could see through the walls with my magic sight, and it looked like they were small dressing rooms. They were dead ends, so I left them alone.

At the end, the hallway took a right, and then came out on a small indoor stage. It looked like it was for a comedy club or maybe an open mic night. This was perfect. I had room to move around, and the place was dimly lit. I could see okay, but any mages coming down the hall would be at a disadvantage as long as they didn't summon a light. There were two other exits from the club, and I noted them as I started summoning a Flasher. My other Flashers and Bashers were outside.

I sent them a mental call.

'Get in here if you can. Find a way. Some of you stay outside in case I can get outside again.'

It would have to do. I had my Flasher ready when I heard the next mage come through the outside door. He came down the hall at full speed, turned right, and ran out onto the empty stage. I closed my eyes as the Flasher lit him up, just as I heard the outside door open again. The next bad guy was already on his way. That seemed awfully quick. Damn. I only had a moment to take out the guy in front of me.

I punched him and ran into a shield. Damn it. That was not what I needed right now. It felt like a regular shield amulet, so I bashed it hard, trying to make it run out of magic. I almost had it down when two more mages joined the fight.

Crap, this was going to get crowded. The two of them let loose just as my Flasher went off again. One guy was shooting rocks, like Cassandra did in her fight. The good news was two of the rocks hit the first mage with the shield. The first rock took his shield down, and the second rock hit him in the chest. It hit hard enough the rock punched through his skin and went inside, like a bullet. Wow.

Unfortunately, the third rock hit me. I dodged so it wasn't a solid hit, but it still hurt and it spun me around. It didn't seem like a little rock should have that type of power, but I felt like I'd gotten shot. The spinning didn't help either. It didn't spin me all the way around, but still I felt a bit sick. Seeing all around me at once with my magic sight was a very handy ability, but it made me really vulnerable to vertigo.

The other mage was a woman, and she let loose with some sort of goo. It was green, and it shot out in a wide radius, like it was coming out of a Nickelodeon splat cannon. There was no way to avoid it, and that hit me too.

It didn't hit my face, thank goodness, but it splashed all over my chest and down my legs. Everywhere it hit, my skin started blistering and smoking. It was some sort of magic acid. Even worse than my skin was what it was trying to do to my aura. It was trying to melt through my magic.

I screamed and threw up as I fell off the stage. I couldn't help it. The pain was that intense. Holy crap.

The goo had also landed on the shield guy, and he screamed and let loose on the other two, or at least where he thought all the pain was coming from. My only saving grace was the three of them were now blind. My Flasher had done his job well.

I crawled across the room, tipped over a table, and hid behind it as the three of them went at each other. They couldn't see where I was, so they were just reacting to whoever hit them. I ripped off my shirt and pants and threw them away from me. The acid was still eating them up. It was still trying to eat me up too.

I could barely think, the pain was so bad. I'd felt pain before. I'd already had all kinds of injuries as a supernatural. This pain, though, was so sharp and urgent. It was like I was being whipped. Or like I was on fire. Actually, it was worse than that. It was like I was being whipped while I was on fire. I had to get this stuff off of me.

My clothes were melting, and there wasn't anything else in reach with which to wipe this crap off. Underwear! I still had on my underwear. I ripped it off and used it to wipe off the worst of the goo. Of course, it started smoking and melting, so I tossed it after my other clothes. With no other option, I started rubbing myself on the floor. I left slime trails and I had to leave the shelter of my table, but it was worth it.

The pain continued, and it was coming from my magic. The damn stuff was trying to eat through my power. I had a dense aura and a matrix, so I was warding off the worst of the damage, but this stuff had to go!

Penny came to my rescue. She flooded my body with magic. She gave me more magic than I'd ever tried to hold before. I was beyond buzzing with magic. I was on fire with it.

"Push!" she chimed at me.

I wasn't sure what she wanted, but I felt like I was going to explode anyway, so I pushed. I did something I'd never done before. I flexed my aura. Instead of lying on my skin, my aura grew by about an inch. My magic followed my aura, and now my magic matrix could directly face off against the hostile acid. I pushed, and my magic lifted the goo right off of my skin. With nothing to cling to, the goo dripped off onto the floor.

My aura felt a bit raw, but it was okay now. My skin was blistered and nasty looking, but I would live. Without the attack on my aura, I could think through the pain for the first time.

The table I'd originally hidden behind had been hit by a random stream of goo, and it was in the process of melting. A fresh stream of goo headed towards me, but I rolled away and only got hit by a few splatters. This time my raised aura protected me. It hurt, but it couldn't stick, so it just slid off.

It didn't appear like the goo mage's shots were directed at me. She was just shooting everywhere. Three more mages had entered the fight, and they had been Flashed as well. Now nobody could see, and all of them were firing with everything they had.

I think everyone could have kept their heads and worked together except for the goo. It was everywhere, and once it got on you, the pain was insane. Even the woman shooting the goo appeared to be affected by it. The mages lost their minds and battled the shit out of each other.

I'm not too proud to say that I huddled behind my tables and waited it out. I kept having to switch tables as they kept getting destroyed. The third one was hit by some sort of power bolt. It destroyed the table and knocked me up against the wall. I got a few bruises, but nothing too bad. By the time I dived behind my fifth table, the battle was dying down.

The goo woman had gotten into a battle of wills with another mage and won. With fresh powers, she went even more apeshit crazy. One of the later mages had a huge sword, and he was battling the others for their magic and then chopping them in half. The sword was insanely large. Like seven feet long and at least a foot wide. It looked like that crazy big sword from Final Fantasy Seven. The mage was winning too many battles too quickly. All that magic got to him, and he went apeshit crazy too.

Finally, it was just him and Lady Goo left. My money would have been on Lady Goo, as her offense was insanely good. She didn't have any defense, though, and Crazy Big Sword cut up through her crotch and out one shoulder. Lady Goo fell apart in two pieces.

Crazy Big Sword had won the battle, but he was going to lose the war. He'd taken on too much magic too fast. He couldn't stabilize it. Plus, he was coated in goo, and it was eating through his skin and his control.

The lull in the fighting was interrupted by a massive explosion. It appeared the first mage at the door had finally detonated. He must have blown off the whole side of the building because I could see a bit of the outside through a hole in the wall. The ceiling sagged, and the plaster started raining down on us. I was afraid the whole building was going to collapse, so I started looking around frantically for Bermuda.

Crazy Big Sword started cutting his way out, screaming the whole time. He used force bolts and his sword to demolish anything in his way. I spotted Bermuda. He was right behind Crazy Big Sword, following him out. He looked fresh and clean, not a spot of goo on him. How the hell had he managed that?

He looked back at me like 'You coming or what?' I did not want to get trapped in a building, so I hurried after them. Crazy Big Sword didn't bother with the hallway. He probably still couldn't see anyway, so he wouldn't know where it was at. Instead, he blasted through what was left of the changing rooms and made his own exit.

Big Ugly Tumor Guy was waiting for him. I think he thought they would join forces and either come after me or get out of the area. They had to have been on the same side at one point. They had organized enough to ambush me after all. That's why he seemed unprepared when Crazy Big Sword came after him, swinging wildly.

I thought it was over for Big Ugly, when Crazy Big Sword took off his hand and part of his arm. He just swung his sword, and suddenly there was a hand and part of a forearm on the ground.

I thought there would be blood spurting everywhere, but there wasn't. Instead, the severed hand just lay there, like it had been cut off and bled out hours ago. Big Ugly's arm closed up into a stump so fast that only a little trickle of blood came out.

It must have hurt like a bitch, though, as he roared and went after Crazy Big Sword. He grabbed his sword arm, stomped on his leg, and pulled. It was shocking how fast he moved. He was a huge guy, so he should have been slow. He wasn't slow at all.

Crazy Big Sword's arm gave out first. It stretched out, longer than an arm should be able to, before being ripped off. This time, blood went everywhere. It poured out the severed arm and fountained out of Crazy Big Sword's shoulder. He'd been toast anyway, but now he was really going to die.

Big Ugly dropped the arm and grabbed Crazy Big Sword by the head. He stepped back off his leg, lifting him into the air. Then he activated his sucker rune. Crazy Big Sword had just absorbed all the power from five other mages, and now all of that power plus his own went into Big Ugly. That was a huge amount of magic he was gaining.

I thought he'd go crazy too, except I realized he was growing. Big Ugly's arm grew back, and soon he had a brand new hand. He was also gaining in mass and height. Somehow, he was transferring all that power into his body and making it grow.

That's how he was beating the curse of the stolen magic. He was expanding his physical body, expanding his aura, and making it large enough to handle it all. If he wasn't so ugly, it would have been genius.

It also meant that he had the physical power of Juggernaut and the healing factor of Wolverine. Either one of those superheroes was way out of my league. Together, it was impossible. It was time to get the hell out of dodge.

I scooped up Bermuda and started to beat feet out of there, but he wriggled out of my arms and started back.

"What the hell are you doing?" I yelled at him, trying to grab him again. He easily avoided me and kept going.

"Bermuda! Stop!" I yelled.

He paused just out of range and looked at me.

'Fight.' He sent a mental image of the copper man squishing the House flat.

"No, No," I replied. "We took out some mages today. That will have to be enough."

'Fight,' he insisted. He sent images of survival. There was no retreat. No surrender. You fight until you die, or you win.

'Penny, are you getting this?' I asked.

'Fight,' she chimed back. She sent an image of Karl beating this guy and gaining every bit of power he held. He would be unstoppable.

'Fight,' she said again. She sent images of pressure, heat, and metal being forged. I think that was supposed to be helpful and provide some meaning, but I had no clue what she was trying to say. I was a human being, not a rock. Someday we'd have a nice long talk about this, but not now.

Bermuda turned back and started toward Big Ugly.

Fuck!

Fuckity fuck fuck fuck.

Fuck me in the eye running.

This was bad.

There was no way I was going to let Bermuda fight this guy on his own. There was also no way we could win. According to Penny, there was no way we could afford to lose either.

This sucked big balls.

There was nothing I could do other than run after my stubborn cat, and hope we figured out a way to beat this mountain of a man.

28

Big Ugly

Big Ugly had almost finished draining Crazy Big Sword.

He'd regrown his hand completely and gained at least another six inches of height. He now seemed to be as big as John when he had been in his rock form. So that meant he was about nine feet tall. His frame was massive, covered in fat and tumors and muscle. My punching wasn't going to do much. But I had to try.

Plan A was to get his attention and see if Bermuda's claws could drain his natural magic. If so, he would eventually go "Boom" just like all the rest.

Big Ugly pulled the last of the magic, and Crazy Big Sword fell apart. Most of his body dried up, turning to dust. His bones separated and fell to the ground. Big Ugly crushed his skull with his hand for good measure, and then let the bone fragments fall.

I had a bad feeling. I wanted to scream in frustration. There was no way for me to beat this guy.

Not with that attitude, there isn't, my Analytical Side said dryly.

'It's not my attitude that's the problem,' I shot back. 'The guy is enormous. He's strong. He's fast. He heals. How am I supposed to beat that?'

If you think you can't, then it's true. His British accent made this platitude sound more intelligent than it was. *Fortunately, the opposite is also true. If you think you can, then you'll find a way.*

'Believe me, I want to have a better attitude about this. I want that a lot. I just don't see how. Reality is staring me right in the face and telling me it can't be done.' I was sore, I was angry, and so very frustrated.

Start with acceptance. You've had your face punched in by a golem. You accepted that and found a way. Accept this too. Maybe you'll find your way then.

He was right. Being angry and frustrated was going to get me killed. The battle hadn't started yet. Big Ugly was still getting used to his new power. I had a moment.

I took a deep breath, held it, and then let it out. It felt good, so I did it again.

I looked up at the mountain of flesh in front of me. I accepted he was big. I accepted it without judgment or reservation. He was big. That was all.

I looked at his new hand. He could heal. I accepted that.

I remembered his speed. I accepted that too. He was fast. I was faster. That's just the way it was.

I felt the anger leave. The frustration faded away. I was calm. And I could think for the first time. I didn't have a full plan yet, but I had the start of one. We were going to test this guy and see what worked.

'Flashers!' I sent out the call. They were ready, waiting for me.

'Light him up,' I commanded. 'One for each eye. This guy can heal, so he will probably recover very quickly. As soon as it looks like he can see, then hit him again. Go for short flashes and save your magic. I think this is going to be a long fight.'

Two Flashers lined up on him, and the whole street lit up as they let him have it. He roared and staggered back.

"Bermuda!" I hollered. "Now!"

Bermuda ran in and scratched his leg. Big Ugly roared again.

I expected to see some of his personal magic leak out. Instead, a thick sludge of rotten magic spilled out. It only lasted for a minute before the scratch healed and he was back to normal.

Bermuda scratched him a few more times with the same results.

'Thoughts?' I asked my Analytical Side.

Big Ugly doesn't have all the stolen magic whirling around outside him like the other mages. He's made his body bigger and pulled it all inside. So when Bermuda scratches him, it's letting some of his stolen magic out, rather than pulling from his personal magic.

'So we can't just go with a scratch and wait plan. He's not going to explode like the others.'

It doesn't appear that way, my Analytical Side said regretfully.

It might be possible to scratch him a lot and gradually drain out all his stolen magic. That will take a very long time, though, and he's not going to stand still while Bermuda's doing that. Eventually, he'll get in a shot, even blinded like he is.

Bermuda was still going to town on him. Big Ugly was covered in scratches. They leaked magic but were healing too fast. He flailed around, trying to catch Bermuda, but he wasn't having any success. He'd eventually get lucky, though. He needed a distraction, which gave me another idea.

'Bashers!' I sent out the call. They were ready and waiting.

'See if you can get in his ear canals. If so, hammer at his eardrums. Don't break them, though. That will let out his foul magic, and it will eat right through you.'

Two of the Bobs saluted with their hammers, then flew up to his ears and wiggled inside. I'd normally have said there was no way they could fit inside an ear, but Big Ugly was big, and that included his ears.

Soon he roared again. This time it sounded like he was in real pain, and he threw his hands over his ears.

Now that he was really disoriented, it was time for me to join the fight. I was pretty sure my punches wouldn't hurt him at all. But it would distract him from Bermuda, and maybe it would force him to spend some of his energy on healing my damage instead of the scratches. It was worth a try.

I stepped in close and started hammering on one knee. It actually went better than I expected. I was used to hitting sand opponents, which were very solid and weighed a lot more than normal people. Hitting his knee was exactly like that. It was hard, solid, and I think his leg alone weighed more than I did. So punching his knee cap felt normal and comfortable.

It even did some damage that helped in distracting him more. My punches were hard, fast, and powerful. I think I even managed to crack his knee cap. He waved his arms around, trying to grab me, so I switched to dodging. I did not want to end up in his hands! If that happened, it was crunch time for me.

By the time I could get another hit in, his knee had healed. That was okay. I was hoping Bermuda was the one that could do the real damage.

Unfortunately, it looked like Big Ugly was healing even faster than before. The Flashers were having to trigger more often, and the scratches were closing in half the time. This was not good. He was covered in rotten magic that had leaked out, but it wasn't anywhere near enough to cause him any real harm. Time to regroup.

"Bermuda," I hollered and backed away from the fight.

Bermuda broke off his attack and came over to sit beside me. He started licking his paws while I was thinking. Got to keep those bitch smackers clean and ready to go!

Okay. What now? Clawing wasn't going to work. Punching wasn't going to work. Maybe I could make up a little creation that would cut him? It would have to be able to cut him a lot, and every time it cut him, the sludge would come out and damage the construct. It was so thick and nasty, I doubt a creation would be able to survive contact more than once or twice. There had to be a better way.

The last time I'd tried to get through a bad aura, it had been with Isobel. I'd made a little stone rocket, which did great at breaking through her protection. But the rockets were so tiny. They wouldn't harm this guy at all. What I needed was something bigger. I liked the tactic of attacking from a distance. Maybe I could figure out Cassandra's technique with the stones? Her attack had seemed powerful and fast.

This could be like a real-life David and Goliath moment. If I could get a stone going fast enough, it could punch through his eye, into his brain and kill him. I'd seen two mages use the stone trick so far. How hard could it be?

The Flashers and the Bashers were keeping Big Ugly busy, so I had a few minutes to experiment. From what I'd seen, Cassandra had just picked up a rock, coated it with magic, and sent it on its way. The rocks hadn't seemed special and the magic used had seemed basic, so maybe this was easy.

There was a lot of debris around me, so finding a rock wasn't an issue. I picked one up that was about the size of a pea and fairly round. I figured I'd start small and then get bigger for the final shot.

I held it in my hand and started coating it with magic. It wasn't hard. It was sort of like when I had done my evaluation with Sandy. She'd told me to use my magic only, not one of my creations, so I had done all her tests with pure power and intention.

I layered the magic on thick and tight. Then I pointed my palm at the giant.

"Go!" I said, putting as much intention and power behind it as possible.

At least the stone flew. It made a lazy arc in the air, hit the ground, and rolled to a stop right in front of Big Ugly.

Okay. That worked, but in the lowest way possible. I needed that multiplied by like a thousand.

I picked up another small stone and started layering it with magic. How could I pack more power onto this thing? I'd coated it pretty good last time. Maybe I needed more layers? Maybe the layers needed to be denser?

I tried for both solutions. I tried to make the magic as dense as possible, building it up as thick as I could. It took a lot longer than the first time, but finally it was ready.

I pointed my palm at the target.

"Go!"

This time it did a lot better. It flew much faster and hit a lot harder. The pea-sized stone broke his skin and went inside, but only by a little bit. Within a few seconds, his healing factor had pushed the stone out and sealed the wound.

Well, that sucked. That had taken a lot more time and energy. How much magic was it going to take to be able to injure this guy? Cassandra had made it look easy.

Of course, she had access to a lot of stolen magic. She could afford to just throw power around like it was water. I was using my own magic filled with my personal soul. I couldn't keep doing this forever.

What I could do was start using my imagination. I'd been concentrating on the rock and what I needed to do to it. But what if I flipped that around? What if I made a construct, but it had a rock inside? The construct wouldn't survive the clash with his rotten magic, but the stone inside it would still have all that mass and speed. It should be able to hit and still do damage.

I started with a rocket. I like rockets, and rockets go fast. Then I added a stone inside. It wasn't as nice and round as the first two, but hopefully, it would work. I made the nose of the rocket nice and sharp. Then enlarged it out to a body wide enough to carry the stone. On the back end, I added four fins and, of course, a rocket engine. I made the whole thing a cherry red since it was dangerous, then added stripes of blue and white. Now it was patriotic!

It didn't have enough details yet, and the stripes looked neat, so I added more white and blue stars all over it. It looked cute and sharp, but it didn't look as fast as I wanted. At the end of the day, this thing needed to have massive acceleration and hit hard, so I added four more engines in between the four fins. Now it looked like it had some kick!

With the form finished, I started stuffing it full of magic. This felt much more normal and familiar, instead of trying to wrap a rock in layers.

I looked up for the first time in a few minutes and realized Big Ugly had wandered to the edge of Fourth Street Live. He still couldn't see or hear, but he didn't seem as disoriented as he had been before. This needed to work as my Flasher and Basher advantage was slipping away.

I'd built the rocket lying down on my hand so there was as little distance between us as possible. Now it was ready to launch, I flipped it up so the base rested against my palm. I pointed my palm at Big Ugly and let it fly.

"Go!"

The result was spectacular. The rocket streaked toward Big Ugly so fast it looked like one long line of red. There was a small "boom," so I think the rocket broke the sound barrier. When it hit Big Ugly, it made a small hole in the front of him, but a much bigger hole in the back. The rock had gone all the way through him! That was the kind of power I needed.

There was no sign of the rocket, and I couldn't feel it. My little creations are strong, but they aren't strong enough to make it all the way through a hostile aura. That's what the rock was for.

With all that success, there were a few things that troubled me. I'd aimed for his chest, hoping to get lucky and hit his heart. Instead, the rocket had curved downward in the air and hit him in his massive gut. Also, the exit hole didn't line up with the point of impact.

I've used little rockets before, and they've always flown straight for me. The only thing that had changed was the addition of the stone. The stone hadn't been that round, so I'm guessing it threw off the trajectory of the shot. Once it got inside, the shape of the stone probably tore up his innards which further changed its path.

This was all fine if I was just going to try hitting him in the gut over and over again. I was totally fine with tearing up as much of his innards as possible. I wasn't trying to do that, though. I was trying to hit him in the eye with a rock that would then travel back to his brain. Everything around his eye was protected by hard bones. This wasn't going to be as easy as I'd hoped.

Regardless, it was time to go for a real shot. This time I searched for a golf ball-sized piece of rock that was as round as possible. I needed a bigger rock as I wanted to do lots of damage to his brain. He healed so fast I didn't think a little rock was going to stop him, even if it hit perfectly. I glanced over at Big Ugly. He wasn't happy about my pea shooter. Not happy at all. I'm sure it had really hurt, although both the entrance and exit holes were healing up already.

I couldn't take too long, so I went with the first reasonable rock I could find. It was a bit bigger than I wanted, and it had some bumpy bits sticking out. It was mostly round, so it would have to do.

I made the rocket, although I didn't realize just how big it needed to be now. If I kept the same shape, it would be almost four inches long. My max creation size is three inches, so I modified the shape a bit, making it fatter and squatter. It didn't look quite as sleek and deadly, so I decided to add rocket engines on the fins too. It now had an engine in the base, four engines outside the base between the fins, and four engines on the fins. So nine rocket engines total. It was overkill, but I loved it. Now, despite not being long and sleek, it looked like it had some power!

I started pouring magic into it. It drank up everything I was sending, said 'thank you very much' and 'may I have some more?' This was the biggest creation I'd made since becoming a supernatural. I didn't realize just how much magic it was going to take to power this thing.

I put my other hand over the top, so the rocket was sandwiched between my two hands, and fed it energy from both sides. The amount of magic this thing could hold was insane.

It occurred to me that this is what normal mages do. They put a whole lot of power into a one-use spell and hoped it worked. If not, they did it all over again. I was very lucky to have my little guys. They did a great job, and they kept doing their job over and over again as long as they were needed. That let me be very magic efficient.

Take my Flashers, for example. I made a construct, filled it full of magic, and then it could flash over and over again. Plus, I didn't have to direct the spell each time. The Flasher could fly itself to wherever it was needed and have at it. Speaking of Flashers, I wondered how Big Ugly was doing? My attention had been so concentrated on my rocket, I'd lost track of him.

I looked up and saw a car flying through the air at me.

I froze for a sec. I couldn't believe it.

An actual car.

In the air.

Coming right for me.

I screamed at Bermuda and dashed to the side.

I'd been standing in front of a restaurant where the entire front was glass. I'm sure that made for a wonderful dining experience, but it made for a terrible defense against flying objects. The facade shattered as the car hit it, covering me and Bermuda in sharp pieces of glass. We were doing better than the restaurant, though. The car kept going, smashing tables and chairs, busting through the back wall, and finally stopping in the kitchen. The amount of damage was just insane.

I looked back toward Big Ugly. He was standing by the street where the cars were parked. The next car was already on its way.

I screamed at Bermuda again and kept running. I also kept pumping magic into the rocket. It might be our only hope now.

The car missed us and hit the neighboring shop, which was the store for Jim Beam. OMG! Bourbon was sacred in Kentucky. You don't mess with bourbon. You just don't.

The car smashed through the storefront, through the carefully crafted "experience" section, and through a huge wall of bourbon bottles. Jim was *not* going to be happy.

The third car was already airborne and on its way. I hollered at Bermuda to keep going.

Then it happened.

Bermuda had been running through glass, and he'd cut his paws. When he went to jump out of the way, he slipped on his own blood.

I was going too fast. I hadn't picked him up because I still had both hands around the rocket, and now there was no time to turn around and get him.

The car smashed into the next store and the wall collapsed.

I could see him in the rubble. He wasn't moving.

My world stopped.

Bermuda was hurt.

My baby.

My blood turned cold.

I looked at Big Ugly. His eyes cleared up for just a split second. He saw me. He saw the look on my face.

He grinned.

Then charged.

The Flashers blinded him again, but it didn't matter. He had a lock on me, and he was coming in hot and fast.

There was no time to go to Bermuda. No time to see if he was alive, or heal him, or tell him how much I loved him. We were in a battle, and that battle needed to end now.

I was Bermuda's only hope. If I moved, Big Ugly would find him and finish him. So the solution was simple. I wasn't going to move.

Instead, I poured power into the rocket. I had to time it just right. Big Ugly needed to be close enough for an accurate shot. He also needed to be far enough away for the rocket to accelerate to full speed. There was little margin for error, and I only had one chance.

It was amazing how fast Big Ugly could run. He surely had to be using magic to augment his movement. He had so much mass, there couldn't be any way he was accelerating that quickly with just muscle.

He was five steps away, then four, when I felt the rocket hit the limit on its capacity. It was ready. I flipped it around on my palm. Three steps away.

"Go!"

This rock was much bigger, and it needed more time to accelerate. For a brief second, I thought I'd waited too long, but then all the engines kicked in and it streaked off. This was it. This was my one shot to save myself and Bermuda. This had to work. The rocket headed straight for his left eye.

But it curved at the last moment and hit the bridge of his nose. It wasn't a straight hit. That might have been better, as it may have had enough force to go through his nose and still reach his brain. Instead, it was a glancing blow, and it was enough to throw the rock completely off course. It entered his head at an angle, punched through his eye, went through part of his face, and came out the side of his head.

It was a nasty wound, and if he had been twenty paces away and still disoriented, I would have been celebrating. But he wasn't. He was now two steps away, and although his head had snapped around, he was still on course to hit me, and then Bermuda. Once he got his hands on us, he'd crush us, even with part of his face missing.

The world seemed to slow down. I wondered if my life would flash before my eyes. That's what they say happens at moments like this. There was no time to gather another rock and try again, or try to save myself with another creation.

I'd worked so hard and trained so much. I'd forged my body into the best version it could be. I'd learned how to walk like a pigeon and hit like lightning. It just hadn't been enough.

I'd met some amazing people. I'd found someone I thought I could love. I'd nested in the House and found a home. I was going to miss all that.

I felt so bad for Penny and Eggy. Eggy had finally found a source. He'd decided to live. He'd woken up. Now his source would be gone, and he'd lose hope again. Penny would fade over time, just like Eggy.

All this was because Isobel had to have more power. And she'd found people like her that wanted more too. And now this guy had figured out how to cheat the system. He'd figured out how to internalize all that stolen magic and use it to grow. He was using it like a natural instead of a mage.

One step away. I could see individual hairs growing out of his flesh. I could smell his blood and sweat and rotten magic.

Then it hit me in a flash. Tyler said mages always think of magical solutions, even when another solution is right there. I'd been doing the opposite. I'd been training so much as a fighter, I'd only been thinking of physical solutions.

But I wasn't just a fighter. And I wasn't just a mage. I was both.

When was a fighter not a fighter? When a fighter was a spell.

I had my solution.

I stepped back into the Pigeon Stance, like I had so many times before. There was no time to think or second guess myself as my body relaxed and my fist flew like lightning towards his solar plexus.

I shot an image to Penny of what I needed, and she started flooding me with magic. Sandy had tested my flow and found it was slightly below average. Penny's flow, on the other hand, was not limited by human frailty. She was made of metal—metal which transmits electricity and magnetism at almost the speed of light.

She slammed her power into me, and in less than a microsecond, I was maxed out. A microsecond later I was at double capacity, then triple.

A microsecond after that, my fist reached Big Ugly. The Relax part was over. Now it was time to take all that speed and Tense On Contact. Except this time, I wasn't tensing with just my muscles.

I was tensing with my magic.

My power flared out below me. Driving roots down into the earth. Creating an unshakable base from which to work.

From there, I built the power up through my legs and hips. I didn't bother with water or smoke or fire this time. I built everything using my magic as the source. I used my colors, my matrix. My emerald green and sapphire blue.

I coiled the magic up through my core, through my chest, across my shoulders, and down my arms. Penny was still pouring in her power. By the time it reached my fist, I was ten times over capacity.

I could never hold onto this much magic. I'd only been a supernatural for a few months. I didn't have that depth of ability yet. It may take me a hundred years to get to that level.

But for a split second, just long enough to Tense, I could use this amount of power.

And that is what I did. I Tensed On Contact. Not just with muscles and ligaments and bone. I Tensed with my magic.

I formed a solid, indomitable core of magic, and drove it into him.

He was still running at me, so he had all his momentum behind him. I was driving my fist forward. Together, we created his destruction.

My fist punched into his flesh and kept going. I was immovable, so his massive body wrapped around me. He was like one of those crash test dummies when they drive a car into a concrete wall.

I felt his organs pop and his bones crack.

The most amazing part was the rotten magic. My arm was deep inside him, covered in oily, viscous stolen magic, and I felt it for the first time.

Like really felt it, and understood it like I never had before.

What I felt was a cry for help.

It didn't want to be here. It didn't want to be passed around from mage to mage like dirty laundry.

It wanted to be invited in. It wanted to be welcomed. It wanted to work hand-in-hand with a mage. It wanted to help and celebrate their creativity and their zest for life.

Instead, it was a slave. Cut off from its source. Forced to bow to a mage it didn't choose.

All that power, all that stolen energy, it just wanted to leave. It wanted to go away. It wanted to fly on the wind. Forget that it ever belonged to anyone, and be free again.

I understood that. I appreciated what it wanted. So I broadcast my power with a simple command.

'Go.'

'Live free.'

'Be at peace.'

I blazed like a beacon. I was pure intention. I was the light of encouragement. And all that stolen energy cast off its enslavement.

It burst out of Big Ugly like an atomic bomb. It exploded out of him in such a thick fog that it covered the buildings and rolled down the streets. Already, it smelled better. It didn't smell rotten anymore. Instead, it just smelled like wood smoke.

My moment of Tense was over.

Big Ugly rebounded from my fist and staggered back, stunned. Without any stolen magic to power him, he was just a big mass of flesh. He hit the ground and didn't move.

"Penny!" I screamed, and she went to work again. Only this time she was sucking the magic back in.

Somehow, taking the magic back was much slower than when she'd pushed it into me, and I felt myself stretch and expand in a way I never had before. Finally, Penny got it all, and I collapsed.

I felt burnt out. Like I couldn't feel my regular magic anymore.

I felt thin. Like I was a ghost. Or like I was just going to float away.

I couldn't stop, though. Bermuda needed me.

I crawled over to him and put my arm around him.

My magic sight was doing strange things. I couldn't tell if Bermuda was breathing or not. I couldn't tell what the damage was, or if I could heal him. I had to try, though.

Even though I couldn't feel my magic as usual, I was going to make it work for me.

I started with Tea.

'Duplicate,' I whispered. 'He has my magic. Heal him like you healed me.'

My Ent nodded and got to work. I saw the slightest breath from Bermuda. He was alive!

Next I focused on my primary red Gem Cell.

'Duplicate. Take my power. Cover him.'

The red Gem Cell sparkled, and that is what it did.

Even though my magic felt strange, it was still doing what I wanted. And I wanted to make sure Tea's Grove had plenty of battery power to work with. I borrowed magic from Penny and gave it to the Gem Cells. Soon Bermuda was covered from his nose to his tail in a colorful array of battery cells.

I heard the sound of sirens. I had to get out of here. I couldn't be found near all this destruction.

I was afraid to lift Bermuda. What if moving him did even more damage? He was alive, and I didn't want to jeopardize that.

'Let me take care of him,' Penny said.

She flexed, and somehow Bermuda disappeared from the rubble and appeared in my Throne Room.

I thought my Throne Room was just imaginary? It was the seat of my power, sure, but I thought it was just a mental construction. Not a real place where a cat could go. Regardless, it solved the problem for now.

I staggered to my feet and stumbled over to Big Ugly. I needed to make sure he was down for good. His one eye watched me, but he didn't move. I could see inside him now. All that bulk was just dead flesh.

I guess that made sense. When John had powered down, his golem stone had just become regular rock. If we hadn't peeled it off of him, he would have been a human body encased in a rocky tomb.

The same thing was happening with Big Ugly. Now that his stolen magic was gone, he was encased in a huge mass of dead flesh. He was already human, so he wasn't doing the whole "revert back to a regular man" sort of thing.

Instead, I could see his natural magic wrapped around his core organs, trying to keep him alive.

It was a losing fight. Everything was just too big for the magic he had left.

I didn't wait around to watch the end. The mundanes were coming, and my job here was done. I needed to make sure of one more thing, though. He was still a sucker mage, and there was a lot of dark magic in the air. I didn't want him to be able to capture any of it and maybe reverse his condition.

'Clear the space all around him,' I called out to the Granny Godmothers. 'Don't let any magic touch him.'

They sent me happy smiles and cheerful waves as they got to work. I watched for a moment, then turned and limped away. This mission was complete, and Big Ugly wasn't coming back again.

Other than Bermuda, tonight had been a success. I was in crappy shape, and my magic was out of whack, but I was still alive. Bermuda was also alive, although I felt sick thinking about how he'd looked.

Together, we had taken out thirteen mages and released all the stolen magic they'd accumulated. All that crazy punching, stepping, and healing had paid off. Eggy could run new scenarios, but hopefully, what we'd accomplished tonight would be enough.

Now it was time to go home and take care of my baby.

Epilogue

The journey home sucked.

I looked a mess. I was naked and covered in blood. Most of it was mine. The glass had done a real number on me, and I was covered in cuts. They went along very well with the swaths of burned skin from all the goo.

It didn't help that I was having trouble walking because I'd overloaded my body trying to hold all that magic. Not to mention physically stopping a charging giant.

I'm pretty sure I looked like a crazy, bloody zombie shambling down the street, and that wasn't good considering all the first responders out tonight. The battles had done a lot of damage all along Fourth Street, so there were police, firemen, and EMS everywhere. So I took alleyways and back roads as much as I could. A few times I had to jump behind dumpsters until the lights had passed. At one point I decided to just suck it up and don a not-too-nasty trash bag as clothing.

It was a long, crappy journey, and I was extremely glad to arrive home and see Annabeth at the back door waiting for me. I was so tired and so happy to see her I started tearing up. Heroes weren't supposed to cry, but I was no hero. I was just a new mage who had done what was needed to survive and protect his adopted family. Tonight felt like the biggest trial yet, but I'd made it. I'd survived. And Karl would have a lot less magic to work with if he won his war.

"Oh, my goodness!" She ran over to help me into the House, or maybe give me a hug. Neither of those were a good idea. I was covered in too much glass for her to touch me.

"You poor thing. It's okay. You're home. You're going to be okay." Annabeth kept reassuring me over and over. She was being all strong and supportive in her Mom role, trying to project even more cheer than normal. Her eyes were big, though, and her hands shook a bit, so I could tell she was shocked at how I looked.

Still, I was very grateful for the support. And I was more than happy to let her take charge for a while. My head was buzzing, and I was having trouble thinking.

I made it up to my bathroom, leaving a thin trail of blood along the way. Annabeth wanted to help, but I was afraid to let her touch me. Either she might get cut on the glass, or push the glass into me and I'd get cut more.

I wasn't sure how to deal with glass. I knew you didn't just throw it in the trash can, so Annabeth took over at that point. She laid out a bunch of paper towels over the bathroom floor and started picking off the largest pieces. Then she wrapped them in the paper towels and threw them away.

I helped with the process, and as we continued, I got a pleasant surprise. Tea and his Grove had already been hard at work, pushing the glass out of my system. I was still covered in the sharp pieces, but it was now crusted on with the dried blood and wasn't doing any additional damage.

Go, Team Healing!

They were also working on my cuts, and by the time we were finished picking off the glass, they had already closed them. They weren't fully healed, but at least they weren't bleeding anymore.

The unpleasant surprise was that I'd been bleeding from more than just my cuts. Holding all that magic, even for a moment, had put a lot of stress on my body. I was bleeding out my ears, my nose, my eyes. Even the sides of my fingernails had blood coming out of them. I looked in the mirror, and my eyes weren't white anymore. They were blood red. I looked like a vampire.

I was surprised Annabeth wasn't freaking out more than she was. I looked a mess. A horrible, awful, bloody mess. I wasn't worried about me, though. As long as my magic returned to normal, I would be fine. Instead, I was worried about my kitten.

I wanted to make sure I was clean before working on Bermuda, so I took a very careful shower. Once I was clean enough, and I wasn't going to drop blood and glass all over my baby, we made a soft bed of towels on the bathroom counter, and I asked Penny to retrieve Bermuda out of the Throne Room.

He was breathing, but unconscious. I started to freak out again as I took in his broken appearance. His body was covered in blood and glass, and he looked awful. What got me the most was how still he was. Bermuda was always so full of life. He projected pure cuteness and contentment even when he's sleeping. This was not like that. He was still and limp. He seemed so small. Annabeth stayed strong again, and together we picked out all the glass and cleaned up the blood.

The Grove had been working hard on him too, and it had already pushed out all the glass and gotten the healing started. We went through a lot of towels and washcloths to get him cleaned up, but it was worth it. He looked so much better when we were done.

I was very worried about what was going on inside him, but my magic sight was barely working. I could see he was covered in battery gems and that he was already blanketed in a layer of moss. That would have to do for now.

We carried Bermuda on a clean towel to the middle of my bed, and I lay down beside him. Annabeth lay down on the other side. There were three of us in the bed, and there was still plenty of room.

I thanked Annabeth for being so wonderful and supportive. But we were now in a good spot, and she could head out if she needed to. She said thank you, but she was going to stick around and make sure her boys were okay.

Even though I was safe and clean and Bermuda was as good as I could get him right now, I was still wound up from the fight. I told Annabeth all about it—what had gone right and what had gone wrong. As I was telling her about the battle in the comedy club, I realized just how lucky I'd been. If that had been six regular mages, working as a team, I'd have been toast. It was only the perfect mix of the Flashers, the goo, and the stolen magic making them a bit crazy, that caused them to end up fighting each other and not me. It was a sobering thought.

Annabeth was fascinated by what I'd found out about the corrupted magic when I'd punched Big Ugly. She started wondering if there was a way for her to use that info.

We talked until the morning light, and to my surprise, Annabeth fell asleep first. I lay there for a while, soaking in the quiet and peace. I gently touched Bermuda's head. That was the only spot that I knew was okay. He opened his eyes briefly, giving me a tired look. Then he closed them and went to sleep.

I kissed him very gently and snuggled him softly. I breathed in and out, letting the rest of the tension go. I soaked in the peace of the room and eventually drifted off to sleep as well.

***

The next six days were all about recovery. Tyler showed up from his latest mission with the House and was shocked to hear what had happened.

I stayed with Bermuda the whole time, never letting him out of my sight. Both of us were covered in healing moss, although mine wasn't as bad this time. When my mushrooms came, they weren't as much as before. They just made me feel good. There were no warped walls or flowers in the bathroom this time. Bermuda, on the other hand, was saturated with them, and he got totally stoned. If he hadn't been hurt, it would have been funny as hell. I got some very strange looks, and when he finally got to his feet, he couldn't walk straight.

One time he just yowled at me for a whole hour. He'd go, "Yoooowwwrrrrrrrr," and I'd go, "What's up?" and he'd go, "Yaaawwwrrrrr," all over again. It was so much fun. Tyler was trying to read, and he finally had to get up and stuff his ears full of toilet paper so he couldn't hear us anymore. When Annabeth stopped by, Tyler started talking really loudly, as he still had his earplugs in. Bermuda and I thought that was hysterical. Annabeth turned the whole thing into a drinking game, and soon we were all three sheets to the wind, making yowling noises. You couldn't buy entertainment like that!

On a serious note, I made sure Bermuda had plenty of food and water, and I made sure he ate every time he was awake.

Anna Lykit showed up, of course, but I was on to her, and she didn't get away with any of her tricks. Instead, we watched lots of Netflix shows together, and her chatty comments were hysterical. Tyler couldn't hear her, of course, so I had to repeat everything for him. I'm sure he thought having an imaginary friend was strange, but he just rolled with it.

At the end of three days, I physically felt much better. My cuts were fully healed, and most of my burns had faded away. My muscles had recovered, and all my movements felt normal again.

What still felt off was my magic, although it was getting better. I was used to my magic having a certain texture. I knew my boundaries, and normally, I could tell if my magic levels were low, normal, or high. Now I just felt stretched. I couldn't really tell what my magic levels were.

Annabeth had a theory. She said it was like losing your voice after going to a concert. While you're at the event, you're screaming and singing at the top of your lungs. Then, the next day, you can barely talk. I'd forced myself to use a lot more magic than I should have been able to handle, and now I just needed time to recover. It made sense, so I used my magic as little as possible. I even turned off my magic sight, which felt very strange.

Bermuda finished his three-day moss treatment and seemed to be doing much better. Tea checked us both out and said we needed another three days. All the bad stuff was fixed, but there was still more to do.

So I spent another blissful three days with my baby. We snuggled together a lot, watched even more shows, and ate like there was no tomorrow. He got lots of kisses, belly loving, and snacks. He moved like he was still stiff and sore, but I like to think he was a happy kitty.

I know I was a happy boy. Having down time with lots of snuggles and love was just wonderful. I got snuggles from Tyler, and he gave Bermuda lots of love too. Even Annabeth got in on the snuggle action. On the fourth night, Tyler, Annabeth, and I were chatting and having a good time together, and ended up falling asleep in my huge bed. We had a huge cuddle puddle and it was so nice.

Annabeth kept up her training and continued to go up in levels in the arena. This time, I didn't feel like I was falling behind. I'd tested myself in real life, and I'd held my own. I didn't train at all. Not even once. I used my magic so much in the arena, both for sight and power, that I didn't want to strain it any more than I already had. I could feel it getting better. It was going to be alright.

I'd thought about the final fight and realized that was another way I'd gotten lucky. My Hyper Magical Power Punch had worked, but I'd been fortunate I hadn't needed to fight another mage. That was a great technique, something I wouldn't forget, but it would only be a last resort, end-of-fight kind of weapon.

I was thinking that a scaled-down version might be very useful, though, and I was excited to get back to Sparkles and try it out. I think the idea of Tensing On Contact both physically and magically would give me even more force. Using my body as the spell container was still a great idea, especially if I didn't overload it with magic.

The Grannies reported back. Big Ugly was no more. More importantly, none of the stolen magic had been reabsorbed by him, or anyone else. Most of it had blown away with the wind, but there was still some of it that had stuck around downtown. That clean up would have to wait for the future. Now they were freed up, they went back to working on the park again. It was my highest priority.

Most of the magic they cleaned up went into the House, although I didn't see any changes yet. I was looking forward to what it was going to do with my living room and kitchen. The bathroom and bedroom were now pretty amazing, so my expectations were high. Some of it went into Eggy, but I wasn't doing any magic right now, so I couldn't convert it into my personal colors. I was hopeful that soon he would have enough power to do his final transformation into a vase. That was going to be so exciting.

On the sixth day, Bermuda got up, stretched, and then walked into the kitchen on his own. Best of all, he walked normally. He wasn't weaving or limping or needing any help. I got up too, stretched, and felt just fine. Actually, I felt better than fine. I felt full of energy. I went to my massive bathroom mirror and gave myself a good once over. I looked good. My skin was healed. My cuts were gone, and my burns had healed without any scars. Go, Team Tea!

To be back to full health after just six days was awesome. I still had nightmares from Isobel and the golem. If that happened today, though, I'd heal so much faster. When I'd started this process, I'd wanted some sort of defense. I'd found that with Pigeon Stepping and blocking, but being able to recover like this, that was a form of defense too.

I decided a shower was in order. I'd been lying around for days and hadn't been paying that much attention to personal hygiene. Bermuda decided to join me. He hopped up on his customary place on the back of the toilet and started his own bath. The rain water shower heads in my walk-through shower were so nice. I just stood there, soaking it up for a good while. Then I went to the air side and got my blow dry. Now that I was feeling better, the frisky fairies were back, and I started thinking about a whole different type of blowing.

As if he had been summoned by magic, Tyler walked in and said, "Hi." I said, "Hi," back in a happy, but sexy voice. He got the clue, and between one blink and the next, his clothes vanished. That was a seriously good superpower to have!

We made love on my huge bed under the slow-turning ceiling fan. We took our time, and I luxuriated in all the good feelings of being back to full health. Afterwards, of course, I had to take another shower, but I didn't mind. Tyler was with me, and we were chatting the whole time.

We had just finished when I heard a knock on the door. It didn't sound like Annabeth. I wrapped a towel around me and went to see. It was John!

He looked good. His eyes were clear, his smile was easy, and he had a nice tan. Obviously, his two-week honeymoon had done him a world of good.

"John!" I squealed and gave him a great big hug.

"John!" Tyler yelled and made it a group hug.

"Ah! It is good to be back!" John laughed and picked both of us up, giving us a squeeze. He was a little too enthusiastic in his greeting, because when he put us down I felt a little dizzy and saw spots. Still, I felt fully hugged.

"Meet us downstairs," he said. "We have much to discuss, and there is little time."

That sounded rather mysterious, but he wouldn't say anything else about it. Instead, he left to go tell Annabeth.

Tyler, of course, pulled his magic clothing trick, and suddenly he was ready to go. I had to run to my walk-in closet and get dressed, but it didn't take me long.

Sandy greeted us at the door to her apartment, and once again it was hugs all round. She looked good too. The tired lethargy of low magic was gone, replaced by the vibrant and healthy Sandy I was used to.

Annabeth and John joined us, and we moved the reunion inside. Sandy had made coffee, and Annabeth started making tea. John and Tyler would have rather had a beer, but Sandy's refrigerator wasn't fully stocked, so they settled for coffee. The air was filled with happy voices, and I paused a moment to just take it all in.

We were all here.

We were all okay.

This was what I'd been working towards for weeks now. All the training, fighting, and healing had been worth it. The family was back together. Once again, this felt like home. Whatever showed up, we would face it, together.

Drinks done, Sandy raised her glass in a toast.

"To homecoming and a fresh beginning."

"Hear, hear!" we all chimed in and touched cups.

"This isn't exactly how I envisioned arriving home again," Sandy said. "I thought I'd settle in for a day, then restock the pantry, and have a big supper. John could check out his brews, and we would have a lovely evening, eating, drinking, and catching up until the wee hours of the morning.

"Instead, I got a notification today. The Gathering starts tomorrow, which means we need to leave today, and our portal..." She paused to double-check the time. "Our time for departure is in six hours."

Thank You!

Thank you for reading my book! Not only did you make it to the end, but you're reading all the ending stuff. Clearly you are awesome. :)

I really hope you enjoyed the journey. If you did, please tell others about it! This world only exists when people read it. The more readers it has, the larger the world can be.

Wow, I've finished my second book! That's an amazing feeling. And it sure has been a learning process. This book took longer to finish, as I was still going through a learning curve with book one. (I put Misfit Mage through two more editors, got it in paperback, then audio.) Book three shouldn't take as long, as I've gotten better at all this.

I had to split the story arc for this book into two books. I had it all planned out, Jason learns to fight, gets his healing on, develops a deeper relationship with Tyler, big fight at Fourth Street Live, going to the Gathering, final showdown with Karl and Marius. As I was writing it, though, I realized I had too much stuff to fit into one book. So I've split it into two books in the only place that makes sense—the battle of Fourth Street Live.

In the next book, Sandy and Jason are heading to the Gathering. Jason is going to learn a lot about the larger supernatural world beyond Louisville and make new friends (and new enemies). Then some interesting stuff is going to happen that I can't tell you about, and then we have the big knock-down-drag-out fight with the last of the Louisville Mages. It's going to be epic!

Note About Reviews

Reviews are so important! Good reviews let Amazon and Google know you liked the book, and they will then suggest it to other readers.

I'm an avid reader, but for the longest time, I never posted a review. I didn't know what to say, and I felt like the world would judge me. So, for all of you who like the book, want to recommend it, but don't know what to say—here is a simple format to use:

Title: Just say you enjoyed it and how you read it. Example: "This is a fun read. I read it in two days."

Description: Just act like it is a text to me. Just tell me your favorite character and what you liked about them. If you still need more words - just add in your favorite scene.
Example: "Sandy is my favorite character in the book. When she fought for John and then proposed to him, I gasped! They will make a wonderful couple."

More About Author

Before I was a writer, I was a Photoshop artist. I'd ask guys to be my models, shoot them against a neutral background, and then Photoshop a scene together. I've attached a few samples below. If you like them, you can check out my shop on Etsy.

https://www.etsy.com/shop/MichaelTaggartPhoto

Dark Perspective—Matt:

Develop Muscles—Stone:

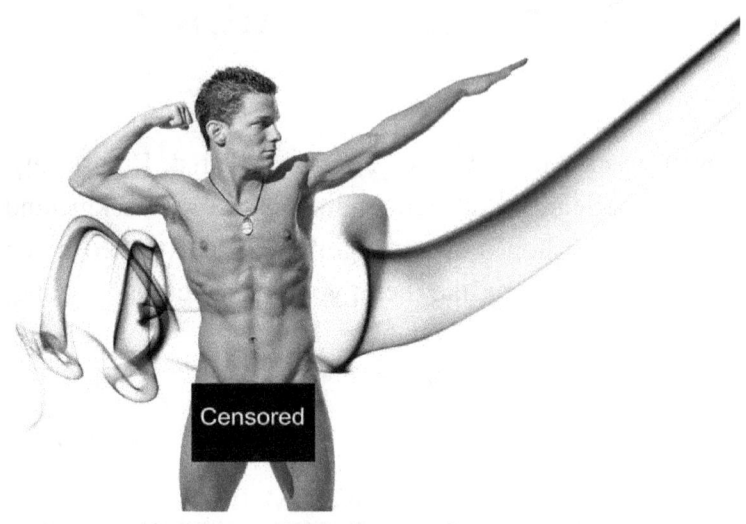

Legend of the Phantom Swordsman—Stone:

Family Pics!

Here is Bermuda getting in some snuggle time.

Here is his sister, Halo.

Here is his younger brother, Memphis.

And, of course, here is my Handsome Husband Harold!

Please follow me on Amazon. When I release a new book, Amazon will let you know.
www.amazon.com/Michael-Taggart/e/B008BBEGCS

If you want more updates than that, then check out my email list. I promise I will only send out about one email a month or less—and it will only be about book stuff (and maybe the occasional Bermuda picture).
Mailchi.mp/4a097952f220/michaeltaggartbookssignup

You can also check out my facebook page:
www.facebook.com/michaeltaggartauthor/

Thank you again for taking a chance on me! I hope you have enjoyed the journey and look forward to more.

Hope you are having a purr-fect day!

Michael and Bermuda

CPSIA information can be obtained
at www.ICGtesting.com
Printed in the USA
LVHW031610300821
696463LV00018B/2679